An Irish Exposure

Part Three in 'The Rents' Saga

Chapter	Page
Chapter One	6
A room with no view	
Chapter Two	13
Consent to travel	
Chapter Three	20
Travelling 'Flight'	
Chapter Four	27
Flight of Fancy	
Chapter Five	34
Stepping back in time	
Chapter Six	41
Table for Two	
Chapter Seven	49
Room Serviced	
Chapter Eight	56
There's no place like home	
Chapter Nine	63
Return to the cottage	
Chapter Ten	70
Adele's Awkward Awareness	
Chapter Eleven	77
Morning Mayhem	
Chapter Twelve	85
Coffee for three	
Chapter Thirteen	92
Some 'Fin' new	
Chapter Fourteen	99
Ambitious Adele	
Chapter Fifteen	106
Naked Attraction	
Chapter Sixteen	113
A matter of trust	
Chapter Seventeen	120
I kissed a girl	
Chapter Eighteen	127
Guilty	
Chapter Nineteen	134
The Talk	
Chapter Twenty	141
Back to the beach	
Chapter Twenty-One	147
Beach Bums	

Chapter Twenty-Two   **154**
The naked truth
Chapter Twenty-Three   **161**
All hallows eve, eve
Chapter Twenty-Four   **168**
First night jitters
Chapter Twenty-Five   **175**
At your convenience
Chapter Twenty-Six   **182**
Party Time
Chapter Twenty-Seven   **188**
The last day
Chapter Twenty-Eight   **195**
Hours for the taking
Chapter Twenty-Nine   **201**
Plane and simple
Chapter Thirty   **208**
Hometown Blues

Epilogue   **212**

Chapter One

A room with no view

Sasha felt like she was almost expected to feel nervous from the moment she first contemplated the idea of asking her parents about the idea of Jim coming over to visit her but the fact of the matter was that she wasn't nervous. At first she put it down to the open way she had been bought up, especially in the years since they had started going to the complex as a family but for some reason the subject of boys visiting didn't scare her.

There was no doubt in her mind that there would be rules set out surrounding his visit but in her mind there was a logical and yet not quite practical solution. They should all just book a week in a hotel, treat it like it was just another holiday even if they were in her home town but she knew that the expense of doing that wasn't really practical.

She knew that, if her parents agreed to the idea of staying in a hotel it would mean a similar level of freedom to that which she enjoyed at the complex but with two big differences. Firstly she was fairly sure that she wouldn't get away with walking around a hotel naked, but she could always do that in her room as long as she got her own room. Secondly they would need to either be in their home town or fairly close by because she was sure her father wouldn't want to take time off work just so that she could have her boyfriend come over to visit her.

Added to that was the fact that if they stayed in a hotel it would mean Jim would need to book in to the same hotel as them which she was sure would make his visit too expensive. All in all, while she could see good reasons why a hotel would be a nice idea Sasha could also think of plenty of reasons why it wouldn't and that was only the reasons she could think of, she was sure her parents would come up with others.

There was no easy way to bring up the idea, it wasn't as if she would be able to slide the suggestion into a conversation so Sasha knew she was going to have to actually bring it up and prepare herself for the reaction. She was pleasantly surprised at the reaction she received when she suddenly blurted the idea out in between main course and pudding one evening but Sasha felt sure that her parents were probably expecting her to ask something like it from the moment she had introduced him as her boyfriend. Now that it was out in the open it felt like a weight was lifted from her shoulders, all she had to do now was be ready for whatever her parents might say in response.

Sasha felt sure that part of the routine would be the talk she had heard others at school mentioning that they had endured with their parents. Most of the time Sasha was sure that the much anticipated talk about sex was too late, just like it was for her but she knew that no matter what level of knowledge she had it was best to act like it was new to her. Unlike others at school, due to her time at the complex Sasha was confident that whenever the talk happened she could avoid awkward graphics which was some relief.

By the time she got around to trying to discuss how soon the visit might happen Sasha was surprised that the talk still hadn't been mentioned but was content not to bring it up until one of her parents did. Part of the surprise with the talk, from what others had told her, was which parent was going to be designated with the task of having the talk.

For some of the girls she went to school with the option was limited due to them living with only one parent but she had both of hers at home and knew it was wrong to assume it would be her mum initiating it whenever it happened.

Her first suggestion had been to invite him over for Christmas, the break from school was two weeks meaning he could be with her not only for a special time of year but for almost as long as their time on Zakynthos. Admittedly the weather was going to be notably different if he came over to see her at Christmas but that wasn't the only concern with that time of year.

At the end of the day, Sasha knew that Jim had family that she was sure he would want to spend time with over Christmas, and even if he didn't, she was sure that his parents wouldn't appreciate her taking him away from them at that time of the year. The last thing she wanted to do was to make enemies out of his parents when she barely knew them except for the few brief times they had passed niceties at the complex.

Sasha's second inclination was to suggest the February mid-term break due to how close it was to Valentine's Day but she wasn't sure that Jim would want something quite so romantic so early in their relationship. She had no doubt that Jim was the romantic type, he had proven that to her a few times during their time at the complex but it still seemed a little bit too excessive to plan their next meet-up specifically around that date.

She smiled as the pondered over the idea of taking Jim to the school Valentine disco but knew that even if he was over with her she wouldn't be allowed to take him. The rule on that had been made clear before the previous year's event after some of the older student had tried to discuss bringing their partner who was in college with them.

There was, in her mind, something extremely frustrating in having a boyfriend and yet not being able to bring him along to such an event. She could see now why the older girls had protested against the "no outsiders" rule that had been set as Jim would be the perfect deterrent against Fintan's anticipated annual attempts to get her to go to the disco with him.

In true form, he hadn't let her down when the posters advertising for the disco had been plastered on the school walls on the lead up to her last valentine's day. This year he had beaten his own record for the amount of times he could either hint directly at or invite her to join him at the disco. Seven times in total she had found ways to tell him it wasn't going to happen even using less subtle hints like 'not even if you were the only boy at this school' and yet he still seemed undeterred. She had decided to learn how to say 'No' in as many languages as possible to see if she could find one he would understand but the problem was a lot of the languages she chose basically used the same word.

In reality she knew that she should probably give him some credit for the effort and creativity he had put into a few of his attempts, she just wished he would focus his attention on someone else. His first attempt had come in the form of a box of chocolates that had mysteriously appeared on her desk which some of the girls had said was sweet.

Sasha could still remember trying her best not to comment as she offered them around to the other students knowing that she had seen him buying them a few days earlier in the discount store and as he had delivered them anonymously he couldn't comment on her sharing.

His third attempt was less subtle than a box of chocolates and had been less easy to hide as it had been delivered by the postman. Thankfully Sasha had seen her father's car drive away before the post had arrived however that had only accounted for one of her parents. If she had been organised Sasha was sure that she would have probably missed the postman too but she wasn't sure if that was a good or a bad thing.

She had been upstairs in the bathroom when the letters had been pushed through the door and heard her mother announce that there was one for her in the pile. Conscious of the time she had made her way back downstairs and over to the table to see what was waiting for her before making her way out of the front door.

Propped up against the condiments was an envelope that seemed almost too big to fit through the letterbox but it didn't appear to be crumpled somehow. She didn't need to glance into the kitchen where her mother was busy stacking the dishwasher to know that the content of the envelope was obvious to both of them. Without much care or attention she stuffed the unopened card into her bag hoping that by the time she got home it would have been forgotten about – it hadn't.

His final attempt was the one that he should have been nominated for an Oscar for as it lacked any element of subtlety but left no doubt in the eyes of any onlookers what he was looking for. Fintan had lingered outside of one of the classes they shared together while she sought some clarification on an assignment they had been issued with.

Looking back on it, Sasha knew that if she had foreseen what he was going to do she would have left her questions for another time. By the time she was ready to leave the class there was a crowd who seemed to all be waiting for the big moment when Fintan openly asked her to join him at the disco. She had taken a deep breath before answering and glanced around the crowd trying to assess how they would respond to her answer.

It came as a huge relief when she spotted Adele on her way down the corridor whom had clearly seen the predicament she was in and was frantically making her way through to rescue her. Feeling Adele grip her arm gently she blurted out a non-committal reference to thinking about his offer before feigning that she was being unwillingly dragged from the scene away by her best friend.

The biggest problem she had with the option of February was that it was still such a long way off and she didn't like the thought of it being so long until she saw him again. In a way she had accepted that from the moment that she had got on the plane it was going to be more difficult for her to arrange a date than anyone else she knew.

Now she was back at school she accepted that what others referred to as the honeymoon period was most definitely over. For the first week she had tried to avoid seeing couples during her break time because every time she saw one it reminded her of what she was missing out on. After a week she knew she couldn't avoid the hand holding and decided to treat it the same way she treated nudity on the complex – accept it is there and get on with her own life around it.

She had been half way through a class when she had felt her phone buzz against her foot from the inside of her school bag. Glancing up at the teacher who was passionately scribbling on a white board she cursed the fact that there had been no vague boundaries around the use of phones in a classroom.

The punishment for being caught using it was clear – it was confiscated for a length of time that was determined by the teacher. She had a vision of a box somewhere with a multitude of ringtones all going off at different times until either the battery died or the phone was reunited with its owner. There had been one incident where a phone had been confiscated and the owner's parents had been trying to urgently get hold of their daughter, thankfully it was resolved without major issues.

Peering at her watch she huffed as she realised that she had just under half an hour until she could answer the question burning in her mind of who was trying to contact her. Logic told her that it was either one of her parents of Jim as everyone else, with only one exception, who had her number was in class just like she was.   There was the possibility that it was an email and that then left the scope wide open as there was no way of telling who or what might have sent her a random email.

By the end of the class she was sure that her phone had buzzed at least another 3 times making her relieved that she had at least remembered to put in on silent mode after break time. It was like some kind of rebellion, everyone seemed to go through the same routine of putting their phone volume up at the beginning of the break only to have to put it on silent by the end of it.

Sasha smiled at the teacher as she gripped her bag and watched him vigorously wiping away the text he had spent the last hour talking about. Turning toward the door she held her breath hoping that she wasn't going to hear her name called back delaying her further from finding out who had been trying to catch her attention during the class. She felt the sigh leave her body as she shut the class door behind herself knowing that she only had a few minutes in between classes but that was enough time to see what was waiting for her on her phone.

Peeking at the screen as she made her way down the corridor she felt a smile crossing her lips as she spotted a message from Jim. It was unusual for him to text her during the day as he knew she couldn't pick up or respond to anything he sent her very easily. The only exceptions to this had been in her first week back at school when he hadn't realised she had returned and had maintained a similar text routine to the one they had been keeping ever since her return to Ireland.

Quickly she slipped outside the door where she knew no one was going to interrupt her and opened the message he had sent her. He face flushed with excitement as she noted that he was thinking the same as she was, February was a long time, in his message he mentioned October which was much sooner.

She knew that his comment was only a non-committal suggestion, he was good at them but usually when he made them it was his way of testing the water. Normally his suggestions would become commitments if she thought they were a good idea and this one she was definitely interested in. Nodding as she replied she cordially told him it sounded like a good idea as long as she could convince her parents before slipping the phone back in her bag ready for her next class.

By the time she got home Sasha had already gone through as many ways she could think of as possible of putting the suggestion forward to her parents. In a way she knew that they were already aware of her intention to meet up with Jim so all she had to do was convinced them that October was a good idea.

She knew that, in some cases it was better to speak to both parents at the same time and asking them about the new date that she had for Jim's visit felt like one of those occasions. In the past she had experienced times when she had mentioned something to one parent just for the response to be to ask the other one. These never seemed to end comfortably due to a hidden code that existed between parents whereby if one of them wasn't prepared to answer it meant that the other had to exercise caution before giving their response.

This decision was one that she didn't want to take any chances with, not now that she had already received their assurance that it was ok for him to visit. After a lot of contemplation while she waited for her father to get home she decided that a carefully timed dinner time question was the best way forward.

As she asked the question Sasha could see that she wasn't going to get a definite answer immediately. She hadn't expected her question to be greeted with open arms but the look of shock in her father's eyes as he tried not to choke on the fork full of food he had just scooped into his mouth said that there was more than just a yes or no awaiting her.

Diarmuid glanced through the side of his eyes as he heard the request being made and swallowed slowly as his glace caught Mary's eye. They had both been preparing for this moment ever since the idea of him visiting had first come up but hadn't anticipated it being something that would be expected so soon. Requests of a similar nature to this in the past would have been enough to gain leverage to get things done and he knew that there was a chance that if they agreed they could do the same with this one but that wasn't the main issue that was crossing his mind.

When they had bought the house they had accepted that one child was enough and therefore a third bedroom was an expense that they didn't need. Even when friends and relatives had stayed over they had been able to accommodate them by evicting Sasha from her room to the couch in the front room for a couple of nights. They knew that in theory they could do the same with Jim but this time it seemed like there was a difference despite the fact that they had met him and had no doubt he was a trustworthy person.

The fact that he had been introduced as the boyfriend made everything feel different and they both knew that while they had been on the complex they had almost glossed over the fact that he was the first person Sasha had introduced under that title. When he had been a younger man Diarmuid knew that if he was given the same accolade it came with a suspicious glance and rules that were set by his girlfriend's parents. For him, those rules were centred around how he was expected to act when in the presence of the parents and their daughter although he was sure that they knew that more happened when they weren't looking.

This ability to turn a blind eye to activities was saved by the fact that after a visit to a girlfriend's parents' home he would be returning to his own home before the end of the day. With Jim, he didn't have the same comfort zone and Diarmuid knew that the circumstances were going to be as awkward for Sasha and Jim as they were for Mary and him. There wasn't going to be an easy way to approach the subject but he knew that both Mary and he had been thinking the same thing – where was Jim going to sleep.

In the early days, when Sasha had been young there had been days when he had been able to work from home, something that his current job didn't allow him to do but at the time he had set up a room downstairs as a study area. In more recent years the same room had become a place for Sasha to use for her homework but ever since she had moved her desk to her bed room it had become a redundant room.

"You need to give us a little time to work things out before we give an answer Sasha" Diarmuid made his reply as calmly as he could in an effort to try not to seem like he was dismissing it completely.

Smiling across the table Sasha nodded in agreement knowing in her heart that she had made quite a big request and an immediate answer wasn't likely. Part of her mind wanted to press for a time frame but she knew that if she did that it was more likely that she wouldn't get the outcome she was hoping for. She had tried that before with much more trivial decisions and always ended up regretting her decision so this time, she knew she just had to be patient and let them decide.

Mary stood as she cleared the dinner plated and peered at Diarmuid nudging him slightly to get his attention as she walked past him. She had to admit that he had handled the enquiry in a better way than she had expected him to and knew that it was an enquiry that she was happy to let him make the decision on. Casually she made her way into the kitchen and felt in some way relieved when he took her hint and followed her in so that they could discuss things.

"We could put him in the study" Diarmuid muttered the words as if he was a ventriloquist as he casually scraped his plate before glancing into the dining area where Sasha had now left the table and presumably ambled into the front room.

Mary smiled as she turned to him; it felt in some ways like they were discussing Jim as if he was a new piece of furniture. She could tell by the calm way he bought the subject up that he had given it some thought but was sure that Diarmuid had as many concerns as she did about the entire concept of having Jim stay with them. In many ways she knew that they had been boxed into a corner because when the concept had been bought up in the first place neither of them had shown any objection.

The study seemed like a reasonable answer and she knew that somewhere under the pile of boxes that had accrued in the room they had an old camp bed. Part of her mind knew that if they wanted they could back away from their initial acceptance of Jim visiting but it seemed wrong to do so when Sasha barely ever asked anything of them. If they did agree she knew that both Diarmuid and she would have more to discuss about it but at least the study meant there was a staircase in between Sasha and Jim while he visited her.

"I will let you tell her" Mary smiled as she dried her hands feeling a shudder drive its way down her spine at the thought of what she had just agreed to.

Chapter Two

Consent to travel

Although Jim refused to openly admit that he knew in his heart that his father's vague but realistic comments about his new found relationship were true. There was no way he could argue against the comment that seeing her was going to be a challenge given how far apart they lived but in a way that had made him more determined to make it work.

Over the years as an unofficial confidant to a number of girls he knew that the one thing they found it hard to do was to trust a new boyfriend. In some cases their lack of trust was well guided given the reputation that preceded the new boyfriend but that made Jim wonder why they had accepted a date in the first place. He learned very quickly not to question the logic in dating a person they didn't trust and just go along with their decision sweeping up the pieces as the relationship almost inevitably fell apart.

Trust, he learned extremely quickly was something that effected both sides of a relationship with more than one occasion when his close friendship with a girl causing tension to their relationship, especially in the early stages. While he wasn't able to confirm it, sometimes the issue of trust seemed to dissipate after the first time the new boyfriend had seen his girlfriend naked but that sometimes made it even worse. Now that he had not only experienced naturism but met Sasha naked even before they started dating this quest for nudity in a relationship amused him in ways he knew he couldn't discuss with anyone who hadn't experienced Sasha's lifestyle.

In worse case scenarios Jim knew that some of his female friends had used the excuse that he was their gay best friend. This was an option that had both theoretical advantages and disadvantages for him but the biggest advantage was that, as long as the new boyfriend didn't know him, he was able to maintain a close friendship.

There had been some occasions when Jim had almost wished he was a gay best friend or at least that he tried to pass himself off as having been. He had heard of times when someone who really was in this category was allowed to do stuff that was out of bounds for him as a heterosexual man in a friendship with a woman. While he was sure that he didn't want to be sat in changing areas for hours with any of the girls he knew the idea of being allowed to see them getting changed wasn't one he was adverse to but that wasn't enough for him to actually change his sexual orientation.

On the negative side, his rumoured disinterest in women did mean that any girl who heard of his orientation who he had gone to the lengths of actually asking on a date wasn't sure whether it was actually a date or not. There had been more than one occasion in the years before meeting Sasha when he had thought he was on a date only to find out that the girl he was out with wasn't thinking the same thing, which had led to some interesting situations, especially if he attempted to kiss them.

Jim knew that, as much as he trusted Sasha and was fairly sure that she trusted him they had a bigger factor to contend with. The distance between them was going to mean that dates were not only a long time apart but almost intensified by the fact that when they did meet they would have to try to cram as much into their time together as possible. In a way the idea of high octane dating was almost appealing to him because it meant that they would make more of their time together and appreciate it more.

Although they had only really known each other for just over a month and had only spent less than two weeks in each other's company he had started thinking of ways he could be closer to her. The reality of the situation was that, even before his summer holiday he had marked it in his head as the last time he was going away with his parents and he had to admit, if it was going to be the last one they had made it one he wasn't going to forget.

One option that had occurred to him was the prospect of looking at going to a college in Ireland but he wasn't sure if he was ready to make such a big move so soon. As much as he liked the idea of gaining independence, the idea of moving to a different country was much scarier than simply moving to a different town and being able to go home at the weekend if he wanted to. The end result was that he had done neither and was now going to the local college but it was only a year's course so he could change his mind after that.

The subject of his next meet up with Sasha had come up a few times but usually as a fleeting reference to the fact that they both wanted it to happen. Their agreement on the fact they wanted the same thing came as a relief to Jim even if the easiest way that was going to happen was going to be if they both revisited the complex on their next summer holiday.

He had intentionally chosen not to discuss the idea of returning with his parents because there were some moments of the holiday that he didn't want being bought back to his memory again even though he had eventually got used to the idea of naturism. The last thing he wanted was for them to take his enquiry as some kind of acceptance of them being naked or barely dressed around the house. Two weeks abroad with not only the risk of but the reality that he had seen both of them without clothing was more than his mind was able to comprehend for now.

Sasha had looked like a different person when they had spoken in video chats and he knew that it wasn't the fact that she had been dressed that was causing it. He had seen her in clothing many times during his visit to the complex but now it was as if the fact she didn't have the choice that was deflating her enthusiasm.

When he mentioned to his parents that Sasha and he were hoping to meet up as soon as possible it had occurred to him that there may be some concerns about him travelling alone even if he was almost 17 years old. His suggestion had been followed by an awkward moment of silence before his mother acknowledged it with a non-committal "that sounds nice" which he knew was neither an agreement or a disagreement.

By the end of the evening he had managed to navigate his way through another revision of "the talk" which he could see his father had been coaxed into giving him. The sincere expression that had crossed his father's face at the beginning of the talk had quickly dissipated and been replaced with a look that was closer to relief when he calmly confirmed to his father that he knew how that part of life worked. Trying not to laugh as the talk had started Jim found an irony in a talk about human bodies and how they worked only weeks after a holiday where they had been surrounded by nudity.

September had bought with it a clean start for Jim in as much as now that he was at college he could try to build a new reputation for himself. He knew there was nothing specifically wrong with the reputation he had but part of him wanted to be seen in a different light to the moniker of every girl's best friend.

He had considered the idea of making it publicly known that he had a girlfriend now but even that came with complications that didn't appeal to him. Firstly, there was the fact that he couldn't introduce Sasha to anyone, which he knew was a complication that other people had if they got involved in distance relationships.

Secondly was the fact that he had avoided discussing where he had been on his holiday for fear that somehow the naturism aspect would be discovered and eclipse anything else about the trip. He didn't expect any of his friends to accept that the first time he had met Sasha she hadn't been wearing anything except a friendly smile and was definitely not ready for his friends to realise that he had probably spent time naked too. So far, he hadn't managed to reform his reputation but changing how people saw him when he was studying wasn't anywhere near the new challenge that was awaiting him.

The few people that he knew who had formed distance relationships could tackle theirs by a train or bus journey but he wasn't able to get to see Sasha as easily. He had a flight to look forward to, something he had anticipated might happen the following summer if he really did manage to go away on his own holiday. As this trip was definitely not in the summer and wasn't what he considered a normal holiday it was a far reach from anything he had expected at the beginning of the summer break.

Now they had flights booked Jim knew he had to start preparing for his first trip away on his own and there wasn't long to get everything ready to go. Normally when he was going on holiday there would be a few weeks or even months between the booking date and the flight but this time he had only been given a fortnight.

Ireland was different to any of the other places he had been to because from what Sasha had told him it wasn't very different weather wise to where he lived. This time it wasn't the weather he was going away for and he knew that there was a chance that as he was visiting his girlfriend there were going to be other things to probably look forward to.

In a way, he felt bad that the first thing that had come to his mind once the flights had been booked were the intimate pleasures that Sasha might be willing to share with him but he knew that others his age would think the same thing. It was like a feast that he had tasted for the first time and now he had tried it he wanted to sample the pleasures over and over again as long as Sasha had the same in mind.

They had discussed the intimacy of their relationship a few times in text and on their calls with different levels of awkwardness. Sasha had seemed quite comfortable discussing it but had also made it clear that the naturist side of her didn't want him thinking that sex was the only reason she wanted to be naked with him. She had tried to explain the concept by referring to the fact that everyone was naked in the shower and that wasn't sexual, Jim had listened solemnly as she tried to explain it but his mind had filled with images of her in the shower making the rest of the conversation awkward for him.

He had heard that some of the lads as school bragged about their adventures with their girlfriends and sometimes wondered how the girls maintained their innocent persona. While he didn't want Sasha to think that all he was interested in was the intimate side of their relationship he knew that he also wanted to make sure he was prepared for anything that might happen between them.

With a few days before the flight Jim made his way to a chemist after college and gasped as he spotted the range of contraceptives that were available. When he had tried to find them on the complex there had only been one machine in the gents bathrooms but here he could see shelves with several different options available to him.

It occurred to Jim that he had never really taken much notice of the section he was now staring at and suddenly he felt more exposed than ever before. Part of the reason was that it was strategically placed in between the sanitation products and the baby products neither of which Jim was planning to have a use for any time too soon.

He glanced along the aisle knowing in the back of his mind that choosing the item was only the beginning, there was also the checkout process to consider. On his way in he had noted that at the till was a middle aged gentleman who, he couldn't label as someone he actually knew as he only knew their name by the fact he wore a badge, but he had conversed with the man a few times on previous visits.

Each time they had spoken in the past it had only been a casual hello and comments about the weather but Jim had felt there was something more, something unsaid, depending on the man's tone. It was almost as if he was trying to assess the need for whatever had been picked up from the aisle or who the item may be fore without directly asking This time, Jim felt sure that there wouldn't be a lot of doubt who he was purchasing for and why he was buying it.

He glanced back up at the range of products slightly shocked that there were not only different sizes and textures but flavours too. He bit his lip as an image of a person casually chewing one popped into his head while knowing that there was a completely different reason for the flavouring but the image still amused him. Looking around he noted that he was the only person in the aisle which made it easier and reached out grabbing a box that seemed relatively normal and reasonable value.

Taking a deep breath he made his way toward the till realising very quickly why he had heard other guys at school referring to having added other items to their purchase to conceal their real reason for entering the pharmacy. The man at the till looked at him calmly as he scanned the box smiling but choosing not to say anything until the point where it was time to ask for payment. Jim left the pharmacy, stuffing the box into his pocket as he walked out the door while making a mental note to avoid that shop for at least a few weeks.

Tucking the box under a couple of layers of clothing in the case he had been preparing for a few days when he arrived home Jim glanced over at his desk spotting a small ring box. He could still remember buying the little box to keep the ring that Sasha had presented to him at the airport in.

Originally he had intended to wear it on the chain he had bought while in Greece but that option had proven ineffective when the chain broke sending the ring plummeting down his chest half way through a class. He had been relieved in a way that it had happened in class as he had followed his peers who chose the untucked look which he knew would have led to him losing the ring had he been walking.

After a few awkward moments of fishing along the waistline of his jeans he managed to successfully dig the ring out and place it safely in his coat pocket where it had remained until he arrived home. In his head he could almost imagine Sasha's face if he had to admit to having lost the item, there was no way he could replace it and pretend to still have the original, it was far too unique.

Grabbing the box he opened it and took the ring out recalling Sasha's words as she tried to explain the meaning behind the symbols it held. He smiled softly as he replaced the ring and closed the box tucking it safely under a few layers of clothes so that he didn't for get to take it with him. Deep down he knew that he was only really packing it to show to Sasha and prove that he still had it but it seemed like the right thing to do being that he had seen the necklace he had given her still around her neck when they talked.

He had fond recollections of their recent video chats which had teetered off a little since they had both returned to education. Sasha had been very quick to mention that she was certain that she would be returning to the complex for her summer holiday in the next year. Her comments seemed reasonable given the fact that her family had been going to the same complex for a number of years.

Jim wanted to be able to give her the same assurance but knew that the chances of his family going to the same place two years in a row were a lot lower. During his childhood there hadn't been many occasions when they had gone on a trip to the same place unless it was to visit a friend or relative for a long weekend. He had considered the idea of maybe booking a trip himself but hadn't given the idea enough time to be able to give Sasha the answer that he felt sure she was wanting to hear.

Thinking quickly he kept the discussion going on the subject of the complex by commenting on how much he had loved seeing her most days in what was now his favourite outfit. His comment received a poked out tongue and a two finger salute from her which he could see was a playful gesture diffusing the situation in his mind.

Grabbing his bags Jim made his way downstairs making a mental not that the presentation of his bags would be seen as confirmation that he was ready to go. He paused halfway down the stairs before making his way back to his room and removing the box he had packed from the pharmacy, choosing instead to keep that on him for now. It was bad enough that the pharmacist had given him a knowing look when he had bought the item but the thought of the Rents discovering it during the regulation bag inspection was something he wanted to avoid at all costs.

Across the room on the dining table Jim spotted his passport and boarding card patiently awaiting him as the clatter of pots alerted him to his mother in the kitchen. He made is way over picking up the documents and sliding them in to the inside pocket of his jacket before turning and peering through the kitchen door.

Fiona had decided to keep herself busy as she heard Jim making his way downstairs by focussing on the over baked remnants of the previous evenings dinner that had latched itself to the inside of a saucepan. She had gone through all the arrangements that had been made for Jim with Paul a few times and they had agreed that it was best to try not to seem too emotional when he was due to leave.

It had made more sense for Paul to take the car to work and let Jim head to the airport by taxi than for her to take him there herself so now all she had to do was pretend that his absence for the next week wasn't ripping her apart inside. She brushed her forearm across her eyes wiping away a single tear as she tried to control her breathing before turning and putting a faint smile on aa as she faced Jim in the doorway. Mopping her hands with a semi-dry tea towel she made her way over and busied herself straightening the collar of his jacket as she composed her mind.

"You have everything you need?" She felt her throat catch as she spoke and pulled away from him slightly

Jim couldn't help but notice how much effort his mother was putting in to making out that it wasn't a big deal as she stood patiently awaiting his answer. Carefully he slid his hand in his pocket gripping the box that he had removed from his case as he nodded a silent response to her question. Part of his mind was encouraging him to reach out and hug her but the other part was advising against it as she would know that he had seen the flustered redness in her cheeks.

Fiona shuffled past Jim and made her way over to his case that was neatly propped against the wall ready for him to leave. She reached out instinctively preparing to check that he had packed everything properly but stopped herself as she glanced at the case, she pulled her hand away and accepting that it was likely that he had been as meticulous as always and she should just trust his judgement.

Still stood in the doorway Jim watched his mother make her way over to his case and smiled as she grabbed the handle. Instinctively he gripped the box in his pocket silently relieved that he had taken the time to remove it and safe in the knowledge that he could slip it back in when he got to the airport. He felt his jaw drop slightly when he saw his mother release the case without any inspection and make her way back toward the kitchen. He smiled as his mother brushed lightly past him and made her way back to the sink where the abandoned saucepan was patiently awaiting her attention

With a sudden shock, he heard the toot of the taxi that had been booked as it pulled up outside and caught a glimpse of his mother who turned as she heard it too. This was it, the moment that he had been waiting for and now he could sense the emotion filling the moment as his mother dried her hands a second time before following him toward the front door.

Jim waved over at the taxi driver who was standing patiently by the car door waiting for him with an air of authority safe in the knowledge that the journey had been prepaid. He turned to face his mother smiling as he noted that she was still trying her best not to make a fuss over the fact he was going away. Carefully he wheeled his bag toward the car and handed over to the driver before requesting a few moments which the driver seemed happy to give him.

He turned and spotted his mother still stood in the doorway knowing that she was going to wait there and watch as he disappeared toward the airport. Clearing a lump in his throat he made his way back up the path as a tension built in his chest that he hadn't expected to feel but somehow it seemed right.

"I'll see you in a week then" he smiled vaguely as he spoke and noted the puffiness ih his mother's eyes

Without a moment of hesitation he launched himself toward his mother embracing her in a way that he hadn't done since he had been a much younger man. The hug seemed to knock her back at first but he managed to stop her falling as he dug his heels into the ground and relax as he felt her hand on his back. Gently he released her and glanced up spotting a tear that he knew she had been suppressing as he stepped back from her.

"I'll call you when I get there" Jim smiled and waved vaguely before heading down the path to the waiting taxi.

Chapter Three

Travelling 'flight'

In some ways it felt like the decision to leave early on the morning she was travelling to the airport to meet Jim had almost been made for her without the specific instruction to do so having been actually given. Sasha had found it hard to hide her excitement at the fact that he was due to arrive as she sat down for dinner the previous evening and although she hadn't said anything her mother had been quick to point out how distracted she seemed.

The meal had started off in the normal way with comments passing between her mother and father about how their days had been before diverting to her with questions about her last day of school before the mid-term break. As much as she loathed saying that it had been uneventful because she knew that saying something like that was likely to spark a comment about what she was learning the last day before mid-term was generally uneventful.

There had been the usual bouts of banter among those in her class as they discussed what they had planned for their week off but Sasha was confident that none of them had plans quite as nice as hers were. One teacher had passed a comment about setting an assignment to be completed during the break but it hadn't taken long for him to realise that no amount of comment about it possibly effecting their grades was going to save him from the jeers he received.

"You haven't forgotten that we are only letting Jim stay here because we have room for him have you?" Sasha glanced calmly at her father as he made the comment while knowing deep down what he was meaning and actively wanting to avoid the pending chat especially over dinner.

"Yes Da, and thanks for being so awesome about it" she smiled amicably as she replied while noting how her reply had taken him back

In the short time in between her parents agreeing to let him stay and him being due to arrive Sasha had been practicing different ways to not only avoid the chat but also keep her parents happy that they hadn't made a mistake in letting him stay. Adele had been able to offer her some guidelines and now she was seeing them work to her advantage by not feeling awkward when the subject of him staying came up.

"Do you think I should get an earlier bus to go meet him?" Sasha felt proud of the fact that she had simultaneously kept the subject on his visit while also distracting from any reference to their bedroom arrangements

Neither of her parents could deny that the busses, while reliable to turn up couldn't always be sure of arriving at a location at the expected time. Sasha knew that she had left plenty of time for her route but it didn't hurt to have her parents look over the journey one last time before she actually made it.

In her mind Sasha could see an element of humour in the fact that she knew most of the girls at school had been put through the trauma of the sex chat with their parents and, despite being less than a day away from having Jim staying in their house she had managed to avoid it. There was something, sweet, awkward and in some ways concerning in her mind at the idea of her parents thinking that it fell on them to teach her about sex, she could distinctly recall having bought a letter home advising her parents of sex education on the school curriculum and yet nobody she knew seemed to be able to avoid the parent version of the subject.

She knew that it stemmed to the fact that no parent wanted their child to become pregnant too early and lose out on education but she also knew that most parents couldn't wait to be and, in many ways encouraged, the arrival of grandchildren. Admittedly Sasha also knew that most parents didn't openly admit to wanting grandchildren until their son or daughter was married but that wasn't the point, either way the act of becoming a grandparent would involve their child experiencing sexual encounters

It was, in many ways, the final gesture of the day that came as the biggest surprise of all to Sasha, especially when she succeeded in avoiding the sex lecture for the rest of the evening. She was making sure everything was ready before heading to her room when her mother stopped her and handed an envelope over to her before stepping away to let her open it.

Sasha smiled as she gently pulled a hotel voucher out peering over at her parents to see if it was real or just some kind of joke.

"We wanted to give you some time with Jim before coming home, we trust you will act responsibly with it" Sasha smiled over at her father knowing what he meant as she acknowledged the gift they had given her.

There was no denying the fact that the voucher was for one room so they accepted that they were going to be sharing it but Sasha accepted that was more for economy than anything else and chose not to linger on it.

It didn't come as much of a surprise to Sasha that the journey up to Shannon Aiport proved to be an eventful one. Busses seemed to prove challenging to some people on the simplest of routes so when she encountered chaos at both of the places she needed to change bus she was almost prepared for it. The fact that announcements at the terminal she was meant to chage busses in for the second time were practically non-existent didn't help but it did make her grateful that she allowed plenty of time in case she managed to miss a connection.

By the time she arrived at the airport Sasha couldn't wait to get off the bus knew that she had to accept that being one of the first ones on the bus had left her with a window seat, which was something she preferred as opposed to an aisle one. This did however mean that as the bus filled up the vacant seat next to hers wasn't long being occupied by someone else making their way to the airport.

Patiently she sat in her seat refusing to make eye contact with the man who was sitting in between her and the aisle trying her best not to count the number of people who pushed past him refusing to let him leave his seat.

As she made her way into the airport Sasha was quite relived to note that despite it being a lot smaller that Dublin, the airport she had visited before on her way to Zante, Shannon still seemed to be fairly modern. She had heard stories from other people of airports that looked like they hadn't had any work done on them since the day they had been labelled as an airport, some of them still taking on the appearance of an over-sized farmhouse. Thankfully despite being a lot easier to get around Shannon seemed to fall into a category somewhere in between the bustle of Dublin and the barely an airport she had heard and read horror stories about online

Gazing around she spotted a clock silently assuring her that she had ample time before Jim was due to arrive to find her way around. In neat rows were metal benches, many of them empty but one or two with people sprawled across them seemingly trying to sleep while they waited for either a flight or someone to arrive. She had seen similar things to this at Dublin but with a lot more hiding places for those who had no rush to be anywhere to hide away and try to sleep in among the crowds and frequent announcements.

It didn't matter how many times she spotted people sleeping in airports, the sight of it always made her think of the homeless people she had seen in large cities. She knew that these people had different reasons why they were sleeping on the streets but that didn't stop her wanting to be able to help every one of them.

As a young girl she could remember her mother pulling her away from a person huddled up in a corner at a bus station and wondering why the man was sat there. She could still remember asking her mother about it as they made their way home and being told in the easiest way possible that some people lived on the streets. Her instinct was that they should help them, give them money but her father deterred her from doing that commenting on how many of them would use it for drink. Ever since that day she had always kept a spare pair of socks handy so she could give them to someone who might need them based on her fathers suggestion that these were more useful than money to these people.

Shrugging off the idea that any of these airport bench sleepers were likely to be homeless she made her way over to a small row of shops.

Glancing briefly up at the arrivals board Sasha knew it was unlikely that there would be any information on Jim's flight yet but she was curious to know where other flights were arriving from. It was something that had fascinated her from the first time she had entered an airport, the vast amount of destinations and large number of planes that made their way in and out of Ireland on a daily or weekly basis.

She recalled how as a younger girl she had stared at the board seeking out the less common destinations and tried to work out how to pronounce the place names in her head. That had inspired her passion for geography which was a subject that she was now proud that she was doing well with at school, even if she didn't know what sort of job it would assist her in getting in the future.

Making her way into one of the shops she cringed as she gazed across the row of magazines that she knew she had seen many times in her local news agents. Just like every week they had familiar celebrity faces on the cover with comments that were intended to inspire a perspective reader to buy a copy.

Along the aisle from her Sasha saw a man who was taking the more economic option of flicking through the magazine without having made the purchase. She smiled as she glanced back at the shelf spotting the fact that some magazines had taken the option of outer packaging to prevent such activity.

Sasha knew that a lot of the girls from school bought some of these magazines and consulted them for tips on how to gain the perfect body which was a phrase that she detested. Each magazine seemed to have its own take on what the best method was to achieve results that were supposedly demonstrated in the pictures surrounding the article. Sasha kept her disdain for these articles to herself as she knew it was the inner naturist giving her that opinion however it was nice to have seen Adele showing similar opinions in recent weeks.

Turning away from the magazines she made her way over to a chilled cabinet and reached out grabbing a sandwich feeling her tummy making its hunger known as she picked it up. Glancing along the shelf she spotted a meal deal which, at first, seemed like the best option but she paused as she read the information about it.

Just like she had seen in other airports the prices was inflated but she had learned to accept that as something that was done in places where there was a captive audience. Contemplating her options she replaced the sandwich making a silent note that it was probably possible to get something hot for a similar price in a café.

Picking her phone out of her pocket as she placed a tray of food on a table Sasha smiled as she spotted a text from Jim that had appeared while she was queueing up for what she classed as being an economy lunch. She wasn't a fan of fast food but it had been the easiest and best value of the options that were available to her as a non-flyer at the airport.

Reading the text she made note that he had finally boarded the plane which meant that he was due to land in just over an hour's time. She glanced up at the board again noting that his flight had finally made its appearance on the board with an estimated arrival time that reflected the one that had been on his ticket. In a way it made sense that they couldn't change the arrival time when the plane hadn't even left England but she still wanted the time to be closer than it was.

During her journey up to the airport Sasha had taken time to think over a few of the memories she had of her time with Jim in Zante. She had found herself thinking of them more often ever since the flight had been finally booked but they had also acted as a distraction from her talkative seat companion.

In her mind she almost wanted the woman who had sat next to her to ask her something about what she enjoyed doing or anything to do with her life but it was clear that the woman was far too engrossed in her own misfortunes to care about others. It occurred to Sasha that it was possible that the woman made the same journey up to Shannon on a frequent occurrence and chose someone to sit next to intentionally no matter how full the bus was. If that was the case Sasha knew she had become the latest in an elite group that, if they found each other, could potentially write the woman's life story between them.

As her mind drifted past the monologue that was being presented to her Sasha found herself thinking about ways that she could surprise Jim when she met him at the airport. The fact that they had a hotel for a night was already going to be a nice addition that he didn't know about but she wanted to be able to give him something unique.

The most obvious solution was to buy him something as a gift to welcome him to Ireland but that seemed too boring and in many ways stereotypical. Her present had to be something that she would be sure he would appreciate and enjoy, something that would remove any doubts that he had about how she felt about seeing him again. She wasn't sure if it was the boring monotony of the journey or the accompanying monologue but suddenly an idea popped into her head that she thought would be perfect.

Looking down at the tray she had carried over to her table she grabbed the coffee, preparing herself for something that wouldn't be as nice as the ones she got at home. Taking a sip she was pleasantly surprised that it was similar to the one she usually got from her favourite café but this time there was no chance of Fintan appearing. She cringed at the thought that even as far away from home as she was there was technically nothing preventing Fintan from randomly turning up at the airport.

She had heard of things like that happening to other people whereby they had been somewhere that wasn't in the slightest way connected to their home and someone they knew seeing them. In a way she knew that it had happened to her in the form of Mr Scott having ended up being one of the students at the art class she modelled for. Thankfully that course had come to an end and she had discussed her intention to continue modelling with him, they had agreed that ethically it was best for him to avoid classes she was sitting for.

In a way Sasha felt a little bit bad that her intention to keep modelling was limiting which classes he was able to attend but Mr Scott seemed to admire her initiative and assured her it wasn't an inconvenience. While it had been initially awkward having one of her teachers in the class it had in some ways been kind of nice having a familiar face around for her first term as a life model.

Opening the burger she had bought, Sasha glared at the contents and accepted that she had chosen this over a sandwich. Even though it didn't look anything like the one that was on the display image, she hadn't actually expected it to do, but it still seemed like the better and more nutritional option out of the two. Biting down into it she made a note to herself that if she ever did the same journey again she would make sure to pack her own lunch next time.

Peering up at the arrivals screen Sasha felt her hear jump as she spotted that the arrival time had been adjusted and was now showing as 20 minutes earlier than it had been. She had heard in the past that it was a common practice for airlines to overestimate their flight time to allow for any delays, this time it seemed to have worked to her advantage.

She glanced around the airport happily noting that everyone was busy going about their own business and not taking any notice of what anyone else was doing around them. When she first came up with her idea for a surprise for Jim it had been a concern of hers that it would draw attention even if she was as discrete as possible.

Staring over at the arrivals gate she spotted one lone figure in among the crowd of people who were currently awaiting the appearance of their friends and relatives who had flowers and a helium balloon. It made her smile to see that this person was clearly waiting for someone who was as special to them as Jim was to her and even their over the top gesture was being shrugged off

Glaring from her table over toward the row of shops again Sasha realised that in all of their conversations neither of them had considered the small things like plugs. When they went to Greece Sasha knew that her family had always taken an adapter with them but she had never been to England or taken much notice of the plugs Jim used. Pulling her phone out of her bag she quickly searched online for the answer and felt somewhat relieved when she noticed they used the same type.

Smirking to herself as he put the phone back safely away in her bag she made a note to herself about how strange it seemed that they had discussed so much about his visit but neither of them had thought about plugs. She had learned very quickly that Jim was the type of person who put a lot of thought into everything he did and yet it hadn't seemed to cross either his or her minds.

Jumping slightly Sasha glanced to her left as a family hastily shoved the remainder of their meal into their mouths and dashed out of the restaurant leaving their table a mess. In a way she could both sympathise with them and felt angered by what they had done but knew she had no right to say anything about it.

Whenever she ate out she always made a point of at least stacking the items she had used in an effort to help the staff, this restaurant was designed to be practically self-service and yet these people had abandoned their table. She understood that it was possible that they were in a rush but that didn't stop their negligence from angering her.

After a few moments one of the staff made their way over and casually cleared away the mess wiping the table down before leaving it ready for the next onslaught. Sasha pondered as she watched the same family hurriedly clamouring towards the departures area whether this cleaning task was seen as additional duties or part of the job. Sipping the last of her coffee she stood and made sure to tidy her table thoroughly smiling over at the same girl who had cleared the adjacent table as she emptied her tray.

Making her way over to a window she stared out in the direction of the runway spotting a plane that was preparing to take off. Glancing to the sky she muttered to herself that in a short while Jim's plane would surely be arriving and felt her stomach flutter with excitement at the thought of seeing him again.

Gripping her bag she made her way over to a spot where she was able to see the flights board and looked up scanning the arrivals for Jim's flight. It came as a little bit of a shock when she saw that he was less than 5 minutes away from landing which she knew gave her only a few minutes to decide if she was going through with her surprise or not.

She glanced back over at the gift shop contemplating a less adventurous but also less memorable gift for him. This was their first time on an official dating meet up so she knew in her hear that she wanted to make it as memorable as she could and she was sure there was nothing in a shop that would be as memorable as what she had planned.

It surprised her in a way that she was having so many doubts about something that was notably less adventurous than some of the things she had already done. Looking around the building she could see that there was still the same lack of interest in the people passing from one side of it to the other.

Peering out of the corner of her eye she felt her heart jump as she noted that the board was now saying that he had landed. Digging in her bag she pulled her phone out almost relieved to see that he hadn't sent her a message yet as her body filled with adrenalin. A rush of determination passed through her mind as she made her way to the bathroom to prepare Jims welcome present for him.

Chapter Four

A Flight of Fancy

The idea of going on a flight on his own had initially been exciting to Jim but now he was standing at the airport alone it seemed much more daunting. Everything had seemed so logical in his head right up to the moment when the taxi driver had handed over his bags to him, now all he knew was that the first step was checking in his bags.

He glanced over to the row of desks many of which he could see were empty as he searched for the correct one for his flight. His father always managed to make this look so easy and yet now it was him doing it Jim could see that there was some element of organisation required to get it right. On his way to the desks he spotted a stand that was asking him to measure his cabin bag which he had been confident up to that moment was the correct size.

Jim had never enjoyed those moments when people asked him if he was sure after he had made a decision because they made him contemplate whether his decision was the right one or not. Even if there was not meant to be an incorrect answer those few small words 'are you sure' always made him wonder if his decision was going to have consequences he hadn't anticipated.

It was the same when his computer asked him if he was sure about something he had consciously decided was the correct thing to do. He knew that it was all part of the programming but that didn't stop him pausing for a few seconds each time he was asked if he thought he had made the right decision.

This harmless stand that was presenting itself to him asking him if his cabin bag was the right size was now making him question not only its size but its weight. Casually he glanced at the two bags he had packed and slid the one he was planning on carrying on to the plane with him comfortably into the designated slot. For a moment he found himself peering around as if his mind wanted someone else to confirm that he had done it right before sliding the bag back out of the stand.

Feeling happier that he had done a good job so far he made his way toward one of the only manned desks and presented his passport and boarding card to the desk.

"Did you pack the bag yourself" Jim smiled confidently at the young woman who was asking him about his checked in luggage as he handed it over to her.

This was the first time in his life that the question was going to be answered truthfully as he actually had packed his own bag. Normally at this point one of his parents would have to claim to have packed his bag for him but this time it had actually been him, he nodded choosing not to make too much fuss over the matter. With a new sense of confidence Jim made his way towards the departure area conscious of the fact that he would need time to find the correct gate.

It didn't take long for the monotone voice to announce the gate and Jim felt a rush flow through his body as he made his way to it. He glanced through the window spotting the plane patiently awaiting him on the concourse and felt his heart drop slightly when he noticed that it wasn't the same design as other planes he had used.

Jim didn't consider himself to be a nervous flyer, he had flown a lot of times before but the sight of open propellers caught him slightly as he stared through the window. He had heard of planes of this nature before but only ever in the history books and usually when they were discussing the World Wars, it hadn't occurred to him that such vehicles were still in active use.

In his mind, all modern planes were similar to the one he had flown on during the summer but the one that was waiting for him went against that mould. Jim knew that smaller planes were used for small sight-seeing flights but had always considered them to be a novelty item and not the sort of plane he would be using to fly to a different country.

He couldn't help noting that whereas with most of his previous flying experiences it would be virtually impossible to see if anything remotely awkward happened to the engines. This time, depending on where his seat was, he would be able to see the propeller throughout the flight and know if there was a problem. Reaching into his pocket he pulled the boarding pass out and glanced over his seat details feeling mildly reassured that it was likely from his seat number that he didn't have a window next to him.

It didn't seem to take any time at all for the announcement to be made that boarding was starting and Jim took a deep breath as he joined the queue. All around him he could see other people who, unlike him, seemed quite happy to be taking the flight and have none of the concerns that were plaguing his mind. Deep down Jim knew that the same plane that had been taunting him through the window probably made the journey he was about to go one several times a day but his mind still held doubts.

Sitting down on the plane he glanced along the aisle spotting a young child sitting on his parents knees being pointed in the direction of the propeller by his happy father. The child seemed completely carefree about the experience but Jim couldn't help wondering if that was partially due to the fact that, given his age, the child probably couldn't even say propeller let alone spell it.

As soon as the plane was airborne Jim felt his body relaxing and accepting that the journey wasn't really that much different to any other flight he had been on in the past. His relaxed state was interrupted when the man next to him caught his attention and requested access to the aisle so that he could use the bathroom.

Smiling politely Jim stood and let the man out while acknowledging in his mind that the flight was meant to be just over an hour long, that was the same length as most of his classes at college were. If he was to get up half a class he knew that someone would make a comment about it even if that someone wasn't the lecturer then one of his class mates would surely make the observation. He knew deep down that sometimes you just have to go but that didn't stop his mind making the comparison.

As the flight came into its final decent Jim couldn't help following his instincts and gripping to the arm of the chair as if it was going to give him any extra security on landing. His mind had prompted him to the fact that there was always the ferry if he didn't like the idea of flying for his next visit.

During their video calls Sasha and he had looked at the different options and he had mentioned the idea of using the ferry. He didn't travel by boat much except when he had been younger and his parents had taken him on what they referred to as day trips to France which he had quickly learned meant duty free runs.

Sasha had been quick to point out that the ferry was at least 3 times slower to even arrive at the Irish coast and then there was the journey to where she lived to take into consideration. Out of curiosity Jim still made the effort to look at the options and decided that flying was by far the easier, quicker and cheaper option

Jim could feel an adrenalin rush filling his mind as soon as the plane landed at Shannon and peered past his seat colleague to try to catch a glance at the airport building as the plane taxied to its final resting point. The building was much smaller than the one he had left but Jim was used to airports in other countries being small, all he wanted was to get his luggage so he could see Sasha again.

He made note of the two different languages that adorned most of the signs and acknowledged that one of them must be Irish, a language he hadn't known about until he had met Sasha. He could still recall the first time he had heard her speak the language and how it had confused him enough to make him want to learn more about it. In the time since they had been apart he had made an effort to find out more about Irish but realised very quickly that, just like other foreign languages, unless he knew how things were pronounced he wasn't going to get too far on his own.

Standing patiently at the luggage carousel Jim watched as most of the people he had flown with, including the man who had sat next to him, continued into the terminal with only their hand luggage to worry about. His mind wondered back to the case he had packed in preparation for his summer holiday in Greece and how most of the stuff had remained in the case unused. In hindsight he was almost certain that he could get away with hand luggage only if he returned to the complex.

It hadn't occurred to him at the time but now when he looked back on it, he realised that he should have known there was something different about his summer holiday this year. His parents had only packed one case between them and usually that would have only been enough for one of them, he smiled as he reprimanded his lack of observation skills.

For the next week Jim knew he was going to be a guest to Sasha's family and she had told him that they would need to act properly around them. He had often wondered what constituted as properly but chosen not to mention it to Sasha as he could see she was nervous about him staying as it was. Experience had told him that there were sometimes when making light hearted comments no matter how well intended were not advisable, this was definitely one of those times.

Since their holiday this was the first time they were going to have seen him and even though they were familiar with him the rules would be different. IT was nice that they had allowed him to stay with them throughout the mid-term break; Jim knew that without their kindness it would have been much more difficult to get to see Sasha.

Eventually he saw his bag appear and even though it looked like a marooned soldier he felt obliged to wait exactly where he was for it. He had acquired this skill not only from the Rents but from watching other people at luggage carousels who seemed determined to allow their bags to come to them and not expedite the process. Jim had never really understood why people chose this as the correct process but decided to follow the crowd on this one and wait patiently.

Pushing his way out into the arrivals hall he saw Sasha waiting patiently for him and felt his heart fill with a warm glow at the sight of her face. She seemed to almost light up as she spotted him which gave him encouragement to quicken his pace. With eagerness he pushed his way through the disorganised crowd who were parroting the same 'did you have a good flight' spiel to whoever they were meeting. Sliding his way out of the disorganised huddle of strangers he made his way over to Sasha throwing his arms around her gently.

"I guess you had to leave my favourite outfit at home," he whispered cheekily into her ear as he felt her body next to his.

Sasha pushed Jim away gently biting her lip as she maintained eye contact with him before showing off a cheeky grin as she glanced around the building quickly. From the moment she had seen his flight announced as having landed she had been preparing for this moment but hadn't been sure exactly how it was going to pan out.

In her mind she had half expected him to make some comment that she could work with but never in a million year could he have made one that was so perfectly appropriate. Reaching down she carefully unbuttoned her coat making sure not to ruin the surprise before she was completely ready. With a deep breath she opened the coat revealing the fact that she was currently naked underneath it and giggled lightly at Jim before covering herself again hoping that no one else had spotted her daring manoeuvre.

"No, Jim." She winked, "I'm wearing it." Jim dropped the handle of his bag almost in time with his jaw dropping open as she stared at her body, speechless.

Sasha paused for a few seconds feeling a buss filling her mind as she let Jim take in all of the features she was showing him in discrete flash of flesh. Watching his expression move from the confident but cheeky one he had shown her when they first embraced reminded her of a similar look she had seen in him while in Greece. She smiled as she wrapped her coat back around choosing not to make any comment but knowing in her mind that it had been her nudity that had shocked him then as well.

Picking up her bag she pointed out one of the metal benches to him before making her way toward the bathrooms confident that her surprise had achieved the desired effect. Hiding back in the same stall she had used to undress she giggled to herself as she redressed acknowledging the fact that she had now been nude, or practically nude, on their first day together twice.

"Maybe I shouldn't make too much of a habit of that" she muttered as she wriggled back into her jeans.

Making her way back out of the bathroom Sasha made a point of leaving her coat open as she made her way back over to where Jim was sat. She knew that the presence of jeans protruding from the bottom of her coat was reasonable proof that she had redressed but wanted to make sure there was no room for doubt. Sitting calmly next to him she gave Jim a quick kiss on the cheek and gripped his hand and feeling a shudder run through her arm at his touch.

"Ma has booked us a room for us down the road" she commented calmly digging in her back and producing the voucher and handing it to him.

Jim glanced at her, almost relived that she was now dressed again but also stuck with the vision of her body firmly in his head. He had been wondering about what sort of reception he was going to receive from Sasha's parents ever since the flight had been booked but chosen not to mention his concerns to her.

He knew from his friends that there was usually tension when a boyfriend was introduced to the family and could still recall the reception that Jay had been given when he had first visited the family home. In his mind he knew that he had already met Sasha's parents but as that was a holiday it didn't follow the same rules as a normal introduction as they didn't have to deal with him being in their home.

This visit was going to be a lot different and he had prepared himself as much as he could for what to expect but that hadn't made him less nervous. In a way it was nice that they had booked the room but deep down he couldn't help wondering if their one night away from her home was going to be the only time they could act like a couple during his stay.

He had already accepted without question that there would be something in place to ensure that he didn't share a room with Sasha at their home and knew that it wasn't seen as good practice to do other things like kissing in her parent's presence. Hand holding may also be a frowned upon activity which he knew would mean that any other physical contact had to be discrete.

The hotel that her parents had chosen for them was in the small town of Bunratty which Sasha was quite excited about being able to show Jim. She glanced up at the arrivals board smiling as she spotted his flight still displayed but soon to disappear into the statistics of on time arrivals.

During her journey up to the airport, in a moment when her talkative seat companion had decided to take a phone call Sasha had used the breathing space to check some details on their hotel. Her main concern had been how they were going to get to it but she had been relieved to see that there was a regular bus service to the town. Now that she had Jim with her there was no way she was going to be sat next to someone on the bus that she didn't want to be unless the bus was crowded.

Spotting that they had a few minutes before the next bus was due she led Jim out to the bus stops spotting the one they needed quickly and was relieved to see only a few people waiting for the bus to arrive.

The main attraction in Bunratty was, without doubt the folk village and castle which Sasha had been round with her parents but was still keen to show Jim. He had commented on sightseeing in the week leading up to his visit and, while she acknowledged that most of the places Jim had mentioned were too far away for them to travel to she was quietly confident that he wouldn't get bored during his stay.

In her mind Sasha had pictured being able to take Jim to the cottage, which Adele and she had made almost homely with their hidden improvements. She had managed to sneak away to the cottage a few times over the past half of a term usually unaccompanied but sometimes with Adele and was starting to get more confident that no one, except for her two friends, knew about it.

She had intended to tell Jim about it before he came over but each time she had made an attempt to bring it into the conversation it hadn't felt like the sort of thing that was easy to discuss. It did concern her slightly that there was a possibility that the first time he met her best friend she was going to start undressing but if that happened Sasha felt sure she could tackle it.

Sasha had been relatively relieved that the bus journey to Bunratty was a relatively short one given that some of the passengers seemed oblivious to the fact they were sharing the journey with other people. She didn't mind the random phone conversations, even the ones that were in languages she didn't understand were fairly entertaining in their own way, and she knew that she had made similar calls to these before.

For her the awkward moment was when a guitarist decided that both he and his instrument had to be together on the seat. If he had kept it in the case it wouldn't have been too bad but the fact that it didn't fit easily in the overhead space seemed to mean to him that it had to be played for the duration of his journey. Sasha realised extremely quickly that she wasn't the only one who didn't appreciate his unscheduled concert when he was applauded as he left the bus.

The hotel that her parents had booked them was slightly outside the town centre, which in a way was slightly inconvenient but in Sasha's opinion made it ideal. The more remote location meant that the castle wasn't going to be obvious from their bedroom which would give it an element of surprise for Jim,

Sasha gripped Jim's hand gently as they made their way through the gate and up toward the front door of the hotel smiling at the quaint appearance it had managed to maintain. In front of them she saw the reception desk with the blond hair of the receptionist barely visible over the top of the computer monitor she was sat behind.

An air of pride wisped through her body as she presented the neatly folded voucher over the counter placing her small bag on the floor next to her. If anyone had spotted the difference in size of their luggage they would assume that it was Jim being the gentleman and choosing to carry the majority of their clothing for them. Sasha peered over her shoulder at the couch that he had sunk into while she dealt with the checking in process and smiled softly.

"Please sign here" Zusanna presented the registration card to her new guest as she spoke smiling softly and trying not to look like she was pre-judging her young guests.

She had been made aware that there was only one check in left to arrive when she had started her shift but hadn't expected the person registering to be quite as young as Sasha was. Discretely she glanced down as the screen spotting a note that there were to be no room charges allowed while maintaining a professional look as she waited for the card to be filled in.

Sasha bit her lip as the note on the booking about room service was relayed to her and silently acknowledged that she knew there would have been some restrictions put in place by her parents. In her heart she knew that she had only ever considered room service when she had been at the complex with Jim but could understand why her parents wanted ensure she didn't go too wild. Thanking the receptionist as she picked up the key card Sasha glanced over beckoning Jim to join her as she made her way to the lifts.

Chapter Five

Stepping back in time

Jim couldn't help feeling a sense of pride as he walked along the street peering down discretely as he got used to the fact that Sasha's hand was lightly gripping his, just like it had while they were in Zante. Back at home he was so used to seeing others walking along hand in hand that he had become complacent about it but now it was his turn there was nothing that was going to take him out of the moment.

In his mind, even though their relationship was obvious to anyone who saw them this felt like it was their first real date. There was no denying that they had gone out a few times as a couple while they were staying in Zante but this was different to any of those because this time it had involved making what he considered real arrangements.

Sasha hadn't wasted any time throwing her bag on to one of the beds in their room before making her way to the door as a silent way of telling him that anything he had in mind for them to do behind closed doors was going to have to wait. Taking a little more time he carefully placed his bag on the same bed and made his way to the bathroom splashing his face with cold water in an effort to freshen up after his flight.

Now that they were out in the little town of Bunratty Jim could see why Sasha had been so keen to show him around. It wasn't like any town he had seen before, there was more character to it and yet it was clearly just like any other place where people lived and earned money despite feeling like something out of a theme park.

As they walked through the gates into the heart of the town Jim smiled noting that the streets were intentionally designed not to have cars running up and down them. This felt like not only a clever touch but a nice concept as it kept with the old theme that filled the atmosphere encouraging anyone visiting to enjoy the world of yesteryear.

Standing in a group outside one of the themed buildings Jim spotted a group of students who looked like they weren't much older than him. One of the group was craning their arm out while trying to join the pose as he took a picture with his phone which Jim couldn't help smiling at.

He could remember fond memories from his childhood of times when he had been either on day trips or on holiday with his parents and they had handed their camera to a stranger who had offered to take a picture for them. There was an element of trust in such an act and yet it was one of the most common things to do, especially if there was nowhere to prop the camera or an unpredictable timer on it making it hard to join a picture without assistance.

Despite the element of trust that came with handing over a camera to someone who wasn't part of the intended picture there as also an advantage in having a picture taken this way. The fact that someone was standing waiting to take the picture it almost into an event with most people who passed by making an effort to make sure they walked around the photographer and those waiting to be immortalised in a photo. There was always one or two people who either didn't see the photo being set up or didn't care about it so continued on as if it wasn't happening but that all added to the moment of trying to take a family photo.

Ever since the concept of selfies had become popular the who art of taking a picture of everyone within a family or group had become less interactive. It was almost as if the fact that the device being used was a phone made the level of trust notably lower to the extent where poses had become much more awkward.

Jim knew that he had to acknowledge the fact that he had been involved in a few self-taken group pictures, images that he refused to call 'selfies' due to the fact that they weren't only of one person but that didn't mean he liked them. He was still much happier than most of his friends with the idea of asking someone to take a photo of all of them as long as they could find someone willing to do it.

Sasha gripped his hand harder as she pulled him across the street to a building that was intentionally locked to stop anyone from going inside and ruining the display. Through the window he could see neat rows of desks all set facing the front of the room, some of them with models of children sitting attentively looking at the blackboard.

At the front of the class with a long wooden ruler in one hand was another model, this one clearly meant to represent the teacher trying her best to explain the text scrawled across the blackboard to her captive audience.

Squinting slightly Jim peered at the board to see if he could work out what was meant to be being taught but decided that the little piece he was able to see made no sense to him so focussed his eyes back on the desks.

When he was younger he could recall hearing stories about what it was like at school in the years even before his parents were born. Everything sounded so much stricter and in many ways scarier when the subject got onto things like the use of the cane as a form of punishment. It was the thought of being hit by what was in effect a long walking stick that made him more appreciative that punishment at his school only really involved detention.

Turning her head Sasha pulled Jim away from the schoolhouse like an excited child who had just seen a ride at a theme park that she had been waiting to have a go on. She led the way over to the pottery store where she knew there was an on-going demonstration of the traditional way to make plates and cups before machines took over.

Squeezing her way in through the assembled crowd she made her way toward the front stopping when she spotted a cluster of children gazing in awe at the potter at his wheel. In her mind she could recall having gone to a demonstration just like the one she was looking at as part of a school trip. She couldn't remember where they had gone to but the memory of the pottery demonstration was vivid in her mind.

After a short talk the woman who had been guiding them asked for six volunteers who wanted to have a go at it for themselves. Naturally the entire group put their hand up, some of them jumping on their tiptoes and uttering gasping noises of excitement in an effort to catch her attention.

Sasha watched as six of her classmates were selected randomly and felt the same temporary moment of dismay as the rest of her class when she wasn't among the lucky ones to be chosen. The six who had been chosen were quickly ushered away by a second woman who had appeared half way through the talk and provided with overalls to prevent getting too dirty while they joined the potter.

"Don't worry, everyone will get a chance" the guide made sure she was heard as she made her comment reassuring those left waiting that their turn wasn't far away.

In many ways, Sasha was relieved that the trip and pottery demonstration she had enjoyed with her classmates had been before her first experience of naturism. There was no denying that the coverall that everyone was helped into was effective in keeping their uniform clean but now she reflected back on it she could see a very practical side in pottery being made naked.

Just like the small child in front of her, Sasha gazed through the screen that was set between the potter and the assembled crowd. When she had first seen the dividing screen Sasha had taken it as being similar to the splash guards frequently seen at aquatic creature shows but had quickly realised this screen was for a different reason.

The fact that there was a possibility of clay splashing as the wheel rotated at a pace that seemed impossible to work with was accounted for by the guard in front of the wheel. This additional screen was to allow the potter to concentrate on his work and remain oblivious to the crowd gazing in on him as he worked.

Jim made his way carefully through the crowd recalling how art at school had been one classes he had been happy to drop when it came to time to prepare for final exams. The teacher had made an attempt to teach everyone how to sculpt clay with varying levels of success, but Jim was sure that none of his class were going to become professional potters after seeing their final efforts.

Just like everyone else he had been encouraged to take his creation home once it had been through the final glazing and half-arsed painting. He could still remember glancing at the brief sketch he had created depicting what he was planning to create and how it barely resembled the finished piece.

Despite his best efforts to conceal it his parents had somehow known that he had the clay model in his bag when he arrived home after school. If he had been able to get away with it Jim knew that he was more inclined to feign no knowledge of it or pretend he had left it at school but he knew that either of those options held consequences. If he made out that it was at school still he wouldn't heat the end of it until he remembered to bring it home. If he pretended not to know anything about it or even pretended to have accidentally dropped it the reaction from his mother would have been one of unspoken disbelief.

He could still recall his mother almost standing over him as she dug through his bag before carefully pulling out his finished sculpture. Unlike some of the others from his class at least his one bore some resemblance to the image he had been using to recreate his art project. In the image the sculpture was perfectly toned with a muscle structure that could only be achieved by the most dedicated athletes. Jims attempt to recreate the image looked like it had man boobs an a six pack that was superimposed over a beer belly.

The look of pride in his mothers eyes was, in some ways worth the effort but it was awkwardly clear that she was struggling to see the resemblance to the image he had shown her. Regardless of how unusual it looked compared with the original and despite the fact that it was ever so slightly top heavy meaning it had to be leant against a wall to maintain an upward pose it had taken pride of place in a display cabinet. Jim felt sure it was still there, hidden by souvenirs over the past few years but hadn't dare to ask about it just in case it was somewhere unseen in the back of the overcrowded cabinet.

Leaning in he placed his hands slowly round Sasha's waist clasping them at her tummy and smiling as he felt her leaning into his embrace. He placed his chin on her shoulder as she ran her fingers along the top of his arms in a silent acknowledgement that she felt happy and secure in his grasp.

"D' you fancy a coffee?" Jim half whispered the question in Sasha's ear feeling his energy lapsing after his flight

Sasha turned her head carefully as she heard Jim speaking conscious of the fact that her hair was partially trapped under his chin. She had been so engrossed in the demonstration she had almost forgotten that they only had a short time before the village would be closing for the day and so far they had barely seen anything.

Digging in her pocket she pulled her phone out checking the time and acknowledged to herself that even if it seemed impractical coffee was probably a good way to plan the rest of their visit. Tapping on his hands as if they were the release mechanism for his grip she led the way out of the pottery and into the gift shop, which she knew also had a café tactically placed at the back of it.

Jim glanced discretely around the gift shop as they made their way through it having already decided that it would be nice to get Sasha something while they were there as a memory of their trip. He couldn't deny that Sasha's welcoming present had been more than he had been expecting and knew that if it had been she who had flown to meet him he probably wouldn't have even thought up such a surprise. Now that they were in a place that was designated to the sale of gifts it seemed like a great opportunity to buy her something special as long as he could do it without her knowing.

He made his way over to the counter ordering two coffees as Sasha made her way to a table where she lay out a leaflet she had picked up that unfolded to create a map of the village. Glancing beyond the cashier he spotted a sign that referred to a collection service that seemed like the perfect way to pick up whatever he bought her at the end of their visit. The big challenge now was how to buy it without her knowing, either that or just tell her he wanted to get a gift and ruin the surprise – which he wanted to avoid if he could.

Placing her coffee on the table he sat down spotting the schoolhouse and pottery immediately on the map as he took a first sip. Toward the top of the map, partially hidden by his elbow was the castle which seemed like the most obvious place they should see while they were in the town. Sasha stood quickly excusing herself to go to the bathroom within a few moments of having started her coffee leaving Jim at the table as she dashed out of the door.

Jim glanced around seeing the perfect opportunity to make an attempt to buy the gift he had decided to get as long as he was willing to take the risk on either leaving the table unattended or losing the table if he cleared it before shopping. Gazing over the items he knew that there was nothing her would miss if it went missing while he was browsing the shop but also didn't want to explain why he had left the table when Sasha returned.

Behind him he could hear the clutter of a table being cleared and turned to spot one of the staff busy resetting it ready for the next visitor. Suddenly an idea fell into his mind as he caught the woman's attention asking her not to clear the table he was at while he had a look around the shop. She smiled sweetly at him and placed a "Reserve" sign on the map Sasha and he had been planning to look at as he dashed into the shop to browse for a gift.

Jim was conscious of the fact that he didn't have a lot of time to find something if he didn't want Sasha finding out about it immediately. He hadn't spotted the location of the bathrooms on the map but felt sure that it wouldn't be too far away meaning that he may only have a few moments available before she returned.

In one corner of the store he spotted a range of mugs, all of them with phrases on with a sign above them marking them as having been handmade. He hadn't considered it before but now that he saw the sign it felt like the potter had his work cut out if he was responsible for stocking the store with his work.

Next to the first set of mugs he spotted a second display which appealed to him even more when he saw a sign marking them as being perfectly imperfect. Glancing through the window he was both relieved and surprised to see that there was still no sign of Sasha returning as a burning sensation hit his bladder prompting him to need the same journey she was currently on as soon as she returned.

He had been in similar situations to this before when he had been a young boy with on a day trip with his parents. There hadn't seemed to be any logic in it but either he or his sister had always been asked to remain outside with the bags and one parent while the other was escorted to the bathroom. He could understand it if there was only one of them requiring the use of the facilities but when both of them had synchronised the need to go it seemed more logical for both parents to take one child each.

Conscious of how long Sasha had already been away Jim browsed through the range of mugs that had been classed as imperfect feeling sure that he was already on borrowed time. It felt weird trying to work out how long someone had spent in the bathroom but he knew that if he was going to make his gift a surprise this was more than likely to be his best opportunity.

He had tried in the past to surprise people in the past and each time it had been a challenge to find the right moment to put whatever he had planned into action. Sometimes it felt almost as if the person he was surprising actually knew what was intended and was making it as difficult as possible for him. No matter whether they did or not the end result was always a look that appeared pleased with whatever he had done but he wasn't always sure if the look was genuine or not.

Reaching through he picked up a mug and grinned as he spotted the wording that suggested it had been intentionally created with an imperfection. There was a clear dent type mark near the bottom of the mug that he knew would make it difficult to wash but he loved the words that were printed on one side of it.

"It is our imperfections that make us perfect for the right person"

Glancing toward the window he spotted a figure that looked like Sasha and made his way quickly to the till point handing over his money as the door opened. Feeling a rush filling his mind he knew that it was practically impossible to talk his way out of what he was doing without causing some suspicion. His heart seemed to stop for a moment as he peered anxiously around feeling relieved when the figure turned out not to be her.

Calming down a little he confirmed with the cashier that he wanted to use the collection service as he tucked his wallet back into his pocket and made his way back to the table. Taking a deep breath he looked over the map that was still sprawled over the table and picked up his coffee taking a sip that he knew was going to add urgency to his need for the bathroom but it felt like it was almost needed.

Hearing the small bell above the door tinkle again he turned again this time happy to see this time it was Sasha making her way back to the table. Discretely he glance at the till pleased to see that the mug he had purchased was nowhere in sight even if it was only him who would know what they were looking for.

No sooner had Sasha sat down than Jim stood excusing himself in the same direction she had just returned from. He smiled trying to ignore the burning sensation as he made his way out of the store contemplating his thoughts over what made a mug imperfect.

There were some imperfections that he knew were obvious but they would make the mug unfit for sale, things like a hole or crack that had formed while it was being cooked. He pondered over the thought that it was possible that if the design was put on the wrong side of the mug it could be implied as in imperfection or just sold as a left handed mug. He had seen left handed equipment before and noticed that normally if an item was marked as left handed it also had a premium added as if it was a speciality requirement.

It fascinated him now that he was thinking about it how all mugs seemed to be designed with a right handed person in mind if they had a design on them. He hadn't really considered himself an entrepreneur but as he washed his hands he wondered whether there was a business opportunity waiting to be explored and he had accidentally fallen into it.

Heading back to the shop he peered up at the castle that was the centre piece of the town and paused briefly gazing up at it. He had spotted it on the map and knew that Sasha wanted to go there before they went back to the hotel.

In a way he was sure that he had noticed it when they had first walked in to through the gates to the folk park but not really paid much attention to it. Now he was focussing on it he could see how well maintained it looked despite being notably smaller than the ones that he had visited back home.

Turning to face the shop he saw Sasha waiting patiently outside with their coffee's in take away cups in her hands. The look on her face made it clear that she was either oblivious to his gift, which he knew she should be, or she was hiding the fact that somehow she had found out about it and didn't want to ruin the surprise for him.

"Will we head to the castle then?" Sasha handed over one of the coffee cups as she spoke.

Jim smiled at her peering discretely through the window and he acknowledged her enquiry with a nod while wondering if his gift had already left or if it hadn't, how much time it would need to get back to the entrance.

Chapter Six

Table for two

The fact that Jim hadn't made a big deal over giving her the present told Sasha that he hadn't bought it because it had any deeper meaning to him than simply wanting to buy her a gift. Sasha had to admit that she would have been a little bit upset if the mug had been inscribed with a phrase like "Worlds greatest Gran" but thankfully he had clearly spent some time reading the messages before choosing one.

"It's the little imperfections that we see in ourselves that make us perfect in someone elses eyes"

The phrase was in some ways both well intended and well-meant but Sasha knew that she wasn't the only person who would question the reference to imperfections if presented with the item in the wrong context.

She had heard a similar reference to imperfections before but only recently and the person who had made the reference surprised her in a way.

They had been at the cottage and preparing to spend a little time there practicing naturism when suddenly out of the blue Adele commented on how naturism left all of a persons imperfections visible to anyone. Sasha had been stripped to her underwear when she heard the comment and Adele was already naked and casually folding her clothes into a neat pile ready to enjoy the sun.

"What do you mean Dell?" Sasha stood upright reaching for the clasp on her bra while feeling suddenly conscious of her body for the first time in years.

Sasha had a vague memory from her first visit to the complex where she had seen a man with a large mark on one of his buttocks that looked like he had been severely burned which turned out to be a birthmark. It was on her first day on the site and her parents had been cautiously concerned about how she was going to handle the idea of being nude and surrounded by strangers who were also nude.

From the moment she had arrived at the complex she had made it clear that she had n problems with disrobing and had been naked within less than an hour of arriving in their apartment but that wasn't the same as walking around the site naked. Her mother had kept an eye on her from the sunbed as she slowly made her way up to the man and, with a child's curiosity and innocence asked her about the mark.

The man had smiled and been happy to tell her all about it before escorting her back over to them and complimenting them on how polite she was. Neither of them had made too much fuss about the incident but it seemed obvious that their main concern was going to be how she would react to seeing his penis and yet it was his birthmark that had caught her eye.

"Nothing Sash, it was something Seamus, ya know that guy from Dublin, mentioned"

In some ways it was a relief to hear Adele say that her comment was only a random one and Sasha could remember letting out a sigh of relief as she unclipped her bra. Despite it being shrugged off she found herself still wondering if she had any blemishes she wasn't aware of that had sparked the comment in the first place.

Sasha could see that there was a wisdom in what Adele had said even if the actual idea hadn't come from her. The fact that she had taken in a comment that someone she barely knew relating to a lifestyle that she was fairly new to meant that she was giving the concept some real thought and hadn't just jumped into it, which was in a way something Sasha had worried about from the first moment Adele tried naturism.

"D'you see imperfections in me Jim?" Sasha blushed as she asked the question accepting that it wasn't the sort of thing that was going to be easy to answer and, if there were any imperfections he had noticed, probably not a question she really wanted answering.

Jim froze on the spot as he heard the question. This was one of those questions, which he had learned to refer to as being impossible to answer correctly. These questions were like some kind of subtle trap that regardless of the answer or the intention behind the answer there was always the possibility of getting the third degree or more questioning because of a non-committal answer or one that had the slightest chance of being misinterpreted.

The truth of the matter was that he hadn't been looking for or spotted any part of Sasha's body that had made him wonder what it was or how it had happened. He tried his best to recall the less obvious features, any scar that she might have but the only parts of her that came to mind were those that he had been trying to avoid thinking about ever since he had seen them at the airport.

On one hand he knew that, even if he had been able to think of some part that wasn't completely perfect it was dangerous to even consider mentioning it. There was always the light hearted option of suggesting the stripped naked so that he could make a thorough search but the sincerity of her question meant that such a reply wouldn't go down too well.

On the other hand, if he said there was nothing wrong with her there was a good chance that she wouldn't trust his answer to be genuine. Saying she was perfect seems like such a crowd pleasing response and yet the fact that he hadn't seen anything out of the ordinary on her body also suggested that he hadn't really spent much time looking at it – but was that a good thing or a bad thing?

Some girls would love the idea that their boyfriend hadn't spent too much time mulling over their bodily features, comparing them with any other person they had seen while other girls almost expected to have their body glared at. Sasha didn't seem to fit into either category, there was no denying she liked to walk around naked but she had also reprimanded him on their very first day together for talking to her breasts so it really was a lose-lose situation.

Smiling sheepishly Jim made his way over to the bed where Sasha was sitting and strategically sat down close enough that he didn't look like he was avoiding her but with enough space between them to at least avoid an elbow nudge. He glanced over at the dresser where the mug he had bought her sat proudly as if it was a first prize trophy and knew exactly where her question was coming from.

When he had picked it up he hadn't given the words on it any real thought, he seldom did unless he was buying something for a special occasion and yet this mug had the power to become his undoing.

"Sash, you know that nobody is perfect don't you?" he smiled calmly as he made his first comment

Sasha glared at him briefly out of the corner of one eye as she heard what she had to admit was a very insightful response even if it didn't actually answer her question.

"I'm not dating you because you are perfect to everyone Sash, I'm dating you because you are perfect to me" Sasha felt a blush passing across her face as she leaned in kissing him on the cheek for what she couldn't deny was about the best reply she could expect.

Jim stood and reached over her feeling safe after her silent response as he grabbed the room service menu. Grabbing his arm Sasha looked up at him with a soft expression in her eyes, biting her lip slightly as she touched him

There was a clear tiredness in his eyes as he looked at her which didn't really come as a surprise after all the travelling he had done. In many ways Sasha felt guilty for having taken him to the folk town but the fact that he had gone to the effort of buying her a gift suggested that he had enjoyed at least some of the trip.

"We can't order from that" Sasha tried to keep her facial expression as soft as possible as she spoke to prevent it seeming like she was reprimanding him.

The truth of the matter was that, if they had been in a position to order room service she thought it was a great idea but the conditions of their booking had been set for them and she wasn't about to try flaunting them.

Smiling at her, he placed the menu back on the dresser accepting that she was reinforcing something that was beyond her control as he returned to his seat.

Sasha felt a little bit awkward about the idea that she was basically telling him that if they wanted to eat they had no choice but to leave the room. In a way she wasn't overly fussed about whether they had dinner or not but the fact that Jim had reached for the menu suggested that he was hungry. If he pretended not to be now she knew she would feel awkward about it but room service had been ruled out by the way the room had been booked.

In her mind Sasha could see some humour in the fact that he had just stopped him from using room service and not for the first time since their first meeting at the complex. Unlike the last time she had found him with the menu, this time it wasn't fear of dress codes encouraging him to reach for the menu but also, unlike the last time this time they couldn't use it even if they wanted to.

Jim knew that he had inadvertently put himself in yet another rut having just escaped one that Sasha built for him while asking about her imperfections. The fact that he had made such an obvious effort to reach for the menu left little doubt about his need to get food and even if he hadn't tried to avoid it he felt like he couldn't go the rest of the evening just on the few snacks he had eaten during the day.

In the back of his mind he could remember something having been said about room service but in a moment of weakness it had slipped his mind. Room service seemed like the perfect option but now he had to either find a good excuse for having picked up the menu or accept that they were going to have to leave the room and have dinner somewhere else before he got any real time alone with Sasha in private.

At first, he found himself pondering over the idea of suggesting takeaway.

There was something appealing about the idea of only having to go out for a short while and being able to come back to their room and relax in front of the TV munching on a portion of chips but on the other hand was the issue of the lingering smell and wrappings from their meal. He didn't fancy the idea that in the morning, while they were downstairs checking out and thanking the reception the evidence of their meal would be stuffed in a bin waiting for housekeeping to find and dispose of

Adding more depth to his thoughts, jim realised that this really was the first time he was going to be able to actually take out for a meal, it was true that they had shared their meal times at the complex but that wasn't the same as actually going out for dinner.

Sasha stood from the bed and peered casually over the leaflets that were neatly laid out ready to be used as reference points for the room occupier. It came as no surprise to her that interspersed between leaflets for other attractions that were close were a few leaflets for the folk town. A quick glance through the collection told her that there were at least four leaflets for the town and its castle which really pushed home how keen they were for people to see it during their time in the area.

"Didn't we see a restaurant on the way back her from the castle?" Jim stood from the bed and made his way to the bathroom.

Sasha watched as the door to the bathroom closed behind him silently muttering to herself about how she refused to have a conversation through the wall unless it was part of a game and they were using Morse code. Digging her phone out of her pocket she made a quick search and was pleased to see that he was right, there were a few small restaurants within a reasonable walking distance.

Glancing briefly at the bag she had bought she knew without looking that there was nothing in there which she would consider to be going out to dinner clothing. It was only the fact that they had an overnight stay that had inspired her need to pack anything at all; she hadn't considered the idea that they might be eating out too.

Suddenly the idea of a take away came to mind but Sasha felt sure that, knowing Jim he had already given that idea some thought before settling on a restaurant meal. Although he hadn't said anything about it since the moment they left the airport Sasha felt sure that her daring surprise as she met him was still somewhere in his mind and probably going to be there for some time to come.

It was in some ways a pleasant surprise that he hadn't made any effort to capitalise on his thoughts and yet part of her mind wanted him to make some kind of move to seducing her if only so that she could tell him to wait. In the back of her mind the thought that her move hadn't had any effect on him lingered and his lack of advance since then suggested that maybe he wasn't in a rush to get intimate with her. For now she was content to enjoy the momentum and make sure they had a good time ready for when the moment was right.

The hotel they were in was advertised as offering a bar meal but Sasha knew that if there had been a restriction placed on their stay preventing room service it was also likely that their age was known as well. The last thing she wanted was an awkward moment if one of them tried to order a drink and couldn't provide suitable ID which she knew wouldn't be a problem in a real restaurant.

Brushing her finger down the screen of her phone she peered upward as the door to the bathroom opened again and Jim re-appeared. Sasha smiled and glanced between him and her phone before pointing at a place she had randomly settled on based on a her limited knowledge of the town and budget.

Jim gazed at the screen as if he was assessing her choice while trying to show some interest in where they were going. In his heart he had wanted them to be staying in now they were back at the hotel and was finding it hard to hide his frustration that they weren't able to avail of the room service, even if the options were probably minimal.

With that said he knew that in a way it was nice that he was actually going to be able to take Sasha out for a meal on their first night together and he knew that it was probably the nicest way to spend their first evening. His school friends had referred to going on dates to cinemas or bowling, both activities that he enjoyed doing but neither of them seemed like great choices for a real date especially early in the relationship.

He had a naturally competitive streak that had only grown with the hours he had spent online gaming and knew that such a trait could ruin a bowling date. Even though he didn't mind losing he could think of much better things to do and was still slightly precautious after having lost at chess to Sasha in front of a crowd.

Cinema dates seemed even less appealing although he felt sure that when his friends had referred to taking a date to the cinema it wasn't necessarily the film that was the biggest appeal in such a date. Dark lighting gave a sense of anonymity and in some ways intimacy but there was a crowd sat around them making anything too intimate awkward or near on impossible without raising suspicion.

If the date was specifically to see a film then that meant it was going to be basically a silent date apart from the noise of popcorn, crisps and slurping of drinks. There was also the question of what type of film to see – one that he felt sure was never an easy choice due to the high possibility of different interests. For him, if a date was going to include watching a film it was much nicer to have it in the comfort of one of their homes but that would then more than likely involve the presence of parents.

There wasn't much that he could think of that was more embarrassing than having a parent making a comment about two people cuddling up together. In the event of parents having left them alone to watch the film there was still a high chance of interruptions under the guise of an adult needing to get something from the room. Jim knew that excuses of this kind were actually an excuse to make sure that nothing untoward was going on between the two people attempting to have a date.

"That one looks good" he smiled handing the phone back to Sasha before following her out of the room.

Sasha gripped his hand gently as they made their way back down the road for the second time since having checked in to the hotel. She had a fond memory of the first evening they had spent together in the hotel and how much effort Jim had put in to it despite the fact that at the time they were barely even acquaintances. In her mind, even though she hadn't said anything to him about it, his effort on that evening had been part of the reason that she had been so happy when he had finally made a move.

They peered through the restaurant window as they arrived; encouraged by the fact that there seemed to be a reasonable crowd dining out but accepting the fact that as it was a weekend it was likely to be a busier evening. Glancing over the menu that was presented through the window Jim smiled seeing a few different options that appealed to his stomach which was now demanding some food.

"Table for two" Jim smiled at the maître de as they made their way through the door.

Donal smiled softly as he saw the young couple entering the restaurant picking two menus out and escorting them over to a table that placed them in a cubicle that ran along the side wall. He had grown to enjoy working weekend nights because they were much more casual than the usual crowd of business people that fell in and out of the door during the week.

There was something almost calming about tending to a couple as opposed to a large group similar to the one he had recently led into the private room for a hen party. Every time he passed the door he had to wonder if he was really the only person that was able to hear their high pitched giggling or maybe he was the only person it irritated. Some of the other waiting on staff thrived on the idea of serving the larger groups and he was happy to let them fight over the inflatable toys while trying to serve the main course.

He wasn't sure if it was his inner snob but to him couples were much nicer to serve and it wasn't only because they usually left a better tip, they were just easier to deal with. Smiling amicably he watched as the young couple slid into the booth he had allocated to them watching as they settled before presenting the menu to them.

Jim smiled as he looked down the menu spotting the familiar reference to specials and choosing to avoid them based on his previous experience of them with his parents. Glancing past the menu he found himself wondering if Sasha was planning to order a starter or just go straight into the main course.

It was the one part he hated most about going out regardless of who it was with, trying to work out who was planning on starting from the top of the menu and who wasn't. There was nothing quite as awkward as ordering a starter and then having to sit there eating it while whoever else was sat at the table made small talk while you ate it.

The obvious way around it was to allow Sasha to order first and have a starter ready if she ordered one or to suggest a shared starter which he knew was a nice option for a couple. He had eaten shared starters before but only with another member of his family which didn't seem the same as it would be if he shared with her.

In his mind even though the shared starter was a nice option but only if both of them wanted the same thing. He had already set his eyes on the garlic mushrooms which he knew were not the best option for a date night but he enjoyed them.   He glanced across the restaurant spotting the man that had shown them to their table casually making his way back toward them.

The fact they had been given a booth to sit in was a nice touch as he could see there were plenty of other tables in central locations that could easily have been set to them. He liked the privacy they gained from having partitions either side of them but couldn't help feeling a little claustrophobic.

Making his way over to the table Donal tried not to look like he was stalking the young couple by tactically glancing at other tables as he walked. He was relieved to see them place their menus down as he cleared a couple of glasses from a recently vacated table flicking a cloth over it before preparing to take their order.

The aroma of food filled the air as the starter was presented to their table and Sasha smiled feeling her stomach making its subtle demand to be satisfied. Carefully she sipped at the drink she had decided to treat herself to as their plates were placed in front of them tingling slightly as the warmth of alcohol passed down her throat.

Jim reached across lightly stroking her arm feeling like it was the first moment they had together when they weren't rushing to do something other than enjoy each other's company. He spotted Sasha looking across to him and smiled sensing a look in her eyes that he had seen before but not since their first night together in Zante.

Spotting their main course arriving he moved his hand away quickly like he had been caught by the Rents doing something he wasn't meant to be. He could still remember the last time he had been caught trying to reach something that had been confiscated from him and the disastrous ending to that adventure.

He had been 12 and it had been a handheld games console that he had been bought for Christmas and barely put down for a week before his mother got tired of him staring at it. He waited until she had gone into the kitchen to prepare dinner before making an attempt to reach it off the top shelf of the cabinet it had been placed on.

In his anticipation to regain his game he hadn't realised that it had taken a stool for his mother to reach the shelf and spent the next 10 minutes on his tiptoes slowly losing his balance. After several failed attempts at reaching the correct shelf including some fairly enthusiastic jumping that he timed to match the noisier parts of the cooking routine he eventually gave up. The reality was that he didn't as much give up as trip over as he landed badly crashing into the arm of the couch and falling in a heap.

Sasha dabbed her chin daintily with a napkin as she finished her main meal and glanced casually at the menu again pondering over dessert. She glanced at Jim biting her lip as she saw him patting his stomach in a way she had seen before when he was full but wanting her to make the decision. Glancing at the menu a second time and spotting a dessert that took her fancy she peered back at Jim who she could tell had other things on his mind that weren't on the menu.

Chapter Seven

Room Serviced

Propping himself up on his elbows Jim peered from the bed to the chair in front of the dresser where Sasha was sat calmly brushing her hair. He knew that his face was brandishing the same silly grin he had felt the first time they had shared a bed but he couldn't help it and felt sure in his mind that other boys held similar expressions after a night with their girlfriends even if theirs was more subtle.

From his spot, still snug and hidden under the covers he couldn't help noticing that Sasha seemed to have a glow which in his mind made her look like some kind of goddess. He knew from past experience of compliments that she had dismissed as being unnecessary that Sasha wouldn't appreciate it if he made his thoughts known so chose to silently admire her instead.

In some ways there was serenity in the fact that she hadn't bothered with getting dressed although he could see a towel draping under her buttocks making him wonder if he had slept through her shower time. During his sleep he had envisioned joining her in the shower despite having assessed it during the evening and deciding that such an activity was not practical.

He could recall his friends referring to having shared showers with others and could see the basic appeal of such an activity but his mind kept on telling him it couldn't be a comfortable thing to do. In the past if he had even touched the tiled bathroom wall during a shower it had sent a chill down his spine, he couldn't bear to think of how much more awkward it was to avoid the walls with a second person.

Sasha smiled softly as she spotted Jim propped up in the bed where she had left him half an hour earlier. Carefully she pulled the brush through her raven locks content in the fact that at least there was a good reason for her hair to be slightly dishevelled this morning. Jim had seemed almost obsessed with playing with it from the moment she had joined him in bed which had been comforting but she had known it was going to be awkward the following morning.

She had pondered over the idea of slipping one of the complimentary robes on as she slid out of the bed intent on making her way toward the window to see what type of day they had to look forward to. Part of her mind wanted it to be overcast but not rainy because that seemed like the most ideal weather for travelling as it wouldn't be too hot in the bus but they wouldn't get wet while waiting for connections.

In her mind, she could hear her mother warning her about the dangers of opening a curtain while not dressed. At home, she knew there was the creepy boy from down the road to be aware of but here no one knew her, which made the option of risking opening the curtain nude both more and less enticing. On one hand, the fact that no one knew her meant that if anyone did happen to see her breasts they weren't likely to see her again whereas on the other hand if it was one of the hotel staff – they were likely to at least know her name making it less appealing.

Placing one arm across her breasts, she glared at the curtain as she pondered over her options before glancing at the digital clock, which had been emitting an eerie glow into the room throughout the night. She smiled as she confirmed that it wasn't even 8 AM and it was a Sunday so the chances of there being many people about were minimal. Standing slightly away from the window she carefully pried the curtain open peering down at the carpark happy to see that there was absolutely nobody around.

Ever since she had returned to school she had noticed how, when she was doing her modelling she was becoming more and more comfortable being nude around the students who were drawing her. The fact that Mr Scott was one of the students was still a little bit disconcerting but they had a mutual agreement that she wouldn't make any attempt to socialise with him in the class. On more than one occasion she had spent her break time talking with him about his art work but that only happened when there was no-one else around to suspect anything.

From her first week modelling Mr McArdle had been encouraging her to interact with the group during breaks in between sessions and after the session ended if a student wanted to show or share their work with her. She had made a point of only ever going as far as first name basis to prevent anyone finding out that she wasn't actually over 18 which she knew would cause problems.

At first, she had made a point of making sure that the robe she always wore at the beginning of the class was wrapped tightly around her body before leaving the stage she posed from. Students would sometimes come up to her while she was stretching her arms to loosen her muscles before moving but they always maintained a distance to ensure she kept personal space. By the fourth week she was still wearing the robe but less conscious about tying it at her waist before wondering around the room.

It was week 6 if the classes when she had been pulled to one side by Mr McArdle and reminded to cover up before socialising. She wasn't sure what had distracted her from her usual routine but without thinking she had left her stage with the robe draped over her arm and still hadn't got around to wearing it by the time she reached the second person who wanted to talk to her.

What was more concerning was the dream that had awoken her in which she could vividly see that she was walking down the hotel corridor completely naked. The thought jolted her into waking up so that she could be sure it really was only a dream and not some crazy stunt she had pulled without thinking about it. At the time she turned to see Jim still muttering in his sleep beside her but decided it was time to get up anyhow.

Moving away from the window Sasha sat in the chair in front of the dresser, sliding a towel under her bottom as she sat down just like she would have done when she was at the complex in Greece. Over there it was seen as one of the rules to sit on towels for hygiene reasons which she quickly learned was part of the naturist way of life but here in the privacy of their hotel room she knew she didn't actually need to do it.

In a way it was sad to think that when they left the room it wasn't going to be easy for them to get the same level of intimacy again for the rest of Jims stay but that was an unwritten sacrifice in order to have him stay with her. This bedroom, their one night alone together was the one time when she could relax not only with Jim but without the need to worry about getting dressed. No-one was going to tell her off for walking around their room naked, definitely not Jim and he was the only other person in the room.

It occurred to her that despite the amount of times they had spoken since their last real time together she still hadn't really told him a lot about her growing interest in naturism. It hadn't been an easy thing to bring up in conversation and hadn't seemed like an important thing to mention given that he knew she was comfortable as a naturist anyhow. That was going to need to change, especially now that her best friend was also into the lifestyle just in case he ended up somehow encountering her naked and wondered what was going on. In her heart Sasha knew that the chances of that happening without her being able to prepare him for it were minimal but it wasn't completely out of the question.

Glancing around the room she knew that there was a bible in one of the drawers even without having spotted it because there always was one. In her childhood religion had been seen as part of their lifestyle even if her parents hadn't made much of a fuss about it. She knew all about Adam and Eve and was aware of the story of the snake which people referred to as being the original sin. She could see some irony in reading that story while being nude but didn't want to go to the effort of finding the book or actually reading it.

It was in that moment as she was pondering options when Sasha had accepted that the only thing left to do in the bedroom was read through the welcome folder. In a moment that she hadn't expected Sasha found herself smiling as she spotted a note at the bottom of the menu that she had no doubt Jim would be interested in taking on.

"Prepaid breakfast can be served to your room at no extra cost"

Jim had shown interest in the idea of room service more than once since she had met him and she was sure that he had probably had it during what she classed as their pre-relationship misunderstanding. Each time he had looked at a room service menu with her she had found some reason for him not to use it so this was almost the perfect moment to remedy that even if it would involve covering up when their food arrived. With almost perfect timing it had been mere moments after spotting the option to eat in their room when Jim had woken up and she had spotted him through the mirror.

"D'ya fancy breakfast in bed?" Sasha bit her lip as she made her way over to sit on the duvet next to Jim clutching the menu as she walked.

Smiling as he watched Sasha walk Jim felt sure that Sasha was actually talking about food and not using the phrase as some cryptic way of saying she wanted to continue their previous night's activities. He had heard of people using similar phrases before but knew that Sasha wasn't the sort of person that would make such a comment.

He pondered for a few moments about how such a thing was possible when he had been told the night before that room service was off limits. Pulling his hand out from under the duvet he reached over stroking the top of Sasha's thigh and feeling a tingle filling his body at the touch of her skin before leaning up to read the line she was pointing at in the menu. His stomach rumbled softly as he placed his hand back on her leg while contemplating the idea of a full breakfast with her under the covers – it sounded perfect.

Nodding toward Sasha, Jim tried to relax as he watched her lean over him in what seemed like a pose that was intended specifically to catch his attention as she reached for the phone to place the order. Casually he slid his hand down the duvet brushing his fingers lightly against her tummy and watching her squirm playfully at his touch.

He glanced casually over toward the unused bed that say between them and the window feeling sure that such an item would stand as evidence to prove they hadn't complied with the intention of her parents to use separate beds during their stay. In his mind he could recall how other friends had been caught out with less obvious evidence incriminating them in the past but the hotel gave them anonymity.

Even if her parents had booked them two separate rooms there was nothing stopping them deciding to share one room for the night. The only case where there would be limitations placed on their chosen sleeping arrangements would be if her parents had come along with her and specifically booked him one room and them a family room.

He recalled how he had been given her own room at the complex however at the time she had been a single person and possibly not shown any interest in boys at the complex. Now he had been declared as her boyfriend he had no doubt that other precautions would be taken if they were known to be in the same place at the same time. Listening silently he felt the playful nudge of Sasha's knee as his hand drifted up and down her body warning him that he was distracting her from ordering their meal.

Sasha replaced the handset before glaring at Jim knowing that she had been basically teasing him by pressing against him as she spoke to the reception desk. The feel of his fingers on her body had been not only comforting but arousing giving her thoughts that she knew it wasn't the time to act on now that she had ordered food for them. Sitting up, she paused briefly kissing Jim before sliding off the duvet and making her way around to slide into the bed next to him.

She could feel the warmth encompass her body as she slid carefully over to him and wrapped one arm over his chest gripping his lightly as she placed her head against his shoulder. Jim stroked down her arm lightly as a burning sensation told him that her timing hadn't been ideal and the bathroom was needed before she got too comfortable.

"Don't move, I will be right back" reluctantly he removed her arm skipping out of the bed and dashing toward the bathroom door

Sasha reached over to the menu again, reluctant to leave the warmth of the bed she had just slid back into while she awaited the arrival of their breakfast. She giggled softly to herself as she heard Jim pottering around in the bathroom through the wall that joined the two rooms while trying not to think over what he was up to.

Jim glanced from his standing position toward the mirror that sat above the sink cursing his bladder for its bad timed demand to be emptied. He noted how dishevelled his hair had become overnight and pondered over whether it was worth trying to do anything with it when he was just about to return to the bed he had left.

Jumping slightly as she heard a light tap on the bedroom door Sasha glanced briefly between it and the bathroom which had gone eerily silent. She shrugged lightly accepting that whatever Jim was up to there was no sign of him reappearing as she reached for a robe tying it around herself before making her way to let breakfast in.

Standing in front of the sink Jim wet his fingers and brushed them awkwardly through his matted hair as he stood in front of the sink. He glanced down at the comb he had placed in the bathroom the previous evening knowing that it would be much more sensible to use it but decided that he didn't want to make his preening efforts too obvious. Smiling at his efforts he completed his efforts and made his way toward the bathroom door trying to seem casual while suppressing his thoughts on the fact he was returning to his girlfriend in bed.

An awkward flush ran through Jim's body as he walked casually into the bedroom realising quickly that his manhood had responded to the thought he had recently had of Sasha. He froze on the spot as he glanced in disbelief toward the foot of the bed where she was stood in a robe exchanging small talk with the same woman who had been on the reception desk as they checked in.

Reaching instinctively with one hand Jim made an awkward effort to cover himself while stepping slowly backward toward the door he had only just heard closing behind him. With a panicked fumble he felt a relief fill his body as he finally caught the door handle and shuffled quickly back into the bathroom.

Suzanna had turned her head instinctively as she heard the bathroom door open while presenting her tray of food to the guest she could remember checking into the hotel the previous day. She could feel a flush filling her cheeks as she found herself facing a naked young man who had clearly not expected her to be in the room.

Throughout her time working in the hotel she had encountered a few moments similar to the one she was now witnessing and each of them had caused her cheeks to flush red. It didn't seem to matter how many times she found herself in a position like this the blush that was warming her cheeks from the inside seemed to make itself known.

As room service was part of her job she wasn't immune to moments of accidental nudity as well as moments where guest tried to make her feel like their lack of clothing was planned. Regardless of the circumstances the one thing she knew without doubt that there was no way of consoling a person who had accidentally exposed themselves during one of her room service duties. Somehow the act of going up to a visibly embarrassed person and saying "there, there – it's ok" didn't seem appropriate.

Focussing her attention back toward Sasha, Suzanna smiled politely as she continued laying out the tray on the dresser trying to pretend that nothing unusual had occurred. She could see from the sudden change in her guests pose that there was a visible need to react to the incident but it was being suppressed as much as possible.

Smiling and trying not to burst out in a fit of giggles Sasha gripped the top of her robe as she reached to her bag beckoning the receptionist to wait a moment more. In her mind she was concerned about Jim after having seen his quick retreat but knew that there was nothing she could do about it without causing more awkwardness. She carefully folded a bank note and handed it across as a gratuity before watching the young woman make her way out of their room.

Mortified by what had just happened, Jim peered down at his manhood scowling silently at it as he pressed his back to the door he had just hidden himself behind. He knew that a few of the boys he had gone to school with had suffered awkward moments relating to their own bodies but felt sure that none of them had encountered the same incident as he had just walked away from.

Glancing to the towel rail he tried to calm his mind as he spotted two towels dangling from it casually awaiting usage. In the spur of the moment it hadn't occurred to him to wrap one around his body but then again he had been expecting to find Sasha still in the bed where he had left her.

Jumping slightly he pressed his ear to the door as he heard Sasha's voice passing through telling him that it was now safe to return to the bedroom. He glance over at the towels again pondering for a moment about whether he should wrap himself in one before returning to the bedroom and accepting that it was now too late to be cautious. Sheepishly he opened the door and peered through it with an awkward grin on his face that he hoped Sasha would see as his silent confession of stupidity.

Smiling at him casually from the bed was Sasha who had disrobed again and was now sat cross legged at one end of the bed with the tray of food presented in front of her. She glanced over at him as she bit into a slice of toast casually with a look that seemed to imply that nothing out of the ordinary had occurred in the interim.

When she had first suggested it, the concept of breakfast in bed had seemed like an appealing option as it saved having to think about dressing. Sasha had imagined something similar to the few occasions, generally her birthdays as a child, when she had been presented with breakfast in her room as a treat by her parents.

She hadn't considered the fact that, unlike her parents, the person serving the breakfast would need to be let in to the room, a factor that she knew Jim had suffered in a much more awkward way than she had. Now that the food had arrived she could see more than one reason why her idea of snuggling up together under the duvet wasn't a good idea.

The main reason was the fact that the trays that the food was served on didn't have legs like the one she recalled fondly from her childhood. This meant that these more traditional trays would be balanced precariously across their knees while they tried to eat with the constant threat of spillage if either of them dare to move.

It was the threat of spillage that had been the reason that she had avoided pouring the coffee, choosing instead to leave the pot of coffee on the dresser. Jim on the other hand had clearly not seen the same issue which made her smile slightly as she watched him trying to sit on the soft duvet with two full cups in his hands.

"Leave them on the cabinet for now" Sasha reached carefully across the tray gently grabbing Jims shoulder as she spoke.

Jim glanced down accepting that despite his best efforts he still only had on buttock successfully on the bed and half a cup of coffee threatening to land on his knees or worse. Standing carefully he made his way to the bed side cabinet placing the mugs down turning back to Sasha who he could see was already half way through her food while his plate wasn't even touched.

Tucking in quickly to his food Jim smiled discretely as he watched Sasha mopping up the remains of her meal before casually brushing an escaped crumb off her chest. He felt his body reacting to the natural bounce of her skin and tried to hide his manhood as he made his way through his meal.

Sasha bit her lip dabbing her hands with a napkin as she watched Jim squirm, confident that she knew that her innocent action had caused a similar reaction to the one he had hidden on his way back into the bathroom. Glimpsing discretely over toward the window she stood nonchalantly making sure not to rock the bed too much as she made her way to the now barely warm coffee. Turning again she leaned in pressing her chin against Jims shoulder as she kissed his cheek playfully.

"When you've finished we could always find a way to mess up the other bed if ya want" she brushed her hand down his arm as she made her way over to the unused bed

Chapter Eight

There's no place like home

As he walked in to Sasha's family home Jim made sure to follow as many of the protocols as he could think of that he had learned about when entering a strange house. He paused for a moment making sure to use the door mat in an effort to clean the shoes that he knew were barely dirty before making his way into the front room.

In many ways he was relieved to see that unlike some houses he had been to, Sasha's family didn't seem to have any rule against outdoor shoes making it past the hallway. He had seen this in the past and been caught out by it once when wearing socks that he knew before even wearing them had a hole in the toe area. They hadn't been the ideal pair but as it was laundry day he had been struggling to find a clean pair and if nothing else the ones he had on were at least matching.

While he was packing for his trip, Jim had made sure that none of his socks had acquired holes over the months that he had owned them. It was something that he didn't tend to spend much time looking over but as his pile of socks to throw away he suddenly found himself realising why his father was always grateful to receive new ones on special occasions.

Sasha's mother had met them at the door and welcomes him into their home with a casual handshake which Jim knew felt almost formal but he shrugged it off to the circumstances surrounding his visit. He had been welcomed into most of his female friends houses in the past with much less formal greetings but he knew that on each of those occasions the girls parents seemed confident that he really was just a friend. Many of them barely batted an eyelid to the idea of him joining their daughter in her bedroom but he knew that Sasha's parents had been introduced to him as the boyfriend.

This put him in a different category to other boys and made him in some ways more of a concern than if he had been referred to as just a friend. In some ways he wondered if his reception would have been warmer if Sasha had introduced him as a friend and then their relationship had grown beyond that status. Jim knew that starting off as a friend to a girl was a fine line but one that only Sasha had allowed him to cross into the relationship territory which had resulted in his handshake greeting.

Despite the less than comforting greeting Mary, as she re-introduced herself to Jim just in case he had forgotten, seemed happyt to show him around their home which made him feel a little less like a salesman and more like someone they actually knew.

"The bathroom is the first door at the top of the stairs, make sure to knock before going in as the lock doesn't always work properly" Mary smiled as she gestured toward the top floor without making any attempt to actually take Jim up the stairs silently establishing the boundaries for him.

The fact that the only room he had been told about upstairs was the bathroom didn't come as a surprise to him. Jim had no doubt that there were at least two bedrooms up the stairs too but both of these were considered as out of bounds to him and were likely to remain in that category throughout his stay.

Jim maintained what he decided was a sincere and interested expression as he was shown to a display cabinet in the front room however, the expression on Sasha's face told him it was the Holy Grail. This cabinet was actually like a museum of Sasha, inside it were all the awards and trophies she had won as a child as well as, possibly the fabled family photo album that was only shown to those deemed worthy.

"Oh, and here is a trophy Sasha won when she was 6 with a picture of her holding it" Jim made sure to glance discretely at Sasha as the trophy was being carefully taken out of the case for his appraisal.

The look of horror on her face told him that she had forgotten that the trophy even existed let alone the photograph that accompanied it. In the image was Sasha in ponytails with a wide grin on her face dressed in what Jim assessed to be either a swimsuit or a leotard. From the inscription telling him that the trophy was second place in a gymnastics competition he decided it was more than likely a leotard.

"I didn't know Sasha ever did gymnastics, you must be very proud" he smiled amicably as he handed the items back to Mary

With an air of pride Mary placed the items back in the cabinet before turning and leading Jim to the room that had been made up as his bedroom for his stay.

As he walked in through the door Jim glanced around the room noting the shelves filled with books that in his mind he felt sure had never been read from cover to cover. His father had a similar collection that had spent years gathering dust on shelves in the garage, each of them had been relevant to a hobby or pastime that had never really taken off.

In front of him was a small camp bed that was clearly intended only for one person to use the final confirmation that this room was intended only for him to use.

Sasha smiled as she watched her mother make her excuses and walk away to leave Jim to settle in to his bedroom as she had put it. During their time at the complex Sasha knew that her parents had seen them and accepted them as a couple but this time the rules were very different and she knew it.

There had been some concern, both silently suggested and vocal from both of her parents about whether the relationship would last. Although she didn't like to admit it, Sasha had been concerned about it as much as her parents were but on a very different level. In her parents eyes they were prepared for whatever had occurred to be just a holiday romance, something that would fizzle out in the forthcoming weeks. Sasha had to admit she was just as concerned about it but her concern was more about whether Jim and she had the ability to make it work now they were so far apart. This was in reality their first test of the relationship and as long as they kept to her parents rules Sasha was hoping it wasn't going to be the last time they arranged something together.

Other girls at school had frequently commented on times when they had been at home with their boyfriends and a relative had popped into wherever they were with a random enquiry. It was clear to Sasha that these enquiries were a cover up for the actual reason which was to check up on them and she was determined to avoid such behaviour if she could.

Sasha smiled calmly at her mother as she made her way out of Jim's makeshift bedroom in an attempt to seem busy around the house. In her head Sasha knew that the gesture of leaving Jim to unpack was a discrete way of both confirming that his house tour was over and allowing them some time together while remaining ever present to ensure nothing untoward happened between them.

From the moment she had confirmed Jim as coming over Sasha had been aware that she was leaving herself open to the possibility of him being shown the sacred family photo album. A book that she hadn't seen in many years due to most of their photos now being digital but she felt sure still existed somewhere in the house.

Despite the digital aspect of their family memories Sasha felt sure that some of the pictures that had been taken had been printed out and made their way into the same album that had been around since her christening. As a younger girl she could recall sitting with her parents and, sometimes with her grandparents as they pawed their way through the catalogue of memories, mostly linked to her birthdays or other special occasions including her confirmation, the one time she had been forced into wearing a dress that really didn't suit her personality.

When she was 12 the subject of confirmation had almost been seen as the main thing for discussion within her school. At the time it had still been an all-girls school so break times had been full of girls discussing the dresses they had been taken to try on as the date for the confirmation got closer and closer.

For Sasha there was more than one problem with this obsession with dresses due to having experienced naturism for the first time during the summer holiday before turning 12 years old. Now she not only knew of a lifestyle where clothing was optional she had also tried it and enjoyed it and yet her mother was now telling her that she was going to need a dress that she thought made her look like she was getting married.

Eventually she came to an agreement with her mother that if she went along with the confirmation and dressed up in the way that was expected she could spend the entire weekend after the confirmation dressed as she wanted. It didn't take her mother long to agree to the conditions but Sasha felt sure her mother was starting to regret her agreement by the end of the Saturday following her confirmation when Sasha had spent the entire day wearing only panties.

The problem was that somewhere in the fabled photo album, Sasha knew that there was an image of her dolled up in the confirmation dress. Having had Jim see her in a leotard was one thing, she could handle that but if he was ever shown the pictures from her confirmation Sasha felt sure she would have to emigrate.

Jim glanced around the room as he opened the case he had travelled with tucking the contraceptives quickly under a pile of clothes before stepping away from his bag. At the end of the bed he spotted a table that he quickly accepted was the closest thing to somewhere to place his unpacked clothing.

"So…you did ballet when you were younger" Jim smiled politely as he tried to look sincere about his question.

Deep down he knew that there was no way of hiding the fact that he was actually commenting on how cute Sasha had looked in her dance outfit as a little girl.

Sasha knew that Jim's comment had been meant as harmless banter but that didn't take away from the embarrassment that she had felt when her mother decided to show him that picture in the first place.

She had only been learning ballet for a short time when her teacher commented to her parents on how well she was picking up the different skills. Sasha had lit up at the idea of being referred to as a natural talent and had begged her mother to let her compete despite being in with much more experienced dancers.

When she had arrived at the competition her age group had been one of the smallest but that hadn't taken away from the fact she managed to get second place. It was as she was revelling in her achievement that she had heard a comment made by her teacher, which had changed her opinion.

"Sasha has a good chance of winning next year, especially with this years winner moving to the next age group – it's hers for the taking"

The fact that her ability to win had been implied as being due to the absence of the person who had beaten her made her disinterested in pursuing ballet as a hobby. Within 6 months she had finally convinced her mother that she really didn't want to be doing the activity anymore and been pulled out of the classes. At the time she didn't tell anyone why she wanted to give it up when she was making such good progress and she felt sure the real reason had never been discussed since

In her head she thought back to the journey they had enjoyed together from Bunratty as a way of trying to avoid the thought that were pressing into her brain of being forced at some stage during Jims visit to sit and go through photo albums. There was no doubt in her mind that having someone she knew to sit with was the best way to travel and even better given that Jim seemed happy to be used as a human pillow for most of the journey.

"Tell ya what Jim" Sasha had shuffled in behind him and placed her arms around his waist as she spoke "if you don't mention ballet again, I might just let you have your way with me while you stay, if not its off the table" she kissed the back of his neck before walking away from him.

"I'm making tea, did either of you want one?" Mary shouted her announcement from the kitchen choosing not to wonder back into the study to check on her house guest.

She felt sure that the silence coming from the room meant that they were possibly in the middle of a moment that she didn't want to witness if she could avoid it. In her mind she knew that at some stage during the week it was likely that she was going to accidentally walk into a room with them cuddling but wanted to avoid it as long as she could.

Sasha turned her head hurriedly and was relieved to see that her mother was not standing in view of Jim and her in his room. The idea of relaxing with a cup of tea after a day of travelling was appealing in one way but not in another.

In the past there had been a few occasions where she had been sat with her mother alone while either one or both of them sipped on a warm cup of tea and pretended to watch whatever was on the TV. This seemed similar to any of the past times when she had done that but with one major difference, this time there was Jim to join them as well.

A cup of tea was the perfect opportunity for a casual interrogation which would start off, more than likely with some reference to his journey. Sasha knew that this was only the beginning and it would slowly turn to more significant topics such as how he was doing at school which were things that hadn't been discussed when they had met at the complex. After having spent the morning travelling the idea of settling down with a cup of tea held an appeal that Sasha couldn't describe but she didn't envy Jim going through the experience with her.

Jim glanced over his shoulder at the half unpacked suitcase still laying on the bed and glanced back at Sasha who he could see was hesitating about taking up the offer. If he was going to spend a week in their house he knew that he couldn't really avoid sitting with her parents at some stage during that time.

Meals were bound to be an obvious time when at least three of them were likely to be in the house if not all of them but that wasn't quite the same as sitting with a cup of tea. He had seen his sister go through the phase of a similar casual offer with her boyfriend and knew that the best thing to do was to expect anything.

He smiled softly at Sasha nodding his acceptance that it was better that they get it over with as soon as possible even if there would be a similar experience awaiting him when her father got home.

"That sounds grand!" Sasha shouted from the study before releasing Jim from her grasp and kissing him gently

Skipping from her study Sasha made her way to the kitchen where her mother was busily preparing a proper tea pot and three cups on a tray. It occurred to Sasha that she hadn't seen the tea pot bought out in almost a year with the last occasion having been when the local priest dropped in under the pretence of being in the area.

It had been quickly established between Sasha and her mum that the real reason for his visit was to try to encourage them as a family to get involved in the church again. The fact that he barely recognise Sasha made it clear that she hadn't attended his services in many years but she gave him credit for at least trying.

Sasha saw it as quite a compliment that the special china was being bought out for Jim but chose not to say anything about it to save any awkwardness. Watching she smiled softly as her mother laid out some biscuits in a patterned circle before making her way to collect Jim from his room.

For a few moments Sasha sat mentally preparing herself for the first comment to be made by her mother as she stirred her cup of tea. In a way it was nice to see so much effort but it did make the front room feel more like it was set up for an interrogation as opposed to a friendly chat. As a precaution she intentionally sat slightly away from Jim ensuring that there was a gap between them to prevent any comments being made.

She had heard her parents refer to Adele and her as being joined at the hip in the past which at first had concerned her when they had been younger. As she grew up she realised that it was a metaphorical term and they weren't actually meant to be joined in any physical way but simply meant they were always close.

Jim seemed to without doubt come into the same category of being someone who she could be joined at the hip to but Sasha felt almost certain that the reference wouldn't be used in his presence if at all. Sasha smirked, biting her lip as Jim fumbled his way through his reply to the question of his journey over before quickly thanking her mother for their surprise overnight stay.

Mary blushed slightly as she heard his comment, the overnight stay had been the cause of a lot of private discussions between Diarmuid and her in the weeks leading up to Jims pending arrival. She was sure that Diarmuid had said it as a throw away comment initially but it had got her thinking that it might be a nice idea for the two of them.

Neither of them really wanted to accept that their daughter probably knew more about boys than what she had seen when visiting the naturist complex but they both knew it was inevitable. Eventually they had agreed that one night away was acceptable given how far Sasha was travelling to meet him at the airport but it was to be a room with single beds and not a double bed. Even though they knew that there was nothing stopping them from making their own sleeping arrangements this would at least confirm their expectations.

Sasha jumped as she felt her phone vibrate in her pocket announcing a message awaiting her attention. In a way it was a welcome distraction from the conversation that had now moved on to the subject of whether Jim had visited Ireland before and his first impression of it once his lack of previous visits had been established. She smiled as she saw that the message was from Adele who she had told repetitively about Jims pending visit to the point where her friend was almost as excited about it as she was.

In the few days that had led up to, not only the end of their school term but also Jim arriving Sasha had made a point of ensuring that Adele knew that she wouldn't be around until the Sunday afternoon. Adele had teased her about it playfully with less than subtle hints about how she was surprised that Sasha was expecting to be out of bed as early as Sunday. Sasha had blushed initially at her friend's response but accepted that with the amount of time they spent together naked their conversations had become notable more open and relaxed.

She turned to Jim who she could see seemed to be relaxing into his conversation in a way that impressed her considering the circumstances. Smiling discretely she glanced at her phone while her mother seemed contently distracted by her boyfriend and read the message that was patiently waiting for her. It didn't come as a surprise that Adele was keen to arrange a meet up for the three of them and had timed her message to coincide with her estimated journey time from Shannon.

Sasha grabbed her cup of tea as she pondered over the best way to bring the suggestion of leaving the house into the chat that she could see was going much better than expected. In her heart she knew that there was bound to be a second round waiting for Jim when her father arrived home but could see that Jim seemed oblivious to.

Jim smiled and nodded as he listened to Sasha's mother comments while sensing a discrete vibration pass through the chair he was sharing with Sasha. He waited until he could see that she was taking another sip of her tea before settling the curiosity burning in his mind as to what had caused the silent disruption.

Turning her phone to Jim as he glanced around Sasha showed him the text chat she had been carefully responded to as she mouthed the words "Wanna go out?"

Nodding as quickly as he could Jim jumped at the opportunity, as much as he had managed to get away with vague but polite answers so far he felt sure that sooner or later his luck was going to run out. He turned back to focus his attention on Sasha's mother, who had insisted that he should call her by her first name which he found weird.

At home there had been several adult family friends' visit them and each one had been referred to by the rents as "Uncle" or "Auntie" which was a habit he had got used to. This was the first time he had been told it was ok to refer to an adult using their first name but then again he knew it would feel weird referring to his girlfriend's parents with the same titles.

"Ma, we are going to head out in a bit, to meet Adele" Jim felt a rush of relief fill his body as the words crossed his ears but maintained a look of sincerity as he smiled amicably towards Mary who nodded in acceptance of the announcement.

Chapter Nine

Return to the cottage

As they prepared to leave the house, Sasha realised that there was still quite a lot she had planned on mentioning to Jim but hadn't managed to do so despite the fact that they had spent more than a day barely out of each other's sight.

On one hand was Adele, whom she was sure she had at lease mentioned at some stage during one of their online chats so if nothing else he was familiar with her name when she had mentioned it. Sasha was 100% certain that if she had mentioned Adele there was no way she had mentioned the fact that she had started getting into naturism

Then there was the cottage, Sasha knew that she hadn't told him anything about that but that was because it wasn't an easy thing to try to explain. Even with Jim knowing her interest in naturism the fact that she had found a secret hideaway only a few minutes from her home specifically so she could practice the lifestyle seemed a bit extreme. When she had first started visiting the cottage it had all been a bit of fun, an escape from reality, and the fact that she had friends that knew about it was just circumstantial.

IF she had her way nobody would have ever found out about the place and the chances were that she would have stopped visiting it by now if for no other reason than the weather getting colder. The fact that Adele and she had made the place almost homely had, without doubt, made it more appealing to keep going there even if it was only as a place to meet. There was no rule specifying a dress code when they visited but she had to accept that when they both visited the place it was unusual for either of them to stay fully dressed.

Digging her phone out of her pocket she tapped out a quick message to Adele asking her to meet them outside the cottage and was relieved to receive an almost immediate response.

Whenever they met at the cottage, which had become a regular after school event, especially on a Friday, it was usually she who got there first but Sasha knew that there was always a chance that Adele had been on her way there by the time she suggested meeting up.

It was almost a compliment to her enthusiastic leap into naturism that Adele was not unknown to be disrobing before they even got as far as their makeshift back door. Sasha knew that meeting out the front of the cottage didn't guarantee Adele would still be completely dressed but at least there was a better chance of it than if they met out the back of the building.

In her mind Sasha wondered how confident Adele would be around Jim, this was the first time they were meeting and all Adele knew about him was the very basics. Sasha had been happy to tell her a few things and knew that his name had come up in conversation but that didn't mean she would be as comfortable around him as Sasha had been when she first met him. Admittedly, when she had first met him it had been at a naturist complex and the atmosphere was a lot different to meeting him in her home town but deep down Sasha hoped they would at least get on well.

Her biggest concern was whether Adele would take it for granted that Jim was comfortable with naturism. Sasha could imagine a scenario where Adele started stripping off as she regularly did on the way through the cottage without questioning if Jim knew about why they visited the cottage. Maybe it was time he was given a crash introduction in preparation, just so that whatever happened he was ready for it.

"So, Jim, as you know we are meeting my best friend Adele" Sasha gripped his hand as she spoke keen to make sure he was up to speed with everything but conscious not to spring all the factors on him at once.

Jim turned as he heard Sasha's comment, he could tell from the way she spoke that this was the start of a much bigger point but she was breaking it to him gently. As a younger boy he had heard his sister using the same sort of logic when trying to explain something she either had done or intended to do to their parents.

When it was his sister trying it, normally one of their parents pushed the point along in an effort to get to the actual point of what was being said. For a few moments he pondered over whether to use the same tactic before deciding to go along with it and see where Sasha was heading. Nodding amicably he smiled and casually grunted an acknowledgement pretending that he wasn't expecting any follow-up to her comment.

"Well, we aren't meeting her at her home, we are meeting her at a cottage in the woods" Sasha blurted the line out as if her life depended on the confession being made.

Jim glanced over at Sasha vaguely as he heard her announcement. Ever since the moment Sasha had told her mother they were heading out his only priority had been making sure he kept a good impression while getting away as calmly as he could. The chat with Sasha's mother had seemed to go well but it was still hard to know whether she was just nodding out of politeness, judging his answers or actually in agreement with what she was saying.

In the few moments it had taken him to head to his room and get his jacket he hadn't given much thought into where they were meeting Adele. He had heard the name a few times in video chats but never really paid too much attention to who she actually was. If he was to make a guess he would have expected that they were either going to her house or maybe a café but a cottage in the woods sounded much more exciting.

"Whose cottage is it?" They turned down the small foot path as he tried to show some interest in this meeting place.

Sasha bit her lip slightly as she heard his reply knowing that it was an innocent question and not meant in any way as a sarcastic response to her comment. Every time she had visited the cottage it had occurred to her that all it would take was someone to realise that the property was still there and everything Adele and her had built up would be lost to them.

There was no denying that since her first time visiting the place the two of them had made a few significant updates that were only hidden by the panels they had put up against the back window frames. In the weeks since returning to school, although their visits had been less frequent Sasha had noticed a few new items, nothing too big, but things she was sure hadn't been there before.

"It's not someone's home, it's a bit of a wreck actually" She uttered the words as they made their way down the footpath knowing deep down that somehow she had to mention why they even knew of its existence.

Jim smiled as he glanced around the trees which were all showing signs of giving up their foliage in preparation for the winter. He found the idea of them meeting at what now sounded like an abandoned house both creepy and curious at the same time.

He had watched a few horror movies in the past and knew that one of the easiest locations used for such stories was an abandoned house somewhere away from civilisation. Digging his hand in his pocket he glanced discretely at his pone cringing when he realised that it had no signal but accepting that it hadn't been a great signal since he arrived.

In a sudden moment it occurred to him that he hadn't actually contacted the rents since arriving and made a mental note that he should try to make contact before the end of the day somehow.

Sasha stopped as they arrived at the fork in the path knowing that they were only a few moments away from the cottage. In a way she was sure that Jim wouldn't make too much of a fuss about why Adele and she used the cottage but that didn't make things any easier. This was one of a few things that she had chosen not to tell him about but now, even if nothing happened when they got to the cottage it felt like the right thing to do was to tell him.

"I found this cottage when I first got back from Zante" she gripped both of his hands facing him as she spoke "and, well, it's become my secret naturist spot" she paused, the butterflies filling her stomach as she gazed into his eyes.

Jim took a second to comprehend what Sasha had just told him as he tried to maintain a calm and understanding demeanour. He had held suspicion that Sasha was still a practicing naturist and in a way his suspicions had been confirmed by the unforgettable ay she had greeted him at the airport. In his mind he had made the assumption that there was possibly a relaxed dress code at her home about it and had been relieved to be greeted by her fully dressed mother upon arrival.

While part of her statement didn't come as a surprise to him, he knew the fact that she had been using a place away from home meant that her family were not as fully into the lifestyle as she was. Even with all of the factors his mind had deduced there was one thing that he was struggling to work out and that was whether Adele knew of this side of Sasha's life or not.

He knew that girls that he was friendly with tended to share a lot more than the boys at school and had seen closer bonds forming between the as a result of their comfortable openness. Part of his mind had often wondered whether the main source of their openness was the boys they had been out with but had never fully established that.

Glancing into Sasha's eyes he knew that this was not the time to analyse the situation, especially when her friend was on their way to meet them. All he could do was to go with the situation and try not to act too surprised by anything that happened.

"OK, fair enough" he smiled vaguely as he spoke before leaning in to kiss her as a silent way of saying that he was supporting what she was saying.

"You best show me this cottage of yours then" he gripped one of her hands and watched her face light up as she led the way down the footpath to the cottage entrance.

Jim peered through one of the stone window frames into the cottage when they arrived making mental notes of the bleak interior as he gazed around the shell of what he was sure had been a lovely home at one time. There was no doubt that its location was hidden to most people and even if anyone knew about it there was very little chance of them making any effort to find it.

He could see why such a location would be appealing to Sasha if naturism was something she was trying to keep as quiet as possible now she was home but couldn't see how it was in any way practical in such a location. The muddied interior looked like it had been churned over by the weather and the lack of a roof left the place as a far cry from the golden sands they had left behind in Zante.

"Sash!" Jim jumped back from the window as he heard a voice travelling down the path and turned to see a figure making their way toward them.

He glanced over at Sasha who seemed not only calm but ready to welcome this new person which reassured him that this was the mystery Adele he had been hearing about.

Sasha had mentioned her a few times to him in their chats and texts and he could tell they had a close and long lasting friendship. In contrast to Sasha, Adele had long flowing blonde hair and seemed to beam a confidence that at first Jim found a little bit unnerving but he could see why Sasha got on with her.

Adele spotted Sasha stood outside the cottage as she made her way to it and noted the boy stood glaring through the window accepting that this had to be the Jim she had heard so much about. His reaction as she called to Sasha made her giggle slightly but she was quick to hide it as he embraced her friend and smiled toward Jim.

Without a moment's hesitation Adele slipped her shoes off and made her way carefully through the cottage which was boggier that it had been on her last visit. She glanced behind spotting Sasha and Jim both following her example as she slipped between the board and the stone wall that hid their private space from the world.

Scuffing her feet along the light concrete that stood between the garden and the back wall of the cottage she casually threw her shoes into the shelter they had erected in preparation for the winter. Adele smiled as she heard Sasha making her way into the garden turning to face her friend pondering over what was going to be seen as acceptable behaviour now that they had a new visitor.

In her mind Adele could still recall the awkward moment when Ciara had walked in on them both completely unaware of the reason they visited the cottage. From what Sasha had said, Jim was not only aware of naturism, it had been through the lifestyle that they had met in the first place but nothing had been discussed about how comfortable he was with it now they weren't in a naturist environment.

She had discussed it in detail with Seamus who had openly told her that it took time for anyone who didn't understand the lifestyle to either accept his choices or start to ignore him because of it. Jim wasn't unaware of naturism and she knew that but that didn't mean that Sasha was going to be completely happy with her stripping down even a little bit on their first time meeting each other. Glancing up at the sky Adele accepted that it was probably for the best that the clouds made it slightly chilly deterring her from the temptation to disrobe.

Jim felt his jaw drop as he passed from the cottage into the garden that was cleverly hidden behind the cottage. It almost felt like he had stepped out of the real world and into a secret world that only those who were present knew about. He couldn't believe that Sasha had not only found but adapted such a secluded spot to her own use.

He spotted the sheltered area that he was sure would have been hidden from view even if the windows hadn't been blocked and smiled at the amount of care and attention that had been put into it. There was no doubt in his mind that this had been the work of Sasha, even if Adele had helped her out, the concept and practicality of it was reflective of what he had grown to admire in her.

Jim decided not to make a comment on whose idea he though the sheltered area was just in case he was wrong with his assessment. There was nothing he could think of that would be quite as awkward in this precise moment as assuming the work was Sasha's simply because he didn't actually know Adele all that well. Silently he accepted that it could have been either of them who came up with the idea but chalked it down as something that Sasha was likely to think of, based on what he knew was his bias opinion.

In a sudden moment he realised that he didn't know if Adele was even aware of Sasha's comfort with naturism. The fact that she was here and knew about the cottage suggested that she was aware of it but for now Jim decided it was best not to say anything that could be seen as incriminating just in case.

"What d'ya think then?" Sasha draped her arms over Jim's shoulders as she pressed up against him from behind keen to hear his thoughts on their secret hideaway.

Jim reached up grabbing Sasha's hands and holding them close to his chest as he slowly turned glancing over the garden before moving slowly toward the shelter. He smiled at Adele who was pretending that she didn't feeling like a spare wheel as he shuffled slowly with Sasha still pressed against him toward the shelter.

Adele glanced over as Jim made his way toward their little wind shelter wading into the grass in an effort to give Sasha and him a little bit of time to themselves. She could feel the cold wet grass crushing between her toes as she glanced back excited for her friend and eager to be officially introduced to Jim who seemed like the perfect gentleman.

There was no doubt in her mind that he was attentive to Sasha and she seemed extremely happy with him around which Adele had been concerned about at first but could see she had nothing to worry about now. The way they acted together was similar to the way she knew she had been with boys in the past and it was nice to see that Sasha didn't actually hate all men in the way she seemed to in front of Fintan.

Turning on her heels she made her way slowly toward Sasha who was showing Jim some of the little trinkets that had gradually made their way into the shelter including a gnome that had been named after him. Jim laughed as he picked the gnome up while trying in vain to mimic the position it was posing in but failing in every way including his lack of beard which the gnome sported perfectly.

"So, Sash, who's your new friend" Adele smiled vacantly trying to act as if she was innocent while poking her tongue out in a playful manner to hint at a proper introduction.

She grabbed one of the folding chairs opening it out and sitting calmly into it gazing up at Sasha while also catching a glimpse of the sun in her eyes. Sasha felt her face flush as she realised what Adele was getting at, she knew that her friend meant nothing by the comment and smiled awkwardly back at her.

Overhearing the conversation Jim glanced between Sasha and Adele noting the friendly banter that was clear between them but silently away that with everything that he had seen he hadn't actually made any attempt to introduce himself.

"I'm Jim, its nice meeting you" He smiled vaguely in Adele's direction offering a limp handshake to her as he spoke

Adele realised very quickly that this was the first time she had actually heard him say anything and melted into the accent as soon as she heard it. She had a weakness for a lot of foreign accents, the worst case of which had been extremely noticeable when she was 14 and a French student had joined one of her classes as part of his exchange trip.

On that occasion even the teacher had noticed her gaze transfixed on the boy who seemed oblivious to her interest in every word he struggled to pronounce. It had never occurred to her that the accent she was so used to hearing on TV, apart from American English, could sound so calming in reality

Jim's accent was completely different to the harsh Scottish accent she had heard before and seemed more refined to the London tones she had experienced. In a way it was almost refined without being too posh which Adele knew she would fall for if it was she who had met him and not Sasha. She knew that Sasha had fallen for him for different reasons and was sure there was more to it than the fact they had spent a lot of time nude together but that didn't stop her silently being infatuated by his voice.

"Well Jim, its nice meeting you finally" Adele smiled as she shook his hand "So, you're a naturist like Sasha then?" she continued

Jim paused, glancing at Sasha who seemed both curious and nonchalant about how he was going to respond to the question that in a way he had been expecting from the moment he had arrived in Ireland. He knew that there was no way of denying that Sasha was still passionate about the lifestyle even if it was, in his mind, a relief that her family didn't practice it now they were home.

Adele's question made it clear that she knew about how he had met Sasha and despite the slight assumption it almost felt like he was expected to be a naturist, even if his interest was only when he went on holidays. There was no way of avoiding the question without making it obvious that he was trying to change the subject, he knew that Adele had him cornered whether she knew it or not.

"Greece was my first time trying it" he glanced at Sasha as he spoke "and I have to say it was a positive experience" Jim couldn't help feeling smug at what he considered a masterful response that he had somehow also managed to fit a compliment into that he could see Sasha was thrilled to hear.

In many ways Jim was extremely proud of his answer and as he peered discretely over toward Adele he could see that she didn't seem to have noticed that he actually hadn't given a real answer to her question. He smiled toward Sasha noting that even in her silence she had spotted what he had done and, just like Adele, she wasn't going to challenge him about it.

Adele glanced up at the sky spotting a break in the clouds as she reached to the waistline of her top fidgeting slightly before pausing and peering back at Sasha and Jim. The chill in the air was deterring her but the fact that Sasha, the friend that had introduced her to naturism in the first place, seemed less than keen to join her made her cautious about even removing one item let alone all of them.

"Well, now you're here, let's hope that we can all try it again" Adele smiled as she released her hand from her top brushing her fingers against her thighs in an effort to hide the fact she had even considered disrobing.

Chapter Ten

Adele's Awkward Awareness

Although she wasn't sure how to categorise it in her mind Adele couldn't help but feel a sense of both achievement and closure as she made her way home from the cottage. It had felt like a lifetime from the moment Sasha had first mentioned Jim to the moment when she had finally met this mystery man who had changed her friends life for the better.

She didn't like the mention it but Ever since returning from Greece Sasha had seemed almost obsessed with Jim but now she had met him she could see why he had such a positive effect on Sasha.

There was a lingering thought in the back of Adele's mind making her wonder whether Sasha would have been so up front in telling her about naturism if it hadn't been for Jim but it was hard to connect the two despite the fact that Sasha had met him at a naturist resort. The fact that Sasha had been going there for a long time before meeting him meant that it was possible that he had been a factor in her finally mentioning naturism but if that was true then Adele should be thanking him for it.

The funniest thing in her mind was that, despite the fact that she had seen a picture of Jim the mental image of him that Adele had built in her mind was a far cry from the boy she had just been introduced to. Even as she had approached the cottage the fact that he looked almost exactly as he had done in the picture meant she would have recognised Jim with or without Sasha being there but she was glad to have met him with Sasha. The way she acted around him made it clear how much she liked him even if it hadn't been a pre-known fact that they were together it would have been a reasonable assumption.

There was something special about Jim, something that made him seem different to a lot of the boys she knew but different in a positive way not a bad different. Adele could recall the excitement in Sasha's voice the very first time she had mentioned him to her but had put that down to how new and exciting the relationship was. Now that she had met him Adele could see that he was actually worth the level of excitement that Sasha had afforded him when she had been describing their time together.

One of the best things in her opinion was the fact that he seemed to treat Sasha with a form of respect that she had barely seen in a man, he was attentive and caring but didn't come across as being overly possessive. In the same way his attention had been completely on Sasha despite the fact that she wasn't the only girl in his company.

Part of her mind had made Adele wonder if he would have remained as focussed if she had gone with her gut intention and disrobed even a little bit, but in a way she was glad she hadn't done. The last thing she wanted was to drive a stake between her friendship with Sasha by acting in a provocative or flirtatious manner around her boyfriend.

Adele had been unlucky enough to have experienced what it was like to go out with a boy who was overly possessive but relieved that he had shown his true colours before anything had developed between them.

The boy in question had made a few less than discrete attempts at getting her out on a date with him before Adele finally caved in and agreed to meet up with him to go shopping. In her mind it was her way of at least giving him a chance and getting him off her back so that she could shut him up. As they arranged where and when to meet she felt proud of the fact that she had at least made an effort despite it being obvious in her mind that they were about as compatible with each other as a fish was to the desert.

He had started the day fairly amicably with the occasional subtle hint that he wanted her to hold his hand including a few accidental brushes of his hand against hers as they peered through shop windows. After an hour she gave in and let him take her hand as they walked from one place to the next while finding any excuse she could to pull away from him. In a way she knew it was nice to have someone who wanted to be seen to be with her but she still didn't feel like she was comfortable with the unwritten agreement.

Toward the end of their day out Cathal made the offer to buy her a coffee which Adele was happy to accept after spending most of the day on her feet. He took her over to a nice coffee stand and found a place set for two near the edge of the seating area which pleased her as it meant she could watch the people passing by instead of feigning interest in him.

They had only been sat down for a few moments when Padraig, a boy who she actually got on with from school but hadn't ever considered as someone she could date, waved over to her before making his way over toward their table. Adele knew that her face had lit up when she had spotted him but felt sure that Cathal was too engrossed in himself to notice the change in her body language.

Cathal had sat silently nodding at the banter they were sharing as he sipped on his coffee which, in Adele's mind, was a point in his favour and something that he hadn't shown the ability to offer at any stage during their day together. Unfortunately, she hadn't seen the way his face was clenching with every second that was being taken from him by the interruption to their date.

"Why are you trying to chat my girlfriend up?" A stunned silence fell across the table as Cathal stood and glared at Padraig with a hostile expression across his face.

Adele could feel her cheeks glowing with embarrassment as her jaw dropped open on hearing the reference to her as his girlfriend, something that as far as she was concerned she hadn't made any suggestion that she wanted to be.

She glared at Cathal through daggered eyes, conscious of the number of people around her but also angered by the assumption he had made. Anyone else would have known that the conversation she was having with Padraig was simply light banter and not intended in even a mildly flirtatious manner but he seemed flustered by it.

Glancing as calmly as she could at Padraig who had now stepped back from the table slightly she made a silent gesture toward him to assure him that he hadn't done anything wrong and wasn't the one who should be leaving. With a casual flick of her hair she peered around the café area, relieved in a way that there was no one else taking any notice of the rising drama surrounding her.

In her mind, this situation was similar to the time when Sasha had set the record straight with Fintan at the disco but with less spectators and, she hoped, less ongoing repercussions. It didn't matter to her whether she was at school or not, the last thing she wanted was to be the centre of some unwanted drama.

Placing one hand on the table she paused for the moment as she contemplated the idea of depositing her half-finished coffee somewhere on Cathal as a response to his comment.

Adele paused as anger built up inside her mind while she looked over at one of the café staff who was quickly spraying a table in preparation for the next customer to use it.

On one hand she felt sure that they had probably cleaned up plenty of spillages before and might even get some amusement out of her outburst. On the other hand she knew this wouldn't be an accidental spillage and would generate more attention than she wanted to bring on herself so chose not to go with that option

"Cathal, I am leaving now, with my friend Padraig" Adele could feel her cheeks glowing red with the anger building up inside her as she spoke. I suggest that you sit down, shut up and pretend today never happened" her body shook as she tried to remain calm.

Slowly she stood up

"Oh, and if I ever hear anything about this I can assure you, your reputation will be the least of your worries" Reaching she grabbed the coffee cup thrusting her hand forward as droplets splashed on the table "or would you prefer to be trying to get warm coffee stains out of your pants?"

Adele pressed her hands firmly against the table as she spoke feeling the table top rattle slightly under the pressure she was applying to it.

Leaning down she grabbed her bag swinging it abruptly so that it bashed against Cathal's leg as she brushed her way briskly past him before joining Padraig who was busy trying not to giggle at what he was witnessing. Adele was thankful that against all the odds Cathal seemed clever enough to take her advice and avoid her from that day forwards. For a few days she contemplated taking Padraig out on a date as a way to thank him for being so understanding but knew that if she did it might ruin their friendship.

In her heart Adele knew that she had only seen Jim once and there had only been Sasha and her with him at the time but there was something sweet about him that said that he wouldn't be that sort of guy. Adele also knew Sasha well enough to be confident that she wasn't the type to put up with someone overly possessive.

During their time together Adele hadn't been able to help feeling curious about how muscular Jim was underneath the coat he was wearing. Muscles on men had been something she had been interested in ever since she first started being interested in boys with one of her weaknesses being a strong bicep.

She knew that, if it had been the summer or even if it had been warmer weather there was a chance that either Sasha or she would have stripped down a little bit during their visit to the cottage. They had done it almost every time they had been there before and Adele was sure that Jim being there wouldn't make much difference even if there was more discretion taken by them.

If they had stripped down even a little bit she felt sure that it was likely that Jim would also follow suit and at least ditch the coat that was hiding his physique. Due to the cooler weather Adele knew that after her first meeting with him there was no way to know whether Jim even had a six pack, something she openly admired. Even when she had first seen Seamus it had been his toned stomach that had appealed to her the most out of everything that had been on view to her.

Casually she pushed her way through the front door of her home shutting the door as she kicked off her shoes and pushed them neatly against the wall and out of the way. She smiled as she spotted a small rim of dirt around the hem pf her jeans that she knew would give away the fact that she had been walking through the countryside while she was out.

Before she went out her parents had reminded her that Sunday was their night out, just as it had been ever since she had finally convinced them that she was old enough to be left at home on her own every so often. When she had first been given the freedom of an evening to herself it had appealed to her as an opportunity to invite friends round without having parents listening in to their conversations. That idea had been quickly dismissed when she realised that it was possible that her parents would find out about it from her friends parents sooner or later.

As usual there was a note waiting for her on the table telling her about the pre-cooked meal that was waiting for her in the microwave ready to be heated up when she was ready for it. Her parents always had their main meal at lunchtime on a Sunday, which she had joined them in doing up until they started going out of an evening when she managed to convince them that it was better if she ate properly in the evening.

She knew that the pub her parents went to would be offering them complimentary snack food as part of their evening activities and was happy to be left to do her own thing for a few hours before the new week started. On a normal Sunday her evening involved preparing her bag for school and sitting in front of the TV with her dinner while trying to find something worth watching. This Sunday was different because there was no school to prepare for, even her uniform had been washed and put away into the wardrobe where she didn't have to see it every day.

Glaring down at the muddy patch on her jeans she shrugged as she wriggled out of them draping them over her arm as she made her way into the kitchen. The cool tiles sent a tingle up her legs as she filled the sink with water. Preparing to make an attempt at removing the offending mud so that she could hopefully get another days wear out of them and save any comments from her mother about where she had been in them.

Adele stared into the water as she rubbed the hem of one leg against the other in an effort to remove the muddy crust that had formed from during her afternoon out. She smiled, jumping slightly as a few drops of water splashed from the sink and trickled against her bare legs while pondering over what her mother would say if she saw her.

She knew that there would be two things that would come to attention, the first of which was the fact that she was washing clothing over the sink, something that she had seen her mother do a few times when an item didn't actually need a full wash. In her head she could hear her mother's voice making comments on the fact that she was actually doing something that resembled housework. It wasn't that she never actually did anything to help around the house, but she had to admit that there were other things she could do to help out if she put her mind to it.

The second thing that would be commented on was her current dress code which Adele knew would cause more than a few words to be said. In her early teenage years there had been a few occasions when she had come downstairs for breakfast at the weekend in particular in her night clothes.

Over the years her night clothes had evolved in ways that had not always been seen as suitable attire to wear outside of the bedroom and in her parent's eyes probably not suitable in the bedroom either. From the age of 13 her night dress had become an oversized T-shirt that she had spotted in the window of a charity shop that showed her favourite band at the time and was long enough to cover half of her thighs.

At the age of 14 she was still wearing the same t-shirt despite a growth spurt having sent its hem a lot higher on her leg but still within a relatively safe length. By the time she reached the age of 15 the growth spurt had continued in more ways than just upwards and the t-shirt was showing signs of having been worn well over the years.

One hole in at the top of the arm had formed allowing her right shoulder to peek out and a second hole was starting to show in the side of the shirt were both causing concerns for her parents. Eventually she agreed it was time for the t-shirt to go and replaced it with a dressing gown which both of her parents accepted covered her up a lot better, the fact that she was sometimes naked underneath it was one they remained blissfully unaware of.

Even though she knew that she was technically covered up to a decent level Adel also knew that the fact that her panties were not only visible but in full view would be cause for comments to be made. As a child there had been a few times when her mother has stripped her down to her underwear in the kitchen to get her out of wet clothing but that was different as she was younger then. Now that she was seen as basically an adult the same dress code was not going to be accepted around the house even if it was for a practical reason such as the mud she was trying to get rid of out of her jeans.

Wringing the excess water out of her jeans she emptied the sink and made her way over to a radiator draping them over it to dry off. She smiled as she peered down at her bare legs acknowledging that this was the most she had been undressed outside of her own room during the day time since having been introduced to naturism.

In a way it felt funny that despite a growing passion for it she had never even tried to test the boundaries with her parents in the few months that she had been trying to practice naturism. Nothing had really changed that much in her day to day life except that when she went to her own room she usually stripped off completely before doing anything else.

In her heart she knew that not telling them anything about it seemed like it was being deceitful to them but it wasn't something that was going to be easy to mention to them. She had discussed it with Sasha and knew that her friend was in the same position as she was despite the fact that her parents knew about the naturist lifestyle.

Waddling over she opened the microwave and took in the aroma of the meal that had been prepared for her and covered over by her mother. Glancing again at her legs she paused for a moment realising that there was no one in the house for at least the next two hours to tell her what she was allowed to do.

Adele set the timer on the microwave as she made her way out of the kitchen fiddling with the hem of her t-shirt on her way into the front room. She peered out of the window into the dark street glancing over the street lamps that traced the outline of the footpath before shutting the curtain and hiding herself from the outside world.

She smiled as she made her way to the stair case listening to the hum of the microwave in the background that was preparing her dinner. Skipping her way upstairs she made her way to her room closing the door, pulling her top over her head and making her way to the window as she threw it to the bed. From downstairs she heard the ping telling her that her meal was ready for her and sitting patiently in the microwave as she closed her bedroom curtain.

Standing in her underwear for a moment she looked into her mirror feeling a thrill of energy filling her body as she pondered over her new dress code. If her parents saw her walking round the house like this she was sure they would ground her for at least a week and give her a lecture about how it was wrong to walk around barely dressed.

Unclipping her bra she felt a sense of freedom and adventure as it fell to the floor and smiled at her reflection standing just in her panties.

A second beep from downstairs reminded her of the meal that was waiting for her breaking her thoughts as she reached out grabbing the robe she usually wore just for the bathroom. Wrapping herself in the robe she made her way back downstairs cursing her mind for making her hesitate as she carefully took the plate out of the microwave and made her way to the couch.

Plonking herself carefully into the chair she flicked the TV on using the remote and darted through the channels as she scooped a mouthful of food into her mouth. Despite knowing she was barely covered she knew that there had been nothing stopping her except her thoughts of what her parents would think and they weren't even in the house.

She pondered for a moment about whether Sasha had gone through the same, her parents were not only aware of naturism they had tried it but it was clear that they didn't now they were home. Had Sasha pushed the boundaries? Had she tried being naked at home – even on her own? In her heart Adele felt sure she had done and probably long before mentioning it to her.

What about Jim?

She chewed on another mouthful as she slid one hand into her robe lightly caressing her skin as she pondered over her thoughts.

In her mind she recalled the question she had asked him about naturism and how his answer had been too vague to continue asking but not dismissive of the lifestyle.

Maybe he liked being naked, maybe he hadn't given it any thought since he had got home from Greece, all Adele knew was that she wanted to get naked with both Sasha and him and enjoy naturism with them both.

Glancing down she gasped lightly as she realised that while she was thinking she had exposed her breast blushing slightly as she covered herself again with her robe. She smiled as she scooped another mouthful from her plate and flicked the remote to change the channel again. Her body filled with warmth and adrenalin as she placed the plate on the table beside the couch settling back into the chair and loosening the cord holding her robe together.

Biting her lip she giggled as she opened the robe fully glancing at the only items of clothing separating her from her first nude experience. They seemed so easy to take off and yet still such a big step to take even if she was sat in the house on her own but there was one thing that was concerning her more than the thought of being caught nude.

If she did strip off Adele knew that she could cover up in seconds with her robe if she heard the door being opened and her parents wouldn't know any different. There was something else, something that in her mind was even more awkward than the idea of being seen by her parents with nothing on. Ever since she had left the cottage there had been one thing that kept on returning to her mind, something that she knew she shouldn't be thinking about but couldn't stop it happening.

She couldn't deny that she had a crush on her best friend's boyfriend.

Chapter Eleven

Morning Mayhem

Jim lay in silence on the bed gazing briefly up at the ceiling as he pondered over the wide range of office type things that surrounded him. This was a far cry from his bedroom back at home but it was more than he had imagined being offered when he had been told he was going to be a house guest.

On one side of the room was a bookshelf that looked like it has lots of large and official books similar to the one's he had seen in his school principal's office. Even the titles of them looked boring, not the sort of thing that somebody would willingly choose to read but the sort of thing that was used for reference.

He could remember his granddad had owned a collection of books similar to this at one time but they had been separate parts of an encyclopaedia. Every so often, normally once per visit one of the books would be carefully slipped out of its space on the shelf and used to confirm a random fact that someone had mentioned.

The biggest problem was that by the time granddad, who was the only person who was allowed to access the volumes of knowledge, got round to looking up the trivia the conversation had moved on and no one could remember why they had been discussing it. In some ways it was quite a relief when the internet took over making it so much easier to find stuff but Jim could remember the look of achievement on his granddads face when he finally managed to settle whatever the debate had been with written facts.

On the other side, almost in contrast to the official books was a selection of books that ranged from story books all the way to a row of books similar to the one's he had a fond memory of having left behind when he finished school. These one's he felt sure must have at some time belonged to Sasha but unlike the one's he had handed in these ones looked like they had been fairly well used while still maintaining a looked after aura about them.

He squinted from his bed determined not to move just yet but curious about the titles of the study books and whether he could regurgitate any of the knowledge he had gained of the subjects now he had left school. One particular book caught his eye as he spotted it and that was the one that seemed to refer to studying the Irish Language. In a way it seemed almost ironic that a book about learning Irish had its title written in English but Jim decided it wasn't the sort of thing to comment on.

It had occurred to him that despite them both being the same age Sasha was still referring to going to school whereas he had now moved on to college. He had wondered at the time if it was just her way of referring to still being in education but seeing these books made him wonder if she really was still at school.

Gripping at his tummy he winced slightly as he heard a floorboard creaking from the floor above indicating that someone was awake and probably making the same journey his stomach was telling him he should have made. He had wondered if the house had a downstairs bathroom of any kind as he drifted off to sleep but it didn't seem like the right time to go hunting for it while everyone else was sleeping above him. Now that the only bathroom he was aware of sounded like it was in use he wished he had asked the question but knew that it was too late to be wondering about such a thing.

The morning bathroom routine was never easy as the visitor at someone else's home as it wasn't easy to know when the best time was to make an attempt to use the facilities. For Jim there was an added factor that had to be taken into consideration and that was the fact that he was known as Sasha's boyfriend.

In his mind he knew there were two ways to tackle the situation, neither of which was ideal but both of which relieve the pain that was acting as a constant reminder in his stomach. The first option, the least desirable of the two but the one that was likely to gain him access to the facilities quicker, was to pretend that he hadn't heard anyone traversing the upstairs corridor and make his way to the bathroom.

This one was risky at the best of times because it gave a sense of urgency to whoever was currently in the bathroom and alerted them to someone else needing to use it. If he had been at home this would be his go to choice as he had no fear of having a casual conversation through a closed bathroom door while the occupant tried to vacate the room as efficiently as possible.

As he was the house guest it was likely that he could get away with trying the door but that held the risk that whoever was in the bathroom hadn't locked it which would then lead to sheepish looks for the remainder of his stay.

There was also the fact that if he used this method there was no denying that he had attempted to access the room so there was no point in making his way back to his room in an effort to pretend it hadn't happened. This would result in him standing casually in the vicinity of the bathroom until it was vacated so that he could dash in at the earliest opportunity after whoever emerged.

The alternative was to sit and try to remain calm while listening for any tell-tale sound that would confirm that whoever was in the bathroom was on their way out however this option had other complications. The main one was that there was no way of knowing what the person was in the bathroom for and no way of creating a sense of urgency so the waiting time was unpredictable. As it was a work day there was a good chance that the user wasn't planning on having a shower or even worse – a bath meaning that the bathroom visit was hopefully a short one.

The second flaw with this option was that in order to successfully run with it he had to remain out of sight of the bathroom and therefore had no way of ensuring that he was the next one in line to use it. It seemed fair to assume that after a night's sleep most of the house occupants had a similar list of priorities one of which was to visit the bathroom s it was highly likely that the other two house occupants were waiting on the same thing as he was.

With a brief moment of relief he heard the tell-tale sign of a flushing noise and sprang from his bed reaching out for his jeans in the hope that he would be able to reach the bathroom before anyone else did. Carefully he slipped his legs into them as the pain in his gut burned enforcing the urgency of the situation to him.

Making his way to the door he glanced over at the shirt he had discarded from the previous night pondering briefly over whether it was better to appear fully dressed or not at he heard the sound of a door opening from upstairs.

Roused by the flushing sound down the corridor Sasha turned and reached unsuccessfully toward the handle of her bedroom door. She smiled at the sheer laziness she was demonstrating while knowing that the door had never actually been within easy reach from her most comfortable sleeping position.

For a moment she listened carefully as she contemplated the idea of making her presence known while acknowledging that despite her families comfort with naturism it probably wasn't a good idea to be seen before she was at least partially dressed. She listened as the bathroom door opened as she sat up on her bed as she heard a second set of feet making their way up the stairs.

There was no doubt that this second person was Jim sending a thrill through her body as she reached out for the robe her parents hated but accepted her wearing for brief spells in between waking and fully dressing. Opening her bedroom door slightly she glanced through the narrow gap between the door and its frame as Jim disappeared into the bathroom completely oblivious to her presence.

Silently she closed the door again biting her lip gently at the thought that Jim was so close and yet still so far away. Glancing over at her dressing table she made her way over as she spotted a subtle light on her phone telling her that there was at least one message waiting for her. Gripping the robe close to her chest with one hand she casually scanned the list of messages that was eagerly awaiting her attention.

It hadn't ever really surprised her that large generic companies had no concept of time zones when it came to sending out offer emails. She knew that there was always an option to unsubscribe but there was something about the fact she received these random messages making her feel more popular than she was that was almost comforting.

In a way it Sasha knew it was a massage to her self-esteem but she still felt better when there was something random awaiting her attention when she woke up than she had done on the days when there were no alerts that had arrived overnight.

Scanning her way through the list of messages she felt her eyebrow raise slightly as she spotted a text that had arrived almost an hour before she had awoken from Adele. It wasn't unusual for Adele to message her at random times but usually it was she who was the first out of the two of them awake.

The message was overly amicable as most of Adele's messages were except when she was trying to pretend not to be agitated about something. This time she was referring to how nice it had been finally meeting Jim, which bought an involuntary grin to Sasha's face as well as a comment on how keen she was that they should meet again.

From the moment that Sasha had mentioned Jim coming over to see her it had been part of her plan that he would meet with Adele so that she could see how well he got on with her friends. It was extremely encouraging that Jim had made such a positive impression on her closest friend but that didn't take away from the fact that she also wanted to spend some time with him alone.

She smiled softly as she silently made note that she needed to respond to the message but that could wait until after breakfast, for now there was a much more prominent situation that she was determined to make the most of. At the other end of the corridor Jim was behind the bathroom door, too far away to actually touch, too risky for her to try to get to him without alerting her parents to the fact that she had left her room but close enough to at least let him know that she knew he was there.

Her heart jumped slightly as she heard the sound of the toilet flushing for the second time that morning prompting her to skip back toward her bedroom door. Feeling a rush of adrenalin she carefully opened the door again, this time a little wider than she had before pressing her cheek to the door frame as she awaited his emergence from the bathroom.

"Jim" She glanced briefly toward her parent's room hoping that they hadn't heard her half whispering his name

Startled by the sound of Sasha's voice, Jim froze on his spot glaring along the corridor to the partially opened door here he could see the familiar sight of her raven hair and lightly tanned face peering back at him.

He smiled at her sheepishly, his half buttoned shirt not even partially tucked in to the jeans that he had barely zipped up before leaving the bathroom. In his mind it wouldn't matter too much if Sasha's parents saw him in a partially dressed state as long as he wasn't leaving Sasha's bedroom. In his wildest dreams he hadn't even considered the idea that Sasha would make herself known to him upon his reappearance even if she did hear him fumbling around on his way back to his makeshift bedroom.

Peering discretely at the thankfully still shut bedroom door that he knew her parents were behind she watched as Sasha slowly opened her door further as if she was inviting him to join her. Part of his mind told him to take the risk and dash along the corridor while the logical part told him that to do so was not a good idea as she watched her stepping back into her room while remaining in full view.

Sasha bit her lip knowing that what she was doing went against everything she believed in as a naturist but as it was Jim she didn't mind teasing him a little. Discretely she glanced to her right confirming in her mind that her parents bedroom door was definitely shut, the thrill of having them so close and yet oblivious to her actions sent adrenalin rushing through her body. There was something so exciting about having Jim so close that he could see everything and yet so far away that he couldn't actually touch her.

Cheekily she made sure it was obvious that she was biting her lip by over emphasizing the over bite as she glanced down at the loosely tied knot barely holding her robe shut before focussing her gaze directly at Jim. It was clear to see that he was caught between two minds, one of them telling him to move closer and the other warning him of the risk level that was already present in what was happening. A rush of excitement flowed through his body as he watched the two ends of the cord that had held Sasha's robe closed fall limply down by her thighs.

Sasha kept her eyes focussed on Jim, her heart beating faster than she could remember it ever having done before. Every time she pushed against what was expected she had sensed the thrill of her actions flowing through her body. The last time she had felt a sensation anywhere close to the one filling her now was her first day posing for the art class, her first time naked in front of a crowd of strangers.

Bit by bit she started opening the robe, letting it fall away from her shoulders while still holding it closed at her waist. She glared wide eyed toward Jim as she pulled it open slowly, carefully wanting to show him her body but also wishing that he was able to make a move on her, a move she knew was out of bounds. With a sudden jolt that broke the moment Sasha heard her parents door opening and scuttled back into the safety of her room making sure not to make a sound as she carefully closed her door again.

"Morning" Jim smiled softly as he tried to act as if he hadn't just witnessed a special show from the other end of the hallway.

With a quick step he grabbed the handrail and made his way slowly back downstairs glancing discretely at the firmly closed door that he knew Sasha was somewhere behind.

Diarmuid glanced up as he heard the sound of Jim greeting him, slightly disorientated by the sound of another male voice in the house but quickly waving to acknowledge the greeting.

As much as he had been unsure about the idea of having Jim stay in the house he had to admit that it was at least half reassuring that he had made an effort to dress before making his way upstairs. For many years there had been on and off discussions about whether or not to refit what had once been a downstairs bathroom that sat off the front entrance hallway.

When they had first moved in Mary and he had been grateful for it having been caught with an urgent need to use facilities on their way into the house and yet slowly it had become a junk room. In his mind Diarmuid was fairly certain that somewhere under the boxes of stuff that nobody had touched in more than 5 years there was still a working toilet and a hand basin but there was no telling what state either of them were in.

Every time they had hosted guests in the past it had only been for a meal or coffee and on the odd occasion a sleepover between Adele and Sasha but none of the past ventures had caused enough concern for the disused room to be given a second glance.

The fact that their house guest had been forced into making his way upstairs first thing in the morning was almost a subtle reminder to him of the less than subtle suggestion that had been made of installing a downstairs bathroom.

A lot of their surrounding neighbours, including the lady who lived alone next door had made their version of the downstairs toilet seem quite presentable. Mary had even commented that if it was done properly there was probably room to have a shower in the small room as well but that seemed over the top and unnecessary. If either Mary or he had pre-empted having a visitor who they wanted to actively keep downstairs as much as possible there would have been no question, the downstairs bathroom would have been a feature of their house and one to be proud of.

Sasha sat on her bed, her heart still pounding with the rush of having nearly been caught by her father whilst teasing Jim from her bedroom. The robe she had been wearing was laying at her feet in a heap where it had landed as she had made what she considered to be a successful leap from her doorway to her bed while managing to close the door and not rouse suspicion all at the same time. As the door was closed the fact that she had lost the only item of clothing she had been wearing during the process seemed trivial especially when she considered the fact that she had been removing it for Jim's pleasure anyhow.

Walking silently over to her desk she picked up her phone placing one hand against her closed curtain as she opened up the text Adele had sent her. There was only one thing that she wanted to do as a result of her cheeky peep show but she knew that she wasn't going to be able to do it without causing a lot of questions and potentially a very long and awkward week ahead for Jim.

Sitting in his room with the door shut, Jim sat with a smug grin on his face as he listened to Sasha's father pottering around in the kitchen. It had been an interesting walk back to his room as her father tried to make small talk and he tried not to think about the brief glimpse he had just enjoyed of Sasha practically naked.

Now he had decided to stay out of the way based on the assumption that her father was clearly preparing to leave for work and the last thing he wanted to do was get in the way of what he was sure was a well-oiled routine.

Even worse than the thought of getting in the way of her father as he prepared to leave for work was the thought that if he remained somewhere in the front room there was a good chance that the small talk would continue. He had heard of how awkward moments with the parents of a girlfriend could be when there was nobody else around and while he was sure it would happen eventually – he wanted to avoid it as long as he could.

At the foot of his bed was the still packed case he had bought with him sitting as a reminder that he really should prepare a change of clothing before venturing back to the bathroom to get ready for the day. He leaned over, pausing as he heard the front door being shut, smiling at the thought that if her mother was to go out as well they would have the house to themselves but maybe that was just too much to expect.

Mary left the bedroom, glancing at Sasha's closed door as she shuffled her way to the bathroom pondering over the day she had planned ahead. Below her she knew there was their house guest, she had spent half of the night listening as she lay next to her husband who seemed less concerned than she was at the possibility of their daughter sneaking downstairs during the night.

In her teenage years she knew that if she had been presented with the same opportunity that they were giving to Sasha, there was very little doubt that she wouldn't try it at least once during the night. Sasha however had either managed to sneak out very quietly or had remained in her room all night, which was in many ways a credit to her but not one that she was going to know about.

If this had been a normal morning Mary knew that both Sasha and she would make their way to breakfast in robes, for Sasha, hopefully the one that actually fit her but either one would be acceptable as long as she made an effort. As they had a house guest it seemed inappropriate to follow the usual rules so she knew she would have to at least dress casually. In her hands were her chosen clothing items for the day as she made her way to the bathroom to prepare herself.

Remaining in her room Sasha heard her mother making her way to the bathroom, after some consideration she had decided to keep her curtains closed for now, that way she didn't have to dress until she was ready to go downstairs.

Unlike when they went out for a special occasion, her mother was always overly efficient in the bathroom in the morning to the point where it was almost as if she was timing her routine to try to beat a world record that Sasha was sure didn't exist.

She listened carefully as the bathroom door opened again and her mother made her way downstairs before grabbing the robe she had discarded and throwing it back on again. Pausing she listened as she heard the sound of someone making their way back up the stairs, it was either Jim or her mother. Quickly she opened her door, clutching the robe close to her chest as she peered out spotting Jim, back at the bathroom presumably for the same reason she was intending to use it.

Lightly she made her way along the corridor keeping a discrete eye on the stairs as she snuck up behind Jim. Grabbing him she turned him around pressing her body against his as she leaned in kissing him deeply.

"Morning hun" she whispered the words in his ear as she took his hand placing it against her buttocks

Flushed but excited Jim leaned in holding her close as they kissed.

"Breakfast in 10 minutes Sash, Jims just gone to the bathroom so don't get any ideas" Sasha giggled lightly as she heard her mother's voice carrying from the kitchen.

Pouting slightly Sasha stepped backwards while keeping one hand pressed lightly against Jim's chest.

"I guess we will have to wait" she smiled and kissed him on the cheek before scampering back to her room.

Chapter Twelve

Coffee for Three

From the moment that Jim had arrived Sasha felt like it was the beginning of a new adventure, or maybe more like the confirmation of one she had been going on but wasn't sure anyone else believed. She knew that she had told Adele about Jim and also mentioned him to Maebh and Ciara but only out of politeness and yet she wasn't sure how much of her stories about him existing they had believed. Now that she was with him there was no denying that he was not only real but they were really a couple.

Ever since their school had become mixed gender Sasha had heard girls making attempts to deter the advances of boys by telling them that they had a boyfriend. In some cases, she knew that the line had been true but in others even Sasha had found herself questioning the validity of the aforementioned boyfriend. The fact that she was now mentioning one to her friends and others were hearing her referring to having one meant that it was likely that others were questioning her relationship in the same way she had done with others in the past.

Unlike others, if she wanted to prove that Jim was real Sasha knew that she couldn't just arrange for him to meet with her after school or refer to the college he went to. In a way she was thankful that she only had a small circle of friends and none of them had questioned Jim's existence even if they had never met him.

The reality of the matter was that the boys at school were getting more complacent when it came to being told that the girl they were asking out had a boyfriend. Some of them chose to walk away from the situation and leave it as a failed attempt to get a girl on a date but others seemed either less easy to brush off or not to have read the memo telling them of the gentle refusal methods girls used.

This had led to a few interesting challenges being made and while some of them had less ugle outcomes the end result was always the same – the girl who had referred to the boyfriend, whether fake or real was always the winner. Even if the boy who was turned down was able to prove the non-existence of the boyfriend the chances of it resulting in him getting a date from the girl he had challenged remained at zero. This meant that in reality there was no point in challenging the boyfriend status but some boys seemed to have too bigger ego than to let it drop.

Sasha knew about cases like this all too well, it didn't matter how many ways she tried to tell Fintan she wasn't interested in him and wasn't going to date him even if he was the last boy on earth he seemed determined to wear her down until she accepted him. For a while, the incident at the disco had acted like a good deterrent but, just like other failed attempts at advances on her he seemed to have brushed that off too in recent days.

Fintan had never been the type to take no for an answer and even though he wasn't the type to act maliciously over the incident he wasn't the type to give up either.

Despite knowing how risky her moves were Sasha had made sure that the first breakfast Jim had in her home was one that he wasn't going to forget. From the moment she had successfully hidden and prevented being caught by her father Sasha had been determined to rebuild the momentum she had initiated in any way she could.

Her efforts to distract him started even before he had emerged from his bedroom by sending him a text as she made her way to the breakfast table before sitting down and acting as if she was the heir of virginal grace.

"I'm not wearing any panties 😊" Had been the last thing Jim had seen on his phone before making his way to the table and now it was the only thing he couldn't get out if his mind.

Every time Mary had made her way into the kitchen Sasha had taken the opportunity to build on what she had said by teasing him a little bit more. The biggest victory had been successfully flashing her bra at him in the time it took for her mother to go into the kitchen and make a fresh pot of tea, a move that she noted had made him blush resulting in a raised eyebrow by the time her mother returned.

By the end of the meal Jim was extremely happy to help tidying away the breakfast bits but noted that Sasha had neither proved or disproved her cheeky text. In some ways it had been a relief when she had made the suggestion of heading into town for a while so that she could show him around

Sasha gripped his hand firmly as they made their way through the park toward the town centre hoping that someone who knew her would spot them together. In her experience it only took one person to mention something that was either new news or out of the ordinary for the rest of the town to hear about it within a matter of hours.

Most of the time she knew that rumours spread quicker than facts and generally there was someone on the bad end of a rumour but that didn't mean that her status officially having moved to "In a Relationship" wouldn't become news if anyone saw her with him.

In a way it was the towns rumour spreading rights that had been one of her biggest concerns when she had decided to explore naturism away from the safety of the complex. She knew that Adele was a safe bet, she was unlikely to start any rumours but Ciara had been a lesser known source and one she hadn't planned on telling. So far, however, it seemed like she was able to be trusted with the information, either that or stories of her nude exploits hadn't made their way back to her yet – which seemed unlikely as they both went to the same school. Stopping when they reached the duck pond Sasha sat down pulling Jim to the seat before nestling against him.

"I love coming here for some peace sometimes" Sasha sighed as she pressed her head firmly against Jim's chest so that she could hear his heartbeat.

Jim glanced across the lake, spotting the sign deterring people from feeding the birds and the steady sprinkle of crumbs that had been left by people who clearly didn't think the sign applied to them. There were a few parks close to where he lived but none of them were as large as this one, for that matter none of them were as tidy as this either.

He had made note of the lack of rubbish strewn over the grass from the moment they made their way through the gate something that was a rarity in his area. There had been a few drives to tidy up his town but none of them had really caught the public attention which in a way had created a job opening for an elderly man who wore a luminous green jacket as he made his way through the town. At first nobody had really paid much attention to him but in Jim's eyes, whether this man was doing it for his own sanity or being paid to, he was one of the heroes of the town.

Every leaf and packed that he stabbed viciously or grabbed with a long metal arm was carefully deposited into a bin liner that he carried with him. There had been a few times when Jim had considered asking him about his job before deciding it was better not to question the man in case he triggered a lecture about tidying up. That was something he was used to hearing all about when he was at home so didn't need to bring on to himself when he was out and about.

"Just in case you were wondering hun" Sasha peered up as she spoke taking his hand and moving it slowly to the waistband of her jeans.

Jim glanced down watching where she was guiding his hand as she lifted the waistband of her jeans carefully showing her lacy underwear

"I was only teasing you at breakfast" Sasha grinned as she let go of his hand waiting in anticipation to see what he would do

Jim glanced up and watched as a lone duck ambled past them uninspired by the scattering of crumbs that had been left to tempt him. Pondering over his options he gripped Sasha gently running his finger along the waistband before loosening his grip a little

Sasha stood from the bench slightly flustered but almost relieved that Jim hadn't tried anything too daring as she reached out beckoning Jim to take her hand again and directed their way out of the park and toward the town centre. She hadn't quite decided where to take Jim, the town she lived in wasn't exactly the sort of place that attracted many tourists but she was still determined to show him where she lived.

As they made their way into the main street the scent of freshly baked pastries directed her attention to the little café she knew she visited probably more often than she should do. It had often occurred to her that out of the range of small bakeries that were scattered the street it was this small coffee shop that had the best smell emitting from its doorway. Dragging his arm slightly she pulled Jim through the door and into the café taking in a deep breath before making her way to a table.

The café was busier than a usual mid-morning but Sasha put that down to the fact that the schools were on their mid-term break. Small gatherings of teenagers that made her feel like she was older than she actually was communed around tables that were intended for much smaller groups than theirs. Somehow despite there only being a few cups on their tables Sasha noted that these groups seemed to be the least organised of all of the café dwellers.

She cringed slightly as she heard the undeniable sound of them listening to an excerpt of a new track that was more than likely to become the next short-lived sensation. In her heart she knew that some of the girls she socialised with on occasion had done the exact same with her usually showing some vague interest from an off-centre position within the group. It had been Adele that had pointed out to her that if she didn't at least pretend to be interested she would end up being shunned by them back at school.

Now she was on the outside, merely two years older than the average member of these groups with a smaller number of friends the efforts she had made to fit in seemed futile. With that being said she knew that if she hadn't at least tried to participate she would now be even more of an outcast that she had made herself into. At least in her current status she was still considered as someone worth inviting to parties, even if she rarely accepted the invitation it was nice to be thought of.

Guiding Jim past one of the groups she gritted her teeth as the sound of another one hit internet sensation was giggled and deliberated over. She could still remember the most recent one that had taken a lot of people time to recover from, not because it had been a good song but because despite how bad it was it had a catchy tune. This one, the latest one that was drawing attention sounded like it might at least be worth putting up with for however long it took before it faded into obscurity.

Sasha had often noticed how there was a different set of rules for teenagers that arrived in huddles during school time as opposed to those who arrived when the school were out. Suddenly all of the concerns that shops showed seemed to dissipate and the youngsters were treated almost the same way that an adult would be.

Choosing a seat at a table for two she handed Jim one of the laminated menus in the hope that he would be the one that suggested they should have a pastry as well as a coffee. Deep down she knew that no matter what he said she was determined to treat herself to one even if it meant ignoring his gaze as she ate it.

"What ya having Sash? I'll go order for us" Jim felt almost brave as he made the suggestion feeling sure after their meal out at the restaurant that his accent was going to cause some reaction even if it was a silent one.

In a way he found it quite charming how anyone who wasn't prepared for his English accent said nothing but their reaction still said they were struggling to fully understand him. He was sure that there were other English people living in and visiting Ireland but he could understand that, just like when someone from the North of England, visited his home town the accent he had was slightly discombobulating.

Sasha glanced over her shoulder as Jim walked away from the table complimented by the fact that he had taken control of the situation and taken action but also noting that it was her turn to pay for their next coffee. When they had first met there had been very few moments when either of them had needed to worry about money and it was nice to see him making the effort but she didn't want him paying for everything while they were together.

Turning back she pawed her way down the menu as she tried to avoid the temptation to add more than the one pastry she had ordered to their bill. In reality she knew that she could probably make her way slowly through most of the temptations on the menu but it wasn't a good idea for her figure or her health.

"If it isn't Sasha!" she cringed as she heard the familiar voice, a voice she had been happy to avoid and one that she knew she had been preparing for ever since their last meeting.

As usual, his timing was terrible but there was no way she could ignore the fact that Fintan was casually drifting his way over to her through the crowd of teenage bodies.

The light jacket he was wearing was clearly hiding a familiar polo shirt that Sasha now knew meant he was heading to work but the coffee in his hand suggested he had time to sit down rather than just getting a takeaway.

She cringed as he slipped past her, the scent of his aftershave filling her nose as he intentionally pressed his hand to her shoulder feigning a need to support his movement. Her skin crawled at the thought of his touch but Sasha knew instinctively that if she said anything he could justify his action by the crowd even if it wasn't the real reason.

It was almost like his mission in life was to make sure he did something either creepy or unwanted every time he made an effort to speak to her. His actions were always passive and yet she found it so easy to take offence to the very fact that he was trying to make contact with her in any way at all.

In her mind she knew that she had been lucky for a few weeks with him avoiding her and yet somehow he had managed to time his current appearance to coincide with a moment when she didn't even want to acknowledge knowing him.

With what seemed like a fluid and overly confident action Fintan slipped into the seat opposite Sasha, his mind still reeling from the way he had been treated the last time he had seen her. He had festered on that moment for a few weeks and now knew that the actions hadn't actually been Sasha's but one of the girls she had been sat with so he couldn't really hold the grudge against her.

Sasha glanced over her shoulder, spotting Jim at the counter as her unwanted table guest made himself comfortable.

"My boyfriend will be back in a minute Fintan, you'll need to move" She smiled softly as she spoke the words feeling a little tingle filling her body at the fact that unlike other times when she had referred to Jim, this time he was actually in the same place as she was.

Sipping from his coffee cup, Fintan leaned back slightly in his chair as if he hadn't really heard what Sasha had said. He had heard her mention a boyfriend a few times now and yet none of his friends had ever seen her with anyone. From experience he knew it wasn't a good idea to challenge such a reference but all the evidence suggested that this mystery man Sasha was referring to didn't really exist.

Nodding politely he placed his cup back on the table

"Sure no problem" he responded amicably choosing not to vent his doubts as to whether this boy she was referring to was real or not.

At the counter Jim smiled at the young woman who had served him as he slipped the change into his pocket.

His original intention had been not to give in to the smell of the pastries but that had been counteracted by the fact that a display of well-presented cakes had been sat tempting him throughout the time it had taken him to queue and place his order. Almost without thinking he added a cake for himself

While he had been at school he had seen a lot of girls who had put themselves through strict regimes that they called diets in an effort to lose a few pound and had silently admired their ability to be so disciplined. Jim knew that he was lucky that he could eat and not show any signs of it but his parents had both light-heartedly reminded him that his ability to do that wouldn't last forever. For now he could get away with not being able to walk past a bakery without feeling the urge to buy something or drooling over a cake no matter what occasion it was trying to advertise.

Carefully picking up the tray he glanced through the battlefield of customers that seemed to be getting more difficult to manage by the minute. Glancing down he noted that as seemed to be a common feature, both of their coffees were full to the point of almost spilling which he knew was going to make the journey even more challenging.

In his mind he had noted that there was a member of staff making her way from one table to the next but given the size of the crowd she had been trying to work around self-service had seemed the much more efficient option. Squeezing in between two chairs he smiled casually over at the same waitress who was still fighting her way around two tables that had been slid together by their occupants.

Pausing for a moment as one of the teenagers he was trying to avoid bobbed out of their seat unexpectedly he peered over at the table he had left Sasha sitting at. A new face had now sat with her, possibly another one of her friends he decided but not one that they had planned to meet.

His mind drifted back to their trip into the little village near the complex in Zante and his trip into a shop to get their tickets for a trip to see the turtles. On that occasion the stranger that had been sat with Sasha had been a tanned boy with long dark hair, this time the new face was red headed and extremely fair skinned. Smiling as he made his way carefully to the table he took a last glance at the precarious coffee cups, pleased to see that the spillage was at least minimal.

Sasha felt her face beaming with a mixture of relief and pleasure as Jim arrived back at their table with a tray full of goodies for them to enjoy. Casually she glanced over at Fintan who was sipping at his coffee again after having made a less than subtle reference to the idea that they should hang out together at some time.

This was it, this was the 'told you so' moment she knew she had been waiting for ever since the first time she had politely brushed off his advances. The difference was that this time there was no denying what and who was standing beside the table, even if Fintan didn't believe that this was really Jim there was no way he could deny the fact that there were two drinks waiting to be placed on the table she was sat at.

Raising her hand as if she was making a grand gesture Sasha smiled as she spoke

"Fintan, you'll remember me mentioning Jim, my boyfriend, to you I am sure"

Pausing for a moment as he took in what was happening Fintan glanced at the young man Sasha was gesturing toward. Part of his mind didn't want to accept that he had literally led himself into the situation he was now eager to get away from as quickly as possible. This was the second time he had been humiliated that had involved Sasha but this time he knew he really couldn't land the blame on anyone except for himself.

There was no easy way out of the position he found himself in, his coffee was half drunk and not in a cup that he was able to take away so he couldn't claim he was just making small talk and the boy, Jim who he now had to accept was real was standing patiently at the side of the table waiting to take the seat he was occupying.

Gazing silently at Sasha, Fintan stood from his chair and picked up his coffee cup before politely smiling at Jim and making his way to the counter to change his cup for a takeaway option. Sasha bit her lip, avoiding the urge to turn and watch him walk away although she wanted to mark what she decided was a great victory to her.

Maybe now she was finally rid of him

Chapter Thirteen

Some 'Fin' new

Fintan clutched the takeaway coffee cup he had carried with him since leaving the café feeling the heat from its contents still seeping through and singeing his fingertips. His mind felt numb, like someone had taken it out of his head, played with it and then put it back in but not quite put everything back in the right order.

Ever since the moment he had seen Sasha sat at the table he had been sure that he was in for a good day and yet now it was like everything he had anticipated had been confiscated from him. He knew that he couldn't pin the blame on the boy that had been introduced to him as her boyfriend but that didn't make the fact that he was real sting in his mind any less.

In the back of his mind he knew that Sasha had mentioned a boyfriend to him and even tried to show him a picture as evidence but seeing the boy stood there had been the finishing blow. There was no way he could deny it any longer, Sasha really was with someone else, all of the time and effort he had put in to being with her had been in vain. Shuffling his feet slightly he made his way into the staff room sitting at one of the empty tables as he placed the cup in front of himself.

Eric, one of the cashiers had waved at him on the way into the store, he recalled smiling and nodding a friendly gesture back at him as he acknowledged the greeting of 'how are ya?' with a non-verbal reply. It had never really occurred to him before but now he thought of it he could see how the greeting was, in itself, a question that no-one really cared about the answer to.

Doctors asked it at the beginning of a visit knowing that if the answer was 'I'm fine' there was no reason for the patient to be in his office in the first place. He had said it a thousand times to friends, family and acquaintances, many times as he passed them by, not even pausing long enough to receive a response, anticipating the usual answer while half hoping that his question didn't actually lead to a conversation. This time he knew that he had given a false answer, it wasn't really seen as a lie, but his answer despite having been silent didn't portray the emptiness he was feeling inside.

He sipped silently at the plastic lid to his cup jolting slightly as he heard his name being called from the corridor.

"Fin, just the man I was looking for" the store manager seemed flustered, which Fintan knew was not an unusual look but this time he seemed more flustered than usual.

Eamon caught his breath as he turned the corner from the corridor into the staff room where he had spotted Fintan sitting cradling a non-store coffee cup. His wife had made a few playful comments on about his expanding waist over the last few months which he had dismissed but now he could tell that he actually had put a little weight on or at least lost an element of his fitness.

"My other store down the road is short of a tech salesman, did you fancy a change of scene for a few days while we replace him?" Eamon bit his lip as he spoke

The reality of the matter was that he had just come off the phone with the guy he had hired to run the other store that had been backed into a corner and had to dismiss one of their staff on the spot. It hadn't been an easy decision but the evidence of a stack of phone accessories falling out of the recently dismissed member of his team had been hard to ignore as they fell out of his locker blazing a trail across the changing room floor. They needed someone to replace him quickly, especially with the busy pre-Christmas sales rush due to hit at any time but for now it was important to find a reliable stand in.

As soon as he had heard about the issue there was only one man that Eamon could think of that he could trust with the task and that was Fintan. The department manager in his own tech department was extremely good at his job but he was the only other person in the store that Eamon was confident knew what he was doing when it came to selling their tech stock. It was true that they had recently taken on a new member of their team but so far there were doubts about how long she was going to last. The most recent bet was that she would be gone by the end of the week and if he was being honest Eamon knew that it wasn't an unreasonable opinion.

"I'll get you there and back myself Fin, you've no need to worry about travel, but I will need you to get here half an hour earlier than usual so that we can make the journey" Eamon rested his hands on the table trying to appear calm as he gazed over at Fintan in the hope he was going to be amenable to the option.

Fintan grabbed his coffee cup, half surprised, firstly by the discrete compliment and secondly by the fact that the man he had assumed was just the store manager was actually the owner of at least two stores. He could vaguely recall something being said about it being a family run business but hadn't even considered the fact that the man that had interviewed him was part of the family.

He sipped on his cup, noting the eager anticipation on his manager's face as he took in all of the details, knowing in his mind that a change of scene was probably the perfect way to get over Sasha. Nodding amicably he emptied the cup and threw it into a nearby bin before following the manger out of the store through the back door which he had been sure was only a fire door up until that moment.

In a way it made sense that the manager would have access to the store from the back, it was the perfect way to get in and out without being set upon by either staff or customers as he tried to make his way to his office.

As the door was opened Fintan found himself staring into a small private parking space that he was sure only a few members of the team he was on were familiar with. The area was more than big enough for the single car that sat unassumingly parked safely sheltered in one corner with 'fire assembly point' signs marking the fenced wall confirming this as one of the escape routes from the store. With hurried steps Fintan watched as his manager made his way over to the car flicking a button on the key fob that made the car jump to life with a chirping bleep.

"The door is open Fintan" Eamon beckoned him over as he slid carefully into the driving seat pulling on his seatbelt.

Fintan made his way carefully down the far side of the car opening the door to what he could see was a high range BMW and sliding in watching the door as he sat down.

He couldn't help feeling an air of importance as the car crunched its way along the gravel and down on to a back street gracefully. In all of his dreams he had hoped that one day he would own a car like this but never actually considered the idea that he might end up sitting in one. The price tag he had seen even on second hand models was more than his father earned in a year so way beyond his budget.

For the next fifteen minutes Fintan gazed out of the window, thrilled by the thought of being in his mind, the chosen one as he tried to remain amicable by answering any questions that his manger posed to him. It was almost like being in his interview again, but this time he had the job so there was no pressure on him to impress the man who was sitting beside him with one elbow cocked out of the window. The radio muttered in the background as they made their way from one town to the next before he saw the familiar sight of the store logo peering above the rest of the main street announcing his pending arrival.

Fintan smiled vacantly as they parked pausing as he spotted a girl of about his age making her way over to the car.

"Dad, I've seen the best pair of shoes ever can you get them for me please?"

For a moment Fintan paused gazing over at the sweet face that was peering through the driver side window.

"Fin, this is my daughter Saoirse, she is meant to be here on work experience but apparently that involves shopping" Eamon smiled casually as he unbuckled his seatbelt before carefully pushing his door open forcing his daughter to shuffle backwards.

Trying to remain calm Fintan let himself out of the passenger side glancing briefly over at the girl, her fawn brown hair lapping over her shoulders. The sparkle of excitement in her eyes and the subtle red lipstick she had clearly put on probably without her father knowing she even wore make up.

Unlike the uniform he was wearing, this girl was in what looked like a school uniform, but not the one from the school he went to. This one was a deep claret colour with a charcoal grey skirt that he felt sure was meant to reach down at least as far as her knees but hers flared out resting barely half way down her thighs.

At first it felt unusual to him seeing someone in school uniform when they were clearly not at school but Fintan accepted that it was probably more practical than giving her a work uniform for however long she was going to be in the store.

Fintan held back as he watched the girl hanging on his manager arm in an effort to convince him that the shoes she had been referring to were the best things she had ever seen. It was nice to watch the manager caught off guard and not acting like a manager even if it was only going to be for a few moments. He smiled to himself as the manger casually took a fifty euro note out of his pocket and presented it to his daughter who squealed as she ran back into the store waving amicably before disappearing through the doors.

"Well, she isn't being paid to work here, I can call it her salary I guess" Eamon smiled as he found himself justifying spending on shoes that he hadn't even seen in an effort to regain something that resembled a work atmosphere with Fintan.

Nodding politely with a vague smile as he followed the manager into the store pondering over the fact that this man, the man he had barely ever seen leaving the office, a man that he had convinced himself probably lived in the store actually had not only a second store but also a family, not just any family but one with a teenage daughter in it who was surprisingly attractive. He paused for a moment realising that he was silently complimenting the daughter of the man he had built up a reputation for as a good employee.

In a way, he knew that even the fact he was still thinking about the man's daughter was almost the same as thinking about the child of one of his teachers which was something he preferred not to think about. He couldn't deny that with some of his teachers the thought that they had even had a sex life was more than his imagination could take let alone the idea of any of them having kids.

There were, of course, a few that even he couldn't deny the fact that they had a family, those whose children were known to either have been at the school or were still at the school. Thankfully he wasn't on speaking terms with any of them but that didn't mean they didn't exist, it just meant that they weren't part of his social circle. One of his proudest moments in a way was the fact that he had managed to not only get the phone number of but go on a one off date with the girlfriend of one of the teachers' son's.

The boyfriend, who he knew only as Paudie, had spent a month denying that his girlfriend had even thought of dating anyone behind his back. Being the son of one of the year heads meant that he held a position of unspoken authority even if that position was only theoretical and couldn't be used to influence anything. It was only when he had caught his girlfriend texting Fintan that the thought of something going on behind his back even crossed his mind and yet he hadn't confronted either of them about it.

Fintan had been forewarned of the suspicion not only by his friends but in another text from the girl in question who was contemplating coming clean and admitting to their date, a notion that he was pleased to have been able to talk her out of. He couldn't confirm it but from that day forward it always felt like the Paudies father had been keeping a much closer eye on Fintan even if nothing had been said between them.

This girl, Saoirse, was different, she seemed a little younger than he was but not too young that she didn't understand relationships and there was no denying her interest in fashion, along with her subtle inclination toward rebellious behaviour which he could see even if her father couldn't or didn't want to. The bigger problem was that if he decided to ask her out, which was his current inclination, it may cause one of a number of implications for him which could affect his work life.

From the day he had started his job at the other store his colleagues had told him that it was safer to avoid relationships that involved people he worked with. He could see the potential issues they could cause even if he only based his knowledge off his experience of dating girls in the same classes as him but technically he didn't actually work with this girl, their time in the same store was only going to be brief even if she did end up working there properly in the future. With this girl there was also the fact that he couldn't deny or avoid working for her father regardless of whether she agreed to date him or not and then there were even more complications that may occur if she did agree to a date.

He had experienced meeting girl's parents before and it had never been a comfortable moment especially with the girl's father. His presence in their company made him almost an automatic threat in more than one way and depending on how close he and the girl in question seemed at the time of meeting the level of hostility had potential to be higher. The only respite he had was that he had never been unlucky enough to be caught in a girl's bedroom which he knew other boys in his year had experienced.

If he did decide to chance asking her out he knew that he would need to accept that anything they did may get back to her father whether he wanted it to or not. That would be potentially the good stuff and anything bad that occurred between them and this was the man he intended to continue working for if he was able to hold his job.

Adding to all of the factors was the fact that he didn't actually know how old she was, the way she dressed suggested that she wasn't a young teenager but it wasn't easy to tell her actual age. He had dated girls who were 15 in the past but now he was nearly 17 that felt almost like it was not the right thing to do even if it was only a two year age gap between them there was a lot of difference.

Shrugging his thoughts to the back of his mind he focussed his attention on his manager who had been guiding him through the store and had no idea of the thoughts he was having about the daughter he had only just been introduced to. Then again, he had to admit there was something reassuring about dating a girl that was not in his home town even if it was only the fact that she had very little chance of knowing of his past ventures.

Fintan shuddered slightly realising that no matter how much he was trying not to think of her Saoirse was popping into his mind and distracting him from focussing on what his manager was trying to tell him.

His morning went well; he managed to stay focussed on his job making a few positive sales and recommendations that he knew his manager would be proud of before heading for his first break when he spotted Saoirse sitting alone in the staff room. She spotted him straight away and waved at him as an open invitation for him to join her at the table she was sitting at alone with a book open in front of her. Grabbing a coffee and bag of crisps he made his way over smiling at her amicably while accepting that the welcome she had offered him was probably because she had recognised him from the car park earlier that day.

"Aren't they literally the best shoes you've ever seen?" Fintan smiled as he glanced over at Saoirse.

He could see in her eyes that she was excited about the shoes but her comment had, in some ways, left him wanting to give her the lecture he had received for incorrectly using the word literally in a sentence. In many ways he knew that the lecture he had received had been due to him making a comment as he was leaving English class which seemed in some ways to be the most appropriate time to be reprimanded but that didn't make the situation less frustrating. If anything the fact that a teacher was holding him back from his break time gave his passing comment about being literally starving even more credence as it was delaying him from getting food.

There was a sudden but brief spell of awkwardness as he felt his gaze transfixed on the almost athletic way his table partner has swung her leg up on to one of the free chairs but it hadn't come from the fact that she had her foot on the chair. During her effort to present her new shoes to him Saoirse had inadvertently flashed her underwear at him as her skirt wafted under the momentum of her leg swing. On one hand he knew that the flash wasn't intended but on the other he knew that most of his classmates at school would have given their left arm to confirm the flash of pink polka-dots that he had witnessed.

In his mind Fintan felt sure that Saoirse knew that he wasn't an expert in women's shoes but that hadn't been the point of her showing him. He had been there when she had gone out of her way to get the funds for the shoes from her father so this was her way of justifying the purchase to the only other person who knew about them. The heel on them was easily going to make her look like she was at least an inch taller than she actually was and, as she wasn't a short girl that seemed trivial but he had to admit they looked good on her.

"They're great" he smiled he smile as he spoke

" I guess you just need somewhere nice to go out and show them off" he turned away as he made his comment focussing on the opened bag of crisps Saoirse had been helping herself too ever since she sat down

Saoirse blushed as she heard his comment pondering over whether it had been just a general observation or was he hinting at something that he wasn't willing to ask her outright. Her father had made the recommendation of her working in the store a few days during her break from school and she had welcomed the pocket money and chance to get out of the house for a few hours every day to earn it.

In a way she knew that it was her own fault that she was wearing her school uniform during the holidays but as she had made the comment that had led to the decision being made by her parents she knew she was stuck with it.

On the first day she had entered the staff room she had been quick to notice that she was the youngest one there by at least 5 years meaning it was going to be hard to make any friends while she was there. One of the till boys had made a move on her but soon backed away when he caught on to the fact that she was the bosses daughter. She had been quite relived to see him keeping his distance because it saved her having to tell him she wasn't interested in him.

When she had seen her fathers car pulling into the car park she knew that it was with the back up staff from his other store and had been pleasantly surprised when the temporary team mate turned out to be close to her own age.

Reaching across the table she grabbed another one of Fintan's crisps smiling at him cheekily as she popped it in her mouth before sitting back in her chair.

Even without knowing too much about him she had concluded that he seemed like a nice boy, obviously confident, that was easy to tell by the way he walked and talked to the customers and other members of the team. Nothing seemed to faze him, the fact that he was in effect the new member of the team, the age gap between him and the others he worked with – nothing. There was definitely something about him that made her want to see him in a less formal atmosphere, some kind of date but maybe not as official as that.

"So, Fintan" she smiled, poking another crisp into her mouth as she spoke

"Are you going to be the one to take me somewhere I can wear them or not" Saoirse leaned her head into her hand placing her elbow on the table as she directed her comment at him.

Fintan stared across the table choking slightly as he heard the comment

In his mind there was only one correct answer when a girl was basically inviting him to take her on a date – even if it was the boss's daughter.

Chapter Fourteen

Ambitious Adele

As she hadn't hear back from the text she had sent to Sasha suggesting that they could meet up again Adele accepted that the silence meant that either her text hadn't been read or it had been read but Sasha had chosen not to reply for some reason.

In some ways the lack of reply was eating away inside her but Adele knew that firstly she hadn't used an app that showed her when a message was read meaning she had not way of knowing the status and secondly Sasha would reply when she was ready to. Her mind drifted to images of Sasha cuddled up somewhere with Jim enjoying moments that sent butterflies into her tummy as she felt the craving to experience the same moments for herself.

She knew in her heart that it was wrong to have such an infatuation for him not only because Jim was in a relationship with her best friend but because she barely knew him. There had been something about him that was driving her mad with an unspoken attraction to him despite having only seen him for a few hours.

Part of her mind was drifting to that moment when she had been stood with Sasha and Jim in the back garden of the cottage, the moment when she had instinctively assumed they were going to disrobe as they usually did. The fact that none of them had even removed a shirt had made her wonder how different things may have been if she hadn't exercised precaution. Would she have felt Jim's gaze on her body our would he have remained loyal to Sasha and not even been tempted by her?

Maybe it was his accent, in the past she had found weakness for some accents but hadn't ever thought about it as something that might have caused her to be attracted to someone. There was no doubt he had a cute accent and it had been hard to understand at first but after the first half hour she had got used to how he said different words.

Huffing at herself she decided to make her way back to the cottage, the scene of a crime that she knew hadn't happened but also a place where she could be alone to ponder over what she hoped was just a temporary infatuation.

When she had first arrived at the cottage her first instinct had been to strip off completely however a cool breeze had given her a less than subtle reminder that it was no longer summer and clothing was probably advisable at least for the meantime. It hadn't taken her too long to reach a compromise, removing her outer layers of clothing and sitting in her underwear as she gazed out from the shelter of the greenhouse.

It was almost funny in a way, at the time that Sasha had first mentioned Jim, although she didn't doubt his existence he hadn't seemed entirely real either. There was something about the fact that although Sasha was clearly excited about having met him the fact that he wasn't even in the same country as them made him less real in a way.

There was also the fact that she seemed to have fallen for him so quickly, she had barely known him for two weeks and in that time they had gone from being strangers to being in a relationship together.

Maybe it was the fact they had met on a holiday which had made Sasha drop her guard quicker than she did around the boys she had known for years. Then again, maybe it had something to do with the fact that they had more than likely spent a lot of time together naked both before and after they got together properly. That was in a way something that Adele knew she envied more than anything, Sasha had seen him with nothing on and all she could do was imagine what wasn't hers to have even if she did see it.

Adele knew that there was no reason why he wouldn't be nude in her company at some point, Sasha had clearly told him they both practiced naturism but now she had a full crush on him she didn't know if that was such a good idea. Maybe, if they did have naturist time together she would keep her panties on, she could easily come up with a reason to do that even if it was a lie.

Reaching behind herself she unclipped her bra letting it fall to her knees draping lifelessly over them as she enjoyed the freedom that removing it gave to her breasts, a freedom that she was sure that most women enjoyed but usually in the privacy of their own homes. This was what the cottage had been all about from the moment she had first been introduced to it by Sasha which seemed like ages ago even if it was only a couple of months. If she wanted to sit in her clothes she knew she could do that at home, She could possibly even get away with sitting in her underwear depending on who was home but the cottage was about doing things that she couldn't do at home.

She smiled as she accepted that if she had chosen to make her way downstairs in her underwear, while it was likely that at her age her mother would accept it there would be at least one comment made about the lack of proper dress code. Her father had gone to work early so Adele knew that the comment wouldn't be any reference to her being seen by him with nothing on, a comment that she could easy combat by pointing out that she technically still had something on even if it had been said.

Her mother was more tactical than that, she would make some comment about them needing to go clothes shopping, a subtle but direct reference to the implication that it was clear that Adele had nothing that fitted her. Either that or there would be a reference to her needing to use the washing machine more often to prevent days when she had no clean clothes to wear, both of those being comments that she knew she could argue against but not without feeling the need to dress fully.

In the seclusion of the cottage it was different, Sasha and she had made clothing most definitely optional with the preference being not wearing any something that she felt like she was getting more confident about with every day that passed. Jumping slightly she turned to the neatly folded pile of her outer clothing, a pile that would soon include the bra that was still draped where it had fallen across the top of her thighs

A message had come through on her phone

She smiled as she dug her hand in her pocket silently hoping it was a reply from Sasha but feeling her emotions mix as she noted that it wasn't a text but a message from Seamus, her naturist friend whom she had met by chance through an online naturist group. After their meeting on Hawks Cliff Beach they had continued contacting each other through online messaging but slowly their contact had become less frequent. At first Adele had been concerned that he might take her lack of contact as having something to do with him being gay but he hadn't said anything about it so she chose not to justify their slow drift away from daily messages to once a week or so.

He seemed quite excited in his message at the fact that he had found himself a new partner and they were now sharing a flat despite the fact it was only a few weeks since they had met. In his message he described how his boyfriend seemed comfortable with naturism even though he didn't participate in the lifestyle himself. Adele smiled as she replied telling him how happy she was for him, pausing as she contemplated telling him that she was crushing on a boy she dare not tell before deciding not to mention it.

Placing her phone carefully on top of the pile of clothing she folded her bra tucking it under her jeans before unzipping the door of the greenhouse. A gentle breeze flowed in tickling her skin adding a reminder of why she had chosen the option of staying concealed in the makeshift room if she was going to be removing any clothes while she was there. Pausing with the zip half way up one side she pulled the door open slightly with her foot poking it out into the fresh air, wriggling her toes as the breeze passed over them.

A second message blurted through on her phone.

Turning her head she glanced down, smiling as she noted it was a second message from Seamus, the only man that she knew had seen her naked but didn't want to sleep with her as a result of it. Reaching for the door zip she pulled it further up until the flap was fully open before standing and sliding through the opening into the outside world.

A chill ran through her body making her glance at the clothes that she had intentionally left behind in the warmth of the greenhouse. Standing outside in just a pair of panties seemed crazy with the lack of sun but somehow it also felt comforting and she quickly realised that she wasn't feeling as cold as she had expected to feel. Peering down her arms she could see her skin pimpling and yet she didn't actually feel uncomfortably cold which surprised her at first.

It didn't make sense, none of this did in reality, how could she feel – not warm – but comfortable in just panties? They weren't big enough to be making her entire body feel like she didn't actually need to wrap up and yet somehow she didn't feel cold.

Reaching down she placed her hands to her tummy, her skin felt cool but not cold as she pushed her hands down her thighs sending her panties toward the ground.

For a moment she stood there, her panties around her ankles waiting to see if the removal of such a small item was going to make any difference while knowing in her heart that it couldn't really change a lot, she had been practically naked before and not she was fully naked but the transition hadn't been significant. Bending down she giggled slightly as a breeze brushed past her bottom while she retrieved her panties throwing them into the greenhouse.

In front of her, the overgrown garden, a space she had waded through many times before dressed just like she was now. Behind her the stone wall of the cottage hiding her away from the footpath she had followed to arrive, a footpath that she knew she had never seen anyone else using in all of her visits. Turning on her heels she gazed at the wooden panel that she could still remember helping Sasha place against the vacant doorframe as she made her way toward it.

Pressing her shoulder gently against the wooden panel she peered through into the empty shell of the cottage, its mudded floor hardened by the lack of rain. Pressing her cheek to the wood she gazed out to the doorway that joined the cottage to the narrow footpath she had walked down a few times with Sasha and a few on her own. Admittedly she knew that every time she come to the cottage she hadn't actually been listening for anyone else but she felt sure that she hadn't actually heard any other footsteps or noises that suggested anyone else had ventured past the cottage door.

Even without clothes she felt completely safe, no one knew she was there and no one cared that she had no clothes on.

Suddenly a thought crossed her mind, one that was probably completely insane but to her seemed like it might be at least a little bit fun and adventurous. What if she was to make her way into the cottage itself? She would still be hidden from the path and could always hide if she heard anyone coming.

Standing up she carefully shuffled the wooden panel creating a gap in the doorway that was just big enough for her to squeeze through before sliding her way into the cottage. Her body filled with adrenalin, she was no longer hidden from the world and yet she was still safely out of sight of the path that crossed the main entrance – the thrill was almost intoxicating as she stood staring at the cottage front door. Slowly she made her way one step at a time closer to the doorway feeling her body tingling with excitement with every step she took.

This was completely crazy, her clothes were hidden behind her and she knew that if anyone appeared she only had the stone walls of the cottage to hide behind and yet the thrill, the rush of energy was beyond anything she had experienced before. Sasha would kill her if she knew what she was doing but then again, Sasha wasn't here to see her so this would be her little secret adventure.

Was this the sort of freedom that Sasha experienced when she was on her holiday every year? Possibly

Leaning against the front door to the cottage Adele felt her heart pounding as she peered as discretely as she could down the pathway feeling her confidence grow as she confirmed there was nobody coming. With a quick dash she made her way to the other side of the doorway peering the other way down the path and confirming that she was clear from the other side too.

Adele stepped back positioning herself centrally in the open doorway as if she was looking out on to the footpath while knowing that no one could actually see her. Taking a deep breath she swung one leg forward launching herself out onto the path buzzing with adrenalin at the idea of being in a public space completely naked. She glanced left and right pivoting her body to face both directions before leaping back into the cottage feeling her body tingling as blood rushed through her veins.

For a moment she paused crouching against the stone wall to catch her breath as she took in everything she had just done. This was amazing, it was only a shame that no one knew she was doing it but then again, if anyone did know she was sure they would either be trying to convince her not to do it or encouraging her to do more. Standing again she made her way into the doorway peering left and right to reaffirm that nobody had joined the path while she had been recovering and taking everything into perspective.

Feeling more confident than before she stepped out on to the footpath turning left, to face the direction that would take her back to the main path and then turning right, a direction that was unknown to her. She glanced over her shoulder before counting our ten oversized steps, each one taking her further away from the doorway that led to safety. Again she turned her head – the path still deserted before taking another ten steps and moving into a light jog that took her further away from the cottage.

Stopping after a few seconds she turned and felt her heart sink as she spotted movement in the distance somewhere near the place where her path forked away from the main path. She was stranded, nowhere near her clothes and if she didn't think quickly she was going to be spotted walking along the pathway completely naked by wherever was now slowly making their way toward the cottage.

Remaining as quiet as possible she made her way slowly back toward the cottage, hearing Sasha's words of warning reverberating in her mind 'we must make sure we aren't seen.'

Adele knew she had taken a few steps but the cottage now seemed so far away that she didn't think she was ever going to make it there safely.   Bobbing in behind trees she made her way a few steps at a time back along the path suddenly feeling vulnerable and yet surprisingly warm considering her dress code.   Her heart stopped as she made a leap behind a large tree that gave her a perfect view of the cottage door, so near and yet still too far away to make an attempt to get there without being seen by the figure making its way toward her.

Peering from her hiding place Adele watched as the figure arrived at the cottage and felt a flush of both relief and awkwardness as she realised who it was. In a way it was encouraging to know that her theory about the pathway being unused by anyone except for those who knew of the cottage but that didn't make the fact that the figure she had spotted was Ciara any easier to accept.

Ciara had only visited the cottage once before as far as she knew and that time it has been both Sasha and her that had been walked in on. Before she had left she had made a promise that she wouldn't give away the secret location and the fact that she was stood there alone suggested that she had kept the promise even if she was returning to the cottage for some reason.

Adele watched as Ciara made her way through the cottage doorway and into the main building out of sight from her hiding place. She knew that she had two options, she could either make her way back to the cottage and try to explain where she had been and why she had left her clothes behind while doing so or she could wait for Ciara to leave again and hope that she didn't take the abandoned clothing thinking that it had been left behind by one of them by mistake.

Neither option appealed to Adele, but the more she thought over them the more sense it made to make her way back to the cottage, at least from there she could re-dress safely, while it wasn't the ideal option at least it was better than trying to make her way all the way home naked if Ciara took the abandoned clothing with her when she saw no one was there.

Taking a final glance down the pathway in both directions Adele made a dash for the cottage doorway leaping into the cottage and sliding back against the stone wall as she felt her body fill with relief that she was now back within reach of her abandoned belongings. She glanced at the wooden panel almost relieved to see that it hadn't been moved by Ciara whom she knew was somewhere in the back garden probably wondering whose clothing she had found and where the owner was.

Dashing with sprite like steps Adele made her way from one side of the cottage to the other noting that despite the fact that she knew that Ciara was just behind the back doorway she was still being careful not to make too much noise.   She paused for a moment as she tried to work out what she was going to say when she made her presence known to her estranged friend who was probably still oblivious to the fact that she was there.

"Ciara, it's me, Adele" she pressed her back against the cottage wall as she spoke hoping that her presence wouldn't be seen as too much of a surprise.

"I guess you are wondering why I am here and my clothes are in the garden with you" Adele stopped as she tried to imagine what might be going through Ciara's head.

Jumping slightly, Ciara turned as she heard a familiar voice from the other side of the wall shocked slightly that Adele had identified her without being visible. It had confused her slightly when she had made her way into the garden and seen no one there but signs of activity in the greenhouse that she remembered Sasha and Adele had built the last time she had visited the location.

She had noted clothing sitting neatly piled in the greenhouse but hadn't given much thought to why it was there having made the assumption that whoever owned it had bought spare stuff with them for some reason. Now she was hearing Adele speak the thought occurred to her that the reason for the pile of clothing was not as obvious as it had first seemed to her and it was possible that the voice she was hearing was coming from the owner of the pile of abandoned clothing she had spotted.

The last time she had been here with Adele she had been in just a pair of panties and had made the announcement that Sasha and she practiced naturism. Ciara glanced at the pile of clothing noting that this time there appeared to be panties among the other items and accepted that if her theory was correct then Adele was naked this time. She paused for a moment and turned so that she was facing away from the only way in to the garden that she knew was available.

"I guess ye better come in Adele" Ciara bit her lip as she spoke trying not to giggle as she contemplated different scenarios that could end up with Adele on one side of the wall – the public side – and her clothing on the other side.

Taking a deep breath as she cleared her mind Adele slid between the wall and the wooden fence panel pushing the panel back in place so that she was safely hidden from the footpath again before turning toward the greenhouse.

Through one eye she could see the pile of clothing she had left behind, her body still slightly buzzing at the experience as she composed her mind.

As if she was playing a game of hide and seek Ciara stood with her back facing the resealed doorway her hands cupped in front on her body as she waited patiently for Adele to join her in the garden

"I know it seems unlikely, but there is an explanation for this I assure you" Adele felt her cheeks flush with redness as she made her way toward the greenhouse door.

Chapter Fifteen

Naked Attraction

Ciara could feel her cheeks flushing with embarrassment as she peeped discretely though one half opened eye confirming in her mind that Adele really had just shuffled past her naked.

When she had spotted Adele making her way down the alleyway she had known exactly where she was going but this time there was no Sasha with her making it seem like almost the perfect opportunity to speak to Adele without anyone else to distract them.

From the moment they had first been practically thrust toward each other by Maebh at the fair Ciara had made her own special little bond with Adele even if that bond only went as far as their joint interest in roller coasters. It hadn't been intended to feel like she was some kind of stalker but knowing that Adele would be on her own gave her the perfect chance to get to know a little more about this girl that had been introduced to her just so that Maebh could find out about her secret crush.

As she made her way to the alleyway Ciara had recalled the last time she had been to the cottage, the awkward exchange of conversation between Sasha, Adele and her as they had tried to justify their state of partial dress.

She had given some thought to what had been said that day and how naturism, the lifestyle that Adele and Sasha had both tried to justify to her, was perfectly normal. For a few days she had lingered on their comments gazing casually into the mirror in her room while fidgeting with her clothes before accepting that she wasn't sure if she would ever feel comfortable with her body in the same way they seemed to.

By the time she had arrived at the point where the footpath's forked Ciara had accepted that if she went through with her plan there was a chance that this time Adele may have fully stripped by the time she got there. A small grin crossed her face as she tried not to imagine how Adele might react to being seen with nothing on, something she knew would cause all sorts of embarrassment if it happened to her.

It wasn't so much that she was scared of seeing Adele with no clothes on, it was more the thought that as the cottage had been referred to as a naturist spot she would be expected to at the very least not expect the same concession to be made as had been on her first visit. In her mind the worst case scenario would be if she was encouraged to try it herself, which she knew she wasn't going to be able to do.

Her plan was fairly simple, this time she was going to make sure Adele knew she was on her way into the garden so that when she appeared it wouldn't be such a surprise.

Ciara paused for a moment glancing back along the path she had followed so far as she contemplated her options. In a way she had been hoping to catch Adele on her own ever since the day at the fair but every time she saw her it had been at school and Sasha hadn't been far behind. In a way Ciara knew that part of the problem was the fact they were in different years but the fact that she was always in close company with Maebh hadn't helped her growing interest in getting to know Adele.

The fact was that, for as much as she enjoyed spending time with Maebh she also wanted to expand her circle of friends and Adele seemed like the ideal person. Sasha was nice and friendly to speak to as well but it just felt like she would probably get on better with Adele given that they already had one thing in common.

For a moment she pondered over the idea of walking away, leaving Adele to enjoy whatever it was she was doing at the cottage and wait for another time when she could try to get Adele's attention. Ciara took a few steps back toward the street before turning back to the narrow path that led to the cottage and slowly continuing her journey determined to make the most of the opportunity that had presented itself to her.

With careful steps she made her way from the front entrance through the inside of the cottage noting that the weather had made the ground softer than before but still not too difficult to walk over. For a moment she paused staring at the fence panel that she had hidden behind on her first visit as she cleared her mind in preparation for whatever may happen once it was known that she was there waiting to be invited in.

"Adele? It's me, Ciara" she felt her voice becoming a mumble as she finished her sentence and took a few steps closer to the fence panel.

"Don't worry, I have come alone" She smiled with pride as she spoke, recalling how she had promised not to tell anyone about the cottage, a promise that she had managed to keep despite temptations.

It had been difficult avoiding the temptation to say anything, especially to Maebh who had been bursting with excitement on their first day back at school but somehow she had managed it.

Maebh had clearly got over her crush on Fintan by the time they got back to school and hadn't spent too long finding a new boy to be interested in, This time she had been luckier than she had been with Fintan, Joel had been as interested in her as she was in him and they had been on at least three dates since their first talk each of which Maebh had been extremely keen to talk about the day after with Ciara.

At first, Ciara had been pleased for her friend to have found someone who seemed to not only be a nice guy but also seemed to like her as much as she liked him. The biggest problem was that now Maebh had found a boyfriend their time together both at school and after school had become less frequent and less fun. Their chats had been less light hearted and more about when she was going to see him again, asking for opinions on what she thought she should do with him now they were a real couple.

Making it even more frustrating was the fact that Maebh seemed to be on some kind of personal challenge to see how many times she could either say his name or mention her boyfriend in the space of a conversation.

Ciara had counted once, silently and established that twenty times in the space of an hour was quite impressive but it was nice to see Maebh happy if nothing else. She paused for a moment as she peered carefully past the fence panel pondering over whether she had spoken too quietly or maybe even been wrong in her assessment of where Adele had been heading to.

It was nice to see that the pile of poles that had been spread across the ground during her first visit had now been put together and turned into what looked like a smart greenhouse. Glancing quickly around the garden she made her way out onto the patio area surprised to see that Adele wasn't there.

Quickly she made her way over toward the greenhouse puzzled by the fact that as she peered through the door she spotted a pile of clothes stacked neatly.

There was no doubt in her mind that at least some of the items in the pile belonged to Adele, the jeans were unmistakeable as being the same ones she had seen her wearing as she entered the alleyway.

Maybe she had got changed and gone off for a wonder, Ciara pondered over the idea, accepting that it wasn't the most ideal place to change but, as Sasha and Adele spent time in the same place without clothing on, it wasn't beyond question that Adele might have got changed there.

Her ears pricked as she heard Adele's voice from the other side of the stone wall and spotted her face peering around into the garden as if it was she who was the visitor trying to spy on the place this time.

It had startled her slightly when she noted through her half closed eyes that it looked like Adele had made her way into the back garden naked but she refused to turn from her position until she heard confirmation that she was allowed to look. The comment of the situation not being as it had seemed was almost trivial but Ciara had to admit the glimpse of Adele scuttling past her naked had sparked more than one question which she felt sure she wasn't meant to ask.

"It's safe to look now" Adele tapped Ciara gently on the shoulder as she spoke bemused by the fact that the same person had walked in on her twice now in less than ideal dress code but at least it was only Ciara which she found somewhat reassuring.

For the first few weeks of the school term Sasha had seemed like she was on full guard as she waited for someone to make a sly comment to give the game away that Ciara hadn't been able to keep their secret. Things had calmed down by the beginning of October and the focus had moved to what she was going to do and how excited she was that Jim was visiting her so soon after the summer.

The fact that Ciara was alone wasn't proof that she hadn't said anything, Adele knew that, but the fact that nothing had been said to either of them was a silent reassurance that they really could trust her.

Adele grinned as she made her way back toward the greenhouse digging the plastic chair that they had discarded in favour of the metal shelving once they had built the greenhouse. Pulling her sleeve over the palm of her hand she brushed it down before placing it in front of the greenhouse and inviting Ciara to take a seat.

"Ya know I didn't expect to see you here again" Adele smiled awkwardly as she spoke making not in her mind that it wasn't a good idea to mention Ciara's reappearance to Sasha unless it was for a good reason.

"I gotta ask" she bit her lip gazing down at the ground before continuing her sentence "are you here because of naturism?" Adele tucked her hands in between her legs as she spoke half hoping that something had sparked inside Ciara just as it had with her but half knowing that it didn't seem likely that it had.

There was no doubting that if she had to take a guess between Ciara and Maebh as to which one might have been into naturism, Maebh would be her first guess but then again, Sasha hadn't been the sort that she would imagine enjoying it either.

Ciara felt her cheeks flush with red as she heard the comment, giggling lightly at the idea that she would ever be brave enough to even consider it but understanding why Adele had asked the question. Shaking her head she smiled at Adele confirming that naturism was definitely not the reason she had come back to the cottage.

"Adele, why were you naked outside the garden?" The more she pondered over the question the harder it became for Ciara to find a way to ask the question that had been looming ever since she had pretended not to watch Adele scuttle past her.

Now that Adele was dressed again it almost felt like it was too late to be asking the question but her curiosity had been boiling over, that and a burning interest in what she had missed by closing her eyes to save Adele's awkward reappearance in the safety of the garden.

Taking a deep breath Adele glanced casually over at Ciara, from the moment she had spotted her making her way into the cottage Adele had known that she was stuck facing two options and neither of them seemed appealing. Out of the two of them the thought of having to explain her predicament to Ciara was by far the more amicable over the thought of what may occur if she left her to look around the cottage and accept that there was nobody there to speak to.

It had been too obvious from the fact that Ciara had arrived in the first place that she had clearly seen her making her way to the cottage just like she had the first time but this time she hadn't been as cautious about making her way into the garden.

Adele knew in her heart that, despite her assurances that there was an explanation for what she had been doing there wasn't really any explanation that made sense or seemed logical. The facts were clear, she had left the safety of the garden, the one place where either of the two people that she knew who were aware of the cottage wouldn't be surprised at the fact that she had disrobed.

Sasha had pre-warned her of the possibility of someone who didn't know they were there walking in on them unexpectedly but so far the closest they had got to that happening had been Ciara's first visit. Adele knew that, no matter how much she wanted to turn the situation around, place the focus on the fact that it looked like Ciara had snuck up on her for the second time there was no rule saying she couldn't do. Neither of them actually owned the cottage so she had no right trying to place the blame for the awkward moment in the lap of Ciara who had always come across as kind and friendly so didn't deserve the third degree in the first place.

"I needed to let off some steam and doing something a little bit crazy seemed like a good way to do it" Adele bit her lip as she blurted the closest thing she could think of to an excuse out while knowing that her words didn't even come close to explaining her actions.

As excuses went Adele knew that she could have come up with a better one if she had thought about it but there were only so many reasons she could think of for being outside the safety of the naturist sanctuary while nude. In a way at least the reason she had given was marginally better than the other one that had sprung to mind – 'it seemed like a good idea at the time' had never gone down well with her parents as an excuse so it was unlikely to be seen as acceptable with Ciara.

She had been tempted while redressing to try to blame her unusual behaviour on an alien abduction but that seemed a little too far-fetched for anyone to believe. Ciara was clearly an intelligent girl, Adele had noticed that the first day she met her so there was no way she was going to fall for anything like that especially given the fact that her clothes had been neatly folded so close to where she had been walking around naked.

"It's just, I dunno, everything has been going badly for me recently so I wanted to do something fun, something that no one would expect, but not something so outrageous that it would get me in trouble" Adele added her comment while accepting that she could still feel the thrill of her mistimed adventure surging through her mind, her consciousness telling her that even if she had been caught it had been fun so worth the risk.

Ciara sat in silence as she listened to Adele trying to justify the event that she had accidentally walked in on while trying to suppress a grin. In some ways the incident had been somewhere close to what she had been pre-warned about Adele and Sasha getting up to when they visited the cottage but that hadn't made it less of a surprise. There was no doubt that, even with as much as she had prepared herself for what she may be walking in to the last thing she had expected was Adele walking in through the makeshift door naked behind her when the secret spot was the hidden garden.

"Did ya hear that Fintan has got himself a girlfriend?" Adele could feel her heart beat slowing down to a more normal pace now that the adrenalin was dissipating from her body

Nodding quickly Ciara glanced over at Adele pleased in some ways that the conversation had moved on.

"So, he's got someone, Sasha has Jim visiting, makes me wonder why I can't find someone to go on a date with" Giggling slightly Adele reached over to the corner of the greenhouse carefully picking up one of the gnomes that had now become permanent features in their little garden.

Ciara glanced over as she heard Adele's casual comment, feeling sure that it wasn't meant as anything significant but still not able to quite let it leave her mind. Over the past two years she had played out the same scenario in her head many times whereby she was able to finally tell Maebh that she was into her in more than just a friendly way. Her family didn't know that she preferred women and hadn't questioned the fact that she had never even hinted at any boys she liked.

She had been on dates with boys but none of them had gone beyond a kiss goodnight and even then Ciara felt sure she should feel something more than her usual eagerness to get it over with. In her head it seemed easy, she would tell Maebh that she was in to girls and if she was lucky Maebh would admit to at least being curious if nothing else.

Every time she came close to saying something Maebh seemed to have her eyes on yet another boy who she liked, the latest of which had now become her boyfriend meaning that yet again the chances of her being into girls had been significantly reduced.

"Have you ever considered dating a girl?" Ciara felt her cheeks flush red as she spoke ducking her head to hide the shyness as adrenalin flowed through her body at the thought of what she had just said.

In a way her comment was still fairly safe but the fact she had made such a suggestion would make it clear to anyone what she was suggesting.

Adele felt her jaw drop open as she heard the comment, taken back slightly but trying not to seem too shocked as she glanced toward Ciara who seemed to be receding into her own body as a silence passed between them. The comment was in many ways flattering but that didn't take away from the fact that it was the last thing Adele had expected to be said.

She paused for a moment as she accepted that after her awkward nude re-appearance in the garden this was only the second most awkward thing that had happened to her today. Grinning slightly she stood and made her way over toward Ciara feeling sure that the comment had suggested that she was interested in them trying out something she hadn't really thought about.

There were definitely advantages to dating another girl like her parents wouldn't be suspicious and, given how badly her luck had gone with boys, Adele felt sure that there was no harm in giving it a try at least.

"I hadn't thought about it but sure, we can give it a go if you want Ciara" Adele smiled softly as she placed her hand on Ciara's shoulder shuddering gently at the thought of the new adventure she was about to have.

Glancing up as she felt the hand resting on her shoulder Ciara smiled nodding silently at Adele.

Chapter Sixteen

A matter of trust

It didn't matter which way she looked at it, Sasha knew that the phrase 'you have nobody to blame except yourself' was the most appropriate on for the situation she had willingly put herself in.

Her day had started off in what was considered to be a relatively normal fashion for a week day when she wasn't getting up for school. The sound of her father making his usual attempt to leave the house as quietly as possible had caused the regular short as she half opened her eyes while trying to convince her body that she was really still asleep.

She had come to the conclusion that, despite his best efforts, after so many years of trying to make his way downstairs quietly he was never going to actually succeed in doing so. In her younger years it had been the bedroom door opening that had woken her up and, at the time she had been too young to stay in bed so had regularly made her way to her bedroom door to peek out at him and wish him a nice day before sliding back into bed.

Eventually her parents had got around to fixing the creak of their door making his escape from the bedroom silent and saving the awakening for a few more moments until her father either forgot about the creaking floorboard or flushed the toilet. One of those Sasha knew was inevitable if he was going to obey the accepted protocol instead of leaving a nasty surprise for the next bathroom user.

By the age of 11 Sasha had accepted that her appearance at her bedroom door to see him off was not the nice gesture she had presumed it was but was actually proof that he had failed in his mission to leave without disturbing her. It was shortly after her acceptance that he didn't really want to see her before work that they had visited the complex for the first time resulting in her revolution to sleeping naked meaning that she didn't really want to stand in her bedroom door watching him either.

The updated process of laying as silently as possible while one noise led to another until the final sound that was the car leaving the driveway seemed to suit both of them. This way Sasha found it much easier to resume her sleep until it was a more civilised time to wake up on a non-school day, sometimes she had even managed to return to the same dream she had been awoken from but that was a rarity.

This morning, however, things had been different.

Less than half an hour after her father had left the house Sasha had been intentionally awoken by her mother tapping lightly on her bedroom door. It seemed trivial to hold the duvet against her body as she opened the door but she had gripped it close as she peeked through into the corridor, her hair straggled across her face as her mother made the announcement that changed her plan for her.

"I'm heading to Mrs McGuires' for coffee and gossip, did you want anything from town?"

Mrs McGuire was an older lady, Sasha guessed she was about 20 years older than her parents and yet somehow they had become part of her social circle. Every so often, her mother would go round to see her, sometimes with a cake or some unexpected gift for no other reason except it got her out of the house and gave her somewhere to go. Most of the time the responsibility to go and see her fell on her mother and nobody else was involved in the process but every so often the trip became a family excursion, usually on or around her birthday because she had no family to spend it with.

The fact that Mrs McGuire lived nowhere near the town centre but her mother had used this as an excuse to let her know she was going out said one thing to Sasha. This was her mothers way of telling her that she was being left to her own devices when it came to breakfast, which was fine but today it also meant she was being left home alone with Jim for an undisclosed length of time. The fact that there was no timeframe made it slightly unpredictable but still meant they had time alone together.

Ever since they had arrived back from the airport Sasha had accepted the stark reality that the fact they were going to be under the same roof for just over a week didn't mean it was going to be the same as it had in Greece. This time the roof they were living under was her family home and the option of them sharing a bedroom had been a far cry from her parents mind from the moment she had mentioned him visiting.

In her heart Sasha knew that she had been lucky in more than one way, the fact that her parents had even agreed to him visiting was more than she could imagine some of the girls she went to school with getting away with. Sasha knew that most of the had probably got away with a lot more in their parents' home than she had but not many of them had managed to have a boyfriend stay over while their parents knew he was spending the night in their home.

The announcement that her mother was leaving the house had sent a rush of adrenalin through her body unlike anything she had felt before and she couldn't wait to make the most of their parent free time. She lay on her bed listening carefully as her mother pottered around not making any effort to hide the fact she was doing a few bits including having breakfast before leaving.

Pressing her head into the pillow Sasha listened as carefully as she could hoping that she wasn't going to hear Jims voice greeting her mother amicably from downstairs. Sasha felt sure that even if he did wake he wouldn't intentionally have a long conversation with her mother before making himself scarce again but ideally Sasha didn't want to hear him talking to her mother at all.

"I'm off now, see you later!" Sasha cringed slightly as she heard the announcement but felt her body relax as she heard the door shutting.

Shuffling out of her bed she made her way quickly to her window peering carefully from behind the curtain as she watched her mother making her way down the road.

Without wasting a second she skipped across the floor pulling her 'far too small' robe out of her wardrobe and wrapping it round herself before leaving her room.

Pausing for a moment she stood at the top of the stairs listening just in case the front door was re-opened by her mother who had inadvertently forgotten something. Sasha stood holding her breath as she listened for any tell-tale sounds that could foil her intentions before feeling a large grin crossing her face as she accepted that Jim and she really were alone in the house together.

Like a child making their way downstairs on Christmas morning Sasha's feet barely touched each stair as she made her way from top to bottom. She paused briefly as she reached the last step peering into the hallway assuring herself that there was no sign of her mother returning feeling her face beaming as she made her way toward Jims room.

Sasha could feel the butterflies which she could still remember feeling the first day Jim and she had officially started dating filling her tummy as she pushed the door into his room open only to have the magic dissipate at the sight of him still sound asleep. In a way she knew it was probably a good thing that despite the noise of her mother pottering about he had managed to sleep through it. Sasha couldn't help smiling as she glanced at him laying face down, his head buried in his pillow with one foot dangling slightly out of the other end of the bed as if it was gasping for breath.

"Jim" She muttered his name as she pushed her foot out nudging the edge of his bed with her toes watching it rock slightly under the momentum she caused.

Her effort was met with a muttered groan telling her that he was completely oblivious to the fact she was even in the room.

"Jim!" she uttered his name slightly louder this time pushing her foot harder against the bed biting her lip as the bed visibly moved

"Mmph, uh" Jim lifted his head out of his pillow, blinking slightly as he tried to work out what had woken him as he tried to focus his eyes on the blurry figure in his room which he quickly accepted was Sasha.

Pushing himself into a semi upright position he looked over at her as his sight cleared.

Sasha glanced over her shoulder as she leaned back lightly pressing against the door until she heard it shut behind her before standing and stepping closer to the bed.

"I thought you might like to have breakfast in bed" she giggled slightly as she let her robe fall to the floor smiling as she watched Jim's jaw drop open

For a moment he paused as she took in the fact that Sasha was standing next to his bed naked waiting for him to say or do something. In a way it was like something out of a dream that he knew he had imagined happening but never thought would happen while he was in her house and yet there she was standing in front of him. In what felt like one fluent movement he flipped himself over pulling the duvet over as he shuffled across the bed to make room for her to join him.

Beaming with a grin, Sasha slid gently into the bed and snuggled up against him nestling into his warm body as she traced her fingers slowly down his arms. This felt right, this was where she had wanted to be ever since they had arrived at home and yet somehow because it was their first time in this bed it also felt special.

"D'you think maybe we can make those shorts disappear?" She whispered her words as she reached down feeling her arousal taking over as she pushed against him.

Smiling at her Jim kissed Sasha gently as he tried awkwardly to remove the offending article of clothing huffing a little as he wrestled them down his legs before finally kicking them out of the end of the bed.

Sasha could not help giggling as she tried not to make a fuss over how much effort it seemed to be while trying to maintain the moment she knew she had instigated and was determined to make the most of.

Pressing his shoulders down against the bed she straddled her leg over him as she gazed in his eyes feeling the tension between them as she leaned him planting a passionate kiss against his lips when suddenly it happened, the moment she had known was possible but hadn't expected to happen.

"Well, that was a wasted trip" Sasha felt her heart beating rapidly as she heard her mother's voice and the front door being shut.

"You aren't still in bed are you Sasha?" In her mind Sasha was sure that her mother was probably stood at the foot of the stairs shouting up toward her empty bedroom oblivious to the fact that she was not only up but in the one place she shouldn't be.

In her mind, Sasha was confident that if she had been sat in Jims room with him even with the door closed, she could talk her way out of it but as it was there was no denying that she had made the journey to his room basically naked. Even if she used the excuse that it was nothing he hadn't seen at the complex Sasha knew that her excuse would seem flimsy given that they weren't at the complex. Without thinking she closed her eyes gripping Jims body between her legs as he body tensed while she tried to work out an impossible escape plan that she knew wouldn't happen.

Shrugging as she moved away from the stairs Mary made her way back into the hall, hanging her coat up after her trip to Mrs McGuires home. She knew that there was nothing she could do about the fact that her unannounced visit had ended with her standing outside an empty home but that didn't change the fact that she had wasted a trip. Casually she glanced at her watch, it was half past nine, so maybe still a little early to expect Sasha to have made her way from her bedroom yet but worth a try.

"I'm going to make breakfast if you feel like getting up this side of lunch time" she shouted her intentions up the stairs before making her way into the kitchen.

Sasha bit her lip trying not to giggle as she heard the one-way conversation her mother was having with her empty room while trying to ignore the seriousness of the situation she had put herself in.

Part of her mind was telling her that if she had no way of avoiding being caught out she may as well go out in what she knew was referred to as a 'blaze of glory' and enjoy the moment exactly as she had intended. While she could not deny it was tempting to just go with the flow and continue with her plans there was part of her mind that was telling her that if she was careful there was still a way out of the mess.

Jim peered up casually, very much awake now and aware of what had paused the moment he was anticipating sharing with Sasha but even his biggest concerns couldn't prevent the sly smirk on his face. In a way he knew that he was in a position that other boys would envy him for, laying on a bed with his girlfriend pinning him down completely naked on top of him and yet the underlying issue was much more serious than his mind was letting him accept it to be.

Just beyond the door, which he felt sure wouldn't be opened unless they gave Sasha's mother a good reason to do it was one of the people he was trying to make a good impression with. If either Sasha or he made too much noise and roused her concerns this could mean a very awkward rest of his stay with the or worse – there was nothing to stop them asking him to leave their home. He had been invited there in good faith and now he was in an extremely compromising with their daughter, admittedly, he knew he hadn't initiated it but if they were caught there was no way he was letting Sasha take the blame for it.

Mary made her way casually into the kitchen, while she had been out a tune had become lodged in her mind which she now felt compelled to hum until she could remember where she knew it from. So far her mind had linked it to two songs, either of them was a viable contender but neither of them felt like the correct one despite their similarities.

During the previous evening she had managed to find some time to discuss Jim with Diarmuid and how well he was acting around them. There was no denying that he had shown them both respect and Sasha had definitely seemed happier in the few days he had been staying but that had been expected. Both Diarmuid and she had been slightly nervous and concerned about the idea of having Sasha's first official boyfriend in the house for such a long time but it seemed like the most practical solution. So far, despite their concerns Jim seemed to be the perfect house guest and hadn't made the situation any more awkward than it already was – something they had both agreed they were thankful for.

It had been Diarmuid who had suggested giving them some time alone together which had shocked Mary at first. From the moment that the prolonged date had been suggested it had been him who had shown more concern over it than she had and yet now he was suggesting giving them time alone. Mary had paused before responding to his suggestion to allow time to process whether it was a flippant comment or a genuine suggestion and decided to call his bluff by agreeing to it. She hadn't for one moment expected him to accept her agreement and yet he seemed content that it was the right decision so she had come up with a plan to head out for a couple of hours.

In her heart Mary had to admit that she hadn't made a visit to Mrs McGuire in a few weeks but that had been a tactical decision. She had to admit that their conversations were never exactly the most riveting but there was something about the widowed woman that made it easy to lose a few hours in her company. The fact that she seemed to always have the kettle either on or having just brewed a pot of team made it easy to sit with her while discussing whatever the topic of the day seemed to be.

During their last visit, Mrs McGuires mind had seemed to be set on the concept of her mortality despite only being in her mid-sixties. In reality it wasn't too much of a surprise given the fact that she had lost her husband before he had turned fifty, an unfortunate victim of a car accident but it was the loss of her older sister that had bought the subject back to the forefront of her thoughts. The idea of sitting politely for an hour or so while the subject of religion and funerals was intermittently disbursed in between other topics didn't really appeal to Mary but now she had used Mrs McGuire as an excuse to get out of the house she felt compelled to go round and see her.

It was almost a relief when she got there just in time to see Mrs McGuire pulling on a coat in preparation to make her way into town. At first the suggestion had been made that they could head into town together but Mary had been quick to decline the offer before making her way back home deciding that fate had intervened and she wasn't going to question it.

"It's that song from the dam car advert" Mary muttered the words as she pulled a couple of eggs out of the fridge, content that she had finally worked out what the tune in her head was from.

Sasha pressed her hands against the pillow teetering slightly as she tried to carefully move from her position to one that was slightly less conspicuous. She bit her lip as she shuffled her way off the bed accepting that no matter how she tried there really was no graceful way to clamber off the bed.

"Cover that up" she blushed as she glanced back at Jim noting that despite the situation his body still hadn't accepted that what she had intended to do wasn't going to happen anymore.

Reaching down she grabbed her robe and slipped it on tying it at her waist so that it hid her body as much as possible before reaching for the door handle.

With slow gentle movements she pried the door open feeling an element of relief when she heard her mother clattering with pans in the kitchen. Taking a deep breath she slid out of Jims room pressing her body against the small partition that kept her hidden from the kitchen doorway as she planned her escape. She knew without doubt that this was the most risky part of her journey, if she could make it as far as the stairs she could get away with it. If she was seen there in her robe she knew her mother wouldn't be happy about it but at least she had scope to make up a story from there.

Composing her mind Sasha took a large step into the front room as she made her dash for the safety of the staircase

"Well, I guess this means it is too late to tell you about the birds and the bees then Miss O'Callaghan" Sasha froze in place as she heard he mothers voice behind her.

There was no doubting the tone, her mother never referred to her formally unless it was something serious and this time she knew what the reason was.

Peering over her shoulder she blushed as she grinned sheepishly unable to think of what to say as she saw her mother in the kitchen doorway with a coffee in her hands. Without thinking she gripped the robe holding it closer to her chest knowing not only how bad the situation looked but also that despite her innocence there wasn't much point trying to deny her intentions.

"I take it Jim is awake, go put some clothes on I'll set the breakfast table" Mary turned calmly making her way back into the kitchen as she spoke.

Chapter Seventeen

I kissed a girl

There was no way that Adele could deny that from the moment she had agreed to go on a date with Ciara she had had mixed feelings about it. She knew that when she had agreed to the idea she had been in a compromising situation but there was no way she could blame that on her agreeing to the date.

In a lot of ways the lead up to it had felt very similar to the countless times she had met up with Sasha however Adele knew that this meet up was going to be different to anything she had experiences before.

Even her parents had acted differently when she had mentioned that she was going out with Ciara but Adele knew that their reaction had been due to them misinterpreting what she had meant when she referred to going out. Unlike any time that she told them that she was going out to meet a boy there was without doubt less judgement in the lead up to her date with Ciara.

Adele had got used to, and in some ways become prepared for the pre-date glance over what she had decided to wear. She had a very strong memory of comments her father had made in the past about the skirt she had chosen to wear when going out. Compared with other parents who, based on the comments that had been made at school after a date Adele knew that her parents were pretty lenient on her choice of date dress code.

She had pushed them too far on more than one occasion, the first time out of curiosity for how much she could get away with and other times because she had plans for her date and was trying to avoid being seen by her father as she made her way out of the door for it.

The reality was that the first time she had pushed the unwritten dress code too far was for a date with a boy she had only agreed to go out with to stop him pestering her. She knew that he was from a highly religious family and felt sure that if she dressed in a fashion that made her parents feel uncomfortable it was bound to make him squirm as well. She had bought the offending skirt especially for the night when she was meant to meet him and made sure to choose one that was a size too small and shorter than anything she had worn before.

They had arranged to go bowling, something she knew she wasn't good at even if she was dressed appropriately for the activity. Her choice of skirt would make it almost impossible but at least she knew she was going to have fun trying if nothing else.

The skirt she had put on before making her way downstairs comfortably half an hour before she had to leave home was white and with the way she had to squeeze in to it the material was almost see-thru making her underwear choice, bright pink, extremely inappropriate. Adding to the awkward factor of her chosen attire was the fact that it was designed to flare out from the waistband meaning that if she moved too fast her underwear was clearly visible to anyone behind her.

"Where did you get that skirt?"

The question had come from her mother as she sat down on one of the dining chairs feeling the wood against her thighs confirming that she skirt didn't flow underneath to cover her legs..

Adele paused before answering it feeling sure that if she gave the real answer she was probably going to be grounded which in her mind wasn't a bad thing considering she had no real interest in the date but she knew it would only mean he would ask her out again anyway.

"Oh I found it in the bottom of my wardrobe" She smiled as she gave what she knew was a false answer but definitely sounded better than the truth about the skirt

At that point her father, who had been in the kitchen, had made his way into the front room which Adele knew was a sign that his attention had been sparked by the conversation. He was dabbing his hands lightly with a towel having just finished washing the dishes and glanced discretely over at Adele as he made his way toward the couch. From her seat Adele watched as her parents had a silent debate using just eye contact and possibly unseen hand expressions to discuss the offending skirt before her father stood up to make his way back to the kitchen.

"Adele, you need to change before you go out, no arguing" The tone of her father's voice told her that she was in trouble if she decided to try to go against his word.

For her date with Ciara, Adele had made the decision not to wear anything too flirty, despite the fact that Ciara had already seen her naked she wanted this date to feel like it was their first time out together.

There was something both satisfying and concerning about the fact that, unlike any other person she had gone out with Ciara had already seen her with nothing on. In her heart Adele knew that, firstly she hadn't expected Ciara to be at the cottage and secondly her nudity had been in a place where Sasha and she had agreed as a sanctuary for naturism. In theory, the fact that Ciara was there fully dressed was the anomaly but then again, the rule had always been that clothing was optional.

The fact that Ciara had seen every part of her body put her on a back foot in some ways now that they were going to try dating making Adele ponder on how naturism and dating were probably not two activities that mixed too well in a textile world. She had no doubt that naturists dated, the fact that Jim and Sasha were together was, in a way, proof of that although Adele knew that she still wasn't sure of how much of a naturist Jim was. As for Sasha, Adele felt sure that she would be naked all day if she was allowed to and it was only circumstances keeping her clothed.

Ciara on the other hand hadn't shown any interest in the naturist lifestyle that Adele had to admit she was growing more and more comfortable with.

The more that she thought about it the more Adele accepted that the fact that Ciara had seen her naked and still wanted to ask her on a date was actually a compliment. It meant that, unlike a few of the boys she had been out with, Ciara wasn't asking her out in the hope that she would be naked before the end of their date.

Although she was sure it didn't happen very often, Adele knew that some boys asked girls on dates with only one thing on their mind and it wasn't a long term relationship. She wasn't able to confirm the success rate of this process but she knew that at least a few of the guys that had asked her out fell into this category. There was no denying that some of them had been tempting but the fact that their reputation came before them made these the sort of guys she had made a point of avoiding.

"Ma, I am heading out to meet Ciara now!" Adele had paused as she made the announcement to let her mother respond in whatever way felt appropriate.

The single worded reply that came from another room with no visible interest in what she was wearing confirmed Adele's theory that neither of her parents had taken the fact that she was going out with a girl who wasn't her best friend as anything more than a new friendship.

From the moment she had mentioned Ciara it had been hard to describe how she knew this new girl that she was trying to make her parents aware of. It seemed logical to say that she was someone from school and that they had got talking at the end of summer disco, both of which were true. There was also the funfair where they had both shared a brief moment together as they went on the ride that Sasha and Ciara's friend Maebh had no interest in. Anything beyond that was going to be hard to explain if either of her parents had asked more about this new person.

Adele smiled as she grabbed a light jacket silently acknowledging the fact that she could have been standing in her underwear and because it was a girl she was meeting her dress code wasn't something that was seen as a concern.

If she had been more inclined to make sure her parents knew what type of meet up she was heading to with Ciara, Adele felt sure it would have sparked a lot more interest.

In her mind she recalled the conversation she had enjoyed with Seamus when they had accidentally met on the beach. He had openly discussed his sexual preferences with her and even told her that he had been with girls before accepting that he was gay but telling his parents about it had been the hardest thing he had done.

Just like the date she was about to go on with Ciara, Seamus had been out with guys before telling his parents that he was actually going on dates with the guys they thought were just his close friends. There had been no questions asked when he had mentioned staying over at some guys place because his parents had assumed that there was nothing sexual in what he was doing. Everything changed for him when he finally decided to tell his parents that the guy he kept going out with was more than just a close friend.

Suddenly every guy he mentioned was considered to be a potential partner for him, even his best friend who had known his family for years and had been with the same girlfriend for 2 years by the time he came out as gay.

It was that part that concerned Adele the most and made her wonder if Ciara's parents knew of her sexual orientation. There was little doubt that Maebh was a close friend of hers and probably one that was known to her parents but if that was the case did her parents know that Ciara preferred to date women?

If this date went well Adele felt sure that she would want to tell her parents the truth, she had been honest with them about a lot of things and telling them she preferred women seemed like something she should tell them. For now it was far too soon to get them involved, this was her first date with a woman and she didn't know if it was going to be a one off or a longer term arrangement. Her biggest concern was that if she did decide she wanted to date women more than men how would it affect her relationship with Sasha?

Would anything change between them or would Sasha just take it in her stride in the same way as she had done so many other things in the past.

There was also the issue of how her parents would respond, would they start to question her friendship with Sasha in the same way that Seamus's parents had done with his best friend.

Just like Seamus had described, she had practically grown up with Sasha, they had shared bedrooms on more occasions than she cared to try to remember. Her parents almost considered Sasha to be their second daughter and, although she couldn't confirm it, she felt sure that Sasha's parents felt the same way about her. Adele knew that it wouldn't take long for the news to travel from her parents to Sasha's and possibly cause tension between them despite the fact that Sasha was clearly in a relationship.

Adele took a deep breath as the thoughts of what might happen if this turned out to be the start of a new way of life for her fluttered through her head.

"It's just a first date Adele, get it together" she muttered the words under her breath before leaving the house

As she had made her way to the place that she had agreed to meet with Ciara Adele realised how little she knew about her date for the evening. In reality it was probably as little as she had known about some of the guys she had been out with on their first date but this time it felt different.

In a way her lack of knowledge made the date feel a little more exciting but this time it felt different to when she went out with a boy she barely knew. The idea of dating a girl had been one that Adele was both curious and a little nervous to learning more about but it was Ciara's past that made her the most curious.

With boys that she went out with it was almost easy to tell how much experience they had by how they acted around her. She could tell the ones that had been on a few dates and thought that their presence was going to be enough to get her into their bed and was in many ways happy to prove them wrong. On the other hand, a boy that was too nervous had a certain cuteness to how careful he was with her when they went out but his lack of experience made the date seem almost awkward.

So far, to the best of her knowledge Adele had only been the first intimate experience for one boy and that had been excruciatingly obvious even if he hadn't told her. He had fumbled and almost looked like he was going to pass out when she allowed him to touch her in some places and almost needed a guidebook to how to remove a bra. By the time they had got intimate she had been almost regretting her decision to go all the way with him but as they were naked it seemed like the right thing to do.

Ciara on the other hand was an unknown entity,

Adele felt sure that she had dated other girls in the past and, although she was clearly embarrassed from the redness in her cheeks at the awkward moment that Adele had been left with little choice but to be seen naked by her, the fact that they had the same body type made it easier. This did leave Adele wondering if Ciara had always dated girls or had she tried dating boys and decided that she preferred girls – maybe she would find out eventually but for now it was a subject she decided it was best not to discuss.

As she arrived at the place that she had arranged to meet Ciara, Adele had to admit that it was both nice and in some ways expected to see her date having dressed up a little bit. This already placed their date ahead of some of the times she had agreed to meet with boys for what was meant to be a date. The one that stood out more than any was relatively recent in her mind and one she had neither told Sasha about nor planned to tell her about.

They had met by chance while she had been in town and he had recognised her from school but that hadn't been unusual. It didn't matter how much she tried to look different to the way she looked in her school uniform there was always someone who recognised her the moment they saw her outside of the school gates.

This time the boy, Robbie as she quickly learned when he introduced himself to her, was from the year above her but he claimed that he had been admiring her from a distance for over a year.

At the time that he had first commented to his friends that he liked her they had been quick to deter him from asking her out based on her age. To him it didn't matter that she was possibly under16 but to his friends the 1 year age gap was the difference between her being eligible to be dated and not being.

He had made small talk with her for a short while before Adele made an excuse to go about her business and leave him to his day. It had been at that moment that he had asked her if she wanted to go to the cinema with him the following evening and she had decided to accept his invitation.

Just like any other date, Adele had made an effort, taking the time to make sure that what she was wearing was both nice and not what she referred to as being overly slutty. There was a fine line which she knew not to cross on a first date especially when she wasn't sure if she really wanted to be going out with the boy in the first place. As she had made her way up to the cinema there had been quite a crowd, which was to be expected as it was a long awaited movie that he had talked her into seeing with him.

In a lot of ways the crowd obscuring Robbie from view had worked to his advantage because by the time she spotted him Adele knew it was too late to pretend she had decided not to go along with the idea.

She didn't so much hate ripped jeans and she knew that in the cinema light his choice of low cut jeans that left no mystery about his boxers with rips in the knees was fairly trivial but it made her feel foolish for having made an effort. The fact that he had clearly chosen not to shave made the experience feel more like a day out with a male friend or something impromptu but the one thing it didn't feel like was the sort of date she wanted to repeat.

After the movie she hadn't even allowed him the option of waling her home having made a false claim that she was going to a friend's house for a sleepover. It wasn't until she returned to school that Adele had needed to make her disinterest obvious despite having ignored all of his messages in the days after their disaster of a date.

Ciara on the other hand had made a lot of effort, Adele was even sure she was wearing makeup which surprised her at first but as she thought it over she knew that she had done the same in the past for first dates.

"This is my first time dating a girl" she found herself smiling coyly as she made the comment feeling almost like she had never been on a date before while knowing that was far from the truth.

Ciara smiled and reached out pulling Adele in to a friendly but not overly forward hug as she greeted her.

The anticipation of their first date had been welling up inside her ever since she had woken up so much that it had given her a bad stomach from the nervous cramps but thankfully that had settled down.

"It's OK Dell, I know you have only dated guys but it's really not that different" She blushed as she recalled the short time when she had made attempts at dating guys as she spoke

"Just remember, if it is something you like being done to you, the chances are I will like it done to me" Ciara giggled lightly as she made the comment trying to hide the multiple innuendo's that she knew existed in her words.

As their date progressed Adele had to admit that she was becoming more comfortable with the fact that she was on a date with a girl and stopped worrying about it. She had to admit that there had been a light tingle through her body when Ciara had made a very subtle reach over to stroke her arm gently.

The touch was like velvet across her skin, so different to the heavier hands that she had become used to when a boy made a move on her.

At first it had felt quite funny when she had spotted Ciara glancing at her curves in the same way that a boy did but her gaze was less intimidating and intrusive than a boys. Adele felt sure that the fact that she was able to relax while her date was checking her out was partially down to knowing that Ciara had seen everything so there was nothing to hide.

After a couple of hours together Adele felt comfortable and happy that Ciara had made the first move at real physical contact by taking her hand as they walked. The hug at the beginning of the date hadn't been dissimilar to the way Sasha greeted her but holding hands, especially in the way that Ciara was doing, was both new and exciting.

By the time they decided to call it a night Adele had decided that she was definitely happy that she had accepted the date and knew that she wanted to see Ciara on a more intimate basis than she had ever anticipated but there was one thing that stood out more than anything.

She had almost frozen to the spot as Ciara had leaned in, her body filling with both excitement as nerves at the same time.

Adele had felt her heart beat quickening as their lips touched but soon she accepted that it actually felt nicer than a lot of boys who had kissed her. There was no stubble, no roughness on the lips and no bad breath, all things that she had almost become used to putting up with especially as a relationship developed.

Ciara, however was more attentive, the kiss more considerate and yet just as intense as any she had experienced in the past and the taste of what she knew was lip gloss was almost like the cherry on top. Adele had to admit that if she had kissed any boy who was wearing lip gloss it would have been an immediate turn off and yet because it was a girl whose lip gloss she had tasted it felt like it was appropriate.

What caught her more than anything was that now she had kissed a girl, there was no way she could deny how much she liked it.

Chapter Eighteen

Guilty

Despite the serious nature of the situation Sasha had found it difficult to hide the smile that was trying to make itself known as she had sat down for breakfast with Jim and her mother.

It was clear from the silence at the breakfast table that neither of them had said much but the pale complexion on Jims face made it obvious that he was nervous.

"Mrs O'Callaghan, it was…"Jim had been the first to break the silence but his attempts had been stopped by a raised hand.

The formal manner that he had used when addressing her mother told Sasha that he was trying to make a sincere effort to diffuse the situation in the best way possible. In her heart she knew that he wasn't to blame for the situation they found themselves in but Sasha felt sure that he was attempting to at least share responsibility.

"Jim, I admire your nobility in speaking up but knowing my daughter, I think this was probably her plan" Mary smiled, calmly scooping a spoonful of cereal into her mouth as she finished her statement.

There was no denying the fact that the whole incident had been her idea but Sasha almost choked as she heard her mother coming to the conclusion without batting an eyelid. Part of her mind wanted to protest innocence, possibly even mention that despite how bad it looked nothing had actually happened between them this time. The more she pondered over her intentions the more she accepted that the fact that she was leaving his room made it quite clear that this wasn't the first time they had tried anything as intimate as she had intended on doing.

For the rest of the meal the three of them sat virtually in silence with the occasional comment about the weather and local news but not even a hint of them discussing the mornings events.

In a way Sasha was both relieved and concerned about the lack of discussion, her mother didn't seem angry about it but then again, she knew how well her mother could conceal her emotions if she wanted to. Everything was pointing to the fact that her mother was waiting until she had spoken with her father about it so that they could tackle the moment together, her two parents against Jim and her.

After breakfast Sasha made an extra effort to help with tidying the plates, something she knew that she only did when there was something she wanted but today it felt like the right thing to do.

"If its ok I want to head into town with Jim" she spoke softly as she made the request, feeling like she was a 13 year old again requesting permission to go out on her own for the first time.

The response came in the form of a single word acknowledgement and a nod as her mother put the plates back in the cupboard.

Without any further hesitation Sasha made her way back into the front room spotting Jim in his bedroom, the only room that felt like he could remain out of the way while his fate was decided upon. A fate for a crime that he had been not only suspected of but tried for with minimal evidence and one that he wished he had committed if for no other reason than the fact that Sasha had been forced into leaving him wanting more.

"We're heading out Jim, get your coat on" Sasha leaned in from the doorway as she spoke conscious of the fact that it was probably not a good idea to head into his room again.

Seizing the opportunity to get out of the house Jim grabbed his jacket and was almost in the entrance hall before Sasha.

"We'll be back before dinner Ma" Sasha called out the comment as she held the front door poised ready to open it the moment she received the acknowledgement from the kitchen

Just as before, a single word comment came from her mother as she opened the door and ushered Jim quickly out of the house.

Sasha had to admit to being slightly proud of him as she pondered over the way he had made an effort to speak out about the situation while they had breakfast. There was no doubting the nobility of his gesture even if he hadn't managed to finish his sentence, the fact that he had addressed her mother formally suggested he wanted to probably take the blame for her actions.

Mary took a deep breath as she heard the front door closing, the nervous tension she had been harbouring from the moment she had spotted Sasha leaving Jims room had causes her stomach to tense up.

Glancing over she grabbed the half-drunk coffee she had been sipping throughout what had been a very awkward breakfast and poured its contents down the sink before boiling the kettle again to make a fresh one.

From the moment that Sasha had referred to Jim as her boyfriend while they had been in Greece she had pondered in the back of her mind over the intimacy of their relationship and she felt sure that Diarmuid had been going through similar thoughts.

In her mind she could still remember the first time she had bought a boy home and how her parents had not only scrutinized the situation but barely left the boy out of their sight for more than a few moments during his first visit. He hadn't been her first intimate encounter as it happened but she felt sure that the lack of complete intimacy between them had been more out of his fear for what her father would do to him if he even touched her in their family home.

As a younger woman she had been determined that when she had children she would be more open and accepting of any partner they introduced to her and she was confident that, even if she didn't want to be, she was living up to that unwritten agreement.

Diarmuid had been doubtful about the logistics of Jim staying with them from the moment that they had agreed to allow him to visit and now, even if there had been moments before of intimacy between them, Mary knew that she couldn't unsee what she had witnessed.

It was true that she hadn't actually caught them doing anything but the awkwardly sneaky way that Sasha had tried to leave Jims room left little doubt in her mind of what had either happened or been intended to happen.

The fact that it was Sasha leaving Jims room and not Jim making his way down from her room was enough to confirm that despite the way Jim had tried to stand up and take responsibility it was likely to be Sasha who instigated it.

In a way, Mary knew that she should at least acknowledge Jim's noble gesture, she felt sure that if her parents had caught her with a boy the chances of the boy she was with making a similar effort were minimal. Even Diarmuid, for all of the complimentary attributes that her parents frequently pointed out about him, attributes that had been part of her eventual decision to marry him, wasn't the type to take blame where he wasn't at fault.

Pouring her second coffee Mary wiped her hands on a towel and made her way into the front room, clasping the warm mug as she made her way towards an armchair. She knew that it was almost an unwritten duty for her to tell Diarmuid of what she had witnessed so that they could discuss how to respond in the best manner possible.

Her first inclination was to send him a text telling him, but it felt more like the sort of thing they should actually discuss properly which meant waiting until his lunch time.

Sasha dragged Jim over gesturing to him to sit down next to her as they arrived at a bench in the park. His hand had been clammy ever since they had left home but that hadn't made her want to release her grip, this time despite how awkward it felt holding a warm sweaty hand she knew the reason for it.

There was so much that hadn't been said while they had been sitting with her mother having breakfast and one of the biggest problems as she saw it was – what were her parents going to do about the rest of Jim's visit?

According to the flight he had booked there were still a few days before he was due to go back home but part of her mind wondered if her parents were going to suggest changing his flight dates.

As they stood things were already awkward, there was no denying that and yet this felt like only the tip of the iceberg because changing flight dates would more than likely involve him contacting his parents and trying to explain why he was heading home early.

In her heart Sasha knew that she didn't want to even think about him having to leave early but the reality in her mind was that what they had been suspected of doing was not something that her parents were going to be able to just brush off. If nothing else, she knew from other girls at school that the presence of a boyfriend in their lives came with complications especially if the boy went to their home with them. The big difference was that, for Jim, his home wasn't a matter of a few streets away, he couldn't go home as quickly as most other boyfriends could.

"Ya know, we should have probably just got on with it and had sex when you think about it hun" Sasha smiled as she spoke glancing over at Jim as she accepted that if they had been caught in the act their fates wouldn't be a lot worse than they already were.

Jim blushed as he heard Sasha's comment feeling his pants tighten at the idea of them actually carrying out the act that had been all but promised to him by Sasha's actions when the front door had stopped them in their tracks.

Now that they had time to reflect on the situation that had occurred Jim had to admit that in hindsight they should have just gone ahead as if they hadn't heard the door in the first place. In his mind Jim knew that if the door had opened a few moments later than it actually had there was a good chance that they would have both been so caught in the moment they wouldn't have heard about it anyhow.

As a younger teenager he could recall discussing things that he and his friends agreed they didn't want to ever experience. At least three people had mentioned that they didn't want to ever see their parents naked or even in their underwear for that matter. Now that he had been to Greece, the parents being naked ship had sailed for him even if he had avoided telling anyone it had.

Jim knew that he hadn't told his friends the full story about his holiday but in reality, it was only the lack of photos that made his most recent holiday different to previous ones. Luckily, despite a few of them having helped him in his shopping for clothes for his holiday, none of them had asked him about if he had worn them. He was, in many ways, relieved to have the distraction of mentioning the fact that he now had a girlfriend to tell his friends about.

Sasha's presence in his life seemed to act like the perfect subject changer for the weeks after his return home. By the time he had returned to school the deeper facts relating to his summer holiday were simply memories that only he had and nobody else seemed too interested in.

A close runner up to parents naked was walking in to their room while they were in the middle of an intimate moment, something that was now at the top of his list even if it hadn't been prior to his summer holiday. It wasn't until the morning he was still enduring that he had considered the awkwardness of his parents catching him with a girl but now the implication had been placed on him he could see that being in his top three.

Diarmuid had been almost counting the seconds as the clock on his computer ticked slowly toward his lunch break. As mornings went, he had to admit that so far his day had been fairly good, no major setbacks, his boss seemed like he was in a good mood and no unexpected deadlines. He had even managed to not only fix but catch up with the mess that had been left for him the day before that had seemed like a mountain as he had left for home the previous day.

It was in the final 10 minutes leading up to lunch break as he was pondering over whether to chance one of the awful machine made cups of soup or not that he felt the desk hum slightly alerting him to a silent vibration from his phone.

Usually when his phone blurted out an alert during his work day it was something trivial, an email telling him he was one of 5 million other lucky winners in the weekly lotto or a weather update which he hadn't worked out how to stop. This time it was a text, not just any type of text but one from Mary, who only contacted him while he was at work if it was something that couldn't wait so he felt sure this must be something important.

Glancing round to ensure no-one was lingering to spot him checking his phone he tapped the screen watching it flash to life as his finger pressed against it.

"Call me when you are on lunch, it's about Sasha"

The message was both calm and urgent all at the same time, its ambiguity causing him intrigue into what had spurred the need to send the text but in the same way the lack of detail was in a way comforting.

If it had been anything truly urgent, a trip to the hospital or sudden illness he knew from past experience that it would have been a call or at the very least a much more urgently worded text. This one was almost like a reminder of something he was meant to do but hadn't quite got to the time when he needed to do it. He had set himself reminders similar to this in the past only for whatever he had set as an alert to remind him about to remain prominently on his mind until it had been done rendering the alert as unnecessary.

Diarmuid glanced again at the clock, only one minute had passed since his previous time check and yet now he had a new distraction on his mind to keep him occupied until the lunchtime dash to the canteen.

In a way the request to make a phone call during his lunch break felt almost like a penance as the minutes passed by. Diarmuid felt sure that the call was something important, if it hadn't been then Mary would have waited until he was home to discuss it but it was clearly not urgent otherwise she would have called the office.

From the partition that divided his desk from that of the person sitting next to him he watched as the first few people made their way casually toward the canteen. Their ritual was almost predictable at this time and yet nobody had commented to them about the fact that they had left their desk early with the intention to ensure good seating. Diarmuid had to admire their less than subtle tactics – a casual chat at the printer station while two or more people waited for maybe one item to print that nobody actually wanted, a delayed return to their desk from replenishing stationary that nobody could confirm actually needed replacing it was all so subtle and yet obvious at the same time.

In reality, none of their attempts made any difference unless one of the vending machines was running low on a popular product and even then it was trivial. Diarmuid had been pondering over whether it was more practical to eat and then make the call or make the call before eating as the canteen shuffle started and by the time his computer was ready to tell him it was officially lunch time he had opted for the call first. That way, whatever the issue was he would be able to think over it or relax after resolving it as he ate the lunch that was sitting in the canteen fridge waiting for him.

"I caught Sasha leaving Jims room this morning" Diarmuid listened to the sombre tone Mary had used as he tried to take in what was being said and more importantly, what it implied.

In many ways he accepted that the announcement could have been made by text but could see why it had been something Mary wanted to actually say out loud.

Part of his mind was screaming 'told ya so' as he took in the statement and contemplated the best way to handle it.

From the moment they had started discussing Jim visiting he had silently accepted that there were things that might happen which he didn't want to know about but knew were possible. When they had elected to book a hotel room for Sasha and Jim on his first night, admittedly it had been the most economical option given the location he was flying in to but that hadn't made it any more comfortable in his mind.

He had considered booking them two rooms but the more he pondered over it the more he accepted that even if they had separate rooms there was no way of knowing they would use them. Although he didn't like the idea of sending Sasha up to collect Jim on her own Mary had convinced him that they needed to show Sasha some trust and letting her meet him alone was one way to do that.

His mind raced as he thought over the situation that he knew he couldn't change even if he wanted to, Sasha had made her way to Jims room – it didn't take a genius to work out why she had done it – the fact was that she had and regardless of what they had done while she was in his room it was done now and couldn't be undone.

"We will have a talk with both of them about it when I get home Mary, there is nothing we can do now to change what has happened" Diarmuid tried to remain calm but could feel his body shuddering as he accepted the implications of what he had just been told.

Although in her heart Sasha had to admit that she had been expecting it from the moment she had announced to her mother that they were going out for the day it still felt like a heavy burden when she finally received the text telling her to be home by a specific time.

Ever since she had turned 15 and been allowed more flexibility on when she came and left the house she had made a point of telling her parents if she was going to be out late or if she was going somewhere for dinner. It was her way of staying in their good books and making sure she avoided lectures about food having been prepared for her when she wasn't going to be home to eat it.

This time, the text was specific, she was expected to be home for dinner and, in a way she was thankful to see that Jim was expected back as well.

There had been no mention of changing his arrangements made during breakfast but Sasha accepted that the lack of comments on the rest of his stay was to allow for her parents to discuss things further.

The fact that he was invited back for dinner was surely a good sign that he was still welcomed in the house even if it was only on a temporary basis but Sasha knew in her heart that being summoned back for dinner was only the beginning, Whether she liked it or not, there was a lecture due to happen, one that she had been hoping to avoid but knew she couldn't do any more. Jim may or may not be a part of the lecture but there was no way he was going to be able to ignore it even if he was asked to leave the room while it was happening.

Suddenly her flippant comment about the fact they should have just gone for it while the mood was with them and the opportunity available to them seemed much more prominent – Sasha knew they were in for a long and awkward night at home.

Chapter Nineteen

The Talk

As a young boy Jim had experienced a number of occasions when dinner time had been overshadowed by what seemed like a looming threat of an awkward conversation. On more occasions than he dared to try to remember the conversation had been triggered by something either he or his sister Chloe had been caught or accused of doing that they 'should have known better than to do' in his mother's words.

These conversations tended to fall into one of three categories.

Either one or the other of them had been caught red handed while performing an act that had been previously marked as not allowed to be done or one of them had been accused of an act that they were now being blamed for but hadn't actually done despite incriminating evidence, or both of them had been caught doing something and as a result of their act or omission they were both now awaiting punishment.

Depending on the guilty, or accused as guilty, party the dinner time after whatever the incident was always became an awkward affair. In the cases where it was only one of them who had been marked for blame this gave the other a position of grandeur or authority over their sibling until the issue was resolved.

There had been more than one occasion when the incident had not been caught by their parents and it was either Chloe or he who had witnessed an incident and now had ammunition that could be exploited when the time was right.

Thankfully these incidents were much less frequent and yet they were also much more intense for the guilty party while they either tried to convince the other party not to say anything or waited nervously for their crime to be announced to their parents.

Jim could recall more than one occasion when an incident that had led to an awkward meal time also led to punishment in the form of either grounding or something similar and was thankful of the occasions when it was Chloe at fault and not him.

Regardless of the severity of the situation Jim found himself on the receiving end of as a child he felt sure that Chloe had achieved an almost God-like status the day she introduced Jay to the family as the guy she was moving in with. He had of course been wrong because she was able to push the boundaries even further on the day she announced that she was pregnant.

It had been his experience of the reaction that Chloe received to her 'happy' news that had given Jim the motivation to do all he could in order to ensure he avoided ever reaching the same level and yet here he was, in what seemed like an even worse situation. Not only was he one of the people who had been accused of an incident that hadn't happened but the people accusing him were not his parents and yet he had, up until that point, been trying his best to make a good impression with them.

From the moment they arrived back at Sasha's home Jim could already feel the same butterflies he recalled feeling when in difficult situations in the past. In the back of his mind Sasha's comment while they had been out when she had suggested they should have just finished what she had instigated rang through his mind on repeat as they sat at the table for what Jim could imagine being his last dinner with her family.

Thoughts of how he was going to explain the situation to his parents had been plaguing him all the way back to her home and yet there was no scenario where he could imagine his parents accepting his innocence in the situation.

Apart from anything else there was the awkwardness of the realisation that his anticipated eviction from Sasha's family home would act as confirmation to his parents that he wasn't a virgin any more. Somehow he had managed to avoid discussing anything to do with his previous experiences with Sasha while they were on holiday despite being fairly sure that his parents must have some idea of what he had got up to.

As they sat down at the table Jim had to bite his lip to stop himself heading head long into the situation in an effort to diffuse it. He could remember how Sasha's mother had already shot him down over breakfast when he had made an attempt to defend what hadn't actually happened and was sure that, now there had been some preparation time, any attempt he made to accept the blame would again hit stony ground.

Throughout the beginning of the meal Jim remained vigilant listening with a renewed sense of urgency as either of her parents spoke. Each time he heard one of their voices he felt his stomach tighten in case it was the start of the conversation he knew was inevitable but still unsure of what his part would be.

They reached desert, something that he wasn't used to having at a table while at home, before he spotted Sasha's father out of the corner of his eye dabbing a paper napkin against his mouth – a sure sign that something important was about to be said.

"So Sasha, I got an unexpected message from your mother today" Diarmuid remained calm as he spoke trying not to seem overly surprised by what had been implied and discussed between himself and Mary during his lunch break

Jim could feel the mood change as the comment was made and instinctively glanced over at Sasha.

Feeling her throat almost closing with the tension she felt as she heard the comment Sasha placed her hand to her mouth to catch and remnants of the spoonful of ice cream she had just scooped in.

With an unexpected sense of security she had been relieved when the atmosphere hadn't been as tense as she had been expecting upon their return home.

In her mind she had almost expected to see Jims bag waiting for them on the doorstep with no scope for them to discuss the issue any further so it had come as a relief when she had spotted his room door still closed as they walked past it to the dining table.

Composing her thoughts as she glanced sheepishly at her father she noted that even though he had made reference to a conversation there had been no real context given to what had been discussed. There was no doubt in her mind that she was standing at the edge of a virtual trap and depending on how she approached it she was either going to set it off and make things worse or manage to somehow disarm it.

Her father had been very careful in his words and Sasha knew that she had to acknowledge his tactical move. She glanced over at Jim as she tried to work out her best reaction while knowing deep down that the reality was that despite incriminating evidence, she hadn't actually done anything that she was being accused of.

On one hand she could play it coyly and pretend that she didn't know what her father was referring to but Sasha felt sure that if she did that it was likely to make matters even worse for both Jim and her. As an alternative she knew that she could try to defend her corner and convince both of her parents that the fact that she had been seen sneaking out of Jims room, the one place she wasn't meant to be, without being seen was more innocent than her mother had made it out to be.

In her mind she could already almost hear the conversation; there were more clichés in the idea of trying to defend her innocence than she had seen in a bad comedy movie.

"Dad, I want to tell you that, no matter what happens – this morning wasn't Jims fault, he didn't know what I was planning" Sasha bit her lip as she spoke while silently acknowledging that she had taken ownership of the situation in the only way that seemed practical.

Diarmuid glanced out of the corner of his eye as he heard the response peering discretely between Sasha, Mary and Jim as he contemplated the words.

After his conversation with Mary he hadn't been able to get the thought out of his mind that there was no denying that his only daughter was now a sexually active young woman. He had been suspicious for more than a year about her but it had only been since Jim had been introduced to them at the complex that his thoughts of what may have happened had started to look like a reality.

Over the years he had heard a lot of his work colleagues going through similar scenarios with their gradual acceptance occurring at different rates. Some of them spent weeks in denial and even outrage at the fact that their child's innocence was really over, others had built up a vendetta that he knew they wouldn't be able to legally go through with over the boy who they suspected had been the cause of their daughters deflowering as he had sometimes heard it referred to.

The more time he thought about it the more he found himself realising that, firstly what Mary had seen was, without doubt, incriminating and yet they hadn't been caught doing anything and secondly – as boyfriends went Jim wasn't the worst. Mary had mentioned that Jim had made an effort to discuss the situation earlier in the day which Diarmuid decided was a credit to the young man and even more so now that Sasha had accepted full blame for it. The reality of it was that, if Sasha really had instigated it, all he could do was accept that she had conscientiously chosen him; he hadn't forced her into it.

While it still saddened him that his little girl had grown up, Diarmuid knew how lucky he was that Sasha was a sensible and mature girl for her age and according to what she had said whatever had happened had been her choice.

After he had arrived home he had discussed the situation with Mary before coming to an agreement about how they were going to handle it.

Taking a deep breath he turned his attention toward Jim who he could see was almost frozen to the spot not daring to even try to interrupt and yet clearly nervous about the whole situation.

"Jim, I hear that you tried to talk with my wife about this over breakfast"

Jim could feel a cold shiver running down his spine as he heard the words, the conversation now directed at him.

In one way this was what he had wanted because it took the pressure off Sasha but in another this felt like it was the beginning of the verdict about where he fell in the mess they were both cautiously trying to wriggle out of.

Diarmuid paused before continuing as he recalled his first thoughts when Mary had told him about the situation. He had been in a similar position when he had been younger, not quite as bad as the one he was now trying to handle but, for the time and considering his strict Catholic upbringing definitely not ideal.

"I have to admit Jim; it was very brave of you stepping up like that"

Jim bit his lip as he heard what felt like almost a compliment, the last thing he had expected but as it was a positive comment he wasn't going to just let it go.

"You are welcome to stay here for the rest of the time you are over Jim, but count this as a yellow card" Diarmuid silently complimented himself on the way he had been able to use a sport analogy but could see from Jims vague expression that it had fallen on stony ground with him.

Jim could almost feel every muscle in his body relax as the looming thought of having to explain what had happened to his parents dissipated. He had been rehearsing in his mind different ways they would respond to the situation whilst remaining silently confident that somehow they would make sure it was sorted out for him.

More importantly than anything else, he could see this being the end of his time with Sasha and little or no hope for them to see each other again. In the first moment when he had pondered over the consequences of their failed attempt at an intimate moment together it hadn't taken long for him to realise the bigger picture may involve him becoming single again for having actually done nothing wrong. Now that he was being allowed to stay it felt like at least they had some hope of maintaining a relationship even if it meant tiptoeing around her parents for the rest of his time in their house.

As he started relaxing into the thought that he was, for now, on safe ground the thought occurred to him that Sasha might not want to risk it any more. She had remained fairly jovial throughout the day but that was before the talk, casually he glanced across the table trying to catch her eye but unable to.

"Thank you Mr O'Callaghan, I appreciate that" he smiled softly as he spoke before sitting back in his chair nervously awaiting Sasha's response.

Diarmuid nodded politely at Jim's response feeling a sense of pride in his mind as he silently acknowledged the polite tone that the reply had come with.

"Sasha" he turned his attention toward his daughter as he composed himself glancing briefly toward Mary who seemed silently content with how he was handling the situation.

Ever since she had been left alone in the house to gather her thoughts on what had happened she had pondered over what she wanted to see done.

Her first instinct was to suggest that Jim had to stay elsewhere or go back home but that seemed a little harsh considering the fact that it had been Sasha leaving his room and not the other way around. The more she pondered over the situation the more she found herself making excuses as to how it may be Jim's fault or what part he had actually played in preparing for what she had seen and yet in her heart she knew that it was probably Sasha who had come up with the plan.

During her call with Diarmuid she had made it clear that she wanted it handled in a way that was going to suit everyone. She had pointed out more than once that the evidence was not fully incriminating and yet it was hard to deny the intent at the very least.

Out of everything, the part that upset her the most was the fact that she couldn't deny Sasha had been sneaking from his room so whatever had happened she had wanted it to happen.

"Don't for one minute think that this is a lucky escape, we will be keeping an eye on you both for the next few days." Diarmuid could hear his own father in his voice as he spoke and coughed into his hand before continuing.

"One more incident like this and we may change our mind, is that clear?" he felt his cheeks flush as he spoke.

Sasha paused before responding, her heart was beating harder than she could ever remember it having done before

"Yes Da" she hung her head slightly as she responded and waited for her father to make what she was hoping was his final comment on the matter

"Long as we are clear on this, your free to leave the table" Diarmuid sat back as he heard the comment in his mind acknowledging how trivial it had been and yet how important it had seemed that he say something to bring their conversation to an end.

Standing cautiously Sasha glanced over at Jim who seemed like the colour had drained from his face, her legs shaking slightly as she caught his eye hinting silently that they should both take the opportunity and head into the front room.

For a few moments Sasha sat silently staring at the TV, reluctant to make eye contact with Jim for fear that either of her parents may be watching for their next move. Her mind was split between two opinions; the first was telling her that the fact that they had been dismissed from the table meant that the lecture about her morning escapades was over. On the other hand she felt like she had got away extremely lightly compared to other girls she had overheard at school describing similar scenarios to the one she had been caught in.

Behind them, still at the table she could hear her parents busily tidying up after dinner, something that she would usually help them with but today it felt more appropriate to take her father's offer and leave the table.

In her heart she wanted to hear something being said between her parents but instead there was no audible words being spoken between them.

Sasha felt sure that they were having what she had become used to referring to as one of their silent conversations. She had seen them have similar conversations in the past and knew that they involved a lot of lip reading and hand gestures in order to relay messages without anyone being able to hear them. Normally these conversations were about someone else who was out of sight but still within earshot of them but Sasha felt sure that this time if she was to glance back at the table any gesturing would stop as soon as either of them caught her eye.

Almost instinctively as they had sat on the couch together Jim and she had made sure to leave some space between each other. Not enough for another person to sit down but enough to make it clear that they weren't snuggling up together, something that Sasha really wanted to do but felt sure it wasn't really the ideal time to do anything like that.

Peering beyond Jim, Sasha spotted the TV remote on the small table next to the couch, the place where it was meant to live but not always found depending on who had used it last. She bit her lip as she leaned across him making sure to press against him as she reached out for it knowing in her heart that it was not appropriate after the lecture they had both been part of to stay too close to him but hoping that her gesture would act as some kind of reassurance that everything was fine between them.

As they had made their way home Sasha had come to the silent conclusion that the reason they had got into this mess was because, for reasons that she couldn't fully explain, her sex drive had been through the roof ever since he had arrived. There was no denying that she had been not only coming on to him but doing her best to arouse him in every way she could and at every opportunity she could find.

In a way, she knew that this heightened desire for intimacy was because she knew they only had a few days together before they would once again be separated by a distance she didn't want to think about. Regardless of that, she couldn't help but feel concerned that she may not be able to subdue her desires once he had gone and that went against everything she knew about naturism. There was only one way to resolve it and for now it felt like the right move to make given the warning they had both received – she had to find some way to get back to naturism again.

Flicking through the TV channels she found one that had a movie due to start and rested the remote between herself and Jim as a barrier to prevent the temptation to shuffle up closer to him. Her phone buzzed in her pocket as Sasha smiled amicably at her parents who were making their way to the front room taking up the two armchairs, one at either side of the couch placing them in good locations to monitor behaviour for the evening.

Digging her phone out of her pocket she read through what seemed like an excited message from Adele whose announcement took her by surprise at first.

"Dell has been on a date" she announced not really caring who was listening but keen to try to break the silence that had carried over from the dinner table.

Suddenly an idea came to her, not really an ideal one given the time of year but one that seemed like a good way to get Jim and her out of the house and make some attempts to revisit her naturist side.

For a few moments she had been pondering over taking Jim to the cottage to get him away from the house but as the weather was supposed to be relatively pleasant she had a much more interesting idea – a double date with Adele and her new person she had started seeing but not named.

Sasha knew that her idea was a bit adventurous but decided it didn't hurt to see if Adele was up for it – a trip back to Hawk Cliff Beach. If Adele was up for it that would mean they would be in a clothing optional location and as she wouldn't be alone with Jim hopefully she would be able to keep her other desires at bay.

Quickly she tapped out her message making the suggestion feeling her body shaking slightly as she sent it and waited patiently for the reply.

"Ma, I'm going to take Jim out with Adele tomorrow" she smiled as the confirmation text buzzed up on her phone, eager to meet this new person Adele had been meeting and keen to make sure she could still be in a naturist location and even if she did stay dressed, it was the thought that counted.

Chapter Twenty

Back to the beach

Sasha waved energetically as she spotted Adele standing at the bus stop which impressed Jim given the time of the morning and the fact that the sun had barely risen. From where they were he could make out the fact that there were two figures waiting and one of them was vaguely familiar to him as the friend that Sasha had introduced him to earlier in his visit.

"Hmmm, that's strange, I was sure Dell said she was bringing her new boyfriend with her" slowing their pace Sasha made the comment as quietly as she could despite being out of earshot of the two figures she now recognised.

The fact that it was Ciara standing with Adele came as a shock to her especially given the way that Ciara had reacted the first day she had walked in on Adele and her behind the cottage, a moment she wasn't going to forget in a long time despite the fact that she had still been safely dressed at the time.

It had often occurred to her in the weeks that had followed that if Ciara had made herself known a few minutes later than she had done there was a fairly good chance that the amount of clothing Adele and she were wearing would have been a lot less.

Jim smiled, tugging gently on Sasha's hand as they moved slowly closer to the two girls who seemed to be the only other people waiting for the bus. Despite the fact that he had barely slept after the narrow escape they had been given by Sasha's parents he had spotted something that he felt sure Sasha hadn't seen. It wasn't easy to see in the early morning light but he felt sure that the two girls were holding hands in a manner that was not dissimilar to the grip he was sharing with Sasha.

"Did Adele definitely say it was a new boyfriend she was bringing with her Sash?" He glanced at Sasha as he spoke gesturing with his eyes in the direction of the two girls that they were getting too close to for their conversation to continue much longer.

During the last couple of years at what was now his old school, something that he couldn't believe he was able to say but knew to be an accurate description, Jim had noticed that a lot of his female friends had no problem with holding hands with each other. Something that, in a lot of ways, he was happy that boys were less inclined to do unless it was for the same reason as he suspected to be the case with Adele and the new girl he hadn't met yet. It was, in reality one of many differences that he knew to exist between girls and boys, not counting the obvious ones that he had grown to admire.

His friendship with girls had got him into a mixed array of situations, some which had been less than amicable and others that he knew he was lucky to have been included in even if it was only as part of clothes shopping experiences. Girls seemed to have no problem with being partially dressed in front of each other in environments where boys would make awkward gestures if put into similar situations.

In a way it had amused him a few times that boys he knew were frequently almost squeamish around each other when it came to getting changed and yet had no problem piling on top of each other for games like rugby. Girls on the other hand didn't seem too worried about being seen by other girls in their underwear and this closer knit outlook extended as far as hand holding not being seen as awkward.

With that said, Jim had learned that there were different forms of hand holding that symbolised different types of bond between the two people holding hands together. The first type was the one that he still had bad memories of when his mother had insisted on him taking her hand as he grew up especially if he was seen by someone who knew him whose parents had already moved on from the hand hold protocol.

It was a similar hand hold to that which girls who were just being playful or friendly with each other used – a non-committal hand hold – the type of hold where no fingers were interlocked and release from the grasp was relatively easy if one of them needed to break free for any reason.

In contrast to this was the finger interlocked hand hold, one that was more of a loose vice-grip which suggested that the people involved in the hold were probably in some kind of relationship like Sasha and he were. This one was less easy to break free of but that wasn't a bad thing because generally there was less inclination to want to break free from it. This was the hand hold that he had been enjoying with Sasha all the way to the bus stop and with every step they took it seemed more and more likely that it was the hand hold that the girls waiting for them were also sharing.

"Oh, I see" Sasha whispered her reply before breaking away from Jim to give Adele a hug and smiling softly at Ciara who she still wasn't sure how to greet but felt certain that if Jim's observation was accurate that was going to have to change in the near future.

In the back of her mind she ran through the content of the text she could recall being relieved to have received the night before. A text that firstly, had broken the tension of the evening and, secondly, it has given her the opportunity to forge a quick plan to get Jim and her out of the house for the day. It was all a bit of a blur in her mind but now she thought about it there had been no mention of the gender of the person Adele had announced that she was dating. Sasha knew that she had made an assumption that it must be a guy but based on Adele's past dating experience it seemed like a reasonable guess.

Over the years Sasha knew that she had spent more time than she dared to think about in various states of partial dress around Adele. At the time it had seemed trivial, even the fact that they had been naked together seemed like nothing more than two friends enjoying naturism but now Sasha couldn't help but wonder if anything they had done as friends had influenced Adele's interest in girls.

"I sent Seamus a text too, he said he might pop down to say hello" Adele seemed not only excited but energised about the idea of them being able to go to the beach as a group especially given the time of year.

She had to admit that she hadn't expected an invitation to the beach when she had made her announcement to Sasha that she was getting into what she hoped was going to be a fun relationship with Ciara. After their first date they had met again and the spark that had been between them had grown to the point where she was confident enough to accept that she actually had a girlfriend.

They had been sat together when she had sent her first message to Sasha and it had been Ciara's idea to make the announcement as vague as possible when it came to referring to who she had been on two dates with.

"I wanna see how Sasha reacts to you dating a girl" Ciara had giggled lightly at the suggestion and watched as Adele carefully wrote out her message.

When the reply came back suggesting a double date and naming Hawks Cliff as the place Sasha wanted them to go to Adele had at first been nervous about how to tell Ciara about it.

Ciara had been slightly taken back, firstly by the fact that there was a clothing optional beach in Ireland and secondly by the fact that Sasha was the one suggesting they should go there as a group. Suddenly the momentum she had anticipated achieving from her surprise as the person Adele was dating seemed a little deflated.

She had accepted that Adele had an interest in naturism, there was no denying that from the very first time she had snuck up on them at the cottage but the idea of hanging out as a group with her new girlfriend, their mutual friend and a boyfriend she had only ever heard talked about was daunting enough. Now there was the added factor that the place that was being suggested for them to go to was somewhere that clothing wasn't seen as something that people had to wear.

"Ok, I'll come along with you but don't expect me to get naked" Ciara had been able to feel butterflies as she accepted the invitation to what she was already sure was going to be the strangest third date with a girl she had ever been on.

Ciara had excused herself from Adele's company shortly after committing to the trip to a beach and made her way to the shed in her back yard where she knew there was a pop-up tent stored. Dusting it off she made her way back to the front room of her home, where she had left Adele ready to suggest they should take it with them as a kind of changing room only to fund that the surprises weren't over for her.

"I have a gay friend called Seamus who lives near the beach, d'ya think I should tell him we are heading over his way?" Adele smiled softly, as Ciara froze to the spot still trying to digest the fact that she had agreed to such a day out while also trying to get over the idea of there being another person who might join them.

In a way the fact that Adele had made a point of announcing him as her gay friend was both concerning and reassuring at the same time. Ciara knew that boys sometimes used the gay line as an excuse to try to push their luck in the company of women. She had seen it work more than once but it always came at the cost of firstly having to go on clothes shopping trips with the girl they were trying to get close to and an unwanted safety net which they set for themselves as being the 'harmless gay friend' placing them in the non-boyfriend material category for their efforts. Ciara had started referring to it as karma biting them on the ass whenever she heard of a foiled gay friend attempt.

As it stood Ciara had to admit that unbeknown to him, Jim was going to be outnumbered in the gender split by three to one so maybe having another guy possibly join their little day out wasn't a bad idea. If this mystery Seamus really was gay then there was no threat of him coming on to any of the girls and Jim was with Sasha so he really wasn't a threat. On the other hand, having another guy with them on the clothing optional beach did mean another potential penis on the loose even if it wasn't one that had any interest in women.

"Sure why not, it's gonna be a weird enough day out as it is with all the possible nakedness" Ciara giggled as she responded before settling down next to Adele again to make sure her position as love interest to the girl she was with was well established.

"Changing tent" Ciara smiled nervously as she gestured at the packed item she was carrying in her free hand

Suddenly the day out she had been jokingly talking about the previous evening seemed to be getting much more real but she was there now so she couldn't change her mind without making it seem weird.

Raising her hand and placing it on her neck to hide the mark that Ciara had left the previous evening Adele smiled sheepishly at Jim as Sasha and he stood next to them at the stop.

Although she hadn't told Ciara, in the back of her mind Adele had a strong recollection of the crush she had developed for Jim the first day she had met him. She gripped Ciara's hand tighter as she glanced down the road happy to see the bus on its way to them. How things had changed in just a few days and yet somehow the fact that she was going to experience naturism with her best friend and Jim was what she had wanted to happen ever since that first time they met.

She could still recall how there had been an awkward moment behind the cottage when she had contemplated disrobing before noticing that Sasha wasn't inclined to do the same. This time, Adele hoped that they could enjoy some nude time together as long as the weather remained as good as it was meant to be for the rest of their day out. Adele had checked the forecast before leaving the house but felt sure that Sasha had already done the same before suggesting Hawks Cliff.

It was admittedly going to be cooler than she would had liked it to be but Adele was determined not to let that stop her stripping down at least to her underwear when they got to the beach.

When Ciara had produced the tent Adele had to admit that it was going to be a good idea especially if the temperature dropped. For a moment before leaving home to meet Ciara she had pondered over the idea of packing some kind of swimming costume but decided not to more out of principle than anything else.

Sasha smiled as the bus pulled up and gestured to Adele and Ciara to get on ahead of them before kissing Jim softly on the cheek for his discretion. In many ways she was relieved when he hadn't asked too many questions about their trip and had tactically chosen not to tell him what type of beach it was before leaving the house.

She had watched as he rolled a pair of trunks into a towel and slid them into a bag ready for their trip and followed his lead by rolling a towel for herself out of his sight to prevent him realising that hers was empty.

Jim had told her many times about how his parents had tricked him into going to the complex where they met and each time she heard the story she had joked with him about the fact that if he hadn't gone with them he wouldn't have met her. This seemed to lighten his mood as she watched him recall the lead up to and sheer shock at the place they had taken him to with the highlight of his trip being the naked girl who had befriended him whose hand he was now proudly holding.

They arrived at the midway stop, a place that Sasha recalled with great fondness from their first trip when it had just been Adele and she making their way to the secluded cove. This time she was prepared for their stop and had made sure to pack some snacks to prevent them from feeling the need to spend in the overly priced service station while waiting for their connecting bus.

"Jim, I forgot to mention something to you about this beach" Sasha kept her voice calm as she snuggled up to him feeling the jolt of the bus that was going to get them as far as Dublin city centre.

Feeling his heart almost stop, Jim turned his head slowly breathing in a tuft of Sasha's hair as he made an attempt to face her.

"See, it's now a normal regular beach we are going to hun" Sasha made sure to use soft tones to lull him into a sense of security

Jim knew instinctively that there was something Sasha was trying to break to him gently and tried to remain calm as he listened to her, resting his head back into the seat as she spoke.

"It's a clothing optional beach" Sasha nuzzled against his chest as she made the announcement pretending to want to doze off while they travelled.

For a moment Jim blinked as he took in the comment feeling like he was encountering what he knew was referred to as being déjà vu. There was no denying that he had been in a position just like this before and not more than a few months ago.

Admittedly this time the person telling him wasn't his father, which was a relief after the way he had found out the same information the last time. He could still see the image of the naked people on the rooftop tennis courts who he thought were just an illusion as the reality of his holiday location settled into his mind.

At least this time he had experienced nude locations before and the person he was with was part of the best memory he had from any holiday he had been on. There was also the fact that, unlike last time, this time it was only for a few hours and yet the shock that he had been lured into yet another clothing optional experience stuck to the back of his throat.

Beyond Sasha's head in the seats across the aisle from them he could see Adele and Ciara, both of them seemed quite relaxed which suggested to him that either they didn't know about the beach or were already in on the plan.

In his heart Jim knew that there were boys he went to school with who would envy the position he was on his way to experiencing. A day at the beach with the potential for up to three naked girls one of whom he was happily in a relationship with – to some boys that would seem like heaven but for now all it felt like to him was daunting. Mentally he shrugged while ensuring he didn't actually move so as not to disturb Sasha who felt like she really had drifted off on him.

"I s'pose I won't be needing my trunks then will I" Jim smirked as she spoke while wondering if Sasha as awake or asleep against him

Remaining silent Sasha grinned as she pressed her head closer against Jim's chest choosing not to make a fuss over his reply.

Chapter Twenty-One

Beach Bums

Sasha smiled and waved politely at the driver to thank him for getting them to Dalkey safely as she stepped carefully off the bus.

She knew that, for most people the passing gesture was nothing more than a courtesy but after the journey she had endured it felt more like a compulsory requirement.

In her mind she knew that it wasn't the drivers fault that the chair they had chosen to sit on had been more uncomfortable than a park bench, or that the suspension on the bus felt like it shouldn't even be on the road but that made the prospect of a similar journey back to Dublin seem much less appealing.

Jim had been naturally curious when they got off the bus in Dublin as he had never seen the city before and Sasha accepted that to him this was a tourist trip whereas to her it was just a trip through the big city.

Glancing up, Sasha was relieved to see that the weather was holding up to its promise despite the sight of some less than friendly dark clouds as they stepped on to the third bus in their journey.

From the moment she had arranged the trip she had accepted that there was a chance that the weather would deter them from any actual naturist activity but the fact they were now only a few moments from a location that allowed nudity if they wanted it felt like it had been worth the journey.

During her visits to the complex she could recall that, even in the years before Jim had arrived there were a few people who preferred to opt for the 'optional' part of the clothing rule for the resort. Admittedly most of the time it was only a t-shirt but she had seen more than one person who seemed almost out of place, as if they had arrived at the complex not knowing it was naturist – just like Jim had done.

Carefully they followed the route down to the beach pausing as they reached the sign advising any unaware visitors that they may witness nudity beyond that point.

For a moment they stood on the invisible boundary between the textile and nude areas until Ciara took the first step across which seemed to release the tension that was visible in Adele's shoulders.

Ever since they had stepped on to the bus that was going to take them to Dublin Adele had found herself being questioned about the trip by Ciara who seemed less keen than she had been before about the idea of going to what she was now referring to as a nudey beach. Adele had tried to reason with her but the awkward tension had been almost overwhelming to the point where she had suggested that they could just spend the day together in Dublin and leave Sasha and Jim to go to the beach on their own.

Ciara had paused for a moment, silently acknowledging the fact that Adele was willing to change their plans to save things getting too awkward for her. The idea of spending a day browsing around Dublin wasn't overly appealing especially given the fact that she had a tent and beach items to carry around with her but at least in the city there was no option against remaining dressed. She pondered over the idea before glancing at Adele who was trying her best not to seem upset at the idea of missing out on the beach day.

Peering past Adele's shoulder Ciara could see Jim cradling what looked like it was a dozing Sasha, both of them totally relaxed as if what they were about to do was nothing unusual. In a way despite not knowing much about Jim the little that she did know told her that he had been to nude places before. Ciara could sense butterflies of anxiety fluttering in her stomach as she focussed her attention back on Adele who was still showing a very neutral expression as she awaited the answer.

"No, we'll go to this nude place but next time I get to choose what we do" She rested her head on Adele's shoulder as she spoke, flutters of nervousness racing through her mind as she accepted that she had just thrown away her last chance to walk away from a date she wasn't sure if she would enjoy or not.

Choosing not to look behind in case any of her companions had already started to disrobe Ciara busied herself finding a place that seemed suitable and set about putting the tent up.

In her mind knew that. Although she had suggested it as a place that they could store their unwanted items for the day to her it was also a hideaway, somewhere she could sit and not be confronted by naked bodies if it all got too much for her.

Carefully she pegged the tent down placing rocks on the four corner pegs to stop them from lifting if a rogue breeze tried to lift the tent from its tentative location. Wriggling into the tent she folded the bag it had been packed in and took a deep breath as she tried to prepare herself for what she may be about to witness.

With a sudden thud she jumped as she heard the sound of something landing behind her and turned to see Adele's smiling face and naked bosom popping through the tent door as she discarded a few garments on the tent floor.

"I'm keeping my pants on for now" Adele smiled as she disappeared from the tent leaving her top in a heap on the ground.

Ciara took a deep breath accepting that if Adele was already half naked it was possible that the other two were on their way to a similar dress code.

In a way she knew that she really couldn't blame anyone except herself for the position she was in. When the idea of a double date at a clothing optional location had originally been mentioned she had been cautious about it but also keen for their relationship to be known to the person who Adele clearly knew best and that was Sasha.

There was no denying that, given the chance, she would want their double date to be something more conventional, maybe a trip to the cinema together but trips like that were always difficult. Apart from anything else there was the prospect of trying to find a movie that they were all happy to go and see and at least a day out at the beach took that angle out of the equation.

Ciara knew that the big problem she had was the idea of so much nudity and not in a place where she would expect it to be like a changing room at a swimming pool. Adding to it was the fact that one of the people she was going on the trip was a boy and, although she didn't have any adversity to the sight of a penis it wasn't at the top of her list of things she wanted to see again either.

The first time she had been put in a position where a penis had been brought to her attention had been on the one occasion when she had tried to date a boy. She had chosen to accept a date with one of the more confident boys at school but only so that she could say she had at least tried dating boys. Even at the age of fourteen she had been sure that she preferred girls but one date with a boy who seemed pleasant albeit confident in himself didn't seem like a bad idea.

As far as dates went theirs hadn't been too bad, she had successfully managed to avoid anything too physical even his attempts at a goodnight kiss but had also not made it clear that she didn't want to see him again. She had been home for less than an hour after having said goodbye to him when her phone alerted her to the message that she regretted opening a picture of him fresh from the shower. It took her less than 30 seconds to delete the offending image and reply to him making it clear that she didn't want to have anything to do with him again and would prefer it if they didn't even have to see each other at school.

At first he had responded badly to her rejection but thankfully only by text which she managed to quickly nip in the bud by reporting him to their head of year. As for the hope of not seeing him even at school, that had taken a bit longer but eventually he had moved t a different town making it impossible for them to go to the same school.

"Seamus you made it" Ciara felt her ears pricking at the sound of Adele's voice as another person was being greeted to their spot on the beach.

Suddenly the odds of there being a penis on view had doubled but more importantly in her eyes was the fact that her girlfriend was half naked and clearly pleased to see this new boy, a boy who she had been promised was gay so no threat but still his presence and potential nudity made it more urgent that she leave the safety of her tent.

Ciara took a deep breath closing her eyes and clearing her mind before poking her head out of the tent, still cautious about the amount of skin that she may see but conscious that she wanted to make sure Adele knew she was there.

Over to one side, as she had expected, were Sasha and Jim. Sasha was already stripped to her underwear but had stopped at that stage to wave a casual greeting at this Seamus who she clearly knew as well. Jim was in a similar state of dress to Adele, topless but had his back to the tent so was blissfully unaware of the fact that Ciara was even looking in his direction.

"Are ye going to introduce us to your friend Seamus?" Ciara heard Adele's comment and quickly remembered the reason why she had emerged from the tent in the first place.

Quickly Ciara turned toward the direction where the voice had come from and felt her jaw drop as she saw two naked men standing with Adele.

One of them, the one nearest Adele was fairly well tanned and had a fairly good body, one that even Ciara had to admit to finding attractive. The other one much paler skinned and bald headed but still not bad looking in her opinion taking into consideration the fact that he was a man.

Adele turned her head almost instinctively and smiled over at Ciara beckoning her to join in the conversation. It had felt almost funny seeing Seamus again but not as awkward as it had the first time they had met when she had been much newer to naturism and embarrassed about him seeing her body.

At the time Adele knew that she had wanted him to like her and had felt almost let down by the fact that he had told her he was gay. She bit her lip as she spotted the fact that Seamus was clearly standing with his boyfriend but the fact that she was seeing a girl made it seem more appropriate that Ciara should meet them both.

"This is Ciara, my girlfriend" Adele blushed as she spoke realising that she hadn't really got used to the idea of referring to having a girlfriend yet.

Reaching out her hand she smiled as Ciara grabbed for it and made her way over waving sheepishly while trying to avoid the vision of the two nude men she was being introduced to.

Remaining at a distance with Jim, Sasha watched and felt herself smile as she saw Adele embracing the idea of being in a relationship with a woman. She had to acknowledge that it couldn't have been easy for her to go from dating boys to dating girls and probably even harder for her to accept the double date with Jim and her especially one that was going to a nude location.

She couldn't help noting that out of all of them Ciara was the only one still fully dressed which made it clear to her that, as she had suspected, Ciara was not into naturism in the same way as the rest of them were. Even Jim was more comfortable with public nudity than Ciara and Sasha knew that it wasn't his first choice of lifestyle but at least he was willing to accept and participate in it. For now Ciara seemed like she was devoted to the textile lifestyle but that didn't mean that she wouldn't change her mind in time, just that she wasn't ready to do it just yet. The fact that Ciara had accepted the invitation to go to the beach was at least a move in a positive direction for her to if nothing else accept naturism.

Taking a seat on the towel that she had just flattened on the sand she glanced up at Jim who seemed to be lost in his own world. The presence of two naked men had, without doubt stumped him and was now making him cautious about whether to disrobe completely or not which made Sasha smile as she contemplated it being a size concern.

She had heard about men and their size issues in the past and had been quite relieved when Jim hadn't seemed to let the wide range of shapes and sizes concern him while they had been at the complex. Now that they were in a different nude friendly environment and in a smalled and more personal group it seemed that he wasn't sure if his body was going to fit in with the group that surrounded him.

Reaching out she prodded his leg watching him jump slightly as she peered up casually at him standing above her position.

"Sit down, you're making the place untidy" She giggled as she reached to her back unclipping her bra.

Jim smirked at the comment recalling in his head how his parents had used the same line on him in the past but, now he was hearing it from Sasha it seemed more significant. He glanced across at Sasha; now sitting in just a pair of panties which he recalled was similar to her dress code on their first day at a beach in Zante. At the time he couldn't help but be focussed on her breasts, which he had to admit being happy to see once more, but Sasha had been quick to educate him on their lack of ability to talk.

Sitting up slightly he wriggled out of the jeans he had been wearing feeling the light breeze as it crossed over his thighs. He glanced across at Adele and Ciara still happily nattering with the two men who had joined them and felt his cheeks flush with redness as Adele pushed her pants down before throwing them toward the tent that Ciara had been sitting just a few moments earlier.

"Ciara looks nervous don't she" Jim nudged his elbow toward Sasha as he spoke not looking at what he was doing before realising that what he had nudged was definitely not her arm as it was much softer.

Sasha winced as the sharp elbow caught her biting her lip as she accepted that it was an unintended dig while still wishing Jim had been looking at where he was nudging.

"I remember someone else who wasn't willing to get naked not so long ago don't you?" She poked her tongue playfully toward Jim as she spoke before casually slipping her panties off and laying back to relax on the towel

Jim blushed at the less than subtle reference before sliding his boxers sheepishly down his legs, more out of the need to make a point than the want to be nude but now Sasha had bought the memory of his first few days at the complex tumbling back to him it felt like he should prove he was still comfortable naked in public.

Reaching over Adele gave Seamus an amicable hug before glancing at his boyfriend unsure of whether she should offer the same gesture to him or not. In a way it seemed wrong not to treat him the same as Seamus but the fact that she barely knew him made it difficult to know how he would respond to her. Any doubts she had were quickly set aside as Andy leaned over hugging her with a polite pat on the back before Seamus and he made their excuses and left them to their day out as a group. Turning Adele paused at first, the look on Ciara's face made it clear that even if both the boys had been comfortable with the hug it hadn't been as well accepted by her girlfriend.

Ciara watched from a distance as Adele spoke with the two naked boys that had joined them and made note that after the initial hug there had been no further physical contact between them. It hadn't occurred to her up to that stage that there was any chance of a situation where she would feel almost cheated on and yet still sure that there was nothing incriminating between Adele and her male friends.

As she watched them she could see that the two men were clearly in a relationship together despite the light-hearted reference to them being friends and yet the hug that had been shared still upset her slightly.

From her towel Sasha spotted the uncomfortable pose that Ciara was holding and felt a recall to a similar situation that had occurred between her and Jim when he had seen her hugging Greg after the volleyball game. On that occasion at least the man she had been embracing was interested in women but that hadn't meant there was anything between them as Jim had been quick to learn.

Standing she placed a hand on Jims shoulder before nodding discretely at Ciara as a silent reference to the situation before making her way over to speak to her.

"Hey Ciara" Sasha smiled softly as she spoke while keeping a distance between them to allow for the fact that Ciara clearly was not into the naturist aspect of their trip.

"You might not believe this but, I know exactly how you are feeling" she smiled as Ciara glanced over, the expression on her face clearly softening from the welcomed distraction that Sasha was bringing to her.

At first Ciara wasn't able to stop herself checking out Sasha's body and feeling slightly attracted to her but she quickly realised that what she was doing was probably worse in some ways than what Adele had done. There was no denying that the physical contact aspect of Adele's interaction with the boys had upset her but the fact that the boys had no interest in women whereas she was openly interested in them and had just instinctively admired the one she wasn't in a relationship with put her on a back foot.

"What d'ya mean?" Ciara felt her cheeks flushing with redness as she tried to keep her gaze away from Sasha's body.

Sasha bit her lip as she noted the glance she had received and how it had been vaguely similar to the one Jim had given her on their first day together at the complex. She had accepted that having been naked in front of him on her first time meeting him didn't actually count but there was no way of dismissing the way he had glared at her breasts on their day at the beach which was strangely similar to the glance she was now getting from Ciara. Somehow, despite the fact that she knew Ciara was into women more than men the way she had gazed over her body didn't seem quite as intrusive as it had when Jim had done it. Sasha put the difference down to the fact that although they both had differences to their bodies at the end of the day the features were the same.

"When I first met Jim he saw me hugging another guy, a friend of mine and he reacted in a similar way to how you are now with Adele" Sasha kept the tone of her voice soft to prevent being over heard as she spoke.

"I don't know much about Seamus and the other guy, but I know Adele and I know she wouldn't cheat on you" Sasha smiled softly resisting the temptation to reach out and grab Ciara's arm in a gesture of reassurance.

Chapter Twenty-Two

The naked truth

It came as a bit of a shock to Sasha when they arrived home from the beach to hear her parents talking to her as if the incident that she had been held accountable had never even happened. In her mind she had already considered her the day as being a successful return to what she considered true naturism but her parents had an even bigger surprise waiting for her as she walked through the front door.

"How was the beach then?" her mother had been smiling casually as she spoke clearly oblivious to the fact that a nude friendly beach even existed let alone the fact that Sasha had now visited it twice.

The question almost caught her off guard as she started replying and made reference to Adele having had invited other friends along but Sasha managed to stop herself mentioning the dres code they had shared.

In many ways the journey home had seemed slightly tense but after she had seen the way Ciara was acting Sasha hadn't been expecting it to be the most amicable of trips. It had almost been a relief to get off the bus but to Sasha it was more of a comfort that despite all of the shocks that had occurred Ciara still seemed happy to hold hands with Adele. While Sasha knew that hand holding was only a small gesture the fact that she managed to get home with no distressed calls or upset messages from Adele seemed like a positive sign.

"Ya, was fun, the sea was a little cold but was nice to just relax and have fun" Sasha smiled as she responded to the question, the smell of home cooked food still lingering making her wish they had been able to catch an earlier connection to get home for dinner.

There was something discerning about a takeaway instead of what smelled like it had been a nice stew which was lingering from the kitchen

"Your father and I have given some more thought to that situation we discussed with you last night" Sasha felt her heart drop as she heard the comment while hovering somewhere between a standing and sitting position but now wondering if she actually wanted to sit in the front room or not.

In the past there hadn't been many conversations that had started with the words 'your father and I' which had been what she considered as positive ones but Sasha couldn't deny some of them being memorable at the very least even if it wasn't for the best of reasons. With that said, there were even fewer conversations that bought up a subject that had been discussed previously which had a good outcome and this one fell into both categories.

Jim went pale as he heard the comment and glanced between Sasha and her parents unsure whether he should try to straighten out the mess or not but more nervous about what her parents new thoughts might mean for the last few days of his time in Ireland.

"Sit down, you aren't in trouble" Sasha's gaze turned to her father as he joined in the conversation.

His words were both reassuring and concerning at the same time, on one hand they acted as an assurance that there was nothing bad waiting for them but on the other hand Sasha felt sure there may be a false sense of security attached to them.

Her father had never been one for deception, if he said something he usually meant it but that didn't make Sasha any less cautious about what may be waiting to be said. Taking a deep breath she accepted that it was best to follow the requested instruction and continue the course of action she had already started by sitting on the couch. Behind her, almost looming overhead like some kind of shadow was Jim who seemed to have frozen to the spot unwilling to move until he knew he was safe.

"Come, join us Jim, this involves you as well" Mary smiled calmly as she gestured to him to make his way round to the couch and sit next to Sasha.

Jim could feel his legs weakening as he made his way round to the front of the couch. In what seemed like a nanosecond all of the positive vibes that he had been enjoying during the day out seemed to have been shunted out of view by what sounded like an amicable request but felt like it should have a 'but' attached to it.

Over the years Jim had heard his parents make reference to comments that they expected to have a 'but' attached to them. Normally he knew these were comments that seemed positive on the outside however the added but would give them a clause that had to be accepted as part of the deal – a kind of compromise that wasn't necessarily bad however wasn't welcomed either.

He glanced awkwardly at Sasha who he could see was already slightly nervous about what was going to be said.

In many ways this conversation felt like it should have already been had, a conclusion that should have either happened the same evening as the main conversation of at the latest been made the following morning. As he thought over the timing Jim knew that he had to accept that by leaving as early as they had Sasha and he hadn't really given her parents any time to have their final say on the matter.

Taking a deep breath as he glanced firstly at Sasha's father then at her mother Jim sat down and tried to make himself as comfortable as possible for whatever their announcement was going to be.

"I'm sure we don't have to tell you that we don't want to know what actually happened before your mother caught you yesterday Sasha" Feeling her cheeks flush with awkward embarrassment Sasha had to stop herself from trying to clear her name of the crime she hadn't actually committed.

In her mind it was bad enough that the subject had been bought up again not to mention the fact that despite her intentions she hadn't actually done what she was being accused of. Although it made sense in some ways to defend her position Sasha felt sure that if she tried to do so at this stage it would only escalate things further and she had no intention of doing that if she could avoid it.

From the moment they had left the bus stop she had been buzzing on the natural high of having not only got back to being nude for pure naturism but also seeing both Jim and Adele slipping back into the lifestyle so comfortably. Part of her wished that Ciara had joined in but she had accepted that Ciara was only there for Adele and not for her body to be exposed to anyone while she was on the beach. For a brief moment she had considered suggesting that Ciara at least try disrobing a little bit rather than sitting huddled up for the entire time not even taking her sweater off but she decided not to rock the boat.

It had been her hope that when they got home she would be able to just relax, maybe watch a movie or something and rest on the laurels of her day, laurels that she knew she couldn't tell her parents about but that didn't distract from their existence. Now that the conversation had taken a turn out of left field what was left of their evening ahead felt like it was going to be long and drawn out.

If it hadn't been for Jim being there with her Sasha had no doubt that she would find some reason to head to her bedroom but there was no way Jim was going to be allowed to join her in there regardless of the situation. From the moment she had mentioned him visiting Sasha could recall the subject of sleeping arrangements being a difficult subject and one that she hadn't been given an opinion in.

"I know Da" she muttered her response in an effort to seem humble about the incident that she still wished she had just gone through with. If hindsight was something that she could put into action Sasha knew that, while the conversation she was having wouldn't be any easier to sit through at least her desires would have been somewhat satisfied.

"Saturday is Jims last full day with us isn't it?"

The statement hit like a steam roller but Sasha had to admit she hadn't really thought about how quickly their week together had gone by.

She nodded silently unwilling to admit that just like the last few days of her trip to Zante she already had the hollow feeling welling up inside her body at the thought of saying goodbye to him yet again. This time she felt sure it was going to be harder because they had grown closer during his visit even if the road hadn't always been one that had always been comfortable for the, especially the last couple of days.

One thing that she knew for sure was that after the awkwardness they had been through over something she hadn't actually done she wanted to make sure their last few days together were fun, special and positive. Hearing her father mention how soon Jim was due to leave made the fact that it was so soon hit home in a way it hadn't done up to that point and Sasha found herself struggling to hold back tears at the thought.

In all of the excitement that had led to their day at the beach Sasha had only just realised that the Halloween party that her school always arranged for the end of their mid-term was less than a day away and she hadn't even mentioned it to Jim. Now that her father had mentioned how soon his flight back home was it almost felt like the house of cards that she had been building around herself from the moment he had arrived was on the verge of collapsing.

Everything seemed to have started to go wrong on that fateful morning when she had snuck into his room. Ever since that day Sasha felt like she had been chasing her own tail either in an effort to resolve a problem she had dropped herself in to or to set the naturist that lingered inside her back on the right track.

"Ya you are right Da, and there's the school party tomorrow night too"

it hadn't occurred to her that she had not only not mentioned the fact that there was a Halloween party to Jim but hadn't made any preparation for the party despite how close it was to happening.

Jim felt his mind falling into two different fields as he heard the conversation developing around him as if he wasn't really there.

On one side there was the fact that her father had mentioned that his last full day with them was looming just around the corner which meant two things to him. The first of those was that he didn't have long left before he was heading back home meaning that he was going to be leaving Sasha. The second, and in a lot of ways by far the more reassuring factor was that her father was still referring to him staying with them. Jim knew that the second was only a tentative reference but the fact remained that it looked like he was safe in their home at least for the meantime.

On a different note, Sasha had just mentioned a party, something that came as a surprise to him but he felt sure she wasn't planning on trying to keep it a secret. The problem was that Sasha had mentioned it as a school event meaning that he wasn't sure if he was meant to be going with her or not. Every school event he had attended back at home had been exclusively for school students to he didn't see any reason why her school events would be any different.

In the back of his mind Jim had visions of being forced into a position where he had to either find somewhere else to be – in a town where he only really knew Sasha and her friends – or spend the evening with her parents. He felt a chill running down his spine at the thought of an evening in her family home with her nowhere near and no logical reason for him not to be at home with them. Part of his mind was telling him that there was nothing to stop him spending some of the evening packing his case but there was only so long he could make that last. If he actively tried to avoid them Jim knew it would be obvious and would make any future interaction with them possibly even more awkward than the talk he was already in the middle of being included in.

"So, as you are both going to be at the party tomorrow your mother and I have decided to do something for you but don't for one minute think we are letting you off the hook Sasha"

Jim felt a sigh of relief as he heard reference to the fact that he was meant to be going to the party with Sasha but more than that he was intrigued about what her parents had in mind. Remaining tight lipped he sat back and listened, his mind racing faster than the rabbit on a greyhound track as he pondered over all the information it was trying to juggle.

Diarmuid glanced over at Mary as he prepared himself to make the announcement and nodded discretely as she confirmed that it should be him telling them their decision.

"We've booked you into a hotel near the church hall Sasha, to give you one night to, well I'm sure you know what I mean" Sasha blushed as she heard the words before leaping from her chair and throwing her arms around her father.

"Don't ever let us catch you doing that sort of thing again, you understand me?" Sasha nodded, her head pressing against his shoulder before making her way over to thank her mother.

Jim felt his arms flop to his side as he watched Sasha darting between her parents bemused but happy to hear their announcement.

****

Despite the fact that there had been some uncomfortable silences between Ciara and her on the way home Adele couldn't help but feel a positive glow about their day out with Sasha and Jim.

Ever since she had first agreed to go on a date with Ciara the thought had drifted in the back of her mind of how Sasha would react to her dating another girl. If their date hadn't gone as well as it had Adele had decided not to mention it and put it down to an experience but the fact that they had got on so well during their date made it clear to her that there was something between them.

Throughout the day she had noticed that Ciara had been reluctant to leave the tent let alone show any signs of disrobing and had pondered a couple of times over whether she should put something on as a mark of respect for her girlfriend.

The journey home hadn't been helped by the fact that no matter how much she had brushed them off before putting them back on her panties felt itchy from the sand she had carelessly discarded them in while talking to Seamus. At the time she had considered the idea of making her way back to the tent to finish undressing but hadn't really wanted to break away from the conversation for anything as trivial as putting clothes away.

For the duration of the bus ride from Dublin to their mid-point stop she had resisted the temptation to say anything despite the discomfort after accepting the fact that Ciara probably wouldn't appreciate such a topic being brought up. As soon as she had arrived at the service station she had made her way to a store that thankfully sold cheap underwear and treated herself to a new pair. The relief she felt at having fresh clean underwear on was one that she couldn't explain to anyone else.

Although she knew it was best not to say anything Adele couldn't help but feel relieved when Ciara snuggled up beside her for the last hour of their journey and started snoozing against her shoulder. In a way it was like a silent way of saying she accepted that what she had witnessed on the beach wasn't anything she fully understood but she wasn't going to try to talk Adele out of it either.

Taking the silent acceptance as a win Adele felt her body start to relax and a warm glow fill inside her at the thought that whether Ciara realised it or not it was naturism that had instigated their first date. She knew in her heart that it hadn't actually brought them together, and there was no way she could call it a mutual interest but in her own way she still felt like it was instrumental in them having become a couple.

"Dell, tell me something" Ciara had started the conversation calmly as they walked away from the bus stop

Although there had been nothing incriminating in the vague request Adele felt sure there was going to be a question or statement coming up that she wasn't going to feel totally comfortable answering but knew she had to agree to in order to keep the peace.

"If that Seamus guy had been straight d.ya think you would have been attracted to him?" Adele felt a lump catch in her throat as she heard the question.

She knew that when she had first met him there had been part of her mind that had wanted a relationship with him but it didn't feel like admitting to that straight out was the best way to go so chose a less incriminating path.

"What d'ya mean because he's a guy and we get on?" Adele felt sure that it wasn't the fact that they had a good rapport which Ciara was getting at but didn't want to be the one to mention the obvious factor that them both being nude played in their friendship.

Ciara blushed as she heard the reply, slightly angered but unsure whether Adele was playing with her or not in the innocence of the response. Even as a girl who wasn't into men the presence of a naked penis had been something that had made her stop and take notice and yet Adele was acting as if being naked in the same vicinity as two naked men was nothing out of the ordinary. Adding to her concern was the fact that Seamus wasn't short in what he had to offer which even she knew was something that would make most women show some interest, that and his athletic frame made him quite a catch for anyone.

"No ya dope" she giggled as she tried to keep her questioning as light hearted as possible, "I mean he was there all naked and so were you but he was gay so not going to be interested in a woman but ya know, you weren't only into girls" she gripped Adele's hand a little tighter before releasing the pressure and loosening her grip.

Adele turned her head smiling softly as she spotted the genuine anxiety in Ciara's eyes

"I dunno hun" she smiled feeling her face flush at the fact she had just used a term of endearment without even thinking about it.

"I mean yeah he's nice looking but the first time we met we were both naked so it wasn't as if his bits were anything exciting" Adele knew she couldn't elaborate on it but for the first time since having known Seamus she realised that she hadn't actually paid a lot of attention to his body.

"Thing is Ciara, with naturism ya don't really pay a pay attention to the body unless you're looking to be with the person" Adele bit her lip as she recalled some of the things Sasha had told her about naturism before she tried it for the first time

Suddenly she felt like she understood what Sasha had been trying to tell her about the non-sexual aspect of naturism. It felt funny that she hadn't really thought about it before but now Ciara was asking her about it she could see the difference between being naked for naturism and being naked for sexy times.

"If you ever tried naturism you'd understand" Adele smiled softly as she spoke while acknowledging the fact that it hadn't been that long ago

They stopped as they reached the corner of Adele's road and Ciara turned to face her as she prepared to say goodnight.

For a moment Ciara paused as she gripped Adele by both hands staring into her eyes which showed the energy and passion that had grown between them. She wasn't completely sure what was spurring her on but something inside was telling her that it was the right time to make what she felt was a bold move so early in their relationship.

"Dell, let's not say goodnight, let's have a sleepover at my place" Adele blushed as she heard the words and nodded eagerly.

Chapter Twenty-Three

All Hallows eve, eve

Sasha couldn't help feeling a buzz in her step as she made her way into town with Jim's hand confidently locked with hers. Overnight she had gone over the conversation with her parents' countless times to the point where she had decided that it must have been a dream but Jim had confirmed it was real.

As they had breakfast, she had made a few references to the party in an effort to encourage her mother to say something, maybe even drop the name of the hotel they were booked in to but, to no avail.

When the Halloween fancy dress party had first been announced at school Sasha had imagined it would be similar to the pre-term party with her and Adele going together but ever since the day Jim had been confirmed as visiting her thoughts had changed. For the first time in her life she was going to be able to consider a couple's costume in the true sense of what it was meant to be.

In the past she knew that she had gone as one half of a couple with Adele playing the other part of the duo, neither of them had batted an eye at the prospect of dressing up like a man except when the costume had been intended as bare chested. Now that they were both into naturism Sasha felt sure that even overly revealing costumes wouldn't be out of the question for either of them but on the other hand she was also sure that the school wouldn't approve.

When she had first told Adele that Jim was going to be joining them for the party Sasha had almost seen a look of despondence in her eyes at the thought that there would be a boyfriend going with one of them. Now that Adele was in a relationship as well Sasha felt sure that the situation was going to be much easier to handle.

The biggest problem Sasha had with Halloween parties wasn't so much the idea of dressing up but it was the wide range of variations that people considered to be appropriate for Halloween. On one side you had the people who went with something that would be generally considered scary but for reasons only known to the costume designer had now been given a 'sexy' twist.

Sasha had seen these a few times but usually on older people who she knew wouldn't be going to the same parties as she was but she could still recall a few questionable costumes having appeared at previous years parties..

The second option, and in some ways the one she loathed even more than the sexy scary costumes was the costumes that, in her mind, didn't feel like they belonged in the Halloween category. These were the famous characters, people from history and generally non-scary costumes that had become more prominent as the years went by but what made it worse was when people tried to make them scary by pretending they were an undead version of the character they were portraying. To Sasha that was just lazy as it usually only involved white face paint and a bit of fake blood on an otherwise non-scary costume.

She was proud of the fact that she had always made an effort to make her costume something really scary, something she considered to be a true Halloween effort.

Halloween had always come with mixed emotions to Sasha, the fun part of seeing kids running around trick or treating was always nice to see and the fact that it usually fell near a bank holiday was nice too but then there was the changing of the clocks meaning winter was truly upon them.

Most years that just meant cooler weather and darker days for the next few months with the prospect of Christmas just around the corner. This year there were two other factors that made the time of year seem less enjoyable.

The first of them was that winter meant there would be fewer opportunities for her to enjoy naturism something that she had found a new spur of interest in after her day at the beach. Coping with the thought that their beach visit may be the last time naturism would be practical outside of the confines of her bedroom was a sobering thought.

Even the cottage wouldn't really be an option no matter how determined she was to have a little bit of nude time there was no way the chill of winter was going to make it sensible to even strip down to her underwear in an outdoor location. If she was mad enough or determined enough to try it then Sasha knew there was a high chance it would lead to her getting sick which was something she wanted to avoid.

The thought occurred to her that there must be some people who enjoyed naturism who were able to do so in the luxury of their own homes. Unless she was willing to confess her thoughts on the lifestyle to her parents and try to convince them to let her walk around the house nude she knew that her options were going to be limited.

In the few weeks after her holiday she had contemplated the idea of trying to extend her naturist options but knew she had turned away from the idea just in case making such a suggestion ruined the one outlet she was almost assured of the following year – the return to the complex where all of her family would take part in the lifestyle. Now that the holiday was a distant memory and their trip for next year not even in the minds of her parents for at least a few months it seemed almost futile to bring the subject up.

Adding to the fact was the incident that she had somehow managed to slip away from despite some heavy scrutiny from her parents. Despite her innocence Sasha knew that having been caught up in such a tangled mess had left her on the back foot with her parents having enough evidence to use against her at a later stage if they chose to do so. In reality there was only one definite place she could spend nude time and that was her bedroom and even then she would need to be careful.

As a second option Sasha knew that there was a chance that when she went round to see Adele they may end up chilling out as two nude friends together in her room but now that Adele had a new girlfriend, and one who was clearly not into nudity that seemed like a less likely option than even the cottage. Despite how cold it would be in the seclusion of their makeshift greenhouse even with the door shut at least there nobody would question her if she did decide to pay a visit at some time.

The second factor that was draining the fun out of this years Halloween was the pending departure of Jim. Unlike her, he didn't have the same bank holiday extending his mid-term by an extra day to look forward to and the more she discussed the kind of activities that would happen around Halloween in her home town the more it seemed like she was describing an event that he hadn't heard of before despite his knowledge of the fancy dress element.

Jim had listened intently as Sasha described the fun of the parade that would be going through the town on the day he was due to travel back to the airport. It confused him slightly when Sasha had described the weekend by calling it Samhain and not Halloween but she had been quick to explain it was a Celtic festival. What took him by surprise more than anything was the way Sasha proudly told him that the whole Halloween concept had been one that had come from Ireland.

There was only one holiday that he had known to be Irish before visiting and even that was only vaguely celebrated in England – St Patricks Day. It didn't come as a surprise to him when Sasha had told him of the festivities that surrounded the day in her area but now that she was describing a similar festival linked to what he knew as Halloween he couldn't help but feel slightly shocked. In a lot of ways the festival Sasha was describing sounded like a lot of fun and he wishing he could stay to see it but in his hear he knew two things for certain.

The first of them was that if he asked the Rents to change his flight they would almost certainly say no as it would mean him missing a day of college. Even if they did agree to it Jim felt sure that he would be pushing his luck by asking Sasha's parents if they could put him up one extra night. For now, especially as this was his first visit, it felt like the safer option to accept that he was going to miss the festivities and just hope that he could see them another time.

As they arrived in to the town Sasha paused, glaring down the high street in the hope that it might give her some inspiration about where she might be best to go to find something she could make into costumes for them both. In the back of her mind she didn't want their costumes to be anything too boring, she knew there would be other couples there and the last thing she wanted was for them to have a costume that almost mirrored someone else's.

The biggest problem Sasha could see as she mulled over costume ideas was that everything she could think of that fit into her own category of both traditional and defining Jim and her as a couple was also fairly boring and predictable. Both of which she wanted to avoid as much as possible to lessen the chances of their costume mirroring one that had been chosen by another couple at the party.

In her mind she could recall the fancy dress party she had gone to with Adele at the end of the summer, not their first-time seeing Maebh and Ciara but definitely a more memorable time than their first time seeing the two of them. She could clearly remember there being more than one iteration of May and Joseph with some of them adding their own little twists into the costume but the concept remained the same.

The last thing she wanted was to end up going as something like a male and female vampire which she was sure would lead to them melding in to half of the crowd. A second option she wanted to avoid was anything that involved her dressing as a cat, although she understood how they were vaguely linked to the time of year in her eyes a cat costume was even more boring than being yet another vampire in the room.

In her experience Halloween costume bits were generally readily available in more shops than most people would imagine looking for them in. In a way it was a little bit like the only limitation was on the shopper's imagination but Sasha was also aware that budget had a big part to play however she wasn't overly short on funds.

Reaching the end of the high street she glanced over at the café they had sat in earlier in the week, a crowning moment in her opinion because she felt like Jim's presence may have finally got the message across to Fintan.

"Did ya want a coffee so we can have a thought over our costumes?" Sasha smiled as she gripped Jim by both hands pointing him in the direction of the café to enforce her suggestion even further.

Jim peered over Sasha's shoulder at the café she was directing his attention toward and felt a chill down his spine as a breeze ticked past him.

He hadn't said a lot about it but in order to avoid spending a long amount of time in her mothers presence he had avoided eating too much during breakfast and the lure of one of the cakes that he could almost smell from the café was extremely tempting.

There had been no denying the fact that he hadn't felt entirely comfortable with her parents ever since the fateful morning but at least they had escaped from the situation fairly unscathed and had a night in a hotel to look forward to as well – neither of which he had expected to happen.

From the moment her parents had left them alone the previous evening he had made the decision to treat the rest of his stay in a similar way to the compulsory PE sessions when he was at school – keep his head down, concentrate on the game and hope not to be caught in a position he wasn't meant to be in. Jim wasn't sure how he had done it but somehow he had managed to get a good report from the PE teacher despite having little or no idea what most of the lessons were actually about

Taking in a deep breath Jim felt his stomach rumble at the smell of the fresh pastries, one of many things he knew he was going to miss when he got back home.

Since starting college he had changed his routines a little and was starting to enjoy the more flexible schedule that he now had compared with school life but the amount of homework seemed to have doubled despite the severe reduction in class time. It was nice not having to wear the same uniform every day but he had noticed an awful lot of similarities in what many of the students in his classes wore despite there being no uniforms.

Out of all the new aspects of his life the one thing that he enjoyed more than anything was the daily trip to the small café just outside the college grounds. There was almost a sense of achievement in being able to leave his place of study with nobody really caring if he went back to class or not, except for the rents

He had sometimes pondered over whether any of the other students had parents who monitored their progress as much as his did. Some of the people he saw in class seemed obvious candidates for non-committal learners with a similar outlook on life to that of his sisters ex-boyfriend Jay and yet these boys seemed to be able to effortlessly pass any test that was thrown at them.

Unlike the café that he was now walking into with Sasha, the cakes in his break time café never seemed to be completely fresh. There was no denying the sticky nature of the buns, or the sweet cinnamon flavour of the Danish pastries, which had become his favourite treat and yet the cakes always had a sense of almost seeming like leftovers. Raising his suspicions even further was the fact that a small bakery just down the road from the café seemed to have a similar range with a price difference making the café treats more appealing.

"Did ya want something to eat while we're here?" Jim didn't have to be asked twice as Sasha seemed to intuitively know that he was hungry, then again his stomach had made his thoughts on the subject fairly clear.

Nodding keenly he browsed down the typed up paper insert giving the list of daily specials that were in addition to the good range of items the café suggested they would have available on a daily basis.

"I think an apple Danish would be nice" he smiled as he responded before spotting the waitress who he hadn't seen appear standing patiently waiting to take their order " oh and an Americano" he grinned as he handed the menu over to Sasha.

Without any hesitation Sasha added her order and watched the waitress disappear before closing the menu and sliding it to the side of the table

"So, any ideas for our costumes for the party?" Sasha felt a tingle run through her body as she spoke silently acknowledging that despite the fact that she had been thinking about couples costumes for a while this was the first time she had actually made any suggestion of them to Jim.

There was something both nice and in another way sad in her mind as she posed the question to him and reminisced over all the times it had been Adele and she pondering over a similar thing. Although she was excited at the idea of actually going to the party as part of a couple there was also an air of finality in the fact that for the first time in years both Adele and she would be part of two different costume sets.

Jim felt like he was caught off guard by the question.

It had been years since he had even contemplated a Halloween costume and the last time he had worn one it had been a last minute effort and probably the worst looking ghost costume anyone had ever seen. There had really been no surprise when he wasn't even considered to be in the running for a prize although there was some protest over the eventual winner when it was revealed that his parents had been part of the organising committee for the party. It took a few days and a little bit of investigating before the implications of cheating died down and the winner of the gift vouchers was eventually acknowledged as really being the best costume of the night.

"What sort of things have you dressed up as before?" he smiled and silently allocated a pat on the back for himself for what he considered to be a fairly clever response.

The fact that he didn't know whether Sasha wanted to go as something scary or just in dress up had made him choose the cautious route rather than just plunging in with a random idea only for her to either like it or hate it. This way he knew he would be able to work from her suggestion and, in his mind they would eventually come up with something they both agreed on with the only challenge then being finding the right items.

Sasha felt her face meaning as the ideas that had been lingering in her mind flickered to the forefront before being sent back to their reserved spot in her thoughts.

"Well, a few years back I went to party with Dell and we both dressed as skeletons" she giggled as she recalled the skin tight all in one leotards they had both bought which had been decorated with paper bones on the back and front.

At the age of eleven the costumes seemed like the best thing ever but the more they thought back on them the less they had considered them with such high opinions.

"Then one year we went as two witches" she placed her hand over her mouth as she recalled the incident with the green face paints and how Adele still had a little of it in her hair the next day despite adamantly stating that she had showered three times.

"Did you ever see the Rocky Horror Picture Show?" Sasha felt her face light up as she heard Jim making the comment and the range of characters flashed through her imagination.

There was no denying that the show had a few great characters but the thought of Jim in a corset was the only thing that kept returning to her mind. She blushed as she tried not to make the suggestion almost relieved when the coffee and pastries arrived as if perfectly timed to distract her.

In her heart Sasha knew that with the big day quickly approaching there was a good chance they would have to use their imaginations a little in order to make their costumes but that appealed to her because she knew they could make them unique that way.

"Tell ya what, why don't we just see what is out there we can make our mind up that way" she smiled as she made the suggestion.

Jim sipped from his coffee cup, the pastry sitting next to him teasing his senses as he nodded in agreement.

Chapter Twenty-Four

First Night Jitters

Adele couldn't hide the grin on her face as she woke and saw Ciara was still peacefully snoozing next to her. It wasn't the first time she had woken in someone else's bed and not even the first time waking next to a girl but usually the girl next to her had been Sasha and there was more than just one pair of panties being worn between them. In a way it seemed funny that after everything they had enjoyed Ciara had insisted on putting something on before going to sleep but Adele knew she had done similar in the past.

This time it felt different, but not in the ways she had expected it to, this was a more relaxed different and a positive outlook on a relationship she hadn't really known she would want to be part of.

During their evening, after they got home from the bus things had started off in a similar way to her visits to Sasha with banter and giggles. Ciara had mentioned Maebh and pondered over how she was going to tell her best friend about the fact that she was now officially in a relationship which was, in a way, the moment when the realisation really hit Adele.

Ever since she had first agreed to a date with Ciara, a date that she still ranked as one of the top first dates of her life, Maebh hadn't even been mentioned. The fact that in the back of her mind Adele knew that Ciara had a best friend, one that she had met more than once so couldn't really deny knowing hadn't really crossed her mind. Now that Maebh had been mentioned the reality was that, just like she had been nervous about mentioning her new relationship to Sasha, Ciara – the person she now felt confident referring to as her girlfriend – had to go through the same with her best friend.

The difference was that, for Adele, this was her first time in a relationship with a girl whereas she felt sure Maebh was familiar with where Ciara's romantic interests lay. It hadn't occurred to Adele before but now Maebh had been mentioned she found herself wondering if there had been any romantic connection between Ciara and her – was Maebh actually an ex as well as a friend? Did that mean that she was going to become hostile toward them or, even worse – was Maebh going to become almost a third wheel? A romantic rival that Adele needed to watch out for if their relationship was going to continue.

For now, none of that mattered as there was a more important issue that Adele knew had to take priority and that was the fact that she needed to go to the bathroom and Ciara was in between her and the door preventing her getting out easily without disturbing her.

In the corner of the room in a heap where they had landed were her clothes, Adele blushed as she spotted them while pondering how properly she should be dressed before leaving the bedroom. She hadn't heard Ciara's parents but knew that they were aware of her staying over even if, just like when she had a boy stay over, her parents had been, in most cases unaware of him being in her room.

There had been one occasion, the fateful day when her parents had no way of denying the fact that she was probably no longer the sweet innocent girl they had bought up. Robbie had been the boy who had been not only seen leaving her room in an attempt to get to the bathroom but doing so while wearing boxers and a silk robe which was clearly not his. The awkward moment as he slipped past her father into the bathroom while she tried to close her bedroom door without being noticed had stuck in her mind since the day it had happened.

Now it was her turn to be the barely dressed stranger in the bedroom of the daughter of a household but Adele hadn't decided whether it was less awkward if she was caught by Ciara's mother or father while attempting to reach the bathroom.

Sliding the duvet off carefully herself she shuddered a little as her buttocks pressed against the cold bedroom wall before carefully manoeuvring out of the warmth of the bed. Adele glanced over at Ciara who seemed undisturbed by her movement as she pondered the idea of trying to climb over her sleeping partner without injuring herself.

On the corner of the bed she spotted what was unmistakeably Ciara's bra and felt a blush crossing her face as she recalled the fit of giggles she had suffered while trying to remove it from its owner.

In a sudden moment of realisation Adele felt like she could almost empathise with the fumbled attempts boys had made at removing her bra only for her to get impatient and help them with what she felt was a fairly easy task, something she did without thinking on a daily basis. Now that she had gone through the process of trying to remove one for someone else she could see how difficult the task could be to a non-wearer of the item. Thankfully Ciara had been patient with her and Adele had been relieved when she had finally found the clasp after a few moments of pondering over whether it was a front loading or sports bra and she was fumbling in the wrong location.

There had been a small rush of adrenalin gushing through her body as she say Ciara topless for the first time, one that Adele hadn't expected to feel. It wasn't as if she had never seen another woman topless, she had lost count of how many times she had sat nattering with Sasha with them both naked since she had first accepted naturism but with Ciara it felt like a different sensation, more sensual.

"This is my first time with a girl you know Ciara" Adele could recall biting her lip as she said the words while accepting that she really was inexperienced at what she was trying to do.

In a way Adele felt like the words meant nothing because even if she hadn't been in a relationship with a girl before she had been with boys but she still felt like the least experienced member of the relationship she was currently in.

Ciara grinned as she heard the words covering her breasts more out of instinct than anything else as she tried not to be making fun of what Adele had said. She could see there was a lot of sincerity in the statement even if the timing of it was terrible but she had to acknowledge the fact that it was the first time she had seen Adele showing anything that resembled vulnerability.

From the moment they had agreed to go on the first date Adele had always been confident, never showing signs of doubt or fears and yet here they were about to share a moment that Ciara had been anticipating but determined not to rush after less than a week of dating.

As much as she didn't like to admit it, in her mind she knew that it had been something Maebh had said, not directly but by text, that had spurred her into pushing their relationship forward. There had been a moment of internal sadness when she had seen the confirmation that she had been anticipating from the moment Maebh had started dating her latest boyfriend but in a way it had inspired her to mover her relationship forward as well.

"I'll be going to the party this weekend with Joel, he has found a couples costume for us, hope you don't mind"

There had been a smiley face at the end of the message which Ciara knew was intended as a friendly gesture to soften the blow of the announcement. It was something she had done in the past, placing a little smiley face at the end of a message to make it seem like a much more amicable message than it may seem to be. Now that Maebh had confirmed that she was going to the event with her new love interest it felt like the right time to take control of her own relationship.

Reaching down she took Adele's hand and carefully placed it against her own body tingling slightly as she felt the clammy fingers touching her skin.

"We don't have to rush this Dell, but you do know that as I am a girl too we probably both like a lot of the same things being done" she bit her lip as she spoke feeling her cheeks flush as she let go of Adele's hand pausing in anticipation to see what she did with it.

Adele smiled as she reached down picking her panties and a top from her pile of clothing content that despite her initial concerns their night had gone better than she could have ever expected. She glanced at the bed where Ciara seemed to still be sleeping as she made her way silently to the door and disappeared toward the bathroom.

Ciara lay motionless on her side, her back to Adele as she felt a light breeze wisp over her back confirming her suspicion that the duvet had been moved. At first she had contemplated the idea of letting Adele know she was awake but chose to pretend to still be sleeping in an effort to just watch and see what was going on.

She moved slightly to hide her lower face under the duvet to prevent the grin from forming as she watched through half closed eyes while Adele tried her best not to disturb her. It was clear from her actions that Adele was blissfully unaware that she had only been half asleep for a while.

Despite having done it before, there was always a little bit of uncertainty whenever she shared a bed with someone because she didn't know how they slept.

As a younger girl she had been to sleepovers, mainly with Maebh and had got used to the fact that she moved a lot when she was in bed and had a tendency to suck her thumb – a habit that she adamantly denied and grew out of. By the time they had started going to secondary school the thumb sucking was gone but there was a little snuffling sound Maebh made as she drifted into a deeper sleep sometimes which Ciara accepted was possibly connected to a dream cycle.

Adele was different in a lot of ways – the first of them was the fact that she didn't seem to mind sleeping naked, something that Ciara could see made sense in some ways but couldn't be completely comfortable with. It was quite a relief when she hadn't questioned the need to put panties back on before sleeping because Ciara knew there was no real reason except her own comfort. Unlike Maebh, Adele seemed to take a while to settle into sleep and turned a few times but the worst part had been when she had put her cold feet against the back of her legs. Thankfully there hadn't been any noticeable murmurs or mutterings but Ciara felt like she could handle random noise much more than fold feet.

Refusing to move from her position in the bed which was warming up again nicely now that Adele had laid the duvet back down she watched as Adele clambered over and stood for a moment in the middle of the bedroom. The sunlight through her curtains caught Adele's body highlighting her curves and silhouetting her curves in a pleasant manner as she stared through half closed eyes.

Without moving, Ciara watched as Adele slipped on some clothes but didn't fully dress which told her that she wasn't planning on slipping away without saying goodbye, something that she had been concerned might happen. In the past Ciara had heard of people experiencing their chosen partner disappearing quietly and had always hoped that it wouldn't ever happen to her but knew that she couldn't really do much to prevent it happening.

There was the option of making a fuss as a person was trying to leave unnoticed but, although she could understand how that resolved the leaving without saying anything she felt sure it wouldn't make the experience any easier. The fact that half of Adele's clothing was still in a pile at the foot of the bed suggested that she was planning to return to the bedroom even if it was only to finish dressing.

She waited, eyes still only half open, as the bedroom door opened and she watched Adele slip as quietly as she possible out of the room and into the corridor which Ciara knew would be much colder than her room was. Her parents had often commented on how warm her bedroom was with less than subtle hints about the heating but she had managed to tactically avoid the urge to respond which she felt sure would have led to a debate about her not paying the bills. In recent years she had offered to make a contribution but her mother had been quick to decline politely which Ciara knew gave her a good back-up argument if she ever did feel the need to respond to the comments on her personal tropical paradise.

Sitting up she slid her legs out of the bed and wriggled her toes as they slowly came back to life after hours of not having to actually do much except prop a duvet up. On her dresser was the phone that she was sure she had heard silently rattle during the night alerting her to yet more emails that she felt sure she wouldn't want to read.

The one thing that was pressing on her mind was the urge to let Maebh know that she was going to be arriving at the party as one half of a couple as well. She had been contemplating the best way to respond to the announcement of Joel being her best friends 'plus one' ever since receiving the message about it but hadn't been sure of what to say.

In a way she knew that a simple acknowledgement of the announcement was all that was really needed and yet part of her mind was telling her that the two letter response of 'OK' wasn't quite enough. She had received similar messages in the past as replies and always felt herself wondering what the context of the OK had been. It felt almost like a passive aggressive reply that could mean the sender was actually okay with whatever had been said or could mean that they weren't okay with it but didn't want to make a fuss over it either.

At the time that she had received the message Ciara knew that she fell into the latter of the two categories and the fact that she had half expected the announcement from the moment Joel had been officially announced as the new boyfriend in some ways made it even bitterer. She had never begrudged Maebh moving into a new relationship but this one felt kind of forced, as if it was a rush to see if she could find someone. In her heart she knew it was nothing of the kind but the fact that Joel seemed overly nice to the point where he was almost grovelling sometimes made him seem like a convenience rather than a proper boyfriend.

Slipping casually off the bed Ciara reached over to the phone glancing at the screen as if it was meant to inspire her as to how she should handle Maebh before reaching to the wardrobe door. She jumped slightly as she heard her bedroom door before smiling at Adele as she made her way back into the room.

"Hey" she grinned softly as Adele made her way over to the bed.

It felt like a formality to ask if she had slept well so Ciara decided not to bother as she peered through her neatly hung rail of clothing while wondering if Adele's wardrobe was as tidy as hers was.

In the past she hadn't really paid much attention to other people's wardrobes but usually the people she had been dating hadn't been as outgoing as Adele was.

Grinning at the fact that, for a change Ciara was at least for now the less dressed of the two of them Adele stepped up behind her placing her hands around her waist and snuggling against her neck.

"Hey to you too" She bounced her chin of Ciara's shoulder s she spoke pondering over whether they should be thinking of dressing or not as it was still fairly early.

Ciara felt her cheeks blush as her body shuddered slightly under the cold hands that were now wrapped around her body. A moment of silent reassurance flowed through her mind as she accepted the fact that any doubts she had been pondering over about how happy Adele was about their new relationship dissipated.

"So, um, I was thinking" she pawed her way through the range of tops as she spoke before turning carefully to face Adele

"Maybe we should go to this school party as a couple?" Ciara cringed as she hear herself making a clumsy attempt to make a statement sound like a question by changing the pitch of the last word.

It was something she knew she had commented on to Maebh countless times in the past and yet here she was doing it.

Standing upright Adele released her grip slightly while still holding Ciara in an attempt to keep her in the state of undress she was in for as long as possible.

A million thoughts passed through her head as she tried not to seem too shocked or overwhelmed by the idea of them turning up at a school event clearly as a couple.

Over the years she knew that she had gone to events with Sasha and sometimes their costumes, or outfits if it wasn't a fancy dress party, had seemed vaguely linked but not so much that anyone could say they were a couple.

If she went to the Halloween party with Ciara there would be no way of hiding that they were more than just good friends and that both scared and excited her at the same time.

She glanced into Ciara's eyes noting that there was a nervous anticipation as she waited for a response to her comment. In her heart she knew there was only one answer that was acceptable and she knew that she was happy to give the answer that was being expected but she hadn't really thought about how or when they would make their relationship known to others at their school.

Making the announcement to Sasha had been easy, she shared everything with her and had done for more years than she cared to think about but she couldn't recall ever seeing a single sex couple at a party before.

"I'd like that – do you know many scary female couple costume ideas?" Adele smiled and watched Ciara's eyes light up at the reply.

The nervous tension between them seemed to melt away as Adele felt her own nerves intensify while trying not to show her concerns and yet she knew that she was happy with her commitment to be part of a couple with Ciara. It occurred to her that, in a way, making it known that she was in a relationship with another girl wasn't really much different to letting the school know she was dating a boy. Part of her mind kept reminding her that there were much worse things she could be admitting to than her new relationship.

Ciara beamed as she reached across kissing Adele

In the corner of her eye she could see the phone she had been avoiding using but now she wanted to let Maebh know that she was going as part of a couple as well. In the past she had gone to Halloween parties with Maebh both of them dressed up as witches, and she knew that she still had some of the accessories but it felt almost like cheating if they went in the same costume idea she had used with her best friend.

"I'll get dressed and we can go shopping for costumes, how does that sound? Ciara bit her lip as she shuffled carefully out of Adele's grip

Adele moved back toward the bed, glancing over at her crumpled pile of clothes as Ciara pulled a top out of her wardrobe.

"Sounds like a plan to me" she nodded as she spoke before reaching lazily over to her clothing and bundling it on to the bed so she could get ready to go out.

Chapter Twenty-Five

At your convenience

It didn't take long for Sasha to sense a kind of tension in the air as she made her way downstairs for breakfast. During the evening things seemed to have settled down after the incident that only Jim and she knew had never actually happened but neither of them were willing to dispute the assumption given the relatively positive outcome.

Unlike most Friday mornings her father had taken the day off due to having a long weekend to look forward to meaning that the usual shuffle of light noises outside of her room had been later giving her a lay in.

She glanced briefly in the direction of Jim's room, noting that the door was still shut suggesting that he hadn't emerged yet before making her way toward the table, lured over by the smell of rashers cooking. Propped up against the salt and pepper was an envelope which had been marked with her name the contents of which she was already sure she knew.

Over the years there had been a few times when little packages like this had been left in the middle of the table for her, mostly on her birthday or the weekend closest to it but this wasn't anywhere near her birthday and she was sure there was no special occasion lingering round the corner. This must be something to do with the hotel that her parents had booked her, she buzzed with excitement at the first sign that it really was booked and not just a gesture to see how she reacted.

In the past she had heard of people from school who had been lured into giving away information by promises that had been made. On the occasions when it worked it was usually due to there being suspicion of activity that needed to be confirmed by the persons parents – not unlike the situation she was in.

During the evening she had made a few vague attempts to get more details from her parents about the hotel they had booked for Jim and her without directly asking the question to prevent causing any awkwardness.

Her first attempt had been the one she was most proud of, which had been when she had referred to making sure they had all of their costume bits packed while talking in a louder than needed voice to Jim. He had been quick to catch on to what she was trying to do and played along briefly before they both quickly accepted that her parents were too busy pretending to ignore their conversation to say anything.

Now the envelope with all the answers to her questions was sat in front of her taunting her so close she could reach over and open it and yet it felt like she should wait firstly for Jim and secondly for permission to be given.

In some ways, despite the fact that she was confident that she knew what was in the envelope the fact that it had been left on the table for her to see rather than being given to her directly gave it a similar stigma to texting while eating.

Sasha bit her lip as she sat down before smiling casually at her father who was glancing through the local free paper while the smell of cooked food and coffee drifted in through the kitchen door. Unlike texting, reading the paper was seen as an acceptable activity at the table as long as the reader washed their hands before actually eating. This had been an unwritten allowance for longer than Sasha could remember and sometimes, the paper had become the source of something interesting to talk about which had been sufficient to maintain its status as an acceptable breakfast activity.

Hearing the creaking of a door Sasha glanced to see Jim appearing, surprisingly he was not only fully dressed but also looked like he had used the bathroom from the tidy appearance of his hair which surprised her.

Mary had got up early, not because she had to but because she had been restless over night and the sight of daylight through the curtains had been enough inspiration to tell her there wasn't much point in trying to sleep any more.

From the moment they had agreed to book a hotel room for Sasha to spend some time privately with Jim she had felt something inside her mind almost dying slightly.

One of the advantages of them going on holiday every year to a naturist complex had been the pleasure of quite literally watching Sasha grow and develop into the young woman she now was but that came with an extra curse. From the time she had reached 14 both Diarmuid and shew had accepted that their sweet girl was growing up and boyfriends as well as the likelihood of the heartbreak that relationships bought with it were not far around the corner.

It caught her in the throat slightly when she had first accepted the idea if Sasha actively seeking her first real relationship. In the back of her mind she could still remember a 3-year-old Sasha holding hands with one of the boys in the neighbourhood and adamantly saying they were going to get married. The boy and his family had moved away before starting school but that didn't take away from the moment of sweet innocence that had stayed in her mind ever since it had happened.

Jim had been a different story and both Diarmuid and Mary had been nervously awaiting the day a real boyfriend was introduced to them. The fact that they had met at the complex had bought with it both advantages and disadvantages – the biggest one of both of them being the fact that it was potentially a holiday romance.

As a teenager Mary could recall holiday romances that she had enjoyed, all of them only ever lasting the duration of the holiday meaning that there was always a sadness when it came to an end but they also had another distinct characteristic and it was that which had become the bigger concern – the fact that a holiday romance was almost like a fast track relationship.

Things always seemed to progress a lot quicker with someone you met on a holiday, Diarmuid had made a comment about having seen Sasha going to Jim's apartment while they were on holiday but as it had been during the day and not a long visit neither of them had really worried about it. Now that they had agreed to giving them a bit of time to themselves both Diarmuid and Mary knew they were basically acknowledging the fact that Sasha was a long way from the innocent girl who was determined to marry at 3 years old.

"Morning Jim" Mary smiled as she spotted him entering the room before gesturing for him to take a seat while she finished up the cooking.

It didn't take long for Sasha to realise that despite his presence at the table Jim was actually in auto-pilot mode, something she had seen before but knew she couldn't comment on for fear of giving more away than she wanted to.

Despite her best efforts to discretely direct his vision to ward the envelope that had been eating away at her ever since she spotted it, Jim seemed oblivious to its presence. Sasha bit her lip as she pondered over whether flashing her breasts in his direction may spark his attention before deciding that she already knew the answer and doing so would spark more than just his attention

In a way it was almost a relief when her mother arrived with the coffee pot placing it in front of the condiments making the envelope less obvious and harder to get at which Sasha decided had been a very clever and purposeful move.

"Are you looking forward to the party tonight?" Sasha glanced over as she heard her mother posing the question.

Jim glanced up, his top lip still touching the warm cup of coffee he had just poured himself as he noted that the question had clearly been directed at him.

The trip into town for Halloween costume ideas had been a little bit of a surprise for him due to the range that was available but also the fact that some shops seemed to be crossing Halloween goods over with Christmas stuff. In his mind it was almost as if both dates were fighting for priority with one of the much closer than the other. In a way he had been relieved when the idea he had suggested of the Rocky Horror Picture show had quickly become less than practical for more reasons than he wanted to imagine.

Fake blood and scars littered the shelves all of them seemed like they could make great effects for a person who had time and energy to go through the process of applying them properly. Sasha had seemed vaguely interested in a few of them and had picked up some that she seemed confident that she could get creative with.

In the back of his mind Jim could recall the body painting session at the complex and how she had worked hard on his design, a skill that he felt sure she could put into effect with Halloween make-up.

As a child he could recall a few Halloween costumes, most of them had been fairly traditional but also bought as one costume whereas he had accepted fairly quickly that Sasha had intentions to make something. The first shop they had gone to had been a fancy dress costume shop which Sasha seemed to be familiar with but it didn't take her long to decide they weren't going to get much there unless they had a lot more money available.

By the time they had started making their way home Jim still hadn't been sure what they were going to go dressed as but he felt confident it was going to look great based on all the little accessories Sasha had managed to find.

"I haven't been to a Halloween party in years so, yes it will be fun" he smiled as he resumed drinking the coffee that had teased his lips before the question.

Mary turned to Diarmuid as she made a subtle gesture which he snorted a non-verbal response to before leaning over the table and carefully picking the envelope that Sasha had been keeping an eye on.

Sasha paused for a moment as she saw her father picking the envelope up, her heart jumping at the idea that something had made them reconsider their offer. In a fleeting moment she ran through everything that had been said and done since the offer had been made, there was nothing she could think of that might have caused it to be retracted.

"I'm sure you are keen to know about this envelope Sasha" Diarmuid grinned as he spoke you have barely stopped glaring at it since you sat down" he paused

Sasha felt her cheeks flush as she heard the comment

"As you know we have booked for you to stay in a hotel" he continued his unrehearsed speech "and you would be right to think that the details are in here" he smiled as he placed the envelope back in its spot on the table

Jim paused as he heard the comment, slightly bemused, and angry at himself for not noticing the envelope as he sat down. Then again, as he wasn't at home, he knew that the chances of there being anything out of the ordinary waiting for him were remote so accepted that he probably hadn't even thought to look for anything. Now that the conversation had turned to their pending hotel booking he silently acknowledged that her father had his full and undivided attention.

"Before you open it there is something we want you to know"

Diarmuid allowed a pause as he finished his comment which he knew was mainly for dramatic effect

The reality of the situation that he was trying to talk his way around was one that neither he nor Mary had anticipated at the time when they had made the announcement to Sasha that they were going to give her a night in a hotel. Apart from the fact it was the Halloween weekend it was also a holiday weekend which had made booking hotels tricky.

At first they had contemplated retracting their offer but neither of them really wanted to do that despite the fact that it had only been made in an effort to avoid facing what they already suspected had occurred between Jim and Sasha.

Mary had been going through options of the best way they could let Sasha down after having made such an unusual offer to her when she had spotted an offer in the same local paper that

Diarmuid had been pretending to read at the table. Something that Mary didn't approve of him doing but hadn't even stopped and now the paper had given them the answer to their problem.

Out of the three hotels that they had considered as reasonably close to both their home and the location of the party it had seemed almost like a sign that the nearest one of them had a special offer on but it was only available for a two night stay. Mary pointed the offer out to Diarmuid who hadn't wasted any time in placing the booking but now he was left with the task of making it seem like it had been their idea to do it and not an act of convenience as it really was.

"As Jim is going home on Sunday, we have decided to give you two nights away" Diarmuid smiled calmly as he gestured toward the envelope in a silent manner allowing Sasha to open it.

Sasha could feel her body buzzing with excitement as she reached across the table while trying to remain calm but still comprehending the information that had just been passed to her. She had been looking forward to having time with Jim with no parents to watch for and now they had two nights together but as a bitter twist, after that she had to watch him leave.

Carefully she peeled the envelope open and pulled out the neatly folded sheet of paper finally able to see the answer to her question of where they would be staying. Her cheeks flushed as she spotted that, unlike their first night together in Ireland, this time her parents had booked them a double-bedded room.

She could vaguely picture the hotel as she folded the reservation details and placed them carefully back in the envelope before glancing across the table at Jim who seemed almost shocked by the announcement. Placing the envelope back on the table she turned, first to he mother then to her father before jumping from her chair and shuffling between both of them and giving them a thankful hug of appreciation.

"C'mon Jim, we best pack for our weekend" Sasha smiled as she glanced over at Jim

Suddenly the realisation hit Jim as he heard the words.

From the moment he had boarded the plane to make his way over to Ireland he had been pondering over what was going to happen on his last day. At the time the thought seemed almost morbid and definitely like he was wishing his time away which he didn't want to do but he knew it was a reality he had to prepare for.

In his mind there were a few scenarios which he could picture happening with one of them more likely than the rest – an awkward but amicable goodbye between him and Sasha's parents before making his way back to the airport. While he knew that one way or another he would feel obliged to thank them for their hospitality the fact that his last two nights were going to be in a hotel seemed to be bringing the moment closer than he had expected.

Leaning over he grabbed the coffee cup that he had been sipping from throughout the unexpected announcement from Sasha's father and pressed it to his lips acknowledging that the coffee was now cold but it seemed only polite to drink it anyway.

"Oh, by the way Jim" Jim swallowed the mouthful of coffee he had just taken as he heard his name mentioned by Sasha's father

Part of his mind wanted to refer to the fact that the timing on his name being used couldn't have been a lot worse but he felt sure that such a comment could come over as hostile rather than light hearted so held back as he turned to face Diarmuid.

"You won't need to take your large bag with you as we are going to take you to the airport on Sunday" Diarmuid rested his chin on his hands as he finished his second announcement of the day, content that he had now ticked all of the boxes that were expected of him.

He glanced over at Mary whose soft smile confirmed that he had done a good job

Jim felt his jaw drop as he heard the offer and cupped his hand under his chin to prevent any dribble from the coffee which he felt sure he had swallowed but didn't want to make any unnecessary mess.

When he had arrived, he had taken Sasha's advice and bought a return ticket, the second part of which was safely tucked into his main luggage bag along with his passport but there was no way he was going to turn down such an offer.

"Thank you, Mr O'Callaghan," Jim smiled before finishing his coffee and excusing himself from the table to pack for his weekend away.

Diarmuid sat in silence as Jim and Sasha left the table

The sound of his name being given with his full title caught him off guard at first as it was usually only his boss that called him that and only then if he was in trouble. Part of his mind wanted to tell Jim that first names were fine but it seemed like something that could be bought up another time as it was clear that both Sasha and Jim were now too preoccupied with preparing for their weekend to worry over small formalities.

In some ways it was nice to hear Jim being so formal but he was sure that they had discussed name formalities when they had first met him in Greece. For now he would just take the comment in the tone it had been intended and rest on the laurels of what seemed like a positive achievement.

Jim stood over his bed separating out the things he should take to the hotel from those he felt like he could leave behind while also acknowledging in his mind the fact that when he did return to the house he would only be repacking again. In some ways it seemed pointless leaving some of his clothes behind for a weekend in a hotel but in his mind he had come up with a plan to make their weekend easier. Stacking his un-needed items in a neat pile he left the room and made his way to the foot of the stairs.

"Sash, why don't we just put all or stuff in one case make it easier than trying to carry two" He glanced over catching the eye of Sasha's father as he spoke.

Diarmuid pretended to be busy as he spotted Jim leaving his room and making his way to the stairs and felt happy he had done as he heard the practical suggestion being made. He knew in his heart that there was no way he could ever assess Sasha's taste in men but he knew without doubt that it was little things like that which she would find attractive. He had been trying not to judge Jim from the moment he had met him but it hadn't been easy with him being announced as a boyfriend, but now he felt sure she had found a good one.

Sasha felt her ears prick up as she heard Jim's voice carrying up the stairs and bit her lip as she heard his suggestion. She didn't like to admit it but the only bag she had that wasn't suitable for a long holiday was her school bag and the more she had glanced over the array of items she planned to take the more she was realising they weren't going to fit in that. It was mainly the Halloween accessories causing her problems but now they had gone to the effort of buying everything they wanted it felt wrong not to pack it all.

Skipping from her room she made her way to the top of the stairs and smiled as she saw Jim waiting at the bottom patiently for her reply

"You mean, like a real couple Jim" she winked down at him as she spoke

Jim glared up as he hear Sasha's reply and saw the cheeky expression on her face, there was nothing he needed to do but smile and nod in reply

Chapter Twenty-Six

Party Time

As they made their way toward the hall where she could already hear the dull thud of what she was sure was Halloween themed disco music Sasha had to acknowledge that finding a couples Halloween costume had been harder than she had expected. In her mind she knew that if she had been willing to break from what she considered to be real Halloween costumes then the choices were wide open but to her it had to be something scary. The fact that the costume shop in town had offered a reasonable selection but been overpriced had, in her opinion worked in their favour as it had given her inspiration which had cost nothing.

For a short time, she had considered Jim's suggestion of something from the Rocky Horror show but the moment she had spotted black robes her mind had gone in a different direction and she was proud of the creations Jim and she had come up with. Thankfully the mess that their makeup had caused in the bathroom of their hotel room was minimal and easy to clean before they left but the receptionist had given them an unusual look at they walked out of the front door.

In a way Sasha knew that the pairing of an Angel of Death as she had decided to refer to her design wasn't one that was usually seen with the grim reaper but as they made their way down the street she became more confident that their costumes worked well together.

From the moment Jim had been confirmed as visiting her for the week she had known that she wanted to take him to the party. There was always a competition for the best individual and couple which she didn't usually bother entering but this year she had to admit to being tempted.

As soon as she had mentioned Jims visit to Adele it had been clear that her best friend had realised that unlike previous years they wouldn't be going together in the same way as the y had before. In many ways Sasha was relieved when Adele had made the announcement of being in a relationship because it seemed to relieve the concern she had over how to handle the party arrangements with her. On one hand Sasha knew that she wanted to go with Jim but on the other she also didn't want Adele to feel left out or like a spare part in their plans so the fact that Adele had someone to go with had made it easier to handle.

This year was the first time that she hadn't planned her costume with Adele which Sasha knew had the potential to cause concerns over them both choosing similar ideas. In her heart Sasha knew that there was still a chance that she may end up clashing with Adele but the fact that their costume was so unique made it less likely in her opinion.

During the first half a term that they had shared at School, Sasha knew that she had mentioned Jim a few times, mostly in conversation with Adel e who thankfully didn't seem to have got bored with her mentioning this mystery boy. Although Sasha knew that the conversations with Adele had been intended as private she also knew that her status as no longer single had become known to a lot of other people within her school year, some of them through her and others through the lines of gossip that she knew frequently spread.

Sasha could feel butterflies in her stomach as she made her way to the door into the hall gripping Jims hand in a way that she knew was probably more aggressively than it was intended to be. She glanced down at their interlocked fingers before acknowledging in her head that the white makeup they both had over their hands to give them the dead look would hide any redness caused by her grip.

In its own way, this was a big moment and one that she hadn't really discussed much with Jim but felt sure he was aware of all the same. Inside the hall there were going to be a lot of people who had heard about this mystery boyfriend, most of whom probably didn't care about whether he was real or not but she knew there would be a few who were suspending their disbelief until they had evidence one way or another of him being a real person or made up.

Sasha knew that anyone who was still curious and hadn't seen them together would finally have proof that he was real as soon as they saw them together and, as much as she didn't care about the opinions of people she barely spoke to, she had to admit there was some pleasure in proving anyone doubting Jim's existence wrong.

Gripping Jims hand in a slightly looser way now that she was aware that she may have been cutting off circulation as they made their way to the door Sasha smiled as Mr Scott who was on unofficial doorman duties took their tickets. Just as he had been every year, Mr Scott had made half an attempt at a costume with a cloak that had an oversize hard collar that comfortably covered the back of his neck and his hair awkwardly gelled in an effort to give him what Sasha knew was referred to as a widows peak.

His face seemed almost illuminated by the exit light above his head reflecting off the white face paint which wasn't dissimilar to the one Jim and she were wearing. A single trickle of fake blood cascaded from one side of his mouth completing what she knew was intended to be his version of Dracula.

The first year she had seen his costume she had been impressed with it but over the years she had got so used to it that she couldn't see anything scary in his attempt. She had to admit that, although it wasn't scary she had to give him some credit for making an effort which was more than some teachers did.

"Miss O'Callaghan, Welcome" Mr Scott raised his arms as he spoke forcing his cape to flutter behind him while intentionally changing the W to a V in an effort to change his accent as he greeted them.

"And this must be your plus one" he directed his glance at Jim as he spoke offering an amicable handshake.

Jim couldn't help the smirk that crossed his face as he heard the polite comment s he contemplated the idea of being considered a plus one. He had heard the phrase used before but only in what he considered formal settings but never given any consideration to the fact that he was now a plus one.

In some ways the accent of the man who was clearly a teacher from the fact that he had known and referred to Sasha by her full name, the same way he had referred to her parents but something that he was aware that Sasha didn't like hearing being used. Just like when he heard his full name given. Sasha had made it clear that there were only a few times when she went by her full name – when she was at school, if she was at a job where it had to be used or if the person referring to her intended to reprimand her for something.

As far as Jim knew it was unlikely that Sasha was being told off for anything unless it was something she had done in the past and this man still hadn't discussed it with her. Jim knew that there was a possibility that Sasha worked for this man, she had referred to having had a job but hadn't given him many details about it but as this wasn't her place of work it seemed logical that he must know her from school.

It was both disorientating and comforting at the same time to hear what sounded like an English accent seeping through a heavily made up accent but he knew that it may actually be an English accent to choose not to say anything about it.

"Yes sir" he smiled as he tried to remain politely formal as he took the man's hand shaking it firmly "I'm Jim" he continued before releasing his grip, unsure if he had been too heavy with his handshake or not.

In the past he had been caught out with handshakes and knew that they were a difficult thing to master despite how easy they looked. One of his teachers had given him some tips on how to give a good handshake and he had been proud to try them out when he went for his college interview. Everything had seemed to go well until the end of the interview when he had stood to shake the hand of the woman who was discussing course with him and he had gripped her hand tighter than he had intended to.

The wince of pain had been clear in her eyes as she gritted her teeth and smiled before pulling away from the gesture and hiding her hand behind her back which Jim felt sure was to prevent him seeing any redness he had unintentionally caused her. For the next week he had been sure that his overpowering handshake was going to be the reason he didn't get on to the course and hadn't worked out how he was going to break the news to his parents when the rejection arrived. Thankfully he had been worrying over nothing when the letter finally arrived offering him a space on the course he had been attending since September.

Sasha led the way through the door smiling at Mr Scott as she pushed her way carefully through a thin wispy curtain that she was sure was meant to resemble cobwebs as they made their way into the hall. The dull beat of drums vibrated through the floor from the DJ booth on the far side of the room as she scanned around spotting Adele with Ciara on the far side of the room.

Burning with curiosity Jim made his way over toward the buffet pulling lightly on Sasha's hand distracting her from her intended path toward her friends. He had been sure to only have a light meal at the hotel based on the fact that Sasha had assured him that there would be food at the party.

Glancing his way across the nearly laid out spread of food, most of which was still covered with see through protective lids to prevent spillage he nodded as he spotted the usual array of seasonal joke names in among the dishes. He could still recall the first time he had been to a proper Halloween party as a child how the names of some of the dishes had made him cautious and in some cases even stopped him from trying them just in case they weren't what they looked like and actually were what the label said.

"C'mon Jim we will eat later" Sasha smiled as she spoke before ushering him away from the food and over to the corner where Adele and Ciara were stood talking.

Jim smiled and waved at them both amicably as they arrived while acknowledging the clever way they had dressed as the famous twins he had seen clips of but never watched from the Shining. They had the look almost perfect and the sign Ciara had created with the simple phrase "Want to play?" made it a great costume and one that suited them as a couple.

Sasha smiled as she reached over, awkwardly hugging Adele while aware of the fact that her costume having wings made it difficult to get close to her. Jim had already discovered the downside of them on the way down from their room at the hotel when she had almost crushed them by making an attempt to lean against the elevator wall. It had been in that moment she had accepted that anything she wanted to do while in costume had to be done with care or run the risk of ruining the look she had been so proud of arranging in such a short time.

From the moment she had seen Adele in a relationship Sasha had been caught in a mixture of happy and passively concerned for her. She had no doubt that Adele was happy and Ciara seemed like she knew what she was doing even if she didn't necessarily understand the lifestyle interests that her new girlfriend had. The biggest concern that Sasha had was in how or whether their relationship was going to remain strong by the time they returned to school which she knew was only a few days away.

There was no doubt in her mind that Adele would be able to handle anyone who wasn't comfortable with single gender relationships and, from what she had seen of Ciara, Sasha felt sure that she was just as capable. Over the course of the last couple of years Sasha had seen a few people who were either clearly or potentially in single gender relationships and knew that they had not always had an easy time from other students. The fact that Ciara and Adele were at the party in clearly matching costumes was one thing but the big test to their relationship was, in Sasha's mind, still to come.

"Maebh is over there" Ciara smiled gripping Adele's hand lightly as she spoke

In the corner of the room on the couch that Sasha was sure hadn't moved since the pre term party she spotted two costumed figures who, at first glance, looked like they were rehearsing an intimate scene from a TV show. She grinned as she recalled the awkward moments Jim and she had shared while getting used to how each other preferred to do couple type things while also acknowledging the cute aspect of their actions.

"It looks like she's a little busy, I'm sure we will catch up with her later" she winked at Jim as she spoke.

With almost perfect timing, as the DJ started playing the Time Warp almost out of nowhere, Fintan strutted his way on to the dance floor with a girl that seemed like she was happy to be seen with him.

Sasha spluttered as she saw them making their way into a space where there was no way of avoiding their presence while trying hard to restrain the urge to laugh at what she was witnessing.

His walk seemed too well rehearsed as he made his way on to the floor in what looked like stiletto heels, a thick black wig covering his usual fiery ginger locks and face makeup that she felt sure would make most women envious. The girl with him who seemed to be struggling more than he was with her high heels wearing a black dress with a small white apron that made her look like she was a badly dressed member of a housekeeping team. Her hair intentionally scruffy as they tried to perform the dance that had been made famous by the characters from the movie they were clearly trying to imitate.

"Bet you are glad we couldn't find the items to dress up from the Rocky Horror now aren't you Jim?" she nudged him gently as she spoke before biting her lip as she watched a crowd forming around Fintan and his girlfriend.

In a way seeing him with a girlfriend came as a relief to Sasha as she felt sure that between that and his accidental introduction to Jim she would hopefully be free from his endless persistent hints at her about dating him. The fact that the girl with him didn't seem to have an overly familiar face was both reassuring and concerning at the same time.

Many times over the years since he had first started attempting to get her on a date Sasha had heard stories of the trail of broken hearts he had left behind and yet somehow that hadn't stopped girls wanting to date him. In her head Sasha knew that it was possible that this one he was with may look different when she wasn't in fancy dress but the fact that she had managed to recognise him under his makeup told Sasha that if this girl went to their school she would probably still be able to recognise the face.

The possibility that his mystery girl was possibly from a different school meant that he would still be able to flirt when they were back at school if he chose to, safe in the belief that his girlfriend wouldn't find out about it. Sasha had seen him do similar things before with different degrees of success depending on how well the girl he was meant to be dating was known to others in their year.

On the positive side, the fact that he was at the party with someone meant that at least for the duration of the party it was less likely that he would try anything – especially with the amount of teachers around the room.

For now, Sasha decided she was going to take the positive and enjoy the moment whilst trying not to imagine how awkward it would have been if Jim and she had gone with Rocky Horror costumes. Even if theirs had been different characters Sasha felt certain that Fintan would have made a connection and used it as a reason to speak to her, something he couldn't really use as an excuse this time.

During their shopping trip, Jim had spotted a costume in the fancy dress shop in town that was intended to look like the character "Riff Raff" from the show which had been tempting until he saw the price and decided against it. Sasha could still recall the awkward moment during the previous party when she had realised, much to her horror, that her costume had been linked to the one Fintan had been wearing which she knew had ended comically thanks to Adele but at least this time she had dodged that bullet.

Jim felt a shudder pass down his spine at the sight of a boy in drag despite knowing that the costume was almost accurate to the character that was being portrayed. He glanced sideways at Sasha whom he could see was taking great pleasure from watching a boy she clearly knew strut around on heels. In his mind he had to accept that if he had pushed for them to go with his theme idea the costume he was now cringing over was a realistic option that he could have considered wearing. Seeing it on someone else was enough to make him relieved that the costume he had seen had been over priced.

"Their characters aren't even a couple in the movie" he snorted as he made his comment noting the wry grin appearing on Sasha's face as his observation sank in.

In the few moments after she had first seen Fintan and the mystery girlfriend it hadn't occurred to her that there was such an obvious anomaly in the costumes they had chosen. Now that Jim had made it known to her she couldn't help wondering whether the girl he was dancing with was actually his girlfriend or another girl who had coincidentally been at the party in a costume from the show – just like her costume had been linked to his in the pre-school disco.

For a few moments the stark reality hit her that, despite the fact that they seemed overly familiar with each other there was a chance that Fintan was still single and consequently still a threat to her sanity. She watched as he lifted the girl he was with into the air before spinning her round and letting her slide down to her feet again, the dress she was wearing rising as she slid to the floor making her choice of panties obvious to the assembled crowd. If this wasn't his official girlfriend Sasha felt sure that she was clearly comfortable with him and hopefully that meant she was free of him at least for a while.

"C'mon let's show them what a real couple dances like" Sasha smiled as a slower song played while dragging Jim toward the dance floor.

Chapter Twenty-Seven

The last day

From the moment they had left the party Sasha had decided which she had decided not to tell Jim about and that was her intention to make the most of their time away from her family in more ways than one. Jim had already made it clear that he had one intention which she was happy to indulge however there were other items on her personal agenda which she felt sure he would be happy to participate in, one of those being her decision to make their room a clothing free zone.

Ever since returning from Zante she had been seeking opportunities to explore the naturist side of her life and now they were in a safe environment it seemed like a waste not to at least enjoy some nude time with the man she loved.

Sasha could still clearly recall how cautious Jim had been about naturism when they had first met as well as the disastrous accident that had literally blemished his first experience on public nudity in more ways than one. She had seen such a difference in his comfort with naturism over the remainder of their holiday and that had become obvious to her again on their trip to the beach which she had been pleased to see this time she was determined to take control of the situation but make it fun at the same time.

The adrenalin of the party had led to a fun night when they got back to their room and Sasha smiled as she flopped out of the bed spotting the crumpled heap of Halloween costumes and accessories that were still laying around the floor in the place they had fallen. It had taken a passing glance in the mirror which spanned the width of the dresser to confirm that no matter how excited they both were there was one thing they both had to deal with before either of them got into the bed – their makeup.

In her head Sasha had a fond memory of their body painting day at the complex and how difficult it had been both making the decision to wash the paint off and then actually trying to wash it off. Part of her memory of the day seemed almost surreal but she felt sure that they had both used the shower more than once in an effort to remove the paint but even their best attempts hadn't been completely successful. Her recollection was that despite their best efforts the bed sheets the following morning still seemed to resemble an artwork that Jackson Pollock would be proud of and sell for a small fortune.

"We should probably do something about our makeup" Sasha could remember breaking the momentum slightly as she made the comment and the awkward pause that had resulted before Jim nodded and shuffled into the bathroom.

In a half-dressed condition Sasha could still recall glaring in the mirror that had provided the warning and smiling as she spotted a trickle of black face paint that had made its way down her cheek at some point during the evening. She knew in her heart that there was no way of actually confirming when it had broken loose but, in many ways, she hoped it had been during the party because it really made her initial efforts look even more scary which she was quite proud of.

As she pottered her way around their room gathering parts of both of their costumes Sasha paused while passing by the window acknowledging the fact that she hadn't opened the curtains yet. She looked over at the bed where Jim was still snoozing as she pondered over whether to open the curtains once he woke or leave them shut.

If she was at home she knew that someone in her street would make a comment to one of her parents about the closed curtains, either directly or sooner or later the lack of light entering her room would eventually get back to them. It still made her shudder when she recalled the first time she had been spotted sitting in the window before having got dressed and how she still hadn't been able to confirm who it was that had spotted her.

Due to the fact that they were in a hotel Sasha knew that they had a little bit more anonymity because there was no way anyone except for the hotel staff and Jim who could identify their window. Sasha could see a few advantages to keeping the curtains closed especially if she wanted to carry out her intention to remain clothing free but then again she knew that even if she did open the curtains she would be extremely unlucky to be both spotted and identified by anyone who knew her who happened to pass by,

Given the fact that, for now, Jim was still sleeping Sasha decided to leave the curtains as they were, the longer he remained asleep the better as it gave her more time to prepare her secret plan to prevent dressing being an option.

From the moment she had woken Sasha had been determined to make the most of their privacy especially with it being the last full day of Jim's visit which filled her mind with mixed emotions. She wanted the day to be one that they could both enjoy but that didn't take away from the sad reality that he was soon due to be heading back to the airport with no known time frame for them to meet again. Unlike the day that she had left the complex to head home from Zakynthos this time she at least felt confident that they were going to meet again and next time she wanted it to be her travelling to see him.

In the same way as this visit being Jim's first time in Ireland, Sasha knew that if it hadn't been for having met him she wouldn't have even given the idea of visiting England a second thought but now she had a reason to want to go there. Throughout his visit Jim had made a few comments about how much smaller things seemed to be in Ireland and how much friendlier which had given her a sense of pride however his reference to the size of places made the idea of going to England less appealing.

Ever since she had been a little girl, Dublin had been a daunting place to visit and bigger than anywhere she had been before even in her holidays and yet Jim was adamant that the town he lived in was even bigger.

There had been talk in the year leading up to her Junior Cert at school of a group trip to London being organised by the teachers as part of their push toward showing cultural diversity but that hadn't happened. When the announcement had been made that the trip wasn't going ahead it had been met with mixed responses from the classes that were due to go but as the year progressed focus had been moved back to the much more important issue of their pending exams.

Sasha smiled as she recalled the fun they had enjoyed during the party while carefully zipping the case shut with all of their belongings piled inside them before dragging the bag into the wardrobe to hide it.

The way she had dragged Jim to the dance floor only to realise that it was their first dance together as a couple stood out in her mind but only because of what had motivated her to wanting to dance in the first place. She recalled how there had been a moment of awkwardness as they swayed together before finally seeming to synchronise their motion with each other.

As she had lay her head on his shoulder feeling the warmth of his body through the costume she had found herself glancing at those around them. Ciara and Adele had joined them on the floor and seemed very comfortable with each other and, in the corner of her eye Sasha felt sure she could see Maebh and the boyfriend who she silently acknowledged they should try to introduce themselves to before the end of the party.

In a sudden moment it occurred to Sasha that shew hadn't really seen Maebh since their day at the fayre although they had exchanged amicable glances to each other as they passed each other on their way to their classes. Every time she had seen Maebh there had been one thing that seemed almost inevitable, just like Adele and she, Maebh and Ciara seemed almost inseparable which made her wonder how Ciara had somehow become part of her group of friends and seemingly left Maebh behind.

Despite the fact that she couldn't see him, Sasha felt sure that Fintan and the girl he had made a scene with were somewhere close-by. She smiled as she melted into Jim's arms safe in the knowledge that even if Fintan and the girl he had been seen with weren't an actual couple they weren't going to spoil the evening for Jim and her.

It was in that moment, as she gripped Jim's shoulder that she realised that no matter what Fintan tried, there was no way he could now deny the existence of the boyfriend she had been trying to enforce on him for the last few weeks. For the first time since he had started making his attempts to get her on a date she had someone who she felt safe with, someone she could use as a kind of kryptonite to keep his advances at bay.

They stood swaying gently together to the music oblivious to anyone else around them until the DJ upped the tempo again breaking the calm aura that had surrounded them.

Feeling slightly put out by the change in tempo that seemed to coincide with Jim and her only just getting used to the concept of dancing together Sasha took Jim's hand and made her way carefully through the oncoming flock of people who clearly preferred the upbeat music as she fought her way toward the buffet table.

"Sasha isn't it?" she turned as she heard the voice and smiled as she saw the figure coming toward them was unmistakeable as Maebh.

Now she was closer to them it was clear to see that unlike the face pain they had opted for Maebh and the boy who she was quite clearly with had chosen the more practical approach of latex masks that were now propped on top of their heads allowing them to see properly. Sasha could recall having seen masks similar to those which Maebh and her boyfriend were wearing but choosing against them due to how warm she was sure they would be even for a short time. The flushed cheeks on Maebh's face acting as confirmation of her theory and making her happy she had chosen makeup despite its obvious inconveniences.

"This is Joel" Maebh shuffled to one side making sure her boyfriend was obvious to Sasha as she spoke.

Sasha smiled as she shook the hand of the boy she was being introduced to before quickly introducing Jim in return. In a sudden moment she realised that it was possible that Maebh wasn't fully aware of the relationship between Ciara and Adele but Sasha decided that wasn't really her news to discuss. The boy that Maebh was with seemed like he was older than she was but Sasha accepted that it wasn't easy to tell with the costume he was hidden behind. The one thing that was obvious in her eyes was the fact that, just like she was happy, Maebh was clearly happy in her relationship.

In a way, now that she had seen Maebh and finally been able to introduce Jim to the last of the people she considered as close acquaintances Sasha felt like she had completed a mission she had been unaware of being part of. The fact that Ciara was in a relationship with Adele gave them a mutual connection which she felt sure would lead to them spending more time talking about during school.

There was no denying that Sasha felt like Maebh was someone she was grateful to know considering how influential she had been in distracting Fintan during the last party they had both attended. Now that Fintan had clearly bought his own distraction it felt like they could both relax and enjoy the company they were with, safe in the knowledge that no unwanted distractions were going to ruin their evening.

Maebh had smiled and waved over at Jim as Ciara and Adele joined them on their way over to the buffet to select some food. Throughout the rest of the evening the six of them shared laughs and fun times together with what Sasha decided was the crowning moment being the winner of the fancy dress being announced, although none of them won a prize it was nice to not hear Fintan's name called out either making it a win for everyone as far as Sasha was concerned.

"Morning" Jim made sure to hide the lower half of his face under the covers as he mumbled his first word of the day to hide the silly grin he could feel forming as he opened his eyes.

At the end of the bed, thankfully oblivious to the fact that he was waking up he could see the naked buttocks of Sasha as she pottered around at the dresser. Part of his mind wanted to make some kind of smart comment like 'bottoms up' or 'there's a lovely smile' which he knew were the sort of things his parents would say if they happened to see even a covered bottom pointing in their direction.

There was no denying in his mind that he was extremely lucky, he had known boys from school and now college who he was fairly sure had only ever seen their girlfriends naked on special occasions and here he was with his girlfriend parading around the room naked. In his mind he knew that if he tried to make some clever comment about it Sasha would be quick with a retort to squash his comment in the water, either that of he would lose other privileges which he knew he was only able to get while he was still with her.

Sasha turned at the sound of his voice grinning casually as she tried to carefully tug a brush through the matted knot that had been bothering her in her hair. She felt sure that the knot wasn't due to anything more than some face paint from the previous night but that didn't make it any less painful trying to resolve the issue. Tugging the brush a few more times she felt her eyes water as the brush finally fell free taking a few strands of hair with it as she pulled it loose.

Swing her arm backward she placed the brush on the dresser awkwardly before placing one knee on the bed and clambering on to the bed to crawl up toward the half visible face on the pillow.

"Before you say anything smart" Sasha kissed his forehead as she spoke "I have hidden our clothes so there is no point in even thinking of getting dressed" She smiled as she continued her statement. "This room is a clothes free zone until further notice" she kissed him again as she sat down gently, her legs straddles around his waist.

Jim paused for a moment, his body confirming that it was fully aware of the fact that he had a naked woman pinning him down. In the back of his mind he could recall the last time he was in a similar position to this and how badly that had ended up but he felt confident that there was little or no chance of the same or even anything similar happening this time unless it was the housekeeping staff. He could still remember the last time a member of hotel housekeeping walked in to his room unexpectedly but even that wasn't enough for him to want to change the situation he was now in.

Part of his mind was egging him on to make the observation that there weren't many men who would be wondering where their clothes were if they were in the same position he was but he decided that was a conversation that didn't need to be started.

In his heart he felt sure that, if he had been inclined to challenge Sasha about the hiding of his clothes he would be able to find them but the fact that she wanted to keep him without clothes was much more exciting than trying to find their suitcase. Propping himself up carefully as he reached down running his hands along Sasha's thighs he smiled up at her as he felt her hands stroking his chest.

"Breakfast in bed then I guess" he smiled

Sasha grinned down at him as she heard his response to her statement, the look in his eyes confirming her suspicion that he had other plans that didn't involve selecting something from the menu. In many ways she knew that it was her own fault but she hadn't been able to resist the temptation to make the fact that she didn't want to dress any time soon into a fun experience.

Carefully she arched her leg over rolling on to her side of the bed bouncing slightly as she flopped down on to the duvet before leaning over and picking the menu out of the drawer next to the bed. Her stomach growled softly as it confirmed her intention to eat as soon as possible as she hunched her knees up resting the menu against them to paw her way through the options.

In reality she had already decided what she wanted for breakfast but she felt it was best to at least pretend to be selecting something even if it was only to confirm her true intentions to Jim before passing the menu over to him. She bit her lip as she passed the red folder over slapping it playfully against his chest and wincing in empathy as she watched him exhale heavily as it slapped against his skin.

"C'mon Mr Loverman, there will be time for that sort of thing later" she poked her tongue out at Jim in an effort to ensure him that she wasn't completely against other activities once they had eaten something.

Jim paused as he opened the menu, glancing briefly at Sasha who he could see had now picked up her phone and was looking through messages. There had been a playful element to her voice but he could tell that she really did want to eat and not have the type of breakfast in bed that he had been anticipating. Like an ebbing tide he felt the urges that had been eagerly filling his bod drain slowly away as he made his selection and passed the menu back to Sasha who wasted no time in placing their room service call.

"I'm going to go use the shower" he spoke softly before kissing her lightly on the cheek as he carefully rolled out of bed.

Sasha couldn't help blushing as she noted the awkward way Jim was trying to make his way around the bed toward the bathroom his hands tactfully placed to hide his manhood from view as he shuffled past her.

"Can ye throw a bathrobe out just in case the food arrives, wouldn't want to shock the porter would I?" she smiled as she spoke noting Jim's acknowledgement as he disappeared from view.

Pausing as he walked into the bathroom Jim pressed his cheek against the doorframe glancing longingly out at Sasha laying on the bed as he pondered over the idea of locking himself in the bathroom and letting her worry about the food arriving while he was safely hidden away.

Every time he saw her without clothing he could feel his mind reminding him how lucky he was to have someone like her be so interested in him to actually want to date him. In his mind he felt sure that even if he left her without a robe she would find some way to either cover up if their food arrived or just answer the door as she was, which was something he wasn't comfortable imagining regardless of who delivered their breakfast. Peering over at the counter where the sink was neatly set he reached over grabbing one of the neatly folded robes and threw it casually over at Sasha holding back a stunted giggle as it flopped over her face before quickly shutting the door to the bathroom.

Glancing over her shoulder as she pulled the robe off her face Sasha grinned as she watched Jim disappear quickly into the bathroom before bundling the robe in a pile on the bed as she waited for their food to arrive

Chapter Twenty-Eight

Hours for the taking

Sasha couldn't hide the ambivalence running through her head as she woke for the second morning next to Jim content with the fact that nobody was going to come crashing through the door or, if they did it wouldn't be anyone who cared that they were in bed together.

Part of her mind, the part that she wanted to hold on to for as long as she could, was filled with a happy contentment at the fact that she was here with the man she had chosen to date despite all of the obstacles in their way. Ever since the first time that she actually considered them as a couple, that awkward day when he had been encouraged to meet her in the hotel lobby by her friends after an honest misunderstanding, she had accepted two things.

The first of them was that Jim wasn't like the other boys, the ones she dealt with every day at school – or if he was then she hadn't seen it in him yet. Maybe she would see a different side to him when she went over t visit him in England, something that she had decided she wanted to arrange as soon as possible with him but didn't want to talk about while he was here with her because that would involve acknowledging the fact he was going home.

It was the fact of where his home was which was both the second thing she knew she would have to find a way to deal with if they were going to continue to date each other and the reason that her heart was wrenching against the contentment she was trying so hard to maintain in her mind. So much about the day she knew she had waiting for her to acknowledge its arrival felt so similar to the day she had left Zante and yet this time there were also so many differences apart from the fact that it was Jim getting on the plane.

In the back of her mind she could already feel the emotions that she had gone through that day in the airport in Zante rushing through her body, emotions that she didn't want to show, at least not for now. Suddenly it occurred to her that she couldn't recall Jim mentioning the little ring that she had given him and she definitely couldn't remember seeing it on him at any point during his visit. It seemed almost trivial to bring it up today of all days but Sasha knew that if she didn't mention it she would be thinking about it until they spoke again.

Unlike the last time, she had already mentally acknowledged that this one was going to happen and there wasn't much she could do to change that. In reality she had known Jim would have to go back home from the moment they had arranged for him to visit her but at the time it had felt like it was so far away and yet now it was here. On the positive side Sasha also knew that unlike the last time, this time their relationship status seemed more certain, she couldn't imagine anything changing that.

As she pondered over the idea of visiting him Sasha realised that Jim very rarely mentioned his friends back home. She felt sure he had a few, probably more than she did and yet they rarely came up in conversation and she was sure she couldn't name any of them. Making a note to herself Sasha decided to try to find a bit about his social circle, but not today, today she wanted to make sure everything went as well as possible.

Glancing over she smiled as she noted that Jim's nose was pressed awkwardly against the pillow, his jaw slightly open but his eyes firmly closed as if he had been sedated and left to recover. He snorted slightly as she watched him making her jump as he shuffled and turned seemingly oblivious to the fact that she was sat wide awake next to him.

Sliding gently out of the bed Sasha walked over to the curtain, an air of confidence in her step unlike the previous day when she had felt conscious of maybe someone seeing her through the window. Glancing back she noted the fact that Jim was now facing away from her so the light through the curtain wasn't likely to disturb what she felt sure sounded like a deep sleep probably due to the late hour when they had eventually drifted off.

Their day together had gone as well as she could expect after Jim had feigned an interest in trying to find where she had hidden their clothes. Sasha smiled as she recalled giggling at his over the top vague attempts to find the case which she knew he had seen at least twice when he had opened the wardrobe it was in and yet hadn't even attempted to pull it out confirming his contentment to stay naked with her for at least a while.

When the room service arrived, it was Jim who went to the door, a towel tentatively wrapped around his waist teasing gravity as he opened the door for the porter to bring the tray in. Sasha smiled over as he remained quietly confident in the towel not falling to the ground as he made light conversation and signed to accept the addition to their bill would need to be paid before they checked out. Feeling a little cheeky Sasha sat up in the bed as the porter made his bay back to the door completely oblivious to the fact that she was intentionally flashing one breast at Jim in an effort to distract him.

It had been getting on for lunch time before a second knock at the door had been the push they needed to make them decide it was time to venture into the town for a while. Sasha dashed into the bathroom locking the door behind herself with a cheeky giggle leaving Jim to deal with the muffled voice from the corridor announcing their latest visitor as being a member of the housekeeping team. After spending a nice afternoon together actively avoiding places where they might see crowds they returned to the hotel with take away food for their dinner and spent the evening in bed watching the TV and talking.

As she made her way around the bed Sasha glanced down at the knotted takeaway bag, the subtle smell of condiments still emitting from it but not pungent enough to make the room smell too bad. Hearing the tell-tale snort confirming that Jim was finally waking she grinned as she made her way back round to her side of the bed perching casually on the covers as she watched the one eye that she could see opening.

Snorting hard against the pillow as if it was the first time he was catching his breath Jim paused as his eyes open while he tried to work out why it seemed that he had been trying to burrow his way through the pillow during his sleep. Peering through one eye as he contemplated the most logical way to peel his face out of the pillow he felt a grin cross his face as she spotted Sasha perched casually next to him.

"Morning" he mumbled as he shuffled under the covers

Sasha glanced down at Jim as he manoeuvred awkwardly under the blankets, mildly impressed at his ability to do so while remaining fully covered, not even a toe made an appearance as be bounced himself on to his back.

"I was thinking, with it being your last day" Sasha felt a lump hit her throat as she spoke, her mind accepting for the first time that Jim really was going home in just a few hours.

"Maybe it would be nice to have breakfast in the restaurant today" she smiled as she spoke while trying hard to hide the sadness in her eyes.

Jim turned his head smiling softly as he gazed at Sasha in what he still considered to be his favourite outfit but one that he felt sure she would be changing before they went for breakfast if they went with her suggestion. It hadn't really occurred to him until that moment but now he was looking at her in all her glory he had to accept that this may be the last time he was going to see her naked for a long time.

Part of his mind had been contemplating the idea of them arranging another meet up but that seemed like a trivial thing they could deal with once he was back home again rather than discussing it on the day he was due to leave. In his head he knew that if they did make another arrangement while he was still with her it would give them both something to look forward to but for now he decided not to bring up what his heart was already telling him was going to be a difficult subject – the fact that he was going home.

Leaning over to the small table by the bed he dug his phone out of the drawer it had been sat in overnight and glanced at the screen before peering back at Sasha bemused by how chirpy she was.

"Breakfast sounds great Sash but you do realise the time, don't you?" he passed her his phone casually as he spoke

Bemused slightly by his comment Sasha glanced at the phone that was being presented to her as she recalled here actions. She could clearly remember glancing at the alarm clock that had been supplied by the hotel when she woke up and accepting that it was early for a Sunday but given the fact that they had to get back home before leaving to the airport it didn't seem too early. Now, according to Jim's phone, it was earlier than it had been when she had first made her way over toward the window making her pause for a moment before realising that she had forgotten that the clocks had changed.

Suddenly it felt like she was being given a free pass, an extra hour that she hadn't expected to have meaning that, even though she was still going to have to say her good byes to Jim later that day, for now it was an hour further away than she had anticipated. In a moment of excited relief Sasha flung her legs in the air as she awkwardly wriggled her way back under the blanket before snuggling up to Jim and placing her head against his shoulder.

"Jim, ya know that ring I gave you in Zante?" Sasha kept her voice soft to prevent it seeming like she was getting bossy about it.

In a sudden moment of shock Jim realised that he had intended to put it on as a necklace using the chain he had bought for it but had left it on the desk on the morning he had made his way to the airport.

"It's safe at home Sash, I didn't bring it to save losing it" he smiled as he spoke feeling slightly guilty for the white lie about the reason it was at home but not too guilty given that he hadn't lied about where it was.

Sasha paused as she heard his response before accepting that it made sense in a way, she could recall when she had handed it to him knowing in her heart that it wouldn't fit on any of his fingers so it probably was safer at his house unlike her chain from him which barely ever left her neck.

"Oh Jim" she sighed softly as she ran her hand over his chest feeling her body warm up against his.

"Wouldn't it be nice if we could do this more often?"

Jim felt a shudder run through his spine as Sasha pressed her body against his but managed to hide it to prevent breaking the moment that he hadn't expected to be enjoying. There was only one answer to her statement and he knew it but felt like there was more behind her comment than her words had mentioned.

"Well, yeah, course id like that but wouldn't it get expensive?"

Sasha cocked her head as he spoke before realising that he was referring to the fact they were in a hotel.

"No Silly" she giggled lightly as she spoke "I mean just be together like this more often" she kissed his neck gently

In a moment that felt like enlightenment had just been offered to him Jim realised that it wasn't the hotel that Sasha wanted more of but couples time.

He had been anticipating a moment like this ever since they had first realised how difficult it was going to be to se each other but had chosen not to say anything about it. Ever since the moment he had arrived home from Greece he had heard comments from those people he considered to be his closest friends about the distance and how difficult it was going to be, he had even had one person try to pair him up with a local girl which he knew wasn't intended to be offensive to his relationship, but he had still taken it to heart.

The way Sasha spoke about them being together more often told him that she was happy in their relationship but, just like him, she wanted them to be able to see each other more and not have to make as many arrangements as they had for it to happen. For a moment he pondered over the idea of one of them moving to be nearer to the other, but he knew that neither of them were in a position to even suggest such an idea to their parents. Sasha was still at school, and he had just started college which he knew his parents were proud of so they wouldn't like the idea of him dropping out to move to Ireland.

Although Jim knew that he wanted things to be easier for them he was also conscious of the fact that if he responded in the wrong way it could open a can of worms that he didn't want to dig in to – the one that involved any doubt or regret about their relationship.

"Yeah it would be great, one day we will make it happen" He felt a sly grin cross his face as Sasha's nose nuzzled into his neck in a silent acknowledgement of his answer

In a way it felt funny to Jim that ever since he had turned 15, he had been determined to find the first opportunity to leave home. His first inclination had been to make sure to enrol in a college that was too far away to live at home but the more he considered that the more he realised that was just going to make college expensive.

He could still remember his sister leaving home to live with the boyfriend that his parents still referred to, usually when they were comparing how he or his sister had fared in comparison with any of their friends' children of a similar age. It didn't happen very often but, every once in a while, Jay would be seen as the lesser evil depending on who he was being paired off against at any time.

On the other hand, his parents seemed to be quite pleased to know that he had got into what was looking like a real relationship as his father called it. Jim had been clever enough not to question what made it a real relationship and just take the comment as a compliment on who he had started to date. Just like so many of his friends, his parents had shown their concerns over the distance and how often they would see each other but unlike his friends Jim felt like his parents were actually supportive which caught him off guard at first.

Somehow for the first time in years it seemed like he had done something that his parents really approved of but he didn't want to admit to the glaring fact that it wouldn't have happened if they hadn't chosen the complex in Zante for their holiday.

Of all the different reasons that he had contemplated for wanting to move out of the family home it had never occurred to him that it might be a girlfriend that would be the one that he would be considering. He knew that other boys he had known from school, boys who were in higher years than him, had left home and moved in with their girlfriends almost immediately after school which had usually ended in disaster due to finances.

After the week they had spent together Jim could see that living closer would be a nice thing and there were definitely logical reasons why it should be him moving not her. The most obvious of these was the fact that, unlike him, she was still considered as going to school and although he was still studying she had big exams still pending which seemed much more important than his ones. If he moved he could always start a new course whereas, from what Sasha had told him, it wasn't as easy for her to retake the final years of school.

A flush of shock brushed its way through his mind as he realised that he really was thinking of the idea of moving, something that Sasha and he hadn't really spoken about and yet there it was in the forefront of his mind. Peering through the corner of his eye he could see Sasha laying relaxed next to him, her head buried in his neck and her hair obscuring her eyes making it difficult to know if she was snoozing or still awake. For now his thoughts about the idea of moving could wait, they could always discuss it once he was back home. Shifting his body gently he slid one arm across, feeling a rush flow through his body as he touched her skin and gently slid his hand between her and the mattress.

Sasha nuzzled closer, a grin forming on her face that she didn't want Jim to know about as she felt his arm casually drifting round her waist. She knew in her heart that this was the sort of thing she was going to miss the most once he went back home – the feeling of his fingertips against her skin. Her spine tingled lightly as she felt his hand resting against her lower back, hovering in a nowhere region which she admired. There was something comforting and exciting in having his gentle touch close to but not quite on her buttocks that was almost relaxing.

She had seen a lot of couples walking along with a hand on each other's buttocks which she felt couldn't be a completely comfortable or safe thing to do for many reasons. Even worse were the one's she saw with a hand in their partners back pocket which just seemed completely inconvenient as well as difficult to explain if the gesture caused any injuries. Where Jim had his hand seemed almost perfect, close enough for her to know that he was tempted to let it drift further and yet still far enough away that it wouldn't cause awkward moments if her parents saw him doing it. Then again, the level of awkwardness may intensify if her parents saw it happening while they were both naked as was the case on this occasion, luckily her parents weren't anywhere near them to see what was happening.

Lifting her head slightly she kissed the side of his neck.

"Jim, ya know that extra hour we have?" she bit her lip "why don't we go get some breakfast then we can come back here and have a proper goodbye before we pack and head home" she pressed her back into his hand as she whispered softly into his ear.

Smiling as he heard her comment Jim turned to Sasha, the flushed look on her face confirming what he suspected. Part of his mind wanted to suggest they skip breakfast but ever since Sasha had suggested eating in the restaurant his stomach had been telling him what a good idea it would be to eat before they left.

It hadn't occurred to him that Sasha had actually forgotten the clocks were changing but now he could understand that was the reason she had shuffled back into bed. Her latest suggestion was more of an after-thought based on the fact that they had more time available than she had originally thought and yet it seemed like the perfect final memory to share.

Turning his head as he gripped a little harder to her back he smiled and nuzzled against her as he looked into her eyes seeing the calm anticipation of his answer.

"Sounds like a plan Sash" he kissed her gently as he spoke.

Chapter Twenty-Nine

Plane and Simple

As they walked into the Airport building the reality of the situation hit Sasha like a speeding train. For the second time in only a few months she was going to be saying goodbye to Jim and this time, despite the fact that she was much more confident of their future together than she had been the first time round it felt almost worse this time. She gripped his hand as they stood just inside the sliding doors shuffling out of the way of the nameless people all rushing to get to their flight as she watched her father pull away in the car.

In a way it had come as almost a relief when the suggestion had been made that they should make their way up to the airport with plenty of time to spare rather than waiting around at home. Jim had made his way to the room he had been using as a bedroom before carefully separating out their clothes on his bed, smiling softly as he folded Sasha's Halloween costume on to the duvet before pausing when he reached his own one.

Part of his mind was telling him that he should take the costume back home with him, there was no doubt in his mind that it would fit in his case but he knew that it was likely to never see the light of day again once he got it home. If he chose to leave it behind he felt sure that it would still not be used again but at least it would be somewhere safe for if he visited her again the same time next year.

A sudden realisation hit his mind as he pondered over the future for the costume he had worn once but never expected to even own in the first place. Here he was in a relationship that had barely lasted three months and yet he was already planning for a year ahead of himself.

The thought of actually being in a relationship had been daunting enough at the time when they had first decided they were officially dating and yet somehow it had seemed so easy, as if it had been meant to happen from the moment they had met. He had to admit that if he tried to tell any of his friends that he had seen the girl who was to become his first real girlfriend naked before even finding out her name they would have probably considered him a liar.

Anyone he knew that was in a relationship that had lasted beyond the first date seemed happy despite a few arguments which he felt sure he knew most of the details of – the joys of being the friend that everyone turned to in their moment of need. The truth of it was that, unlike Sasha and him, these long relationships were with people who could barely avoid each other especially if they went to the same school. Sasha and he were lucky to get one video call a week together and yet somehow they had made it work.

"Sash, d'you think id be best leaving my costume with you or taking it home?" Sasha turned as she heard the question, her mind more focussed on trying to seem positive despite the fact that Jim's imminent departure was starting to cut her up inside.

In a way his question seemed trivial, there wasn't anything she planned to do with his costume or hers for that matter until maybe the following year. For now it seemed almost irrelevant except for the fact that both of their costumes were part of their first couples costume. If he left it here she knew that she would just be putting it away with the rest of her Halloween bits which sat in a chest in the attic along with the Christmas decorations. Both sets of items had one occasion in the year when they would come out while they spent the rest of their lives hidden away.

"If you can fit it in your case take it with you" She smiled as she responded accepting that there was part of her mind that could see the significance of their costumes being stored together and yet it made more sense for Jim to have what he had worn.

Jim nodded as he slipped back into his room

As he took a final glance around the room Jim smiled, noting the neat pile of clothing that he had carefully separated from his own which belonged to Sasha. The fact that they had shared a case for their time in the hotel meant that he knew there was a slight chance that somewhere in amongst his clothing he may have forgotten a random sock or other item belonging to her but felt sure that, if he had she wouldn't miss it too much.

He had heard stories of boys he went to school with having intentionally kept small trinkets or items belonging to girls they had dated as a souvenir of their time together and often pondered of the relevance of such an act. At least if he had accidentally kept anything belonging to Sasha he felt sure she would know it was genuinely an accident and not see anything sinister in his actions.

Pulling the zip around the case he grinned as he recalled the saga involving her discarded bikini bottoms in their first few days on Zante. Now that he looked back on the incident he could see how trivial and silly it had been but at the time he knew it had almost wound him up, especially as they had reappeared more than once while he had been actively avoiding her. Now that he looked back he knew how grateful he was for the fact that against all the odds Sasha hadn't given up on him which was the only reason they were now together.

"I have left your things on the bed Sash" Jim smiled faintly as he spoke making his appearance back in the front room ready to head home.

Sasha glanced toward the direction of his voice as she heard Jim making his announcement while fighting hard against the tear that she could feel burning against her eye. Seeing Jim stood there with his case bought everything crashing down inside her mind as she leapt from her chair throwing herself at him with a big embrace.

"We should probably hit the road, traffic" Diarmuid glanced toward Mary as he spoke nodding discretely as they both acknowledged the gesture Sasha had just made.

In his mind he knew that his reference to traffic was probably trivial given that it was the Sunday of a Bank holiday weekend and there was more than enough time to get to the airport before the flight. The sight of Sasha opening up in such a way threw him off at first but, in a way both Mary and he had prepared themselves for her to be a bit emotional after having spent a week with Jim in the house.

Jim felt his ears prickle and his heart sink as he heard the reference to them making their way out of the house, in his mind he felt sure he was going to be wanting to visit again and yet so much seemed uncertain after everything had gone on. He knew that, no matter how much he wanted to be sure he would be welcomed now was not the time to check such things.

Despite everything that had been implied as having happened, he knew that he hadn't actually done anything wrong and yet he still felt like a suspect. The harsh reality of the fact that his chances to see Sasha again may be conducted by her parents or, possibly even his, was sticking in his throat like a piece of bubble gum that refused to budge.

"So, I guess you enjoyed your visit Jim?" Diarmuid almost cringed as he asked what had seemed in his mind to be an amicable question to break the silence of what was going to be a long journey if nobody spoke.

In the past when Jim had heard a question like this he had been content to allow one of his parents to give the response. On the outside it seemed like a simple yes or no answer but he had learned two things from listening to his parents replies. The first thing was that, no matter how bad their visit was the only answer that people expected to hear was a positive one because anything negative would leads to an awkward moment. Secondly, he had noticed that regardless of the answer that was given the person asking the question didn't really seem to care – it was simply a conversation starter.

Over the years he had noticed a few questions that fell into the category of being nothing more than a polite comment or conversation opener. The one that surprised him the most was when people asked each other "How are you?" or variations on that, even the doctor seemed to ask it without actually wanting to know the real answer. Every time he had heard the question since realising it wasn't something people actually wanted to know the answer to he had pondered over how the questioner would respond if they got a different response from the standard one of "I'm fine how are you?".

Despite knowing that his response was probably not going to mean much within a few minutes of providing it Jim saw this as a potential opportunity.

"Yes thanks, it was great to see you all again, I am looking forward to coming back soon" he kept a poker face as he provided what he felt was an amicable and comprehensive reply while also digging slightly for any reaction to his suggestion that he wanted to return.

Glancing discretely through the corner of his eye in an effort to try to get Sasha's attention for her reaction to his response Jim wasn't overly surprised to note that she was content to sit silently in the front seat oblivious to the stunted conversation that had started without her. Now that her father had made his excuses to leave them alone at the airport Jim could almost see the sadness in Sasha's eyes and knew that he had been trying not to show the same emotion ever since they left the hotel.

The sterile shell of the building felt all too familiar as they gazed over toward the check in desks while both silently accepting that once his case had been handed across the desk there was no denying the reason they were stood in the building. In a way Jim was almost relieved to see that there didn't appear to be any desk open to take his case as he browsed the destinations that were being advertised.

Part of his mind was encouraging one of the boards to be advertising somewhere in Greece as a kind of sweet acknowledgement to the place they had first met however Jim knew that it would be unlikely to see any flight heading there at the end of October. The closest he could see was a flight that was advertised to a place he felt sure was somewhere in Italy but chose not to say anything in case he was wrong.

"Let's go get a coffee" he smiled softly at Sasha as he made the suggestion.

Sasha glanced over at Jim as she heard his suggestion, her mind split between wanting to show him how she was truly feeling about the idea of having to see him leave and wanting to come across as positive against the odds so that they could part with a happy memory. Her cheeks burned with the urge to allow a tear to fall that she had been holding in ever since they had left home. Although she could see Jim was struggling almost as much as she was to keep a happy impression on his face she had been determined not to cry while he father was sat opposite her in the car. Now it was just the two of them it felt trivial to maintain the illusion that she was handling him leaving with confidence and yet she wasn't quite ready to give in to her feeling just yet.

Sniffing as discretely as possible she nodded at Jim before following him to one of the small café areas.

Sitting at one of the tables Sasha watched as Jim made his way over ordering two coffees before returning with takeaway cups which, in her mind, was a subtle confirmation that nobody was expected to hang around for too long. Unlike a lot of the other people waiting for flights Sasha knew that they had more than enough time so wouldn't need to rush which suited her as she didn't want to think about the moment she knew was inevitable – that moment when Jim checked his bag in.

Reaching across the table Sasha placed her hands against Jim's as she felt the tear she had been holding in finally break free and trickle down her cheek. Conscious of its appearance she ducked her head to look down at the table as a burning rush of emotion flowed through her body that she knew she wasn't going to be able to hide from Jim.

Startled slightly by Sasha's touch Jim focussed his attention away from the announcement screens he had been trying to discretely check for details about his forthcoming flight. The coffee was warming his fingertips through the cup but it was the subtle yet comforting touch from Sasha that was pleasantly unexpected.

He glanced across at her noticing immediately that she was trying to hide her face from view which he felt sure meant she was either shy or embarrassed. He had seen similar gestures with his female friends and knew that each time he had seen it there was something on their mind that they were trying to hide but couldn't. This time, unlike some of the times with his friends, Jim felt sure he knew what it was that had caused Sasha to shy away from him in such a subtle but obvious fashion.

"You do know I'd stay on if I could Sash" he kept his voice low as he spoke feeling sure he had hit the right note first time.

Looking up slowly Sasha pulled one hand away from Jim's while gripping lightly to his hand with her other one. She knew there was no denying the tears she had been trying to hide, her face felt puffy as she peered over at him forcing a smile as her thumb brushed lightly over the back of his knuckles while wiping her cheeks with her free hand.

"I know hun" she placed her hands closer against his as she responded to what she knew was meant to be a comforting comment.

In many ways she knew that it was the little moments when Jim was able to see through her that she admired the most about him. It was almost as if she couldn't hide from him even if she wanted to and despite how vulnerable that made her feel it was also extremely comforting to know how well he seemed to understand her.

Glimpsing briefly at the screen Jim spotted the silent announcement that check in was opening for his flight. The clock on the screen re-assured him that there was still ample time but seeing that announcement bought his flight that bit closer and he knew Sasha wasn't going to like it.

"I'll be back in a moment" He smiled softly as he stood grabbing his bag "Stay there, I wont be long" he grabbed Sasha's hand gently squeezing it in a reassuring fashion before making his way to the check-in desks.

Sasha watched longingly as she sipped at her coffee knowing in her heart that no matter what she did Jim was going to be heading home soon. The fact that he had left her to her thoughts to check his bag in was both a sweet gesture and a bad thing because it meant that she didn't have to watch him handing his bag over but she also had time alone as the reality started to really sink in.

Jim turned from the check in desk, his boarding card in his hand and his case having disappeared along its own personal journey to hopefully join him on his flight which was getting ever closer. Beyond the row of desks, he could see Sasha, still sat exactly where he had left her, motionless as if she was trying to encourage time to stand still. Part of his mind wanted his flight gate to be announced but only to save the awkwardness he knew they were going to share until he it was time to go.

"Hey Sash, can you teach me a little Irish?" Jim sat down prizing his coffee out of Sasha's hands before taking a sip and noting that it had already gone cold.

Cocking her head to one side Sasha glanced at Jim with an air of bemusement on her face as she heard his random question. She could recall speaking a little Irish to him in the past and having mentioned to him that she knew how to speak it but in her wildest dreams she hadn't ever expected him to want to learn the language.

She knew that it was not unusual for visitors to Ireland to ask a local person to teach them some Irish and also knew only too well the kind of phrases that were commonly taught to a visitor but hearing Jim asking caught her off guard.

"Er, sure?" she emphasized the questioning tone in her voice as she spoke while trying quietly to work out where Jim's mind was going with his request.

Jim smiled softly quietly pleased that his unexpected question had provided a side-track to take away from the sombre atmosphere that had been building ever since they had walked into the airport.

On his way back from the check in desk he couldn't help noticing that the departure gate had already been announced for his flight and that meant his flight was only around the corner. From here it was a gamble of how soon he wanted to get to the place he was going to be waiting for the plane to appear at the window but, if he didn't go through relatively quickly there was a chance of delays putting him under pressure.

As soon as he saw the updated announcement, he knew that it wouldn't take too long for Sasha to spot it as well which he felt sure would make things seem sadder despite their inevitability.

"Well, I was thinking" he smiled as he sat down cupping her hands into his. "There must be an Irish way to say see ya soon which is better than goodbye" instinctively he glanced at the screen directing Sasha's attention to the update he had been trying to avoid her seeing.

Forcing a soft smile as she spotted the gate number Sasha silently acknowledged the discrete method Jim had used to tell her it was time for him to start thinking about making his way to the area she was going to see him disappear out of reach. She stood slowly keeping one of Jim's hands grasped in hers as she gestured to him not to forget the hand luggage bag that was sat by his feet.

Remaining silent while trying to keep her composure she led the way to the staircase that she knew led to passport control before stopping and turning to Jim. Placing her hands on his waist she gazed longingly into his eyes, the puffiness burning her cheeks and she let her body succumb to the tears she had been holding back.

"It's Slán go fóill which means bye for a while" reaching up she dragged her arm across her eyes to wipe the tears aside as she spoke.

Jim nodded as he heard the words before fumbling his way through the same phrase in an effort to make it sound the same as when Sasha had said it.

"Slán go fóill then" he repeated the phrase this time more confidently "because this really is only bye for a while Sash, we will see each other again soon"

Feeling his heart pounding hard against his chest he leaned in kissing her softly as he felt the world around melting away leaving it as just the two of them for the brief moment of their embrace.

"I'll contact you as soon as I am home Sash, I promise you" stumbling slightly on the first stair with his left foot Jim leaned in kissing her one last time before making his way toward passport control.

Chapter Thirty

Hometown Blues

Jim could feel the anti-climax hitting his mind as he turned the key and walked through the front door into his home.

He had sent the requested text to the rents as he collected his luggage and fought his way through the airport to the taxi that was waiting to return him to the hustle and bustle of his day-to-day life and had received a short acknowledgement soon after leaving the airport.

The smell of dinner cooking had been the only thing that seemed positive after what he knew he could only describe as the best holiday he had been on for more reasons than he dared to try to explain.

Sitting calmly in his favourite armchair was his father, the local newspaper in his hands and the TV on in the corner providing a welcome background hum as his mother pottered between front room and kitchen in the same way as she had done every day.

"Did you have a nice time? Fiona smiled across as she saw Jim ushering his case into the front room.

Jim glanced between his mother and father somehow pleased to see them and feeling less tense than he had done around Sasha's parents despite the fact that they had made him feel extremely welcome during his stay. His father peered over the top of the paper as both of his parents awaited his response with a silent anticipation.

"Yeah was nice" Jim smiled gently knowing that his short response barely gave even an overview of how many adventures he had been on during his visit.

He wasn't certain but from the way his parents had spoken when he had first mentioned visiting Ireland, he felt fairly sure they hadn't even visited the country which meant that, for the first time in his life, he had been somewhere they hadn't. In a way he could see that being an advantage and a disadvantage because it seemed inevitable that sooner or later the rents were going to ask him more about his trip and yet there wasn't a lot he wanted to tell them despite how much he had done.

Gripping the handle to his case he made his way up to his room pondering over whether it would seem strange that he hadn't just taken it through to the kitchen as dirty washing that either he or his mother would eventually transfer to the washing machine.

Ever since returning from Zante he had felt the urge to handle his own washing which his mother had acknowledged as a moment she was proud of but for him it was more a case of wanting to prove his own independence. This time he had an additional reason for not wanting his case to be opened by his parents and that was the slim chance that he had somehow forgotten to separate all of Sasha's belongings from his own after their weekend away together.

He had heard stories of clothing that clearly didn't belong to any member of a household being discovered in the washing pile by a parent in the past and wanted to avoid it happening if he could. When his sister Chloe had first been dating Jay he had a vague memory of an unexpected pair of boxer shorts having been folded prominently on top of the washing pile as a way of saying "gotcha" without actually having the conversation at the time.

Chloe being the overly confident person that she was had handled the situation in a way that Jim felt sure only she could have done so and got away with it.

"Ah there they are" she beamed as she picked the suspect shorts off the pile before stuffing them into her pocket and grabbing a slice of toast and heading out of the door before anyone had a chance to say anything about their presence in the house.

Swinging the case up on to his bed he unzipped it taking a deep breath of the mixture of musty smell of worn clothes and the slight hint of Sasha that emitted its way from the case where her clothing had once been mixed in with his. Just the sense of her still being near made Jim pause for a moment as he took in her aroma while pondering over what she might be doing.

Digging his phone out of his pocket he glanced at it, noting that there wasn't much batter left but should still be enough to let her know he was back home.

"I got back, lets video chat later" she smiled as he sent the text and was thrilled by her quick reply

One by one he pulled the items out of his case placing his Halloween costume bundled up on one end of the bed before pausing as something caught his eye. Carefully he pulled the bundle of silky items apart pondering over whether they should be washed and if so, where he would store them afterward and how much to tell the rents about the party if they saw him washing such unusual items. It was as he shook the black robe that had made up the main part of his costume that he spotted a little white item fall to the duvet.

In a way he was pleased to see that the item he had somehow managed to bring home with him was only a sock but the fact that he had it made him ponder over whether its partner was also in his case or had Sasha and he somehow managed to end up with the pair split between them. Jim knew that people often commented on the concept of socks becoming lost in the washing machine, but he wasn't sure that he had heard of many cases of them ending up in different countries but still safely in the care of people who knew the owner. He was fairly sure that socks got left on holidays in the past however this was one occasion when the rogue sock had at least half a chance of returning to its owner eventually.

Glancing at his phone he pondered over the idea of letting Sasha know what he had found while also contemplating how to get the item washed and safely stored until he could return it to her. He grinned as he considered the irony of the odd sock he had accidentally acquired somehow becoming lost in the washing machine rendering its fate the same as those who lost their way in other cleaning incidents.

"Jim, dinner will be ready in 15 minutes!" The sound of his mother calling made Jim jump at first but also came with an indirect acknowledgement that he was back home.

Jim glanced at his suitcase and back at the sock that he had inadvertently smuggled into the country before picking up his phone and scrolling down to Sasha's name on the call list.

In a way it seemed strange having to call her instead of simply walking up to her, but he knew that, at least for now, this was the way it was going to be for them both. Pausing as his finger hovered over the call option he placed the phone on his desk, smiling as he spotted the ring that Sasha had asked him about, still threaded through the necklace he had bought for it after she had given it to him.

During his visit he had not really mentioned it but the fact that she wore the chain he had bought for her made him feel special. Carefully he picked the chain up clasping it awkwardly around his neck and feeling a slight chill as the cold silver danced against his chest. Part of his mind felt guilty for the fact that he hadn't even given the necklace a second thought when he had packed to visit Sasha but now he was determined to make sure he kept it on him at all times.

Turning back to his case he carefully took every item out, the smell of food cooking downstairs reminding him that the last meal he had eaten had been breakfast. His past knowledge of airport meals had given him enough experience not to chance eating anything during his journey and, although they had left at nearly lunch time, he had chosen not to say anything when they hadn't stopped anywhere on the way to the airport.

As he separated out his clothes Jim felt almost sorry that the lone sock he had found was not able to me matched up nut now his clothes were all split out into piles for washing at least he knew that its partner must still be safe in Sasha's home, or the hotel if they had somehow managed to leave it there. Picking up the phone again he sat on his bed reaching out and grabbing the rogue sock as he selected the option to call Sasha.

****

From the moment her father had returned to the airport to collect her Sasha couldn't recall having said much until they arrived at a service station where the suggestion was made that they could get a coffee before heading home. In a way Sasha had been pleased for the break and welcomed the coffee but the pain in her stomach from having just watched Jim disappear was still pressing against her.

By the time they had arrived home she had settled and accepted the fact that he was due to land and all she had to look forward to was returning to school again in a couple of days' time where she knew others would be raving about their mid-term break. The fact that she felt sure none of the people she went to school with, apart from Adele and Ciara would have any idea about what she had enjoyed was both calming and exciting.

The first text from Jim had acted like both a confirmation that he really had gone and an assurance that he had got home safely but that hadn't changed her mood for the better except for the suggestion that they should video chat soon which she had been keen to accept.

Now that she could see her phone ringing and his name flashing on the screen Sasha could feel her body filling with adrenalin at the idea of, if nothing else, hearing his voice again.

"Hey Sash, how's it going?" Sasha could tell from his tone that Jim was trying to keep his thoughts together as he spoke but was still happy to simply hear from him.

"So, I have unpacked my case and found something of yours" Sasha let the phone go silent as she heard the words while she pondered over what it might be.

She knew that, despite having been asked, she hadn't got round to removing the bits that Jim had told her he had left for her in his room but had promised to do it before going to bed. In a way the fact that his unattended bed was still set up made it seem almost like a shrine, part of him that was still there even if it wasn't going to be there for much longer Sasha was revelling in the fact that it was currently still there. She giggled lightly as she heard him tell her that somehow one of her socks had got tangled up in with his Halloween costume and pondered over whether to tell him to just throw it away or not.

Part of her mind was telling her that it was pointless them both having one part of a pair of socks and yet another part of her mind was telling her that it was quite sweet in a way that he had even taken the time to tell her he had it.

"I'll keep it safe for the next time we meet" he commented setting a flutter in her tummy at the prospect that he was already talking about their next meet up.

In the back of her mind Sasha had already been pondering over how soon she would be able to visit him, her first thought had been their next school break but she had dismissed that with it being Christmas. Much as she wanted to see Jim as soon as possible she wasn't sure that her parents would welcome the idea of her being away at that time of the year. Now that he had made the hint her next idea was to plan to see him in the early part of the new year.

"So, when do you want to see me next" Sasha beamed as she heard him asking the question and couldn't wait to start arranging her trip.

Epilogue

Five years later

Sasha glanced up at the sun that was catching her eye as she lay calmly on the nude beach in Zakynthos. In the distance out in the clear blue water was the small platform she could still remember paddling out to years earlier when she had first met Jim as he sat on the shore uncertain about her and definitely uncertain about naturism, how times had changed in the years that had passed. Next to her lying casually on a towel Alice was relaxing as her young son built a sand castle with pride and excitement filling his eyes as he patted the castle into shape with a plastic spade.

"I can't believe you called him Jim" Sasha giggled slightly as she spoke, turning her head to face Alice feeling both complimented and amused at the way Alice and Greg had chosen the name of their first born.

It had been the year she had met Jim that had become an influence in her friend's relationship, they had recalled how it had been a combined effort that had finally got Sasha into what they considered her first relationship. How were they to know that five years later the couple would still be strong and yet here they were, still happy together and Jim, now fully into naturism having moved to Ireland two years and a number of visits later so that he could live closer to her.

"If it had been a girl we'd have chosen your name Sash" Alice smiled as she spoke gently patting her hand against her tummy "maybe this one will be a sister for him"

Sasha sat up abruptly at the news that Greg and Alice were expecting their second child, in her heart she knew that it had been partially her fault they had got together in the first place and now here they were a happy family.

"Don't you dare say anything to Greg, I haven't told him myself yet, but I got the confirmation just before we left home" Alice smiled as she spoke before pointing out at a figure heading toward them their face slightly obscured by the sun

"How did you get on Dell?" Sasha sat back on her elbows recognising the figure as her best friend

Ever since her first experience in naturism Adele had grown more and more confident about the lifestyle, at the age of 18 she had finally told her parents about it just before moving out to live with Ciara at the time. Their relationship faded out over the following few months which Ciara put down to the fact that she couldn't cope with her girlfriend parading round the flat naked all the time.

It took Adele a few months to get over their relationship but slowly she decided that she preferred dating men and started looking for one who would accept her as she was – a home based naturist. Adele's jump into the lifestyle gave Sasha and Jim somewhere they could go now that the little cottage had been sold off and the land where it had once stood reclaimed by a family who said that it had been owned by a distant relative many years earlier. Thankfully at the time they had gone searching for it none of them had been sitting in the garden topping up their tan but Adele had been forced to conceal a grin as she heard mention of a greenhouse and two gnomes having been found by the new owners.

For a while Adele moved from one relationship to another noting that for most of the guys she seemed to attract it was her nudity that they liked and not her as a person. This was her second year at the complex with Sasha and the first time she had felt confident enough to go fully nude, despite practically living nude back at home.

"At t'was a good craic Sash but they're all married so no action" she grinned as she perched on the corner of the towel huddling her knees into her chest.

For a few moments the three of them sat silently gazing out at the sun, each one in their own little world.

"Where is your Jim, Sash?" Alice sat up slightly brushing the sand off her towel as she spoke.

Sasha smiled

"He's playing volleyball would you believe" she giggled "but I guess I should go find him before lunch" She stood up as she spoke before tugging at her towel encouraging Adele to let her take it.

"Oh and, what we said earlier" she tapped on her stomach as she glanced down at Alice

"I won't tell Greg about yours if you don't tell Jim about mine"